THE COURTS OF THE FEYRE

"Mike Shevdon strikes sparks from the flinty core of English folklore, as a hero every reader can relate to finds he's part of an incredible and scarily believable parallel realm. If you've been thinking urban fantasy has nothing fresh to offer, think again."

   Juliet E. Mckenna, author of the Hadrumal Cycle *and the* Tales of Einarinn

"Here is the very best of urban fantasy... A highly believable page-turner of a quest."

   Aurealis Magazine

"If you're a fan of urban fantasy – or even if you're not – I'd recommend this book."

   Spellmaking

"Shevdon's prose is elegant and simple and winds up being invisible. We notice the story, not the writer. And that's a rare and pretty fantastic thing."

   Kate of Mind

"Mike Shevdon gave me just what I need: main characters that I feel for, care about and could get invested in. Thanks for something new, sir, that has renewed my faith in modern fantasy."

   Deadwood Reviews

ALSO BY MIKE SHEVDON

The Courts of the Feyre
I: Sixty-One Nails
II: The Road to Bedlam

MIKE SHEVDON

STRANGENESS AND CHARM

THE COURTS OF THE FEYRE
VOL. III

ANGRY
ROBOT

ANGRY ROBOT
A member of the Osprey Group

Lace Market House,
54-56 High Pavement,
Nottingham,
NG1 1HW, UK

www.angryrobotbooks.com
The end of time

An Angry Robot paperback original 2012
1

A catalogue record for this book is available
from the British Library.

ISBN: 978-0-85766-223-1
eBook ISBN: 978-0-85766-225-5

Set in Meridien by THL Design.

Printed and bound by CPI Group (UK) Ltd, Croydon, CR0 4YY

For Mum and Dad

ONE

"Hey Roland, how's it going?" Sandeep pushed the door to the control room closed behind him, feeling the lock click shut under his hand. The shopping centre was closed; there would be no shoppers nosing around where they weren't supposed to be, but security was a good habit to cultivate for a professional.

Roland stretched in his chair. "Evenin' Sunny." Roland didn't even look away from the monitors, but then he'd have watched Sandeep on the screens, walking through the shopping centre from the back entrance.

"Any excitement?" Sandeep took the plastic box and a bottle of water from his rucksack and tucked them into the small fridge in the corner. "It's about time we cleaned this fridge out again. What's this?" He poked a foil package at the back.

"I think it's a kebab. Marky had to leave early – he must've left it."

"Shall I chuck it away?"

"Better not. You know Marky. He'd eat it even if it was furry."

"That boy will poison us all."

"Reckons he's immune to it. He's built up a resistance, he says."

Sandeep closed the fridge just as it whirred into life. It buzzed for a moment and then settled down. He put his rucksack on top of it and then turned to stand behind Roland.

"Is number four not working?" he asked Roland, glancing at the monitors.

"Been playin' up all day, hasn't it? It comes back periodically, so it's not the camera. Must be a fault on the circuit. I'll have to get the electrician to check it out tomorrow. It might be the booster box gone again. Crappy things – they always buy the cheap ones and then they have to replace 'em every three months."

Sandeep turned away and went to the log book, running his finger along the spiky handwriting to decipher it. "What's this in the log?"

"Oh, unit thirty called us down for some kid an hour before closing. You know, the console games shop? He was swearin' at the staff, started pushing the other customers around – threatening people. Marky and me was gonna chuck 'im out."

"Did you call in the police?"

"Nah, he slipped past us. Sneaky little sod must'a been quick on his feet."

"Isn't that where screen four is?"

"Yeah. We didn't have any pictures for the plod, so we left it. He'll be back – they always are. We'll get him next time."

"Didn't you get him on any of the other cameras?"

"Couldn't find him. If you get chance tonight you could go back through the tapes, see if you can get an ID shot."

"I've told you, they don't have tapes any more. It's all on disk now. What did he look like?"

"Tall skinny kid, spiky hair, looked like he hadn't seen

daylight in weeks. Could'a been one of them gothics. The time's in the log. The plod'll probably already be acquainted with 'im. They usually are with that sort."

"Goths, Roland. They're called goths."

"Yeah, them. What the...?"

Screen four suddenly cleared, showing a pallid face right in front of the camera, leering up into it.

"Bugger me, that's him. That's the little sod there!"

"How did he get inside at this time?"

"He's been 'ere all the time, hasn't he? The little sod's probably been hiding in one of the store cupboards. Quick, ring the plod. I'll go and catch hold of 'im." Roland stood up, pulling down his sleeves.

"Wait for me, Roland. You shouldn't apprehend alone. It's against the rules."

"Sod that!"

Sandeep was on the phone, speaking to the police control centre when Roland marched out. He watched on the monitor as Roland's back retreated down the corridor outside and flicked to screen twelve to catch him as he came out onto the main concourse. Sandeep finished reporting the intruder and put the phone down.

"Bloody hothead," mumbled Sandeep to himself. "You're not in the bloody army now, Roland."

Pulling the control room door behind him until it clicked shut, he ran after his colleague. By the time he reached the main concourse he was breathless. He leaned against one of the advertising hoardings. A photo of a youth smiled back at him, holding one of the new smart-phones that Sandeep coveted but couldn't afford.

He pulled a hand-held radio from his belt. "Roland, I'm right behind you. Wait for me, OK?"

The radio crackled. There was no reply.

He jogged through the empty shopping centre, glimpsing lurid offers under the bright lights of the stores behind the security grills, massive discounts on artificially inflated prices. It occurred to Sandeep then that the kid hadn't triggered the alarm. If he'd been hiding in the shop, why hadn't the alarm gone off?

As he turned the corner onto the main strip, he could see Roland up ahead, standing next to the palm trees. The kid was a dark outline beyond him, dressed in a long coat. Maybe Roland was right and the kid was a goth. Sandeep slowed to a walk, relieved to have reached them before Roland got heavy with the kid. The last thing they needed were charges for assault.

Roland's voice sounded hollow. "Come on, son. You can't escape. Give yourself up and we'll go easy on you."

Sandeep smiled between wheezes. Roland watched far too many cop movies.

The boy laughed at him. That was bad. Roland wasn't going to like that.

Roland started walking forward again and Sandeep picked up his pace to a trot.

"You don't want to get funny with me, son," called Roland. "I ain't got no sense of humour."

The laughter petered out and the kid lifted his arms as if he were holding something to his chest. Then his left hand jerked back and forth. Sandeep recognised the gesture; he was pumping a round into a pretend shotgun. A sudden breeze stirred the leaves on the palm trees. Sandeep looked up. Where did the breeze come from? They were inside the shopping centre.

He slowed to a halt, turning back to find the source of the cool air when a massive thud punched into him from behind.

A wave of heat like the draft from an oven door hit him in the back, lifting him off his feet and hurling him back down the tiled walkway. He tumbled in the air and landed rolling and sliding on the hard tiled floor. As his hearing came back, fragments of glass tinkled onto the tiles around him in a bizarrely musical way over the screeching of the bomb alarms.

He shook his head, trying to clear the ringing in his ears. Pushing himself up, he could see stripes of blood rising on his hands where the glass had slashed him. He turned to look back for Roland, just as the smell of smoke and burning plastic hit him, catching in the back of his throat and making him cough and retch.

Down the concourse, the kid was walking calmly through the debris under the rain from the sprinklers, black smoke billowing from the shops to either side, their security gratings gaping where the blast had burst them open. He stopped in front of another shop, pumped the pretend shotgun and pointed it at a shop. Sandeep squinted through the smoke – there was nothing there. The kid wasn't holding anything. Sandeep watched in disbelief as the kid's hands jerked, as if in recoil, and the shop windows burst outwards to a dull thud, erupting in fire and smoke.

The kid smiled a long lazy smile and began strolling towards Sandeep, pointing to one side, then the other. As he passed each shop he would pump his hand and aim into the shop. At the gesture, the shops would explode in rolling gouts of flame, erupting in a hail of flying fragments, yet he never flinched or turned away. He walked though each explosion untouched, the detonations timed with his steps. It was like he was playing an instrument, waiting for the beat – a pyrotechnic conductor.

As Sandeep pushed himself upright, the boy paused and made a show of noticing him. The boy's eyes caught the light from the fire, glowing with the hellish light. He pumped a round and turned to aim towards Sandeep. Before he was aware of it, Sandeep was running, his legs carrying him in huge leaping strides away from those eyes. There was a dull crump and a roll of thunder behind him and he was lifted and thrown down the concourse, spinning in the air to land hard and twisted on the tiles. Sandeep's arm gave a wet crack as he fell on it. As his hearing returned, he recognised the sound of his own hoarse screaming.

Acutely aware of the pain as bone grated on bone, he made himself roll over and push up to his knees, and then to his feet using his good arm to help him. Once he was up, he cradled his broken arm against his chest, and staggered away from the smoke and the glow from the shop windows.

He glanced back once, thinking of Roland back there. He had to get help. There was a demon loose and the shopping centre was turning into hell.

Garvin looked up from the slim brown folder he was reading as I entered the room.

"This is nice," I told him. "I didn't know you had an office."

There was a large picture of a pastoral scene in a thick gold frame on the wall. The woodwork of the desk was dark and polished and the curtains were tied back with gold sashes to let in daylight.

Garvin leaned forward and closed the folder on the desk in front of him, setting it on a pile of similar folders. He gestured at the striped seat of a regency chair set in front of the desk. "I don't. This is Mullbrook's office. He lets me use it."

I sat down slowly, wondering what circumstance would

mean that Garvin needed an office. "Tate said you wanted to see me?"

"We need to talk. There are things to be done – things I need you to do."

"What kind of things?"

"You've been spending a lot of time with Alex. When you're not with Alex you're with Blackbird."

"Alex needs a lot of attention right now, and Blackbird gets tired easily."

"Blackbird is strong enough to lift the back end of a car. She's fey, Niall."

"Half-fey," I corrected him, "and that doesn't mean she can't get tired. It was a long labour. She still hasn't got her strength back"

"She seems to be managing well enough. She's got the stewards to help her. It's not like she's been abandoned, is it?"

I looked at the pastoral scene on the wall. The watercolours ran into one another, making it look like it had been painted in the rain.

"Alex is improving, so Fionh tells me." Garvin sat back, clasping his fingers together.

"There have been fewer incidents," I agreed.

"Fionh says she's exhibiting some clear signs of control, but she says you're babying the girl."

"She said that?"

"Not in so many words, but that was her meaning."

"What did she say, exactly?"

"Niall, you can't carry on babysitting her. She won't take responsibility for herself if you're there making excuses for her every time she screws up."

"I'm not making excuses. She was tortured – abused. She needs time to adjust."

"It's about time she was responsible for her actions. She can't learn if you keep stepping in for her."

"She's fourteen, Garvin. I'm her father. I'm supposed to step in for her."

"In fey terms she's an adult. She's come into her power, responsible for her own actions, or she would be if you let her."

"She wants to see her mother."

"We've discussed that, Niall. It's not a good idea."

"You said she was responsible for herself. She's an adult, you said. She can take her own decisions. Well, the adult has decided she wants to see her mother."

"It's better that Katherine believes that Alex is dead. It'll be easier."

"For whom? For Katherine? I find that hard to believe. I can't imagine a worse situation than losing your child. The loss of her daughter will be the first thing that comes into her head when she wakes up, and the last thing in her mind before she sleeps – if she sleeps. I know, I've been there."

I consciously softened my tone, forcing down the anger that bubbled up inside me when I talked about what happened to my daughter. "Discovering that she's been lied to will be hard. Knowing what's been done to Alex will be harder. But none of it as hard as living with the loss of your only child. It doesn't compare."

Garvin met my stare for a few moments and then looked down at the desk. He sighed, then took the folder from the top of the pile and began laying out press cuttings in front of me.

Shopping Centre Bomb Terror – Flash Flood Swamps Village – Is this the Beast of Balham?

They were tabloid headlines, and the stories below them were no less sensational. The last was accompanied by a blurry photo, probably taken with a mobile phone. Without any scale to reference the image against, it was impossible to tell how big the animal was.

"Looks like silly season," I said.

"Thankfully the shopping centre was closed, though one security guard died and another was injured in the explosion." He picked up a sheet from the folder. "The fire officer's report on the shopping centre is inconclusive. They can find no trace of an explosive or an accelerant, but the fire spread from shop to shop despite fire barriers and a suppression system. It happened in the late evening, so there were only security staff on site. The surviving guard said the security system was on the blink and the screens went dead, but just before the fire he saw someone on the concourse. Two of the guards went down to investigate."

"Arson?"

"Terrorism – possibly eco-warriors or anti-capitalists – at least that's the official version. They think the dead guard might have been involved. The alarms didn't go off and the devices appeared to be timed – a professional job. The guard who died had military training – demolition. The destruction was total, everything burned."

"Sounds bad."

"Could have been worse. It could have been full of shoppers." He picked up another sheet. "Village of Sawlby in Derbyshire washed away three days ago. It's a Pennine village, pretty little place – or it was. Sixteen dead at the last count. Stream came up into a raging torrent." He picked up the cutting, "A wall of water seven feet high swept through the sleepy hamlet." He replaced it on the desk.

"As usual it's the vulnerable that suffer – the old and infirm, or the very young. They're digging bodies out of the mud, trying to clear up the mess. Sound familiar?"

"Alex was here. Fionh's been with her most of the time."

"Alex isn't the only one, though, is she?" Garvin picked up another sheet. "Reports of very large cat-like creature stalking the streets of Balham. Several people have seen it, usually at night, and there are an increasing number of missing pets. It seems to have developed a taste for rabbit."

"Could be an urban fox?"

"One that can open a hutch with a combination padlock on it? The police have been called in, suspecting vandals. They found a trail of paw prints – big ones."

"So there is a cat?"

"The paw-prints vanish in the middle of a park. They just run out."

"What do you mean, run out?"

"The ground was soft, it had rained earlier in the day. They had a specialist with them – she reckoned it was panther of some sort. She tracked the creature into the park, hoping to trace it back to its lair. They had a marksman with a tranquilliser gun on standby. She followed the tracks to a kiddies playground. The tracks go into the sandpit, but they don't come out."

"There were other tracks?"

"Oh, plenty. Kids and parents had been there all day. The only cat tracks were going in, though, not out."

I had a sudden memory of encountering a large black cat in the passages below Porton Down. It had stared at me with knowing eyes while chewing on something that might once have been human.

Garvin laid his hand on the pile of plain brown files next him. "Secretary Carler was good enough to let us have the files from Porton Down. It's difficult for them to tell whether these people are dead or at large. There were some identifiable items, but they could have been dropped or discarded. There were no bodies found, of course, other than the staff."

I winced slightly. Some of the bodies that had been found were people who had died because of me. Raffmir had been particularly ruthless with the medical staff, and my own hands were hardly clean. I had the sudden flashback of a man in military uniform crawling backwards away from me after he'd tried to blow my head off with a shotgun. The fear in his eyes as my hands closed around his throat would never leave me.

I shook my head, trying to clear the image. "You're saying that these incidents are being caused by the escapees from Porton Down – they are doing these things?"

"I'm simply pointing out the correlation between the traits documented in these files and recent incidents in the press. Secretary Carler has requested our cooperation in tidying up the loose ends. He's dealing with the official inquiry. We're dealing with the escaped inmates. These... stories are an embarrassment for all of us. The courts ensure that this sort of thing doesn't happen. I want you on it before it gets out of hand."

"It looks like it's already out of hand."

"Quite."

"What do I do with them if I find them?"

"Bring them in. It's better for them if they come to us. They can join the courts, gain some protection. We'll find a place for them. They can be with people of their own kind."

"And if they don't want to?"

"We're not really offering them a choice, Niall. It's for their own protection."

"But if they won't come?"

"Persuade them."

"And if they won't be persuaded?"

"What do you want, Niall? A signed warrant? You're a Warder. Act like one."

"You want me to eliminate them?"

"If you choose to put it that way. Bear in mind that seventeen people are already dead, and there may be more we don't know about. What did you think they were going to do, blend in with the community?"

"I couldn't leave them there. They were being systematically tortured."

"And torture victims make such good citizens, don't you find? Alex is barely holding it together, and she's had help."

"You said she was improving."

"She is." Garvin stared at me. "You let these people loose, and you need to take responsibility for them. We can't leave them at large. If they come into the courts then all well and good. We can help them, give them support, keep them safe."

"And if not?"

He pushed the pile of folders across the desk. "I'm giving you Warder's Discretion. It's your call. Deal with them."

I left Garvin's office feeling resentful. Why was it my problem? It was hardly my fault that the people at Porton Down had been running secret experiments with half-breed mongrel fey as their subjects, was it?

Subjects? Victims would be a better word. What had been done in the name of science was obscene. They had stuck needles in them, drugged them, tortured them and made them perform like circus freaks, all in the name of research.

Wasn't anyone else going to take any responsibility?

Of course, I already knew the answer to that. I could tell Garvin that I didn't feel capable of fulfilling the mission and he would shake his head and assign someone else – Amber probably. She would finish the job that Porton Down had started and kill them all, quickly, efficiently and without attracting attention. I ought to be grateful that Garvin was giving me a chance to find a better solution, but I didn't feel grateful. I felt manipulated.

I mounted the stairs two at a time – the injuries I'd sustained breaking out of Porton Down had almost completely healed. I still felt a twinge or two in my shoulder where I had caught the edge of a shotgun blast, but only when I was duelling with whichever Warder Garvin chose to partner me with at our morning practice sessions, and even the twinge would soon pass – a benefit of my fey blood.

Walking through the doors to the corridor on which Blackbird and I shared a suite of rooms, I entered quietly in case she was asleep, not that I often found her sleeping during the day, but since she was the one managing the feeds in the middle of the night I thought it would be unkind to wake her if she had finally managed to grab some rest.

I needn't have worried.

The curtains were drawn back and there were sounds of splashing coming from the bathroom. I left the files on the desk and peeped around the door. She had filled the small baby bath in the big bath and was in the process of introducing our son to the warm water. From the noises he was making, he was enjoying it, though that may have been because of the kicking and splashing. Having no wish to end up damp and smelling of baby bath, I eased the door closed and crept out to check on Alex.

Crossing back across the hallway above the stairs, I made my way the far end of the wing where Alex's room was. The size of the house no longer daunted me – I had become used to corridors with room after room set aside for visitors that never arrived. It did mean that Alex could be well away from most of the rest of the occupants of the house – limiting the amount of damage and disruption to the plumbing for the rest of us.

My daughter's affinity with water was both a relief and a problem. I had been worried that she would inherit my gift for the void, or at least the female form of it, and be able to feed from living things by spreading a corruption known as darkspore. It had prevented me from telling her about her potential to inherit my fey genes until it was too late. Instead she'd discovered her gift for herself with disastrous consequences, drowning three other girls after an incident of bullying. She had lost control then, and was still struggling to regain it now.

Instead of the void, Alex had inherited her affinity with water – she called it a sympathy, I never quite understood why. I did ask her once and she told me she felt sorry for it. She said it always wanted to be somewhere else, that it never rested, leaving me wondering whether she was still talking about the water.

I came to her room at the end of the west wing and knocked on her door. There was no answer. I knocked again and waited. There had been time when I would have simply entered, but having walked in on her naked one day – now I waited. No amount of "I've seen it all before" made any difference, apparently.

Having waited again with no answer, I decided it was worth risking the door. I opened it slowly.

"Alex, are you in?"

The door opened onto a large bedroom, the double bed higher than usual and the furniture in dark polished wood that reflected the daylight from the big French doors in a dull auburn gleam. The French doors were open and I could see

Alex leaning on the stone balustrade overlooking the gardens below. Fionh was with her, so I approached slowly, not wanting to startle her. Fionh noticed me and held up a hand in caution.

"Gently now, Alex," she said. "Let it find its own way."

I edged towards the French doors to see what she was doing. Alex had her arms folded on the rail and was staring intently down into the garden. At my approach, a floorboard creaked underneath me and Alex glanced back momentarily. There was a gurgling whoosh from the garden below.

"Oh, now look what you've done," said Alex. She threw her arms up and turned her back on the garden, resting her back against the balustrade and looking annoyed at me.

"What did I do?" I looked at Fionh, who smiled thinly.

"The pond will take hours to settle now, won't it Fionh?" Alex sounded oddly pleased. Fionh raised an eyebrow.

I moved onto the balcony and looked down onto the garden below. In the centre was a circular pond, water roiling with sediment.

"That was your fault. If you hadn't distracted me, I wouldn't have disturbed all the mud at the bottom," said Alex.

Fionh shook her head in resignation. "OK, enough for today. But I want five fish on the surface tomorrow."

"Five?"

"They're only fish, Alex."

"Yeah, but they go all over the place. They've got minds of their own, right?"

"Are you going to be beaten by five fish?"

"Four," she said.

"Five," said Fionh, heading for the door. "I have things to do in the morning, but there's nothing to stop you practicing before I get here."

"You sound like my piano teacher."

"Did you learn to play piano?" asked Fionh, suddenly intrigued.

"I had lessons," said Alex.

"That isn't what I asked you."

"I can play a bit," said Alex.

"I thought not," said Fionh. "Tomorrow then, and five, not four. Niall, could I have a word?"

"Talking about me behind my back again?" asked Alex, as we retreated to the corridor.

Fionh waited until I had passed through the door. "Actually, no. I want to speak to your father about something else. I'll talk to him about you when when I can tell him how hard you've worked."

"But I *have* worked hard...." Alex's voice was muffled as Fionh closed the door.

"You're very patient with her; I'm grateful."

"I'm not doing it for you, and I said we wouldn't talk about her behind her back," she said.

"But I wanted to ask you how she was doing? Garvin said she was improving. She is, isn't she?"

"Improvement is a relative term. Is she better? Yes. Is she ready to join the courts in her own right, no. At least not yet." She glanced towards the door. "I'm hopeful, though."

"Hopeful?"

"She's still having nightmares, Niall. She cries in the night. She puts on a brave face in front of other people, but we both know she's been through a lot."

"Will she ever be the same?"

"I doubt it. In any case, that's not what we're trying to achieve. She's changed – she's had a lot to take on in a short period. She needs to find a new equilibrium, to find her feet again without them getting swept away from under her."

"How long will that take?"

"The rest of her life, maybe? It was you I wanted to talk about, though."

"Me?"

"Yes. I'm busily giving lessons in power to your daughter and you're missing out."

"In what way?"

"I was supposed to be teaching you. Garvin asked me to talk to you about it."

"I've just seen him; he didn't say anything to me."

"No reason he should. You're progressing with your physical training, but that's only half the story. You need to learn to use your power – you have no focus, no concentration, your control is erratic – you're ruled by your emotions."

"And on the positive side…?"

She smiled, but the smile faded. "It will get you killed Niall. It took you weeks just to master your glamour enough to carry a sword without anyone noticing."

"That's more difficult than it looks."

"Warders have to control their power – not just use it but make it an extension of their will. It's a weapon that's more potent than your sword and potentially a greater weakness if it's used badly."

"I get by."

"Getting by isn't enough. Your power should be an expression of your inner self, a reflection of your determination, concentration and will-power. Use it well and you won't need to fight."

"I'm not sure my inner self needs expression."

"I'm talking about learning to use your power, Niall, not therapy sessions."

"Look, sorry but I'm too old to go back to school. I'm just trying to imagine you teaching me the way you teach Alex."

"I'm not sending you back to school, and I'm not going to be teaching you. I have my hands full with Alex and my other duties, remember? I've arranged for someone else to give you lessons later on."

"But not with you?"

"No."

"Then who's teaching me?"

Two

"This isn't working," I said.

Blackbird glanced sideways at me and then returned her gaze to the parkland that spread out before us. The wide-brimmed sun-hat shaded her eyes, concealing her thoughts from me. "You're not giving it a chance."

"I thought when Fionh said she would find me a tutor, she meant one of the other Warders."

"Thanks." The brim of her hat dipped as she looked down at her hands.

"I didn't mean...I just meant that they would be more... objective."

The August sun beat down upon us, she in a light summer top and shady hat, and me in warders grey. I was hot, irritable and wanted to go inside for a drink.

"You don't think I can be objective?" she asked.

"I think you'd be objective about other people, just maybe not about me."

"You think now that you're a Warder and I'm just a mother, you're beyond my ability to teach you anything... ?"

"It's not that. Dammit, we sleep together. We... doesn't it

bother you? We had a child together."

"I don't recall you doing much sweating and straining," she said. "The way I remember it, it was mostly me having the child."

"That's what I mean. That's exactly what I'm talking about. You don't give me credit for anything."

"You want credit for birthing our child?"

"No, of course not. But you don't allow me any... oh, it doesn't matter. Just get on with it." I sighed in resignation.

"Have you considered that the problem might be with you?"

"There you go again."

"I'm simply suggesting that you might not be be adopting the best approach. If you're going to learn anything you need an open mind – *just get on with it* is perhaps not indicative of openness."

I looked at the landscape, not appreciating any of it.

"How do you feel?" she asked.

"How do I feel? I'm hot. I want a drink. I'm sitting here baking in the sun, wondering what we're doing out here. How is this helping me?"

"You need to be more open to the possibilities."

"I'm open." I opened my arms wide. "Look at me – how open do you want me to be?"

She smiled and looked back at the view. It was a stunning vista, designed by someone famous, apparently, and modelled on the work of Capability Brown. It was supposed to invoke peace and tranquility. It wasn't working.

"Anger will not help you," she said.

"...For anger leads to hate, and hate leads to..."

"Don't quote movies at me that I haven't seen," she said.

"If you haven't seen it, how do you know it's a movie?" I asked her.

"You were doing the funny voice."

I smiled. I couldn't help myself.

"That's better. I was serious about anger not helping you. It tightens everything up, and limits your ability to respond."

"How then, mistress, should I respond?"

She let the sarcasm pass. "You could start by cooling us down. You're sitting here in the heat and it's making you irritable and tetchy – even more than usual. It would be a simple thing to summon a cooling breeze and drop the temperature by a few degrees... not too much. I don't want to lose my hat."

She tipped it forward again, shielding her eyes. The breeze I had called tugged at her loose top. The cooler air over the grey long-sleeved shirt that was the Warder's summer uniform helped lower my temperature and cool my head.

"Maybe I should go and get a hat," I suggested.

"Running away so soon?"

"I'm not running away, I'm just saying that a hat might be good. You've got one."

"You don't have a hat," she said.

"I could borrow one. I'll get sunburn."

"If you don't want to do this, Niall, you don't have to."

"I'm fine. I'll manage without a hat."

There was a long pause.

"The breeze has died," she said.

I summoned it back, but it whipped up the bank, tipping Blackbird's hat from her head and sending it tumbling across the grass. I ran after it as it veered away and I barely caught hold of it before it landed in the flower bed.

I walked across the grass to the bench where she waited. I handed it back to her and she squinted up at me, light and laughter bright in her eyes. The copper tints in her hair caught the sun like burnished metal.

"It was your breeze, Niall, you could simply have let it die and you wouldn't have to chase the hat across the grass."

"I like chasing hats."

"Warm now?"

She had a point. It was far too hot to chase around. I sat on the bench beside her and resumed looking at the view.

"Your power is an extension of your will," she said.

"You've told me that before – or somebody did – Fionh, maybe."

"What is your will, Niall?"

It was an odd question. "What do you mean? Are you asking what I want?"

"No, I want you to tell me what your will is. What is this thing that your power is an extension of?"

"It's what I want, isn't it? What I need, maybe. Didn't you say once that magic responds to need?"

"I did, and you do well to remember it, but that is your unconscious will. Your magic will respond because your unconscious demands a response, but not in any way that's controlled – it's like yawning, you can't control it."

I yawned. She smiled.

"Its the heat."

She carried on smiling.

"You did that deliberately," I accused.

"I suggested an idea and your body responded. I can seed ideas into your mind because you are unfocused and undirected – you have no will."

"Of course I have a will."

"Not a directed will. It's hanging like a banner without a breeze. It's waiting for direction, and by making a weak suggestion I can influence you. In a difficult situation, that's dangerous. It makes you vulnerable."

"In a combat situation I wouldn't be unfocused. Having someone try to kill you concentrates the mind wonderfully."

"Until you're distracted, and you're distracted very easily."

"I'm not."

"The breeze has died again."

This time she held onto her hat. The breeze ruffled the grass and twisted in her hair.

"…and when you call it back it has the tone of your temper in it. You're going to have to lose that."

"That's not me, it's doing that by itself." I let it die down.

"No, Niall, that's you. Let it go and I'll show you."

The gusts died away and the summer heat descended on us, beating down. Then a breath of breeze stirred around us, shifting and flickering, veering and backing. It found direction, pushing gently from behind, cooling our backs and necks.

"Show off," I remarked.

She looked down at her hands again, but I knew she was smiling. We sat in silence while the breeze cooled our backs and we took in the view.

"What do you want me to do?" I asked, eventually.

"Do? I'm not your boss, Niall, and I don't give you orders. If you want to learn, I'll teach you, but it has to come from you. I'm not taking orders from Garvin, or anyone else."

"Garvin put you up to this? I thought it was Fionh's idea."

"And how is that different?"

"Fionh has her own ideas about how things are done."

"She's still a Warder, Niall, and that puts her firmly in Garvin's camp."

"We have camps, now, do we?" I asked.

She lapsed into silence.

"I thought we were all on the same side," I said

"We have sides now, do we?" She used exactly the same

tone that I had. "I don't like what he does, I don't like how he does it, and most particularly, I don't like him," she said.

"Who are we talking about now?"

"Garvin." Her gaze was on the horizon.

"Well unfortunately I work for him, so I don't have that luxury."

"You don't have to work for him."

"He's providing a roof over our heads, sanctuary for my daughter, and for our son, and a place for me in the courts which I wouldn't otherwise have."

"The courts provide that, not Garvin. He places you in harm's way. You're not ready."

"Thanks for the vote of confidence."

"You're not. He knows it, I know it. Even you know it."

"Do you have a better plan?" I asked.

There was another long silence.

"If you do, I wish you'd say because I'm not seeing any glowing alternatives. Most of them involve being homeless and at the mercy of whoever comes along."

"Everything has a price, Niall, especially this." She brushed imaginary flecks from her skirt.

"Yes, well, sometimes you don't really have a choice."

"There's always a choice, if you are prepared to take it." She stood up. "Think about that while you're deciding who you want to learn from."

She brushed the back of her skirt with her hand and then walked back towards the house. The breeze around me died, leaving me to sit in the baking sun.

Rather than summon the breeze again or follow Blackbird indoors, I walked back towards Alex's room. Fionh had mentioned that she would be alone this morning and it would be an opportunity to see how she was progressing for myself.

I walked past the pond but the water was clear, the sediment undisturbed. It didn't bode well for the practice Alex was supposed to be doing in Fionh's absence.

"Can I come in?" The door was resting open, a heavy leather-bound book resting against it to let what little air there was drift through the room.

"Yeah, why not?" Alex was lying on the bed, staring at the ceiling.

"I thought you might be asleep."

"It's the middle of the day, Dad."

"People do sleep in the day, especially when it's hot." I went in and sat in the armchair near the window out of the sun. She rolled over, resting her head on her hands.

"Not me. I can't sleep unless it's dark. Not even then, sometimes."

"Still having nightmares?"

"No." The lie was blatant and obvious.

I'd asked Blackbird how she could lie so openly, given that fey magic rankled against a lie. Blackbird had shrugged and told me that teenagers had a different relationship with the truth. "Maybe to her, it's not lying," she had suggested, but the tone in Alex's voice told me that it was, even though she showed no sign of being tongue-tied or having any difficulty with her words.

"What's up?" Alex asked me.

"I just came to see how you were – how you're getting on with Fionh."

"She's busy. She said she'd come and see me later."

"I know. I thought I'd come and see how you were getting on with your practice."

"It's boring."

"It's necessary."

"She says I'm doing better than you are."

"She said that? You must be doing well, then."

"Not really. She was talking to Garvin about you." The implied criticism hung in the heavy air.

"So have you done some practice this morning?"

"Sure." Again the lie.

"Why don't you practice for a bit with me – you can show me how much progress you've made."

"S'boring."

"You can show me how many fish you can bring to the surface."

Alex sighed and rolled over again to stare at the ceiling. "When are we going home, Dad?"

"We are home." Now I heard the lie in my own voice.

"Not this place. I mean real home. When are you going to take me to see Mum?"

"That's a bit difficult sweetheart."

"She thinks I'm dead."

"That's part of the difficulty, yes," I nodded.

"I feel like I'm dead. I'm so bored!" The pipes rumbled in the bathroom. Alex glared at the bathroom door and they subsided.

"Why don't you do something, then? You could play tennis?"

"All the bats are broken."

"They're called racquets."

"They're all broken."

"I thought you played with Fellstamp last week?"

She sighed. "They were old. They twisted when we played with them. They're all broken now."

"OK, we could find some more?"

"Fellstamp cheats."

"He cheats? In what way?"

"Doesn't matter. They're broken anyway." Her arm flopped out sideways and hung over the edge of the bed. "I've got bats at home. Kayleigh and me used to play."

"Kayleigh and I," I corrected.

"We used to play on the courts after school. Even if we did-n't have a net it was better then playing with Fellstamp. Kayleigh doesn't cheat."

"I'll talk to Fellstamp."

"Don't bother. He won't play with me, and I don't play with cheats."

"All right, I'll ask Slimgrin if he'll play with you."

"He's on assignment. Garvin told Fionh. He won't be back until next week."

"Fionh, then."

"Fionh's too stuck up. Besides, I don't like tennis anyway."

It was my turn to sigh. "Well, what would you like to do?"

"I want to see Mum."

"Alex… it isn't that easy."

"Why? What could be simpler? How hard could it be? We go and see Mum… that's it," she shrugged.

"You can't go back to living with your mother."

"Why not? You just don't want to admit that you lied to her. Again."

"I didn't lie to her."

"You told her I was dead!"

"You were dead… or at least we thought you were. That's what we were told."

Alex straightened her legs and lay with her arms crossed over her chest, eyes closed in a parody of death.

"You're not dead, Alex. I can see you breathing."

She twisted over suddenly. "No! I'm not dead! So why do I have to live in this morgue? Nothing happens here. It's like a home for the elderly. There's nothing to do and no one to do it with. I might as well be dead."

"Don't say that. It's not true."

"I want to see Mum. I want to see Kayleigh and I want my room back." She was shouting and as her voice rose the rumbling in the pipes rose with it. "I want my music, and my things. I want to be in my own room, in my own house, doing my own thing. What's so hard about that?"

I kept my voice quiet, trying to soothe her. "I do understand, but it's more complicated than that. Your mum… It's going to be a huge shock. She needs to be prepared."

"So prepare her! Write her a letter. Get on the phone. Do something! Anything!" The pipes rattled and banged.

"It's not just your mum, Alex. Everyone thinks you're dead. Your teachers, neighbours, friends… you can't just walk into school and say, 'Hi – I'm back'."

"Why not? What do they care? They'll get over it."

"You killed three girls, Alex. You drowned them, remember?"

"They don't know that. They think it was an accident."

"It wasn't an accident, though was it?"

"Is that what you think? You think I killed them on purpose? You think I filled that place up with drain-water and shit just to get even with that slag and her council-flat coven?"

"I didn't mean it like that."

"Well how did you mean it? Huh?"

"I meant that it wasn't an accident. The drains didn't explode, did they Alex? There was no build up of gas. It was you."

She rolled over again, staring at the ceiling. "They should've left me alone. I tried to warn them. Kayleigh did too. Fionh says they got what they deserve."

"I find it hard to believe that Fionh said that."

"She said that if you are challenged and you win, then that's fair. It's blood price. You don't challenge someone if you're not prepared to fight – to the death if necessary."

"She means among the Feyre, Alex. She's not talking about human people."

"I'm fey now, though, aren't I? Them rules don't apply to me."

"Those rules, and they apply to you if you want to be part of human society. I don't think you *can* go back, sweetheart, not once you've broken them."

"You broke them," she accused.

"Yes, I suppose I did. But I can't go back either."

"Mum's got Barry now."

"That's not what I meant."

"But you're not stuck in here. You can go out whenever you like. You don't have to be cooped up in your room all the time like a freaking prisoner!"

"You're not a prisoner. You can go out. There are all the grounds, you have the freedom of the house for the most part."

"It's just a bigger prison, Dad," she said.

"Look, everyone says you're doing really well, but to be able to go out you have to do better than that. You can't just lose your temper and blow the drain covers off because someone looks at you funny."

"I've never blown drain covers off! Now you're making stuff up about me!" she protested.

"You can go out when you can keep a hold on your temper, and a lid on your abilities." I stood up. "Until then you're not safe. So it's up to you. Prove to me that you can control yourself and I'll take you out."

"To see Mum?" she brightened.

"I'll think about it."

Her expression fell. "No, then."

"Like I said, I'll think about it."

"Yeah, you always say that when you don't want to say no, but you're not going to say yes," she said.

"Some things aren't as easy as yes and no, Alex. Maybe if you grew up a bit and took some responsibility for yourself you'd understand that."

Now she looked sulky.

"You could start by actually practicing some of the control you're supposed to be developing. How many fish can you actually bring to the surface?"

"Seven." The lie was plain again.

"Alex, you're not helping yourself." I moved to the door. "I have things to do, and so do you, if you would only do some of them. I can't keep cleaning up after you."

"Oh, so it's my fault the government was torturing prisoners is it? It's my fault that Porton Down was experimenting on innocent people?"

"No," I said, "but it's your choice how you deal with it."

"You're only saying that because you don't want to explain to Mum."

"I'm only saying it because it's true. I'm trying to help you."

"Maybe I don't want help. Maybe I'm beyond help."

"Look", I said. "Neither of us can go back, but both of us can go forward. Learn to deal with things as they are and you'll be happier for it." I stood in the doorway. "Think about it."

"My life sucks," she said.

"Everyone's life sucks at one time or another. There are people around you who care, but they can't help you if you won't help yourself. You can lay on your bed and sulk all your life or you can get up and do something."

"When you and Mum broke up, you did something. You left. You walked out the door and you left me – with her! You've no idea what she was like."

"That's not fair, Alex." Though I knew very well what Katherine was like.

"Yeah, well. Life's not fair. That's what you always say."

"That's because it's true," I said "Your mother gave me no choice. I didn't like it and it wasn't fair, but that's the way it was. It's about time you learned that life isn't perfect and you have to make the best of what you've got. Grow up, Alex."

The remark came out harsher than I'd intended and her eyes brimmed. She turned away to face the window.

I swept out and retreated down the corridor, feeling that once more I was in the wrong no matter what I did. She knew she'd struck a nerve with her last remark, but then she knew where all my soft spots were and never failed to exploit them. Now I had said too much and I was automatically in the wrong.

I bunched my fists as I walked away. *Kids!*

When I got back to our rooms, Blackbird was leafing through the folders I had left on the desk.

"Those are supposed to be confidential," I said.

"Secret is what it says here," she said, checking the front of the file.

"Wouldn't that imply that you shouldn't be reading them?"

"They're not really secret. No one would be stupid enough to leave secret documents lying around on a desk where any-one might read them," she pointed out.

"Touché." There was not much point in grabbing them back now. She was most of the way through the pile.

"Where's the baby?"

"Going to sleep."

"I'll just go check on him."

"If you go in there now you'll wake him up again. Leave him be. If he has a nap now he'll be much nicer to know later. Otherwise he'll just be crabby all day, and it won't be you that has to suffer."

I bit my tongue on the reply to that.

"You could have seen him when he was having a bath. I heard you sneak in earlier."

"I was on my way to see Alex."

"Really? How is she?" she said.

"Sulking."

"I could hear you across the courtyard."

"Yes, that went well, didn't it?" My shoulders sagged in resignation. "She's bored. She wants me to take her to see Katherine."

"You're going to have to take her eventually."

"I know. I said I'd think about it."

Blackbird looked up from the files. "You need to do more than think about it, Niall. Perhaps if you were to see Katherine alone, just to begin with."

"If I even hint that Alex is alive then Katherine will want to see her. After all she's been through she'll need to see Alex for herself."

"Then you're just going to have to grasp the nettle, aren't you?" she pointed out.

"I'm trying to think of a way to do it that won't seem like I lied to her. Alex does have a point."

"By delaying you are only making it worse," she said. "If you'd told her as soon as Alex got back you might have a leg to stand on, but as it is…"

"Alex had no control whatsoever to begin with. She was still in shock after what happened. How could I take her to her mother in that state? With her emotions driving her power, anything might have happened. She was a danger to herself and everyone around her. She still is."

"Nonsense. She's no worse than any other teenager."

"I spoke to Fionh earlier and she said she's not ready to join the courts."

"And what would Fionh know? When was the last time Fionh had anything to do with anyone under a hundred years old?"

"She's the one coaching Alex. She has the most contact with her."

"She's a Warder, Niall. With all that entails."

"What does that mean?" It didn't escape my attention that I was also a Warder, so that particular criticism was aimed at me too.

Blackbird shook her head and went back to reading the files. "Where did these come from?"

"Originally they were from Porton Down. They were passed to Garvin from Secretary Carler, the civil servant who looks after relations with the six courts."

"What are you supposed to do with them?"

"I'm supposed to find the people mentioned in them. Why?"

"They read like scientific mumbo-jumbo. What do you think morphological instability is?"

"In what context?"

"Andy exhibits signs of morphological instability, exhibiting severe disassociation and fragmentation," she read from the file.

"The doctors at Porton Down were experimenting on these people. Maybe Andy couldn't control his glamour. That would lead to sudden changes in appearance that might be called instability. I had trouble with it myself at first."

"Pyrokinetic projection?"

"That would fit with the guy who burned down a shopping centre. Garvin says the fire spread without an accelerant and through fire barriers, killing one guy and injuring another. Plus the CCTV wasn't working. That would point to someone with a fey affinity."

"If this person is throwing fire around, then that would tend to indicate a degree of control. You don't just throw fire – air doesn't burn on its own."

"So maybe there was an accelerant, but not something they'd recognise, or they don't have the language to describe it."

"Or maybe they don't know what they're talking about." She tossed the file back onto the pile. "This is just jargon and speculation. The language is so technical you'd need a glossary to decode it. It's as if it was written to deliberately obscure what they were doing."

"Perhaps it was," I said.

"I read through the file on Alex and didn't understand it, even though I know what happened to her."

"I don't need a file to tell me how Alex is."

"They thought she was delusional, and schizophrenic," said Blackbird.

"Was that before or after they tortured her?"

"It's nonsense, in either case."

"Well since you've had the chance to read through the files, maybe you could suggest which of these people I go after first?"

"Do you think you're ready to go after any of them?"

"Thank you for making that a question," I said.

She ruffled through the files and extracted one, handing it to me. "How about this one?"

I opened the file to a picture of a middle-aged woman staring out of a passport sized photo. Her name was Angela.

"I've seen this woman before."

"You have?"

"She was in the isolation cells below Porton Down. There were a bunch of people locked up in there. I got Raffmir to get me a key to let them out."

A spray of blood spattered onto a glass wall as Raffmir's sword took the head from the nurse who brought us the key to the cells. Her head bounced down the corridor, right in front of me. Black blood ran down the glass leaving a dark smear in its trail. The smell of fear and death was in my nostrils...

"Niall?"

"Hmm? Sorry?"

"You've seen her before?"

"Sorry, yes. When I opened the door to the glass cell, she touched me on the cheek."

I touched my face where she'd placed her hand. When she had reached out for me I had tried to push her away, but it had been like it was glued there.

"You let her touch you?" Blackbird was incredulous.

"I was helping her escape."

She sighed. "You see what I mean now about not being ready."

"She went all wide-eyed on me, started talking about brightness."

"And there was brightness, wasn't there? You lit up everything in a five mile radius," said Blackbird.

"Then she said something else: 'The sun will rise, and they shall fall'."

"I beg your pardon?" Blackbird suddenly focused back on me.

"It's what she said, just before she ran into the dark."

"That's what Deefnir came out with, at the Highsmith's farm. He started blabbering about the felicitations of the Seventh Court and wanted to touch me." She put her hand on her stomach. "Amber wouldn't let him. Deefnir said, 'The son will rise and they shall fall'. I thought he was talking about our son."

"I thought Angela was talking about the sun in the sky, she'd mentioned brightness. I thought I'd hear it before somewhere, but I couldn't remember where."

"Kareesh."

"What?"

"When I took you to see Kareesh, on the day you came into your power. You bargained for your vision, but before she granted it, she said something. Evader of traps, bringer of hope – it ended with, 'the sun will rise and they shall fall', don't you remember? At the time I thought she was finally losing it, she never volunteers things – not usually."

"I don't understand the connection. Why should Kareesh say the same as this woman – and what's Deefnir got to do with it?"

"There's not enough in the file to tell us what's going on. They seemed to think she was a fantasist – they weren't sure she had any power at all."

"But she said the same thing as Kareesh."

"And she was touching you at the time. You're the link, Niall. You were there, both times."

"But not when Deefnir said it."

"But your son was there inside me. You thought it was the sun will rise, but maybe this woman was referring to your child."

"What does it mean?"

"I've told you before, Niall. Prophesy is fickle and uncertain. You can't rely on it. It could mean anything. Even those who see the future don't know what it means."

"I've got to find this woman."

"It won't be difficult. They've given her address. Apparently she's living there."

Turning to the back of the file, there was a photograph of her in a raincoat leaving the front door of a house. Below it was a street map of Tamworth, along with her address.

"Isn't she worried she'll be arrested?"

"What for? As far as I can see she hasn't done anything, except maybe witness things that no one else knows about. If they were going to pick her up they'd have done it by now, so I expect they're leaving her for you."

"I guess I'd better go and see if she's still there then."

On the back of the dresser was a wooden stand, holding the scabbarded blade that came with my job. I took it down and unsheathed the blade, checking the edge for nicks and straightness, then pushed it smoothly back into the scabbard.

"What are you planning to do?" she asked.

"I'm going to talk to her, and find out what she knows."

"You don't need a sword to talk to her," said Blackbird.

"As you pointed out earlier, I need to be ready for anything. Who knows what she's capable of?"

"You sound like Garvin."

"Yeah, well. Maybe it comes with the job," I said.

"To the man with a scythe, everything looks like grass."

"I thought it was hammers and nails?"

"A nail that's hammered is still a nail, with care it can be pulled and hammered flat and may be used again, but once the hay is cut, there's no re-planting it. Not every job needs a sword, Niall."

"Yeah, but there's never one handy when you need it, is there?" I walked to the door. "I'll be back later."

"Try not to get killed," she said.

"Thanks for the vote of confidence." I closed the door behind me.

THREE

Angela's house looked like any other semi-detached built between the wars. It had bay windows and a small arched porch sheltering the front door. There were pins for the gate-hinges in the brick wall where the short driveway emerged into the road but unlike its neighbours, the iron gates which had originally fronted the other houses had been removed.

The house had skipped the fashion for whitewashed rendering and survived as plain brick. As I walked along the opposite side of the road I noted the net curtains hung for privacy, the shrubs in the front garden which had been recently pruned and the brass padlock on the side gate. It suggested cared-for and careful. There was no car on the front drive, but that was true of many of these houses in the middle of the day. It didn't tell me whether there was anyone home.

Strengthening my glamour, I diverted attention away as I reached the end of the street, then crossed to the other side. Reversing my course, I walked back towards the house. The gardens at the rear backed onto one another, providing a possible escape route for me, as well as for her. I wondered what

Garvin would do in these circumstances, but then he rarely did anything this trivial and he didn't work alone. He'd have another Warder backing him up at least.

I began to wish I'd asked one of the other Warders to come with me and watch the back of the house; no amount of magic meant you could be in two places at one time. Still, this job didn't warrant a team. It shouldn't need more than one Warder for a lone woman with no history of violence. More than that would simply scare her, and scared people were irrational and dangerous – there was no reason to turn this into a fight.

Reaching the house again, I looked for signs of occupation. There were empty milk bottles on the step, but they could have been there for days. All the windows were shut, and given the heat of the day that would indicate that no one was home. Maybe I could let myself in and wait for Angela to return.

Movement at the upstairs window caught my eye – not empty then. There was a vague figure behind the net curtains. With my glamour concealing me I should not stand out, even for someone watchful. I continued walking until I reached the end of the street.

With the house occupied, it was more complicated. I couldn't guarantee it was Angela and I wasn't sure if there was more than one occupant. It increased the risk and added uncertainty. I could sneak around the back and try and see who was in, but I had no way of knowing whether she might have set wardings around the back of the house in case of unwanted visitors. The front was safer; anyone could approach the house from the front – milkman, postman, cold-callers. It made sense to stay where the traffic was.

I turned back on myself again, wondering if any of the

houses opposite were unoccupied. I could let myself in to one of those and watch Angela's house from across the road. As I reached the house I noticed a change. In the front downstairs window of the house there was a white rectangle in the window. As I got closer I could see that a sheet of paper had been taped to the glass. On it was written, 'What are you waiting for?'

So much for stealth.

I brought the sword alongside my leg allowing my glamour to conceal it. If necessary I could draw it quickly. I turned into the drive.

As I reached the front door it opened. Angela's face appeared in the gap.

"Oh, thank goodness you're here," she said.

I glanced behind me, wondering if I was being followed by someone else. I was alone.

"You'd better come in, the kettle has just boiled," she added.

This was turning into a strange day.

She opened the door wider and allowed me into the dimly lit hallway. After the heat and brightness of the summer day outside, the cool of the tiled hall was welcome. Angela was careful to keep her distance.

"Shut the door, you'll let the heat in."

I pushed it closed behind me, wondering momentarily if I'd just entered a trap. My hand slid down to the hilt of my sword.

"Come through, I'm making tea, if that's OK?"

It didn't sound like much of a threat, so I followed her down the hall to the kitchen at the back. It would once have been small, but someone had put in a joist and opened it into the sitting room next door to make a kitchen-diner. There was a large French door looking out over a meticulously cultivated garden. After the dark of the hall it was light and airy, and still much cooler than outside.

"Is it?" she asked.

"What?"

"Is tea OK, or would you prefer something cold."

"A cold drink would be fine."

"I have some home-made lemonade if you would like?"

"Great. Thanks."

I watched as she opened the tall fridge and took a jug from the shelf.

"You knew I was coming?" I asked.

She glanced up, hesitantly, and smiled. "I thought you'd be here earlier." She poured the cloudy liquid into a glass and then added a spoon of sugar. "It's a little tart," she said.

"You know who I am?"

"I've known ever since I touched you in the isolation units under Porton Down. Take a seat." She gestured to the chairs around the dining table.

"I'd rather stand." I glanced at the chairs. "You knew I'd say that?"

She shook her head. "That's not how it works, but you already know that."

Placing the glass on the table beside me, she returned to the kettle and made herself a cup of tea.

"Lovely house," I said.

She smiled as she added milk to the tea, moving around the kitchen, watching me from the corner of her eye.

"Have you been here long?"

"I was born here. My mother had me in the bedroom upstairs. I was a home delivery."

"Is your mother here now?"

"She died."

"I'm sorry. I didn't mean to..."

"It was a long time ago. She was an old lady."

I watched her reaction. "How old?"

"She was in her nineties, so she had a good span. I think she held on for grandchildren. Not to be, I'm afraid."

"You're married?"

"No. There's just me if that's what you're worrying about. You won't be needing a sword."

"What makes you think there's a sword?" I thought I had concealed it. I had been practicing carrying it without anyone noticing.

"It's in your posture. You stand like a dancer, but you're not here to dance."

I tried to look more relaxed without relaxing. I didn't work. "So you live here alone?"

"Company would be nice, but it's difficult finding someone who..." She shook her head. "Touch isn't really..." She looked up. "It's very limiting. I'm sure you understand. Even animals seem to pick it up."

I sipped the lemonade, looking out of the window at the garden, realising that she must spend a lot of time there. Plants were so much less complicated than people. They were living things you could touch without sparking visions of other people's lives.

"You'll start to remember soon," she remarked.

"Remember what?"

"What I saw, in the rooms under Porton Down. I've given you the memory."

"You've given it to me? How?"

"It's in the lemonade."

I looked down into the translucent liquid, then put the

glass back on the table, wondering what she had poisoned me with and how long I had.

"It's only a memory, not the full experience. I stirred it in with the sugar."

"Why?"

"Because I want you to understand what I saw. Think back, there's a memory that's not your own."

I thought back to the night Raffmir and I broke into Porton Down, to the people we had killed and those we had saved.

I remembered the rooms with glass walls reinforced with iron wire. I could see myself taking the key from the nurse's hand, the swish of the blade, the spatter of blood across the glass, the slowing ooze as the blood ran down the glass, black and glossy in the dim light.

Strangely I can see both sides of the glass.

I remember the sudden trepidation that the dark figures would kill me too, followed by the realisation that we were being set free. These were not my memories. I could see myself through another's eyes; a shadowed outline under the faded safety lights.

The key is turned; hope outweighs my fear while my heart pounds in my chest. I edge closer; the overwhelming urge to touch. My hand finds its way to his cheek. I am momentarily blinded, a piercing light – so much brightness – then darkness and an after-image, a rising sun. The sun will rise, and they shall fall. I can hear myself saying it.

The image of the sunrise is burned into my retina. My logical mind says that it could be a sunset, but my power knows different. I stumble away down the corridor, away from the man. I can barely see. My eyes fill with a searing light that hasn't happened yet....

I blinked, vaguely disorientated by the foreign memory. I couldn't escape the feeling that something alien was planted there.

"How can I have your memory? Can you remove it?" I said.

"The memory? Now that would be interesting, wouldn't it? If I could make you forget things, how could you trust your mind? I could make you forget why you're here, where you came from, who you are." She shook her head, "No, I can't remove it."

"You could have just told me."

"Do you know what it means?" she asked.

"Some of it. The light could have been me. There was a helicopter spraying bullets onto the roof. I created the light to destroy it."

"I saw the aftermath when I left. What about the rest of it? The sun will rise and they shall fall. What does it mean?"

"I was hoping you were going to tell me," I said.

"Come with me." She went into the hall. "Come on, I won't bite."

I followed her upstairs, careful to keep the sword where I could draw it if I needed to. There was a landing at the top, a bathroom and two bedrooms. At the front of the house was a closed door. A small sign on the door said, Caution! Woman at Work.

She stood with her hand on the door. "I was a writer, you know? Freelance; mainly brochures and advertising copy, before all this."

"All what?" I asked.

"The facility at Porton Down. Did you know I volunteered? Initially they took volunteers. We were treated better than the other inmates, though that changed towards the end."

"I'm surprised you went, given that you must have known what would happen there."

"Oh I had a fair idea what they meant to do, but it was that or be taken there. It was going to happen anyway. Easier on me if I went willingly. It's all in here."

"What is?"

"See for yourself."

She pushed open the door and stepped back, leaving me room to come forward. It opened into a small room at the front that had been converted into a study. There was a desk and chair, a pile of books and notepads – an ancient looking computer and keyboard had been pushed to one side. A desk lamp stood on one corner angled down so it wouldn't dazzle.

The walls were covered in notes of every size, colour and shape. Every patch of wall-space had been tagged with sticky-notes of different colours, pieces of ruled paper pinned to the wall, fragments torn from pads. I pushed the door open further. They were on every wall, as high as she could reach.

"What's it all for?" I asked.

"It starts on the wall behind the door," she said. "See for yourself."

I hesitated.

"It's OK," she said. "I won't lock you in there. There'd be no point."

I stepped into the room and pulled the door back from the wall, trying to discern what I was looking at. Some were scribbled notes, others inscribed in calligraphic letters. To begin with, most were notes on lined paper, carefully cut from the page, but as they progressed around the room they degraded to pages torn from books, scraps of newspaper, napkins, pieces of cereal packet.

There were random images scattered amongst the notes. Some were instant scribbles, like the moon and stars on a sticky-note, others carefully sketched, like an engraved medieval sun, shining down beneficently. Initially it was chaotic, but then themes started to emerge.

The phrase, the sun will rise, was scattered throughout,

but as the notes became more frantic, the writing became less legible.

After that the fragments became more diverse with pieces I recognised. The words, Gauntlet Runner, written over a newspaper photograph surrounded by pictures of rabbits cut or torn from magazines – cartoon rabbits, rabbit symbols, photos of rabbits. In another there were dogs of all different shapes and sizes. One section had spikes, nails and all manner of pins and the distinctive curve of horseshoes.

"What's it all for?" I asked her, where she stood outside the door watching me scan around the room.

"I've written nothing except this since I came back," she said, "I can't pick up a pen without this coming out. I dream it, I find myself repeating it when I'm cooking, I end up humming it to myself. Nails, rabbits, stars, the rising sun. It's all I can think of since I touched you."

Her manner was becoming more anxious. Her tone was clipped and she pushed her hand through her hair. "It's in my head and I can't get rid of it, God knows I've tried. I need you to tell me what it means. I've been waiting for you to come so you can tell me what it means."

She was rubbing her hands together, dry-washing them.

"I don't know what it means."

She must have heard the slight hesitation in my voice. "But you suspect."

"I recognise some of it. I doesn't make any sense, though."

"Tell me."

"I'm not sure it helps."

"Tell me!" She reached for me and my sword was in my hand. We faced each other, her outstretched hand close to the edge of the blade. She met my eyes.

"Are you going to use that on me?"

"If I have to."

"You can't imagine what it's like. It's driving me to the edge. If you can tell me what it means then maybe it will leave me alone. If you're here to kill me, then do it. It'll be a mercy."

"I'm not here to kill you."

"Then tell me what you know, or you might as well use that sword before I kill myself."

I glanced again at the walls. "A lot of it is about me, I think."

"What about you?"

"The rabbits – I'm called Rabbit by some, Dogstar by others…"

"Sirius – that's the dogstar isn't it? I have a picture of Orion on the wall there. Sirius is below it – look there."

"There's a ceremony with nails and horseshoes. It's an ancient ritual."

"I have nails – horseshoes too, what's it got to do with you?"

"I was involved with it, last year. It was going wrong but we fixed it."

"This is all about you…" her eyes tracked around the walls.

"I don't know what the rising sun means, but it's come up more than once – not just with you but with other people. Maybe whatever it means hasn't happened yet."

"Will you let me touch you?"

"No."

"Just for a moment. I swear I won't harm you."

"What for?"

"I just need to see… maybe I'll be able to say what it means. It could help you."

"It could make it worse," I said.

"I don't think so." She gave that nervous shake of the head again.

I watched her and realised how thin the veneer of sanity was, and how close she was to doing something stupid. I couldn't leave her like this, not when it was my fault.

"I have a proposal," I said.

We arrived at the High Court without warning, which might not have been the best idea. Amber was in the room where the Ways terminated, sword drawn as she realised I was not alone.

"Who's this?" she asked.

"A guest – my guest." I glanced at the sword, and she lowered the point minutely.

"You're not supposed to bring visitors, Dogstar."

Angela was looking around wildly, disorientated by the unexpected landing.

"She's not a visitor. Garvin told me to bring them in, well here's one of them. Angela, this is Amber. You can trust her. She'll protect you."

Angela glanced warily at Amber, who raised an eyebrow minutely.

Angela looked around. "Where are we?"

"Somewhere safe. I need you to stay with Amber for a moment while I make arrangements. Will you do that? Just don't touch her or anything."

"I won't touch her," said Angela. "She wears death like a shroud."

"Great," said Amber. "One of those."

I led Angela away from the centre of the floor in case anyone else tried to use the Way. Collisions were unlikely, but it wasn't a good place to stand. I led her so she could lean against the wall and I watched her take in her surroundings.

"How do you feel?" I asked her.

"I'm fine – that's quite a ride."

"It's exhilarating to start with, but you'll tire quite quickly. It takes it out of you."

"I went hill walking once, in the Lake District. We came down a scree slope and everything started sliding. Travelling on the Way – it was like that, only more so."

"Sit down here, against the wall. I'll only be a few moments. I just need to let people know that you're here and get you somewhere to stay.

"I'm not staying."

"We'll see. It'll be OK."

She slid down the wall, crossing her legs and watched Amber warily. Amber made a point of not watching her, leaning against the wall, closing in on herself. I had seen her stand like that for hours without moving, but with the potential to strike at any moment. No wonder Angela watched her.

I left them and went up into the house, searching for Garvin. I found him in the hall talking to Fellstamp.

"Dogstar. I was just coming to see you."

"You were? I only just got back."

"Yes, and you brought someone with you. Fellstamp, go and give Amber a hand, would you? I need a brief word with Niall."

Fellstamp grinned at me as he passed. There was no sign in his movements of where I had run his shoulder through with a sword during my initiation as a Warder. The old swagger was back and his dark curly hair fell across his eyes, which sparkled under his fringe with amusement. To me his nose was too broad, his lips too full, but I also knew that among the female Stewards he was considered very attractive. It was rumoured that he'd slept with most of them.

"I'll go keep our guest company, then, shall I?" He executed a neat half turn that kept him facing me as he passed, and as I came between him and Garvin, he winked. He spun back neatly and walked the way I had come.

"What's up with him?" I asked Garvin.

"Hard to say," said Garvin, "Our visitor wouldn't be female, would she?"

"How did you know that?"

"You know how Fellstamp loves to flirt."

"I don't think Angela's his type."

"I didn't know Fellstamp had a type. So she's called Angela. What's her affinity?"

"I didn't ask. She's like Kareesh, though, she can see the future, or possible futures."

"Earth and Fire then. I'll arrange for an audience with Teoth for her. Is she house-trained?"

"What does that mean?"

"Is she dangerous? Do we need to lock her up?"

"No, she's fine. I need to do something, though. She's had a vision and I think it's about me. She wants to touch me, but I didn't want to do it alone."

"You're going to let an untrained seer touch you?"

"The sun will rise, and they shall fall."

Garvin gazed steadily at my eyes. "She said that?"

"Not just said it. She has diagrams of it and poems of it. She draws it and dreams it. It's all over the walls of her office. She's been able to write nothing else since she encountered me in the cells under Porton Down."

"OK. I'll have her brought up to the drawing room."

"That was too easy. You've heard that phrase before."

"Perhaps."

"There's no perhaps about it, Garvin. Blackbird told me

that Deefnir used exactly that phrase when he cornered her at Highsmith's Farm."

"Then you are well-informed, Dogstar." His use of my Warder nickname was intended to remind me of my position as newest and most junior of the Warders.

"It's not just there, though is it? You already knew about it."

"You're guessing, Dogstar." He led off towards the drawing room.

"It's a good guess, though, isn't it?"

"Perhaps. Let's see what your seer has to say."

"You'd better sit on the floor. You can't fall off that," said Garvin.

Angela stood in the doorway, watching Fellstamp move the dust-sheeted armchairs back and create some space in the middle of the disused room. Amber drew back the drapes and let the sun back-light the lace curtains. It should have made the room warm and inviting, so why did I feel cold?

Perhaps it was the memory of when Kareesh had held my hands in the tunnels beneath Covent Garden Underground Station, gifting me with a vision of my future, or at least my probable future. It had set me on a path that saved me from a gruesome death at the hands of the Seventh Court, but left me wondering how much was preordained and how much was down to chance, or fate, or decisions that I or the people around me made.

Blackbird said that the future was uncertain, that even seers could not predict – they could only show you the points on your path that were most likely to occur. My last attempt at this with Kareesh had worked out for me – I had escaped the Untainted and found a place in the courts – maybe that's why I was willing to give Angela a chance. There was a risk, but by doing it here in the presence of the other Warders that risk was limited.

Garvin's reaction bothered me. He had been all about business as usual until I mentioned what Angela had said, and then he had become interested. If I had proposed letting Angela touch me in normal circumstances then the answer would have been no, I was sure. I was expecting to have to persuade him, to argue my case. Instead he had agreed almost without discussion and made immediate arrangements. He caught me watching him across the room and I looked away. I never had any doubt that Garvin was trustworthy, that he had the best interests of the Courts and the Warders at the centre of everything he did. I just wondered how much of that included me.

"Sit here," Garvin said to Angela.

A clear path had been created for her to take a seat in the middle of the rug. The other Warders kept a wary distance from her. No weapons were displayed, but after her words about my stance and posture I noticed that the other Warders moved in a similar way. It wasn't that they danced, but that they looked like they could dance, or they were ready to dance. Perhaps that's what training as a Warder did to you. I smiled to myself for a moment, wondering whether I should actually learn to dance and whether Blackbird would like that. Would she dance with me, I wondered?

Garvin must have caught my smile. "Looking forward to this?"

"Not especially. Too late to back out now, though, eh?"

"You don't have to do it if you don't want to. It was your idea."

"So it was."

"Gain as much knowledge and insight into your enemy before you make contact," said Garvin. "It's a sound approach."

"What enemy, Garvin? What am I looking for?"

"That's what we're trying to find out." He squeezed my shoulder in a gesture of reassurance.

Once again I thought that there was more that he was avoiding telling me. It would do no good to ask, though. He would tell me when he thought I needed to know.

I sat cross-legged opposite Angela, about a hand-width apart. She smiled reassuringly, but I could see she was nervous. She kept glancing at the Warders around the room, assessing distance, looking back at me, seeking reassurance herself.

"Do you still want to do this?" I asked her.

"I don't have any choice."

"There's always a choice." I found myself echoing Blackbird's words and smiled at the irony.

Angela smiled back, taking it as a positive sign. She reached out to touch my cheek, but I shook my head. I held out my hands, palms upward and open, forearms resting on my knees. "Trust me, this is how it's done."

She looked at my hands and then positioned hers above them. "Ready?"

"No one ever is," I told her.

Her hands clasped mine.

Cold rushes down my arms – I thought I remembered the cold from last time, but my memory was blunted. It sears and burns through my veins, running like rivers of quicksilver, killing sensation. My eyes blur with tears and my teeth grind together until my jaw aches. Humming vibrates through me, a note so low I can feel it in my bones.

There is Angela behind the glass screen, reinforced with iron wire, her face illuminated in the pale nimbus-glow surrounding me. Blood slashes across the glass, running down in black rivulets, and the door is open. Her hand touches my cheek and her eyes fill with light.

"The sun will rise and they shall fall." This is not the future, it's the past.

The world spins and I fall, plummeting into a funnel which narrows so that I am rushing down a tunnel, twisting and buffeting, this way and that, until I stop, suddenly and immediately, standing in the room below Covent Garden Underground Station in the dim orange glow from the lamps with the smell of new turned earth and recent rain. Kareesh sits in her nest of cushions, reaching for me, grinning with pointed teeth.

I looked around for Blackbird, but she isn't here. Gramawl looms in the background at the edge of the lights from the filigree lanterns hung from the ceiling. Blackbird was here when this happened and Gramawl wasn't, why isn't she here now?

Kareesh speaks in her crackly voice, "Here you are at last, gauntlet runner, witness and suspect, evader of traps, bringer of hope. Rabbit will be your name, but not for always. Another name will be yours, Dogstar, when you have earned it." She reaches forward and touches my face. "The sun will rise and they shall fall. So say I."

"So say I." My eyes are glazed as I hear my voice acknowledge hers, but that's not what happened. She never called me Dogstar – that happened later when Raffmir named me at the anvil under the Strand. Are we changing the past?

There's a cawing sound behind me and I turn to look. I am outside, a path leads up through a graveyard to an ornate archway with a wooden door of grey bleached wood. The arch over the door is carved with impossible creatures, serpents, griffins and manticores, the carved face of a man with ivy growing from his mouth stares down at me. The door swings open and two men stand before the door speaking in low tones.

"The work is completed?" The first is tall, dressed as a priest.

"It is done, though why you need such protection on God's house is beyond me, Father." The second looks worried. He has the tan of a man who works outside. His hands are rough and criss-crossed with old scars.

The priest clasps the man's wrist. "Never speak of it. Understand?"

"I still say, it ain't right," says the man.

"He moves in mysterious ways, and we are His servants. This will stand well for you in the life to come," says the priest.

"I hope so, vicar. I surely hope so."

As the door closes, everything is inside out and I am in a tall room lined with books. Shelves vanish into the dimness on all sides. A dark-haired man sits at a desk, a lamp at either side. Open in front of him is a book, its pages brown at the edges, the paper as thin as tissue. Each facing page has three intricate symbols aligned down each page and between them is a central design which spans the join. The symbols shiver and squirm on the page but the central design is clear, a circle containing four symmetrical shields arranged in a cross. The symbols have text beside them in the tiniest writing. I squint to see what they say, but my eyes blur and the text runs into grey.

The grey resolved into mist. I begin to see that there are people around me. There is a noise I recognise, the distant squeal of brakes and hum of an electric train. The mist pulls back revealing a London Underground platform crowded with people.

I have been here before.

The train is getting close, I can hear the clack and rumble as it approaches. I am standing in the same spot as on the morning I first learned about my fey heritage, on the same platform with the same people. On that morning, the man beside me fell deliberately onto the tracks as the train reached the platform. He committed suicide by tube train.

I look at the person next to me, but it's not the same man. It's a skinny boy with spiky hair. He glances at me with knowing eyes and

then at the approaching train. He looks calm, relaxed. I look back to
where the train is clattering onto the platform. Aware of what is
going to happen I turned back to the figure next to me to find him
wreathed in fire. Long curling yellow flames ripple up his arms, his
clothes smoke, his face shimmers in the haze. No one else notices, no
one steps back from the heat that radiates from him.

He steps around and stands on the edge with his back to the track,
looking at me, his eyes filled with orange fire. He extended his burn-
ing hand to me. I lift my hand to take his, but the heat from his hand
is incredible.

"It's too hot!" I tell him. My hand blisters as it nears his. I can't
take his hand.

"How can you save me," he asks calmly, falling slowly backwards
into the path of the train, "when you can't even save yourself?"

Four

Angela's hands release me and I topple sideways. Cramp sends shooting pains up my leg and I kick out trying to release the pain.

"Nnnngh." My tongue is welded dry to the roof of my mouth.

"I think he's having some sort of fit," said Fellstamp, grinning down at me.

"Give him a moment," said Garvin. "Well, Angela? Did you see anything?"

She pushed out her legs, stretching her calves and rotating her feet. "It's not for me to say." She rubbed her hands together, encouraging the circulation. The afternoon sunlight had disappeared, leaving the room in twilight, but having done this before it was not such a shock that so much time had passed.

I managed to unstick my tongue. "Water," I croaked. Fellstamp knelt down beside me and offered me water from a glass. The glass felt oddly warm in my hands and my teeth chattered against the edge as I sipped from it. I swished the liquid around my mouth to ease the dryness.

"Did you get what you needed? Did you find out what it means?" Garvin asked Angela.

She looked up at him, suspicion in her eyes. "You know enough about me, I think, to know that your Warder will know the meaning when the time is right. It's not for me to interpret for him, or to explain what he's seen. I did see one thing, though."

"And what was that?" asked Garvin.

"This isn't about me, is it? It's about him." She gestured to where I was sitting half-upright on the floor. "This started long ago and I am only the latest link in the chain of events. I'm not the first to speak of a rising sun, am I?"

"Nor the last, probably. How about you Dogstar, what did you see?"

I looked up at Garvin and wondered what he wasn't telling me. "To me it seemed to be more about the past than the future. Maybe whatever it is has already happened and we're just not seeing it?"

"Seeing what?" asked Garvin.

"Perhaps if you told me what you were looking for, I could help you find it," I said.

"If we knew what we were looking for, I'd be able to find it myself," said Garvin. "Fellstamp, give Dogstar a hand, will you? He'll need to sleep it off. I'll ask Mullbrook to find room for Angela."

"I'm not staying," she said.

"On the contrary," Garvin said. "I insist."

"You did what?" Blackbird was incredulous.

"It was a calculated risk."

My head was thumping and my vision had acquired a strange heat-haze effect. Maybe that was causing the nausea.

"After our conversation this morning, when I specifically mentioned the dangers of letting her touch you, you let her do it again? What were you thinking of Niall?"

"We need to know what this is about."

"Who is this 'we', that needs to know?" she demanded. "Why don't you let Garvin dirty his own hands?"

"It wasn't Garvin's idea, it was mine."

"Then why, Niall? For goodness sake why?"

I sighed. "You didn't see her room. It's covered in images and clippings and scraps of paper, and as far as I can tell they all link back to me. It's like she's been following my progress without even knowing who I am. How can she do that?"

"She's fey, and a seer to boot. Who knows what her motives are?"

"You took me to see Kareesh. She's a seer."

"Yes, and I had doubts about that. Kareesh has cared for me since I was a girl but I don't just let her lay her hands on me any time she likes!"

"I had Garvin there to help. He could have stopped it if it was needed."

"What's he going to do, chop her head off? You had no idea what she was capable of – she was imprisoned the same as Alex. Do you think they were treating her any more gently than they did your daughter? She could be insane for all you know."

"She didn't seem insane."

"Your daughter didn't seem insane until she… no, sorry Niall, I didn't mean that. Alex isn't insane, she's just…"

"What?" My expression had darkened at the mention of my daughter's mental state.

There was a sound like a mewling cat from the next room which quickly changed to a more persistent cry.

"Now you've woken the baby," said Blackbird, an edge of irritation creeping into her tone.

"Me? I wasn't the one making all the noise."

Blackbird bustled into the nursery, and in a moment the curtains were drawn back and she reappeared carrying a flushed and rather cross baby.

"Don't you worry, Daddy's going to stop yelling at you now." She rocked him in her arms, though he continued screaming.

"I wasn't yelling..." but it was useless to argue since he didn't understand the discussion anyway and Blackbird was just making a point.

"Here," she said, handing me the screaming bundle. It never failed to amaze me how someone so small could make so much noise.

"There, there," I said, trying to make my voice soothing and still be heard over the din, "there's no need for all that, now, is there?"

I held him, being careful to support his neck which had a tendency to flop over to one side, and transferred him onto my shoulder, putting his mouth next to my ear, but making it easier to stroke his back and comfort him. I rocked from side to side and gradually the yelling subsided to a low-level grizzle.

Blackbird opened drawers and pulled towels from the rack, settling onto the bed. She held her hands out. "Pass him over."

"I've just calmed him down. Give him a moment.

"He's hungry, that's all. Pass him to me."

I gave in and lowered him into Blackbird's arms, where-upon he started crying again, just as I had predicted. Blackbird ignored the yelling and lifted her top, exposing a pale breast before lifting the baby's open mouth to a brown nipple. The crying was muffled for a moment and then subsided into a noisy suckling.

"See," she said. "Hungry."

I humphed and looked away. For some reason the sight of my son locked onto his mother's breast made me uncomfortable. Alex had been bottle fed as Katherine had problems with breastfeeding, not the least of which were several bouts of painful mastitis. Consequently I'd got used to seeing babies bottle fed, taking my turn as it came, but while the sight of my son gulping from Blackbird's swollen breasts was perfectly natural, I didn't feel that it was a spectator sport. Perhaps it was too many years of looking at women's breasts for entirely different reasons.

"Why don't you get some sleep," Blackbird suggested. "You look done in. I won't be long. As soon as he's finished his feed I'll put him back down – he should sleep for a couple of hours at least.

I took her advice, taking a brief shower while she fed the baby and then climbing into bed as she settled him back down. After a few minutes she climbed into bed beside me, sighing with exhaustion as her head hit the pillow.

"Hard work?" I asked.

"No, he's fine. Just a long day."

I rolled over onto my side, watching her stare at the ceiling. "I've been thinking about names," I told her.

"Not again, Niall. Not now," she protested, squeezing her eyes shut.

"A family name might be nice, do you think?"

"The Feyre don't name their babies until after the first half-year. We've been over this a hundred times. He won't get his name for ages yet."

"It doesn't stop us choosing a name for him," I said.

"It's bad luck to name him early, and if you choose a name you'll start to use it, you know you will."

"I thought the Feyre didn't believe in luck."

"Tradition, then."

"Traditions can change? Neither of us is fully fey. Maybe he should have a name after three months, as a compromise."

"It's just not the way it's done Niall, you must try and understand."

"It seems a strange sort of tradition that won't give a child a name. Katherine had chosen Alex's name almost before she was born and it didn't do her any harm."

"Your son isn't Alex and I'm not Katherine, now turn the light off and go to sleep. He'll be awake in four hours and he'll want feeding again whether he has a name or not."

"It doesn't stop me thinking about it," I said.

"As long as you don't say it out loud." She deliberately made her voice sound more sleepy to discourage further conversation. I rolled onto my back and clicked the light off, staring up into the dark.

James was nice, and it could be shortened to Jim, though I didn't like Jimmy. Perhaps Paul – you couldn't really shorten Paul to anything.

With that thought, sleep claimed me.

The moonlight bled all the colour from the night. The grass looked grey as Alex hurried across the open space. When she reached the shelter of the oak tree she stopped, breathless, looking back where she'd come.

There were no lights on behind her, no alarms rang. She let the glamour concealing her fall away. Then she noticed the outlines of her footsteps were printed across the lawn where the dew had been disturbed. She stared at the prints, and one by one they smudged and vanished, leaving the grass pristine. She turned her back on the house.

Beyond the row of trees it was no longer lawn, but meadow. The grass would be longer but she'd leave less of a trail. Some cows had been allowed to graze the far field. She looked at her trainers and the bottoms of her sweat-pants which were already wet with dew. She frowned again and they were dry.

"Lovely night, isn't it?"

"Fuck!"

When Alex peered beneath the tree she could see a shadowy figure was leant against the tree trunk.

"Does your father know you use language like that, Miss?" Tate's voice was low and clear in the stillness of the summer night.

"You near enough frightened me to freaking death. What are you doing creeping around like that? You could give someone a heart attack."

"I'm not creeping. I've been here all the time. You, on the other hand…"

She placed her hands on her hips. "I couldn't sleep. I needed a walk." Alex's expression dared him to contradict her.

"A walk that required you to erase your footsteps?" said Tate, glancing back at the lawn.

She followed his gaze. "It looked so smooth. I didn't want to spoil it."

"What I can't figure out, Miss, is why you bother lying to me when you know I can hear the difference," said Tate.

She looked at her feet and then up at the shadowy outline under the tree. Even now she knew he was there he was still difficult to see. It was hard to tell where Tate stopped and the tree carried on. "Yeah, well. It's easier than telling the truth, ennit."

"Ennit?"

"Isn't it? Is it not?" She laughed in the dark. "I can't believe you're correcting my grammar."

"Where were you going?"

She looked across the moonlit meadow. "Out. This place is doing my head in."

"Were you planning to come back?" he asked.

"Sure, yeah. Got nowhere else to go, have I?" She looked at her feet again, and then up at the gnarly figure against the gnarly trunk. "Were you spying on me? Is that how you knew I was out here?"

"No."

She shook her head. "Now who's lying."

"You think anyone can walk in or out of the High Courts of the Feyre without someone knowing about it?"

"Did I trip the alarm?"

"Better than alarms," he said.

"You were following me."

"I was waiting for you."

"Are you gonna tell Dad?" she asked.

"Tell him what?"

"That I was sneaking out."

"I thought you were going for a walk?" he said.

She tried to make out his expression under the shadow of the tree, but it was impossible to read in the deeper shade near the trunk.

"Yeah, right," she said.

"Let's walk then." He separated from the trunk and walked out so that the moonlight slid across his shoulders. The bleached light made his long hair seem grey.

"How old are you?" she asked, moving out into the light alongside him. They began walking gently around the perimeter of the lawn.

"That's a very forward question, Miss."

"Don't ask, don't get. That's what Mum always says."

"Does she, indeed?"

"So how old are you?"

"Very." He said.

"How old's that?"

"What's the oldest thing you know?"

"What, like animals and stuff?"

"Anything."

"The Earth. That's the oldest thing, ennit? Isn't it?" she corrected herself. "Or the sun. That's older, I s'pose.

"I am younger than the sun," he said, "and the Earth."

"Well yeah, everyone is, aren't they."

"Not so old after all then." There was a low sound that might have been soft laughter.

"What about... that tree." She pointed to an oak with a huge canopy at the edge of the grass.

"I remember it as a seedling."

"Really?"

"Perhaps."

"What about my house? My mum's house, I mean."

"That is not even as old as the tree. There was a time before the houses were built when all that estate was farmland, much as you see beyond." He nodded at the fields laid out under the moon. "Before that, not even farms."

"That's harder to imagine, somehow," she said. "It's like my house ought to be older."

"It's what you grew up with," said Tate.

"What did you grow up with?"

"Forests. The deep woods and silent streams that were there long before mankind forced itself on the landscape."

"How old are you, really?"

"I've stopped counting."

"Very convenient."

"Age does not mean so much to the Feyre. We do not age as humans do. Once you stop growing you will stop ageing too."

"At least I won't have to worry about wrinkles like Mum does."

They reached a fence and Tate held the gate open for Alex to walk through. They continued in silence for a while.

"I was going to see her."

"Who?"

"Mum. That's where I was going. Dad won't take me, so I thought I'd take myself."

"Ah, the truth. At last."

"You won't tell Dad?"

Tate was silent for a moment. Then he said, "Why do you think your father does not take you to see her?"

"Dunno, I think he's afraid of what she'll say when she finds out I'm not dead."

Tate said nothing, and they continued walking. By now the side of the house facing them was in shade and Alex kept glancing towards the house, wondering whether they were being watched from the darkened windows.

"She's not gonna believe it to start with, is she? I mean, it's like mental. Isn't it?"

"Yes," he said quietly, "It's like mental."

"Are you taking the mickey?"

"Sorry, Miss?"

"Never mind. So are you going to tell Dad?"

"What is there to tell? We went for a walk."

Alex glanced up at him. "Yeah, we did, didn't we. Do you play tennis?"

"No," said Tate.

"Fellstamp played with me. He kept trying to look up my skirt."

"The way Fellstamp told me, you kept bending over in front of him."

"I never!" She glanced back towards the house. "He cheats."

"So do you, apparently."

"Yeah, well. He started it."

"It does not make for good tennis if both of you cheat."

There was a pause.

"Anyway, the bats are broken."

"So I heard."

"Does he talk about me?" she asked.

"Who?"

"Fellstamp."

"Not especially. Why?"

"Nothing. I mean he obviously said something, you know, about the bats."

"He said he didn't think you'd be playing tennis again."

They rounded the end of the house and turned along the frontage. For the first time Alex could see Tate's face. The individual bristles on his chin caught the light so that it looked like it was frosted.

"I could fix the bats," volunteered Alex.

"Perhaps you should. They weren't yours to warp like that."

"I never warped them. They were twisted already," she protested.

Tate's eyebrow rose fractionally.

"He was cheating," she repeated, defensively.

Tate shook his head, slowly.

"He does look kinda cute in shorts, though, don't you think?" Alex grinned.

"I don't think I've ever noticed," said Tate.

Alex looked up, letting the moonlight fill her eyes. "All that working out with swords and stuff really defines the thigh muscles, you know what I mean?"

"I imagine you see him a little differently, Miss," said Tate.

"Why do you call me Miss, Tate? Only Mullbrook and the stewards call me Miss, and they have to because they work here, but you say it like you don't mean it."

"It pleases me to call you Miss, Miss." There was that low sound again, a soft huffing that might have been laughter.

"Yeah, well, seems to me like you're taking the piss, Miss," she said.

"Then what would you have me call you?"

"My name?"

"Very well, Miss Alexandra."

"Now you're teasing me. Why can't you call me Alex like everyone else does?"

"There is power in names," said Tate.

"What does that mean?"

"It means that how you are called in some ways defines you. Miss is a title, not a name. Once you would have been Mistress Alexandra."

"Makes me sound like a floozy, or a school-marm."

"It is an honorific, or it used to be."

"I quite like that. The Honourable Mistress Alexandra Dobson," Alex tested the title out for style, "accompanied by the honourable Mister Tate….do you have a family name, Tate?"

Tate smiled, "Not exactly, no."

"Any brothers or sisters?"

"No."

"I have a brother now," said Alex. "A half brother, really, I suppose. It's going to be strange, he'll always be younger than me."

"I expect so, Miss."

"There you go again."

"Sorry, Miss."

They reached the drive leading to the main entrance and Alex stopped. "I should go back to bed, I s'pose."

"It will be light soon," confirmed Tate.

"Thank you for the walk."

"You're welcome, Miss."

"You won't need to mention this to Dad, will you?"

"It'll be our secret, Mistress Alexandra."

She hesitated and then smiled. "G'night then."

"Goodnight, Miss."

Alex walked back towards the house and mounted the steps to reach the main door. It was locked, but that was only a moment's thought. As she pushed the door gently open, she looked back. The circle of the drive curved away from the house, rounding a stand of trees beyond the lawns and flower beds, all flooded with moonlight. There was no sign of Tate.

Her gaze lingered on the drive for a moment, and then she shook her head.

"G'night, Tate," she murmured, and slipped inside.

"You look better today," said Blackbird, the hat's rim lifting as she glanced sideways.

"I'll take that as a compliment," I said.

"That was a reckless thing you did yesterday."

"That's spoiled the compliment somewhat."

"You need to be more considered in your actions. If you keep blundering into things you're eventually going to meet something nasty."

"I've already met several things that were nasty. So far I've survived."

"Through sheer luck, but that luck won't hold forever."

"Thank you for the vote of confidence."

"That's the trouble, you're cautious when you should be bold and overconfident when you should be cautious."

"I'll try and do things backwards in future, is that today's lesson over with?"

"Close your eyes."

"Is this the lesson now or are you still berating me for letting Angela touch me?"

Blackbird looked sideways at me under the brim of her hat, and then forward again. "Close them," she instructed.

I did as I was bid and closed my eyes.

"What can you see?"

"Nothing, I've got my eyes closed."

"Really? You see absolutely nothing?"

"Well, not nothing, but nothing that makes any sense. Splodges of colour, sunlight I suppose, the light through my eyelids."

"You can make no sense of it, so you ignore it."

"What am supposed to do, make shapes out of it like you do with cloud formations?"

"What can you hear?"

"You." She waited while I listened again. "I can hear the birds singing, there are cows in the fields across the way there."

"What else?"

"A plane, maybe?" I lifted my face into the light to hear better. "Is that a plane or is it traffic from the road? I can hear noise from the kitchens now that you mention it, and if I listen very carefully I can hear the breeze."

"Anything else?"

"What else is there?" I asked.

"Your heart."

"My heart? I'm supposed to listen to my heart? What's it telling me?"

"It's not telling you anything, at least not in sound. It is pumping blood through your ears fifty or sixty times a minute. Each pump has a pulse, and if you were to listen to my chest you'd hear my heart pumping much the same," she said. "Say Dockweed."

"Dockweed, why?"

"Does it sound louder to you when I say it, or when you say it?"

"When I say it, because I can hear it inside me."

"Then why can't you hear your heart?"

"Sorry?"

"You are able to hear my heart, if you listen, and a word is louder when you say it then when I say it, but when I asked you what you could hear you did not hear your own heart. It is pumping blood through your veins, through your ears, and yet you do not hear it. Why not?"

"I suppose because I'm used to it."

"More than that."

"Because it's my heart?"

"Yes, and no."

"Why then?"

"Because, if you could hear your heart then you would hear nothing else. It's loud in your ears but your brain has learned to ignore it because it contains no useful information. Instead you can hear the bird in the woods or the tiger sneaking up on you, conditioning and survival has made it so."

"Evolution in action," I said.

"Not evolution, perhaps. Some say that in the womb we hear our heartbeat and that of our mother, and that only later do we learn to filter it out. Not evolution, but choice."

"What's this got to do with my lesson?"

"What can you feel?"

"I don't know – the seat we sit upon, the breeze on my back, the dampness of my shirt. Am I supposed to be feeling my breakfast digesting in my stomach?"

"So seldom do we truly listen, truly feel, that we forget that the world exists whether we perceive it or not. We hide our heads under the blankets like children and pretend there's nothing there."

"Are you saying that there really are monsters under the bed?"

"I'm saying that for reasons of comfort and the freedom from being overwhelmed by our sense of the world, we choose to ignore a great deal of it, but we forget that we have chosen and continue as if what we have chosen is all there is."

She let me think about that for a moment, and then continued, "I'm saying that you block your sense of the world, and that to perceive it better you will need to unblock your sense and see the world anew."

"How do I do that?"

"You learn to listen. You take time to feel. You pay attention to what your brain is telling you to ignore until you can hear your own heart, if you so wish."

"And where will that get me?"

"You want the reward before the work, Niall Petersen." She frowned in disapproval.

"No, but it's not unreasonable to ask what the benefit will be if I accomplish this task, is it?"

"It's a fair question." She considered. "A violinist teaches themselves the fine distinction between a note that's sharp or true. A painter knows every shade of blue that his paints can render. A tumbler can sense their balance no matter which way they tumble, and yet none of these begin that way. They practice what they do until they have it right. They don't attempt to play a symphony, or paint a masterpiece, until they have mastered the basics.

"And this is basic?"

"No, this is fundamental. It is the beginnings of power and the end. Knowing the nature of things, being able to name them truly despite their appearance, or attempts to deceive, is a great gift."

"So you're not fobbing me off with trifles?"

"Triviality ended some time ago, Niall. The play is in progress and the stakes of the game are survival itself. I will leave you to practice."

I opened my eyes, squinting up at her in the sunlight as she stood and smoothed her long skirt, then walked easily back towards the house leaving me on the bench seat. I was still there some twenty minutes later trying to hear my own heartbeat when Tate found me.

"Trouble," he said.

"What's up?" I stretched. Having absorbed the tranquility of the garden I had the sense that I might have been asleep when Tate's footsteps alerted me to his approach. I wasn't sure that's what Blackbird had in mind.

"One of your escapees has broken cover."

FIVE

"This isn't trouble, this is a circus! What am I supposed to do with this lot watching?"

Tate's only response was to shrug and look back at the crowd gathered at the end of the road. Police officers in black stab-proof vests were keeping people back and I could see a similar barrier at the other end of the road. In between were an array of police vehicles and ambulances, blue lights flashing. I could hear sirens in the distance, so maybe more were on their way.

"We don't even know if it's him, do we?" I was referring to the file that Garvin had pushed into my hand before we had left the courts and travelled down the ways to Streatham in south London.

"The address matches that of his estranged partner," said Tate. "It was issues with her that sparked the whole thing off, at least that's what the file says. There's an injunction against Difford being within a mile of the house."

"It looks like he's within a mile of it now."

"Then I don't think the injunction is working," said Tate, mildly.

"What's he doing in there?"

"Not a social call."

I went forward to the line of onlookers. "What's going on?" I asked a man in a sweatshirt and shorts who was craning his neck to see.

"It's a siege," he said gleefully, "Some bloke's got himself holed up in the house – they reckon he's got a hostage. Gonna have to shoot him, I reckon."

"Won't that risk the hostage?"

"Nah. They'll use one of them sharpshooters from the windows opposite, you wait and see."

I stood on tiptoe, watching the police moving around the vehicles and talking into radios. There was no sign of weapons being deployed, but they were unlikely to have them on show. I went back to where Tate leaned against a tree in the shade.

"Will the police try and storm the house?"

"Not unless obvious violence breaks out. They want a peaceful outcome. They won't push it, at least not yet. Armed response will be on the way, so that could change."

"We need to move quickly then, what about you?"

"Garvin said it was your problem, but I'll watch your back."

"Thanks. You're a great help."

Tate grinned. "I have confidence in you."

I glanced back towards the gawkers and then turned and walked away from the police line, heading back towards the end of the row of houses.

These houses were built in red-brick terraces, originally two stories high but every one had a loft conversion or a gable window as a third floor. Some had whitewashed rendering on the upper floors or a mock balcony with french doors, painted shut through disuse. The front doors were set two by two along the row with no access to the rear from the front of the house. The bins were all in the front gardens, waiting for bin-day. I counted the numbers on the houses to make sure I had the right house.

The police would be aware that rear gardens backed onto each other and would have people in the house behind, but the presence would be significantly lighter than out here on the street. They were only there to prevent the suspect from bolting over the back fence. If I wanted a quiet entry, that's where it would be.

In a northern town there would be a service alley, dark enough for muggings and illicit drug-taking, but here the original substantial gardens had no access from the street. Each owner had taken advantage of this by building blocky extensions onto the back of the row, leaving a square of green as a token garden, except for the end-house that had taken advantage of the road access by building a garage which faced the side road. It was simplicity itself to cloak myself in glamour and trip the lock to the garage with a pulse of power, pulling the door closed as Tate followed me through.

The garage let me out of a side-door into a passageway and from there I could lift myself up on the fence and peer into the next garden before vaulting over, one at a time. Tate and I settled into a natural rhythm, only one of us moving, the other watching.

The gardens were in contrast to each other, some strewn with children's toys and trampolines while others grew couch grass and thistles to waist-height. Counting the houses back to the one with the police vehicles parked out front, I paused a couple of doors down, letting myself become accustomed to the noise of the city. The sirens were getting closer, but it wouldn't help to climb over the fence and land on top of one the officers watching the rear of the house. I couldn't see them, but I knew they must be there.

I waited while Tate joined me. He pointed over the back fence and was rewarded with a cough from the garden of the houses opposite. There was a low conversation and then silence again. I stared at the windows of the houses facing the back of the row, noting where shadows moved at windows or curtains twitched. There were either a lot of policemen or some nosey neighbours. Probably both.

With everyone watching it was going to be more obvious if I went through the back door of the house, even concealed by glamour. I could ask Tate to create a distraction, but that would only attract more notice. I wanted the attention at the front where all the police cars were. I didn't want them raising the alarm and drawing attention to the rear of the building because they thought something might be happening inside. If I was going to bring my target back with me I needed a way in, and a way out. I looked again at the backs of the houses. The back doors, like the front doors, went in pairs along the row, separated by high fences.

The extensions at the back were two stories high. I moved quietly to the door of the neighbouring house and listened. In all likelihood, if anyone was home, they would have either been moved out by the police or told to stay indoors and out of sight. I wondered which.

I pointed to the door, and Tate nodded and pointed to the ground where he was, indicating that he would stay and make sure no one disturbed me.

A hand on the back door released the locks and I eased the door open, listening for sounds of occupation. The door led into a white-painted kitchen with a very modern range cooker. I closed the door behind me and listened again. There were sounds from the front of the house, but that was probably coming from the road. I crept through the hall, seeing the blue flashes from the emergency vehicles refracted through the glass in the front door. There was a coat-rack, mostly empty, and post on the doormat from earlier in the day.

Taking that as a positive sign I slipped upstairs and listened again on the first floor. The sound of approaching sirens had stopped which either meant that they were not headed this way or that whoever had been making all that noise had arrived and sirens were no longer necessary. I hoped for the former, but suspected the latter.

Reinforcing the glamour, I went quickly up a second set of stairs that looked like they had been added to reach the loft conversion. It was decorated for a child's room, posters of comic heroes and video games. There was a front window, which I avoided, and a back one that looked out over the flat roof of the rear extension, which was what I'd been hoping for.

With my glamour locked tight, I let myself out of the upper window onto the flat roof and moved quickly across the open space, leaping the gap to the next house. This was the one next to my target, so I kept the momentum and leapt again, relying on my glamour to conceal my movements. I knew that they would be watching the back door and that I had to trust my glamour to turn their attention away from the rooftop and me.

On the roof above the extension of the house I kept low until I could peek into the window identical to the one I had exited. My neck prickled as if there were cross-hairs trained on the back of my head. I ignored it, trusting to my magic to conceal me.

The room was similarly furnished for a child – from the pink hairband on the unmade bed and the brushes and combs on the dresser, I'd guess it was for a girl. There was nothing in the file that mentioned children, and for most fey child-bearing was not an option, but this child could be from a different relationship, and was probably safely at school. Even so, I watched the room as I used my power to trip the window catch and quietly slide up the sash window.

As soon as I raised the window I knew something was wrong. There was a smell I dimly recognised, a foetid odour of something bad. My sword was naked in my hand, its weight reassuring, before I slid across the window ledge and into the room. I moved quickly around to the partly open bedroom door and listened. From the stairwell came a shuffling shifting noise, then a dull thud, followed by a long low growl. My heart thumped in my chest – oh now I can hear my heart, I thought. Blackbird would be so pleased.

I prayed that no one else would hear my thumping heart as I slid sideways along the wall above the stairs, watching the open stairwell for something ready to leap on me. Where was Tate when you needed him – wasn't he supposed to be watching my back? Something shifted on the floor below me, heavy but moving quietly. There was a creak, a shifting sliding noise like a sigh, then quiet.

Then it occurred to me – I was the invader here. I was the one out of place. Whoever or whatever was downstairs probably knew this house well and knew every creak of the floorboards, whereas I was the one breaking in with a weapon in my hand. Maybe I should put it away – what did Blackbird say – to the man with a scythe, everything looks like grass?

A low growl from downstairs changed my mind. If I was going to face whatever was down there, I wanted to do it with a sword in my hand.

I slid around and down the outside edge of the stairway,

keeping my weight against the wall where the stairs would be less likely to creak. My movements were covered by the commotion at the front of the house, and I could see a first floor landing through the bannisters with three doors opening off it. There would be more stairs below these leading to the ground floor. The door to the rear room was pushed closed, the other two were ajar. I watched the two open doors as I reached the landing.

At the end of the hallway was a coat-rack, with a couple of adult coats and a smaller pink coat hanging there. It reminded me of my own flat which I had lost. The lower stairs would lead down to a doorway, possibly shared with the neighbours or possibly a separate private access for the upstairs flat. The downstairs would be a self-contained flat of its own. The police were probably in there even now, trying to assess the situation upstairs.

Quietly, I pushed the door to the rear room open. It was a compact kitchen with white units and a stainless steel sink, built out over the rear extension. A bottle of blackcurrant squash was open on the counter and two mugs were placed by a kettle. It looked normal.

I moved towards the second door. The smell strengthened.

Pushing the door to this room open I could see it had been furnished with a large double bed against the far wall. On the bed were two things – my eyes flickered between them. Standing on the bed was the huge black cat I encountered in the corridors under Porton Down, its black fur rippling in the orange-tinted light coming through the heavy drapes. At least I assumed it was the same one – there couldn't be two like that, surely? Lying on the sheets beneath it with her throat ripped out was a woman, her blood soaked into the sheets. Her dead eyes stared at the wall, uncaring, unknowing. It stared down at her and I could hear its soft pant timed with the ripples in its fur.

Its head turned in one liquid movement and it caught me in its gaze, the gold flecks in its amber eyes catching the dim light. I held that gaze for too long; it launched at me, twisting in the air and I fell back, pulling the door closed after me. The cat hit the door and clawed a section out with an easy sweep that cracked the door back against the wall, booming through the building and leaving the door sagging from the bottom hinge. That gave me a moment to stagger around and back up the stairs before it slid round the door. It rippled to the bottom of the stairs and mounted the first steps, its hind legs bunching for a leap.

I edged backwards up the steps keeping my eyes on it, brandishing the bright blade. It ignored the steel and readied for a spring, but then paused, looking back through the doorway to the bedroom. It licked its lips and sniffed again at the air. It was waiting for something – listening perhaps.

Then it sprang, flinging itself at me with easy speed, claws braced wide, teeth bared for the kill. I tripped backward on the step, went down and lifted the sword-point in defence. I felt the blade jar in my hand, heard a scream that sliced its way into my brain, felt the blade ripped from my hand as the weight of the creature bore down on me. Its warm fur smothered my squeal of terror, its heavy scent enveloped me. I was beneath those lethal claws, utterly at its mercy.

Then slowly light emerged. Heat radiated out through the fur, veins were outlined before my eyes. The shape twisted in front of me, a man-shaped cat, a cat-shaped man, it lifted its head and called again – a weaker wail against the dark. And then it turned to ashes and dissolved on top of me, leaving me coated in dry dust.

I had killed it. A lucky hit, I must have pierced its heart. That's the thought that came to me until I tracked back through those last vital seconds. It had me at its mercy. I'd gone down. It could have eaten me alive if it wanted to. It had waited until I was ready.

I lay sprawled on the stairs in stunned silence for long moments while I tried to understand what had just occurred. It made no sense. My hand sought and found the hilt of my sword and the reassuring weight brought me back to my senses just as the police started breaking in the door.

"Police! We're coming in!"

I sheathed the blade and pushed myself up, shedding clouds of fine ash from my clothes and slipping quickly back upstairs, heading for my exit through the open window in the back room. I went for the window and heard a tiny sound. I stopped. I could hear the commotion as the door to the flat finally gave way and the police entered below. They banged and shouted their way in. It would not take them long to find the body.

Even so, I knelt down and looked under the bed. From beneath it a pair of wide round eyes stared back.

"Hello." It was all I could think of to say.

The eyes blinked.

"What's your name?" I asked softly, acutely aware of the banging and thumping coming from downstairs.

"Lucy," she said in a small voice. "Has it gone?"

"Lucy, any moment now a lot of men are going to come in here and turn the place upside down looking for someone. Are you going to be OK?" What a stupid question.

"If you came back upstairs," she said carefully, "then it must have gone. Is it safe to come out?"

I wasn't sure whether it was or not. What would the police

do with a small girl who was hiding under her bed? Would they look after her? The image of the woman downstairs came back to me and I realised that Lucy didn't know what had happened down there, or perhaps she did. Perhaps that was why she was under the bed.

"Best stay there, I think. Someone will come and find you in a few minutes, but stay there for now. Let them run around."

It came to me that I had left it too late, that the thumping sound coming up the second set of stairs was wearing size twelve boots. Making it out of the window and clean away was going to be difficult with fifteen stone of policeman romping in behind me. Instead I settled back into a corner by the dresser, strengthening the glamour around me, cloaking myself in a deep sense of unimportance and the ordinary.

A red-faced police officer burst into the room, staring wildly about. He glanced at the bed, and at the window. He didn't glance at me. A colleague came in behind him.

"Check the room, I'll check the window."

While they searched the room, I concentrated on extending the pool of stillness that included me out to the wide-eyed girl under the bed. She watched me, her eyes growing wider still as the men yanked open doors, leaned out the windows, looked behind doors, searching everywhere except under the bed or in the corner.

"He's gone out onto the roof. Call it in. Tell them to watch at the back. They may be able to see him from the houses behind. He'll have to come down somewhere."

The burly officer that had come in first spoke rapidly into his lapel radio, explaining the situation. The other pulled down the window and closed the catch.

"Seal off the bedroom downstairs until you're relieved. Don't let anyone in there, understand?"

"Yes, sir."

The two officers hurried back out, followed shortly by the noise of them thumping back downstairs. Outside the hubbub rose and fell like wind in the trees, but in the bedroom there was a deepening silence.

Eventually Lucy spoke. "They didn't see you," she said.

"No."

"Are you invisible?"

"Can you see me?" I asked her.

"Yes."

"Then no, I'm not invisible."

"Why didn't they see you?"

I was on the verge of asking her whether her mother told her not to ask too many questions, but then realised her mother was downstairs in the bedroom with her throat ripped out.

"They didn't see me because I didn't want them to."

"Oh," She said. "They're looking for Daddy, aren't they?"

"Are they?" I asked her.

"He brought the beast home with him, and now they're looking for him."

"The beast is…"

"The cat. The really big black one," she said.

"You've seen it?"

She nodded solemnly. "It follows him around, and goes wherever he goes. When he lived with us it used to come upstairs when it thought I was asleep and slip out of my window."

"It came into your room?"

She nodded again, slowly.

"You must have been very brave, not to make a noise."

She nodded again. "You have to be very quiet or it will know you're awake."

I swallowed. I was about to say that it wouldn't be bothering her again, but then she might know very well what that meant.

"It won't come up here now," I said.

"I heard you fighting. Did you kill it?"

Faced with that open-eyed stare I simply nodded. "Do you think you can be brave again, Lucy?"

"Why?"

"We need to get you downstairs and find you someone who will take care of you."

"What about Mum?"

"We need to get you downstairs. We can't go down your stairs because of the policeman, but I could carry you across the roof if you were very brave."

"I'm not supposed to go on the roof. Mum says it's dangerous."

"It is, but I'll be with you."

She glanced towards the door. "Won't the policemen see us on the roof?"

"Not if we don't want them to," I told her.

She wriggled forward on her tummy and then slid sideways out from under the bed. Standing up, she brushed dust from the front of her clothes. "Mum says I'm not to get under the bed, but I've done it before." Now she was in full view I could see that she had mousey brown hair and wore a long sky blue tee-shirt over dark blue trousers. I judged her about eight years old.

"I expect it's OK," I said. I loosed the catch on the window again and slid up the sash. The warm breeze tugged at the curtains at either side.

"Shall I carry you?"

"It's OK," she said. "I've been on the roof before."

"Gone across the rooftops?"

"No, but I climbed out on the roof to look at the stars one night. They said on TV that you would be able to see Saturn, but I couldn't find it."

"There's probably too much light pollution in the city."

"Too many stars," she said. "They all have names, you know." She said it in a matter of fact way and I didn't contradict her. Maybe they did.

I slipped over the windowsill, deepening the misdirection of my glamour, and then helped her join me. The ease with which she slid over the sill made me think she'd done it more than once. Out on the roof it was breezy and warm, more exposed, but it didn't smell of death like the house. Looking down at her I wondered whether she already knew what had happened in the bedroom below. She must have heard.

"I'll carry you across the gaps and then you can walk the rest of the way," I volunteered.

She put her arms up and I lifted her. She was more substantial than I'd suspected, but she wrapped her legs around above my hips and her arms around my neck, resting her head against my shoulder. The urge to hug her was strong, given all that'd happened, but I simply said, "Ready?"

She nodded against my shoulder. Delaying any further would just make it more difficult, so I took a step back and then ran forward, leaping the gaps between the rooftops. It was more difficult with her weight, but I allowed for her and we made it safely across. I walked to the window I had left ajar and she slid down to the flat roof while I opened the window.

"Do you know whose house this is?" I asked her, wondering if she had a friend here.

"No," she said.

"In that case, be careful not to disturb anything," I told her. "We're only visiting."

I slipped over the sill and she followed me. Inside, she held up her hands again. I hesitated for a moment and then lifted her up. She rested back against my shoulder and we moved quickly down through the house. As we reached the ground floor, the noise from outside increased.

"This is the front door," I told her. "There are a lot of people out there, but we'll find someone to look after you, OK?"

She nodded again against my chest.

We went into the front room looking out onto the street through lace curtains. I scanned the crowds. There were police running back and forth up and down the row, and vehicles being backed out through the crowds, but no one paid us any attention.

"Lucy, Something bad has happened. Your mum's not going to be able to look after you. Do you have any relatives – an aunty you could go to?

She spoke into my shoulder, refusing to look up. "No."

"What about grandparents?"

"No."

"Who looks after you when your mum's busy?" I asked her.

"I go to Christa's after school sometimes," she said.

"Who's Christa?"

"She's a childminder. She looks after me until Mum comes and gets me. She looks after other children as well – Sam and Donna. I play with Sam, but Donna doesn't like me."

"I see."

I shifted the weight of her where it rested against me, wondering what I could do. I had rescued her from the house, but she wasn't my child, or my responsibility. I couldn't just kidnap her because her parents were dead. Just because she said she didn't have anyone didn't mean that there wasn't any family willing to take her in. Besides, what would I do with her? I was lodging at the courts until Blackbird and I could find somewhere more permanent, it wasn't our home exactly. It was a mess, but not every mess was my problem.

"Do you think you can be brave one more time?"

She nodded against me.

"You see that ambulance with the blue flashing lights on the top?"

She lifted her head and turned to see.

"Do you see the lady sat on the back step, the one with the blonde hair?"

She nodded.

"I think if you went to talk to her she might let you ride in the ambulance." It was a poor reward for such a brave girl, but I was running out of time and short of options. "Would you like that?"

"Will you come with me?"

It was the question I did not want to answer. I shook my head. "I'm not even supposed to be here, Lucy. I can't come with you. That's why you need to be brave."

She tucked her head back against my shoulder, and despite myself I hugged her close, thinking all the time that this wasn't helping. We stayed there while I watched people outside, the machinery of a crime scene kicking into motion.

"Will the beast come back?" she asked in a small voice.

"No," I said.

"It knows how to find us. It can follow you anywhere."

"Not any more. That much I promise."

She hugged me a bit more and then allowed herself to be lowered to the ground. I went with her to the front door. "Will I get in trouble for being in the wrong house?" She asked.

"They won't see you until you're ready," I told her.

"Will I see you again?"

"Maybe, who knows?" I was reminded of my daughter saying to me, *You always say that when you don't want to say no, but you're not going to say yes.*

She reached up to the door catch and opened it enough to slip through, tugging it closed until the lock clicked again. I watched her from the window, using my glamour to keep her unnoticed. As she got further away from me it got harder, but I maintained as much of it as I could until she was near the ambulance.

When the blonde lady sat on the steps of the ambulance looked up and saw Lucy, I released it. I saw her ask Lucy where she had come from. Lucy pointed to her house, and the expression on the lady's face changed. She knelt down beside Lucy and had her point again, following the line of Lucy's fingers to the one doorway that was wide open on that side of the street. She beckoned over a colleague and sent him to go and get a policeman, and then talked to Lucy for a moment. I couldn't see what Lucy said, but she looked back at where I was standing behind the lace curtain and then shook her head.

It was time to leave.

I let myself out the back and found Tate waiting.

"Well?" he said.

"Case closed," I said, though part of me wished otherwise.

SIX

"It's case closed," I said to Garvin. I was back in Mullbrook's office, trying to explain what had happened.

"If only it were that simple," said Garvin walking up and down, picking points off his fingers. "One – it was your responsibility to clean up the mess after these people were released. Two – of all the people on the list you chose to pursue Angela, who presents little or no threat to anyone, and then you bring her here. Three…"

"You told me to bring them in. Besides, you're always telling me not to go in unprepared – to scout out the situation before engaging."

"Three – you wait until there's a major police incident, hundreds of people involved, media interest, streets full of onlookers…"

"No one saw me."

"Four – you nearly get yourself killed in the process. Five – you then leave a witness who can identify you…"

"She's a child. She won't say anything, and even if she does they're going to think she's making it up."

"Six – you leave a body with its throat ripped out for the

police to examine to their hearts content, no doubt with bloody paw-prints all over the bed linen?"

"It was too late to do anything else."

"And seven – you leave evidence of an escape through an open window so that the police hunt will continue, leaving an open case and an unsolved murder with," he counted his last finger, "…eight – yourself as a potential murder suspect."

Garvin stopped and stared at me.

"Which part of this am I supposed to be happy with, Niall?"

"It was the best I could do in the circumstances."

"The best? I have Secretary Carler demanding an explanation as to why this man Difford wasn't dealt with earlier. He'd already threatened his former partner, he had an injunction out to prevent him from seeing her. It was all in the file. You read the file, did you?"

"Of course, some of it."

"Some of it?"

"I looked through it. I thought it would be best to take them one step at a time – to work my way steadily through them."

Garvin shook his head. "You're not taking this seriously."

"I am…"

"Not seriously enough. These people are dangerous, Niall. They're killers. They've killed before and they'll kill again. Our job," he pointed his finger at me, "is to stop them before they kill anyone else."

"I thought our job was to help them? Bring them in, you said."

"Only where that's an option, Niall. They're damaged goods. Not everyone is going to be able to make the leap – very few of them, probably…"

"So what you really want me to do is to murder them?"

"I gave you Warder's Discretion so that you could make that decision at the time, when it's needed, not so you stand there and admire the scenery. You need to get on top of this, Niall, and fast. Otherwise I'll have to ask one of the others to step in."

"It's still murder, it doesn't matter if someone else's hand is on the sword."

"Tell that to Lucy's mother."

"That's not fair."

"No. It's not nice and it's not fair, but it's what happened. You need to get your head straight before you get you or someone else killed. Think on that while you're reading the files."

He dismissed me with a wave of his hand, turning his back to stare out of Mullbrook's window.

When Blackbird found me I was in one of the abandoned rooms on a dust-sheet covered sofa, a pile of files on the seats to either side of me.

"I can't make any more sense of these than you did," I told her, transferring another file to the pile of files I'd already been through.

She moved the pile of files I'd already been through onto the floor and sat on the covered sofa beside me, her hands clasped in her lap.

"Tate says you're a fully fledged killer now," she said.

"What?"

"He says you killed someone this morning – one of the escapees from Porton Down."

"It wasn't like that."

"What? You gave him a fair fight? Did you challenge him first?"

"He attacked me. I was defending myself, and bloody lucky not to get my throat ripped out."

...the smell of death. Flat dead eyes staring at a wall, blood soaking into the sheets, the torn skin of her throat, gaping red...

"Niall?"

"Yes? Sorry."

"He attacked you?"

"I broke into a house, he – it – was in the bedroom, standing over a dead woman."

"Does it make it easier to use 'it' for a name?"

"Difford. He was called Difford."

"So you killed him."

"He nearly killed me. I managed to throw myself out of the way. A funny thing. He had me cold, I was sprawled on the stairs, I'd lost my footing in the panic to get away. He was at the bottom of the stairs. He could have had me any time he wanted."

"So why didn't he?"

"He waited – it took me a second to reach a position where I could hold my sword straight. Garvin's right, I made a mess of it."

"What was he waiting for?"

"Me, I guess. I'd like to think I know what went through his head in that moment – the woman he'd supposedly come back for was dead, bleeding out into the mattress. He sniffed the air – you could smell blood and shit all the way to the top floor, but he savoured it. Then he threw himself at me, claws and teeth. I didn't stand a chance."

"And yet here you are. Why are you still alive?"

"That's a question I keep asking myself, but I don't feel like a killer – fully fledged or otherwise."

She stood and leaned over, kissing me on the forehead.

"That's not a bad thing, Niall. Not a bad thing at all. I'll leave you to your files."

I watched her leave and shook my head. What was all that about? Would I ever understand her?

Opening another file on my lap, I tried to interpret the stream of technical jargon and half-truths written there. After a second I stopped and closed my eyes. Garvin was right about one thing – I needed to get my head straightened out or I really was going to get myself killed. That was easier said than done, though when there were things that I ought to do that I really didn't want to face up to.

I had been doing the things I wanted to do, or the things I thought I could do, leaving a growing pile of things which for one reason or another I didn't want to do. That pile was getting bigger and it wasn't getting any easier.

Perhaps it was time to grasp the nettle.

"Are you sure this is a good idea?"

Tate must have asked me that ten times while I made the arrangements to see Katherine. I'd asked Big Dave, one of the stewards who was also a driver for one of the court's black Limousines, to drive down and collect her. I asked Tate to say nothing to Garvin about the meeting.

"I don't keep secrets from Garvin," said Tate.

"I'm not asking you to keep it a secret, just don't mention it, that's all."

"He's not going to like it."

"Look, Tate. It's just something I have to do. If you have to tell Garvin then just don't do it until after I've gone. OK?"

Reluctantly, he had agreed.

I had phoned Katherine from one of the increasingly rare payphones and told her I needed to meet, that I had something important to tell her, and that for various reasons I wanted the meeting kept secret.

"Is this one of your games, Niall Petersen?" She had demanded down the crackly phone line.

"No. This is for real. I'll send a car to collect you. The driver's name is Dave and he'll look after you."

"What is it with you and all this cloak and dagger stuff? Why can't you just come to the house like any normal person?"

"You'll understand. I have a lot to explain."

"What does that mean?"

"I'll tell you when I see you."

"You haven't changed one bit, have you?"

"I've changed a lot more than you know. Ten o'clock. Walk down to the end of the road – there'll be a big black car that will flash its lights once. Ask the driver his name. If he says it's Dave then get into the back. He'll do the rest."

"You really love this, don't you?"

"Katherine, just do it, OK?"

"What do I tell Barry?"

"Nothing. He'll be at work and you'll be back in time to cook him supper, though you'll have more to think about than food by then."

"What do I wear?"

"I don't care. Wear something comfortable."

"Typical man, won't tell you whether you're going to be hill-climbing or attending a reception. I don't even know what shoes to wear, will anyone else be there?"

"Just me. That's it. There's no one to impress. Jeans and trainers will be fine."

"Are we going to be inside or out?"

"Outside. But it's warm, the forecast is dry. Just come as you are."

"I'll bring a sweater, just in case. And an umbrella."

"Whatever. Just come."

I would have done this without involving the stewards, but I needed to get Katherine away from anyone else before I told her. That meant I couldn't do it at her house, or anywhere near Barry, her new man. However well-intentioned he might be, this was something between Katherine and me.

I had arranged to meet in a country park, near Northampton. It was mostly deserted during the week and there was a bench overlooking a gravel pit, within sight of the car-park, where we could sit and talk. If she shouted, cried, screamed at me, no one else would be the wiser. It also had the advantage of being a hundred yards or so from a Way-point, so I could get there easily and quickly, and leave the same way.

She would want to see Alex as soon as possible, I knew that, but I wanted her to have chance to get over the shock first, and prepare herself. It had been hard dealing with Alex's loss and I didn't know how she would take the news that she was alive, especially given the circumstances. Alex couldn't go back to living with her mother, and I had to convince Katherine that this was the right decision for all concerned.

She wasn't going to like that.

I sat on the bench under the shifting light cast by the clouds. The forecast had promised to be dry, but hadn't mentioned the gusty breeze or the scurrying clouds. I hoped Katherine had remembered the sweater. The car pulled in late. It had taken over two hours to get here, and I could see by the time she emerged that she was already annoyed. It showed in the set of her shoulders and the determined pace as she walked up the rise to the bench. If she had been trying to pump Tate for information she would have got nothing. That might explain her mood.

"You really have a nerve," she told me folding her arms. "What is this, a quarry? What the hell are we doing here?"

"Take a seat."

"I'd rather stand. I've been sat in that car for over an hour and the driver wouldn't even tell me where we've been going. Where is this, anyway? What all this about?"

"Sit down."

"I will not."

"I have something to tell you, and you're going to have to sit down to hear it."

"Are you ill? Is Blackbird all right? Is it the baby?" Her voice had shed some of its crossness but was rapidly escalating into hysteria.

I stood up. The immediate height advantage meant I was looking down on her, so she sat down. I sat down, leaving a small gap between us.

"You remember last year when there was all the trouble?"

"When they fished you out of the Thames, you mean?"

It had been the Fleet, not the Thames, but I let that go. "Something happened then that I've never told you about."

"I've always thought that was dodgy. You're not after money are you? Is someone blackmailing you?"

"What? Don't be absurd. I'm trying to tell you – something happened that changed me."

"Are we talking about Blackbird? If you want to get married I won't stand in your way."

"No – I was changed. I found something out about myself, about my family and my history that meant that everything had to change with it."

This was not going well. I looked down at my hands.

"I inherited something from my family, an ability, I suppose you would call it, or a trait maybe. Something passed down from one of my ancestors."

I looked up. Katherine's face was frozen. All colour had drained from it, and she wasn't looking at me, but past me. I turned my head to see what she was looking at. A little distance away Alex stood on the grass, her hands in her pockets, a look of terrible uncertainty on her face.

"Mum?" she said.

"That's... what I was trying to tell you," I said.

Katherine ignored me. She stood, and then rushed forward, but hesitated before she reached Alex. Her hands tangled together in front of her as if she was wringing something from them.

"Alex?" Her voice was barely more than a whisper.

"It's me, Mum. It's really me."

She rushed forward and enveloped Alex in her arms, crushing her enough to elicit a squeak from Alex and then a murmur of reassuring words, "It's OK, Mum, it's really OK."

Katherine laid her head on Alex's, holding her close, her tears heedlessly running down her cheeks into Alex's hair, dripping onto Alex's face so that she tried to say something, and then they were both crying and hugging each other. Neither could speak but that the other would start wailing again. Katherine couldn't seem to stop squeezing her as if she might slip away at any moment. That gave Alex hiccoughs so that she cried and squeaked alternately.

I stood apart, watching Katherine come to terms with her daughter's return. My eyes were hardly dry either, making me realise I had finally done the right thing.

Katherine, extracted a hanky from her sleeve and started dabbing at her eyes, and then managed to blurt out, "How?" and then started crying again, which set Alex off and neither of them had breath for words for a while.

"How?" she repeated.

"How is easy," I said. "She was never dead in the first place. They took her from us at the hospital under cover of their rules and their regulations. They deceived us."

Katherine looked at Alex, "You've grown, changed, something's different. Your hair, your..." she was fishing for what was different about Alex, but it wasn't one thing. It was everything. "Where have you been?"

"I've been staying with Dad's people, just for a..."

"You knew?" She threw it at me like an accusation. "You knew she was alive?"

"I've known for a little while. It hasn't been easy."

She strode up to me and poked me in the chest with her finger. "Easy?" She poked me with her finger, punctuating her words, "Easy? You selfish, heartless, mean... shadow of a man. You self-centred, self-obsessed bastard, you..." She ran out of words, the tears running down her cheeks again. She raised her hand and slapped me full across the face. There was a crack, and for a moment my head spun.

"Don't!" cried Alex. "It wasn't Dad's fault. It's not him, it's me!"

"Stay out of this, young lady. You mean bastard of a man! How could you? How... dare you!" she slapped her hand hard against my chest, doing no harm but venting her rage, She did it again, harder. I stood there, taking it.

"How could you keep it from me? How? What gives you the right? Who appointed you lord high saviour of... anything? Do you have no feeling, no comprehension of what it's been like?"

"I've been meaning to tell you," I said softly.

"Meaning to? When's that? When it comes up on your agenda? When you get around to it? When you get off your selfish arse and do something?" She was shouting.

"It's complicated," I tried.

"How complicated is it? She was dead, Niall. D-E-A-D, Dead!" She spat the words through her gritted teeth. "We went to her funeral, God help me. You gave a speech! You cried, dammit!"

"I didn't know then."

"When? When did you know? I want you to tell me right now," she insisted, she dashed tears from her eyes with the back of her hand.

"Afterwards."

"How long afterwards?" she insisted, drilling her finger into my chest.

"Mum, there's stuff you don't know," interrupted Alex. "Things are different. I'm different."

"You are still my girl," she turned on Alex, "but this is between me and your father." She turned back to me, "You have a lot to answer for Niall Petersen."

"More than you know," I confirmed, trying not to react to her anger.

"When did you know that Alex was alive? You won't answer that question, will you?"

"I wasn't sure at first. I thought... I thought I was going mad."

"You still won't tell me."

"After the funeral, the memorial service, whatever it was. I heard Alex's voice. I thought I was imagining it."

"Where? Where did you hear her voice?" she insisted.

"In the bathroom."

She stopped, taken back by the simple honesty of my response. Then she recovered. "You can't disguise your deception like that, I'm not listening to any more of your lies. I want the truth."

"That is the truth."

All the history was coming back to me now. Her doubts and her suspicions, going through my clothes, though my things, always looking for anything on which she could hang her accusations. I remembered why I used to love this woman, but I also remembered why I came to hate her.

"You always twist things," she said. "You don't even know what the truth is!"

"I've had enough!" I shouted back at her. "You have no freakin' idea what you are talking about."

I batted her hand aside where she was about to poke me again.

I was breathing hard. "You ask me whether I have rights, well I do! I am her father. It was me who went through hell to find her, tore buildings down to reach her, saw things that no man should have to see – just to save her!"

I was spitting the words out. Katherine's face flushed like she'd been slapped.

"You talk about pain, you have no clue. You carp on about how you feel and what you went through, but it's all about you! You don't know what pain is. You're living in a dream! You sit on your fat arse in your cosy house with your cosy man and his bloody Toyota…"

"Leave Barry out of this."

"…dreaming of holidays in the Algarve and a new greenhouse. What did you risk? What did you do? A big fat nothing, that's what!"

"You're only angry because you're in the wrong," she accused.

"In the wrong? How can I be in the wrong? I brought your daughter back from the dead, didn't I? Isn't that enough?"

I pushed her backwards, which I swear is the first time I had ever laid hands on her. "You don't know anything. You think you're safe. Your house was watched, did you know that? There were two guys in a car, outside, watching your house."

"My house? What for?"

"They were looking for me and they couldn't find me, but they knew where you were." The moment I said it I knew I'd said the wrong thing.

Her eyes narrowed. "People were spying on me because of you? What kind of people? Police? Is that what you're saying, because you're involved in something dodgy and it sounds like you're up to your eyeballs in it."

"Not police, something else."

"Gangsters, is it? Are involved with organised crime? I wouldn't put it past you."

"Is that what you think of me? Is that what you think I've been doing?"

"All I know is that you're bloody evasive about it. Whatever it is you and Blackbird do, you are both in on it. She's even more vague than you are." She pointed back to the car park. "Who is the heavy in the car? What does he call himself... Dave? I bet that's not his real name. For that matter, where did you get a car like that? You don't even have a job for God's sake! Is it drugs? Is that what's funding this lifestyle? Is that what you've got my daughter involved with?"

"Your daughter? Yours? Don't you mean ours?"

"Alex, get in the car now! We're going home." She looked around. "Alex?"

I looked around and there was no sign of her.

"Shit!" I said.

"Well, she can't have gone far. She's probably sulking somewhere."

"You have no idea, do you?"

"Don't start that again. Find your daughter. You keep

telling me what a wonderful father you are. Do something."
She twisted around, searching for a sign of Alex.

"I knew this was a bad idea," I said.

"Don't just stand there. Search for her. She's probably in
that coppice on the rise."

I went back to the bench, and sat down heavily, holding
my head in my hands.

"Niall! Where's Alex?"

"Good question! Where is she? It took me months to find
her but I dare say you can do it in a few minutes, so go and
look for her!"

"All right, I will." She bustled off towards the wood, shouting for Alex.

The coppice was where the node point was for the Ways,
so if Alex had gone there she could be miles away by now.
She had probably gone back to the courts, fed up of seeing
her parents in one more slanging match. I turned and looked
back to the car park, where Dave waited with the car. His
head was back and he looked like he was asleep. Maybe he
didn't want to get involved in the conflict either.

I watched Katherine march back over to me. "She's not
there."

"No."

"She won't answer me."

"She's probably gone back. She'll be all right."

"Gone back where? How? For that matter, where's your car?"

"I didn't bring one."

"Do you live nearby?" She looked around. I had deliberately picked somewhere isolated, so there wasn't much to
see beyond the lake that was once a gravel pit, the occasional
distant dog-walker, and the rolling countryside.

"No. It's many miles from here."

"That's what I mean about you being evasive." The note of criticism crept back into her tone.

I stood up. "Katherine, I'm tired of arguing with you. I'm tired of protecting you, and I'm tired of your constant carping. You may or may not like what I am and what I do, but I'm tired of trying to explain things to you. Actually, I'm just tired."

"Well, if you behaved like any decent man..."

"Come on." I walked towards the cluster of trees.

"Where are you going?"

"I'm going to look for Alex."

"I've just been up there. She isn't there."

"She could be ten feet away and you wouldn't know it. She'll turn up when she's ready."

"Where are you going?"

"Home."

She trotted after me. "There's no need to be like that. We'll give you a lift. We can drop you off. I'm sure your man knows where to take you. He can drop you off first if you like?"

"You don't understand," I repeated.

"What don't I understand?"

"Everything's changed."

"That's what Alex said, and frankly you're not making any more sense than she did. I don't know what the pair of you think you're up to, but it's not good enough."

We reached the spot in the coppice and I pulled a cursory glamour about us, in case anyone nosey was watching. No one would notice either of us until the glamour faded.

"I'll call you when I've found Alex," I said. "We'll arrange something. You need to talk."

Katherine looked around, then shrugged her shoulders. "Where are you going, Niall? There's nowhere to go. We're in the middle of a wood."

"When you've finished looking for me, head back to Dave and the car. He'll take you home."

"What are you talking about?"

I felt beneath me for the Way that ran beneath us, feeling it rise to my call. I stepped forward and they was a twist of air, a sense of falling, and I was many miles away. There was no sense of a previous passage – Alex must have left some time ago while I was arguing with Katherine. I felt a pang of guilt at neglecting her once again, but ultimately the rows, the constant accusations, the crying and the shouting, were what had driven me away from my home in the first place.

If there was one thing I'd learned it was that you couldn't go back.

Seven

When I reached the courts, Amber was in the cellar where the node point was. She was stood against the wall, waiting.

"Has Alex come back through here?" I asked her.

She ignored my question. "Garvin wants to see you."

"What about Alex?"

"I haven't seen her."

"That doesn't answer my question."

"No," she said. "It doesn't."

I sighed and went up into the house.

"Garvin's in the weapons room, working out," she called after me.

I went upstairs first to Alex's room. The bed was unmade, items were scattered around the dresser, a book was open on the bed. It was a copy of Robert Louis Stevenson's *Kidnapped*. I wondered whether there was any significance to that. She had clothes in the drawers, make-up on the shelves. I tried to remember what she was wearing at the lake, but I had no clear recollection. Jeans? A T-shirt? It didn't matter anyway, since she could look however she wanted.

I looked for personal items; a purse, a piece of jewellery, a hair brush, to see if any of it had gone – and then realised that almost nothing in the room was actually hers. It was all borrowed, or bought for her, or provided for her so that she would be comfortable.

She told me: I want my music, my books, the things from home. I'd heard what she said, but hadn't understood the significance of any of it. I'd heard, but not listened.

I sat down on the bed, heavily. "Now what am I going to tell Katherine?"

I'd assumed that she'd come back to the courts, that she would return here at least to collect her things, even if she was going to try and return to her former life with her mother, but I sat in her room and realised the truth. She didn't need to. Nothing here was hers. She could walk away and not look back.

I rubbed by eyes, feeling tired and stupid. I hadn't considered what it would all mean for Alex. I knew Katherine would be upset and in the event she had acted predictably. We both had. It had sparked another in our long list of unresolved arguments and Alex had been left on the sidelines to watch. Worse than that, I hadn't realised why she was there. She wanted to see her parents reunited. She wanted a homecoming. The trouble was, the home she wanted to return to no longer existed.

Katherine was going to be angry. She would already be pissed off with me for leaving her in a wood. That had been petty, but I'd just wanted to prove to her once and for all that she didn't know everything, and that there were things that I couldn't explain, even if I wanted to. Now I had to tell her that I didn't know where her daughter was.

It would be better to find Alex before I had to explain that.

Alex waited until the noise ceased. She waited until the arguments were over and the shouting was done.

In the lake the sound was a muted echo. In the lake she didn't have to listen to her parents fighting. She had walked into the water to distract them from yelling at each other, but they hadn't even noticed. She could have drowned and they wouldn't care.

She didn't drown, though. They'd proved that again and again at Porton Down, holding her under while she kicked and struggled until she could hold it no more, until the water surged into her lungs on the indrawn breath. Only then did she realised she wasn't drowning. The water entered her lungs, but it didn't hurt her. It couldn't hurt her. It was hers, and it would support her and hold her, until the hurting stopped.

She'd spat water into the faces of the doctors, which had earned her a day in the goldfish tanks, the name the inmates gave to the glass-walled cages with iron wire woven into the walls and iron locks on the doors. They'd given her no food and only plain water, and left her to stew.

It had been worth it.

Beneath the surface of the lake it was dark, the water cloudy. Yes, it was cold, but she could handle it. She'd learned that in the goldfish tanks too, when they'd stripped her naked and thrown her in, turning the temperature down to soften her up. She remembered the goose-bumps on her skin, her embarrassment as she turned away from the glass to hide her growing breasts and the light fuzz of hair in her groin, only to see the camera staring down at her. She'd cowered in the corner as they leered through the glass at her. She'd cried... oh yeah, she'd cried. But then she'd got stronger. She'd learned how to stare back until it was they who turned away. She'd learned how not to cry.

The water wouldn't hurt her, no matter how deep she went, and she could lighten the pressure, easing the weight from her ears and from her drenched lungs. She could hang there, suspended in a cold embrace, for as long as she wanted. Eventually, though, she had to come up. Eventually the world wanted her back.

She surfaced and walked from the water. No one saw her emerge, no one noticed the water running from her sodden clothes, streaming from her nose and mouth. By the time she reached the edge of the coppice where the Way point was, she was dry. She looked back at the lake, wishing she could have stayed there, then walked into the wood.

I walked back down the hall to where Blackbird and I had our rooms. That was another thing – I had left Alex isolated when she should have had people around her. Yes, there were reasons for that, and initially there hadn't been any other choice but to keep her separate until she gained some control, but she could have moved to a room nearer to Blackbird and me days ago. It had been convenient to leave things the way they were until she joined the courts. She'd been making progress towards that – but now?

I found Blackbird sitting on the bed with my son laid out naked and wriggling on a towel spread across Blackbird's legs with his arms and legs waving around.

Is that wise?" I asked her. "One false move and we'll all get a sprinkling."

She sighed. "He was too hot. He's having a cool down." Reaching down, she stroked her hand across his tummy. He blew bubbles and kicked.

I sat on the end of the bed and looked down at my son. His eyes were pale grey, almost colourless. I wondered if they would stay that colour.

"How did it go?" Blackbird asked me. She knew I was

meeting Katherine this morning. I'd had a restless night trying to think of a way to explain and, as a consequence, so had Blackbird.

"It went OK up to a point. Have you seen Alex at all?"

"No, I think… Niall?"

I looked up from the baby.

"What really happened?"

I sighed. "I met Katherine and I was trying to explain what happened last year, and then Alex appeared."

"What?"

"She just popped out of nowhere. One moment there was no one there and the next minute she's standing watching us."

"She used glamour. Perhaps she has more control that we've given her credit for."

"Katherine was emotional, it's understandable. I didn't get time to say anything that would soften the blow. She was just there. I don't think Katherine could believe her eyes at first. It was just so unexpected."

"How did she take it?"

"Badly. She blamed me, shouted at Alex, called me every name under the sun. Yes, I think it went entirely as expected," I sighed.

"And what about Alex?"

"That's the problem. I thought she'd gone off in a huff – come back here to sulk in her room. She's not there, I just looked. I was hoping that maybe she'd be in here, talking to you."

"How did she know where you were going?"

"Good question. But if she has enough control to master her glamour then she could have overheard all manner of things. She could have been there while I was talking to Tate. Maybe she overheard the conversation with the driver?

Either way, she followed me to the meeting, or maybe she was there before me? I don't know."

"This is why we treat people with power as adults, Niall. Once they have power they have to grow up."

"Yes, well, she's had exceptional circumstances. It's been hard for her."

"It's hard for everyone. What will you do?"

"Do? I'll have to talk to Katherine. She might try and go home, which is what I was trying to avoid. Garvin won't want a public scandal and Alex is supposed to be dead. If people start seeing her near her house, there'll be ghost stories, TV crews… it'll get out of hand."

"What about Alex?"

"I owe her an apology."

"Really?" Blackbird raised an eyebrow.

"I suppose. I'm not sure what I did wrong, but whatever it was, it wasn't right for her. I failed her."

"No, Niall, you didn't fail her, but an apology would be the beginning of a new stage of your relationship. You're starting to think of her as an adult."

"I need to find her first."

"Not if she doesn't want to be found."

"I found her before." I found her when no one else could.

"Yes, but she wanted to be found. Now she wants some time alone. You're finding it hard to adjust to these changes, Niall, so how must she be feeling? She's growing up fast, and she's starting to understand that her parent's relationship isn't what she wants it to be. That's part of growing up too."

"I can't just let her run around loose. What do I tell Katherine?"

"Tell her you don't know where she is."

"She'll freak."

"Let her. It's not your fault, Niall. At least not all of it."

"Gee, thanks."

"I mean it. You bear the world on your shoulders, as if everything is your fault. You take responsibility for things that are outside of your control. You need to stop doing that, Niall, or you are going to drive yourself mad."

"My daughter is my responsibility."

"First and foremost she is her own responsibility. She is an adult, and if you treated her like one then she would probably be here now."

"You sound like Garvin."

"Rue the day I hear those words spoken again."

"Speaking of whom, I ought to go and find him. Amber said he was looking for me."

"Never a good sign," said Blackbird.

I stood up. My son gurgled and then wee started spraying from his nether parts. "Aaaah! Get a nappy!"

Blackbird calmly flicked the towel across so it damped down the spray and wrapped him into the towel. "Perfect," she said, nuzzling him. "We just get you clean and dry and look what you go and do?" He gurgled in response. "Come on, we'll go and find a nappy while your father goes and finds Garvin. I know which I'd rather do."

I left and headed downstairs to find my boss.

She could have gone back to the courts, but why walk back into a prison?

Oh, they called her a guest and they treated her well, but she knew a prison when she saw one. You could tell as soon as you tried to leave. She knew that all freedoms must be won, that all concessions must be fought for. Well, she was free. With the Ways at her disposal she could go anywhere she wanted.

She needed a direction. If she went down the Way without any clear idea of where she was going she knew she would be lost, and you could lose more than your sense of direction on the Ways. Fionh had drummed that into her, at least.

What did she want? She wanted her clothes, her things, her music. She wanted the things that made life bearable. Well, she knew where they were. It was just a matter of taking them. It wasn't stealing, they were her things, after all.

She stepped onto the Way, immersing herself in the rush as she hopped from one node to another. It was like skateboarding, only without grazed knees, and if you fell – well, you were falling anyway. She stepped from node to node, tracking southwards, following her limited sense of direction. It was only when she emerged in a park where the roads were patrolled by red buses and black taxis that she realised the she'd overshot and passed the suburb where she lived – where she used to live – some time ago. She was somewhere in London.

She'd been into London on many occasions, but rarely on her own. There was the time when she ran away from home, when she'd ended up at her dad's. The first thing her dad did was ring her mum and tell her that Alex was there. So much for teaching her mum a lesson. So much for running away.

She could use the Underground, though. She walked across the park and approached a lady in a smart suit and high heels.

"'Scuse me, but where's the tube station?"

The woman looked at her like she'd crawled out from under a rock and then walked away. How rude could you get? She'd only asked for directions. There was no need to treat her like that.

Alex continued walked across the park, finding that people

changed track to avoid her. She shook her head. City people were so rude. She walked across the road and headed down the street to the corner, trying to get her bearings. As she reached the cross-street she could see the familiar outline of the BT Tower above the buildings. She wasn't far from the centre then. Not far from Oxford Street, and shops, and cappuccino bars.

She turned and headed towards the BT Tower and civilisation. As she walked she went past a bookshop and glanced sideways into the large window. Her reflection met her gaze. No wonder they walked away from her. My God, she looked a fright. Reflexively her hand patted her pockets for a comb to tame her unruly curls. The water hadn't helped, and anyway, these days her hair tended to have a mind of its own you.

A man appeared in the shop doorway wearing a polo shirt with the shop's logo emblazoned on it. "Go away, you're putting the customers off!"

She gaped at him. Putting them off? How dare he! There was an echo of a rumble, beneath the ground. Alex could feel the water far below her, feel it wanting to burst upwards and engulf the man and his stupid shirt.

"Get lost! Shoo!" He affected a two-day stubble that was so carefully cultivated. He obviously loved himself.

Alex, lifted her chin. The rumbling below her subsided. "Why don't you... take your stupid books and your stupid half-a-beard, and your stupid shirt with its stupid logo, and go and fuck yourself?"

The man bristled, but he didn't leave the doorway.

"It's a public footpath, isn't it?" she said, "You can't stop me. I've got as much right to be here as you have, prick!"

"Right, that does it. I'm calling the police!"

"Help yourself," she said, fussing with her hair in the windows reflection. "By the time they get here I'll be long gone and they'll think you're as big a prick as I do."

He made a big show of going inside and picking up the phone, glaring at her through the half-reflection of the window as he punched the numbers. Alex was guessing that with the other hand he was holding the phone closed – that type were all show.

She did look a state, though. There were black rings under her eyes from staying up until all hours, and her sweatshirt and skirt looked like they'd been trampled by elephants before she'd put them on – one of the disadvantages of getting completely soaked and then drying them by forcing all the water out.

She glanced back at the dickhead in the shop, stuck a finger up at him for good measure and walked on. Within yards she had cloaked herself in glamour. Let the police see if they could find her – they could try. She headed for the brighter lights of Oxford Street.

Meetings with my boss were very different, I reflected, than when I used to have a real job. When I reached the stairs down to the training room I could hear Garvin before I could see him. He was using one of the weapons on the rubber car tyre that we used for stamina exercises, hung in the corner from a chain in the ceiling. The raw smacks as he hit the tyre travelled down the corridor as a fast percussion. He was sweating it, pushing himself. When I opened the door I realised he was doing it in pitch blackness.

"Come in. Close the door." The percussion continued.

I stepped inside, closing the door with a soft thud, and finding myself in darkness as the noise continued. I stood there waiting for him to finish.

The lights flickered on leaving me blinking in the light. I realised that Garvin was behind me.

"Just because the sound continues does not mean I'm still over there. You should know that Dogstar."

He wandered back to the spinning tyre, swinging the long staff in curves and sweeps around and through the tyre without once touching it, this time in silence, letting his muscles cool slowly from the exertion.

"I asked you to come and see me," he said, circling slowly around the twirling tyre but still avoiding hitting it.

"Amber told me."

"She said she told you twenty minutes ago. Where were you?"

"I went to see if Alex was back."

There was a sharp double thud. In Garvin's hand the staff had separated into a shorter staff and a long handled blade. Most of the tyre dropped to the floor, bounced once and then rocked back and forth, leaving the top section jiggling around manically on the end of the chain.

"You cut the tyre in half," I said, stating the obvious.

"I can always chain up another tyre," he said, sweeping the blade in a circle, and finishing with a flourish that joined it once more into a staff, "but getting another Warder at short notice is much more difficult."

"Why do you need another Warder?"

"Because one of them is running around after his daughter?" he suggested.

"I... I needed to meet Katherine and I thought it best if it was done discreetly."

"Discreetly? So you send a black limo to get her? In the middle of a housing estate?"

"I don't know. I thought maybe..."

"No, the problem is, you didn't think. I asked you not to see her. I asked you not to tell her Alex was alive."

"I'm sorry, but I felt I had to."

"A bit late for that, isn't it? You appropriate the property of the courts for your own purposes, co-opt one of Mullbrook's staff into doing your dirty work, and do something that I expressly asked you not to do…"

"You only said it wasn't a good idea."

"And was it? Did she take it well?"

"Not really."

"Well I think we can assume I was right, then, can't we?"

"It's better that she knows."

"Let me say something, Niall, as someone with a great deal of experience in managing the courts and dealing with humanity. It is, in fact, almost exclusively better, if people do not know. Do I make myself clear this time?"

"I couldn't leave her like that."

"This is not about assuaging your guilty conscience. I have a job to do and you're supposed to be helping me – instead you're making it harder."

"She won't tell anyone."

"Of course she'll tell someone! She's bound to, sooner or later. There'll be someone close, someone she trusts. It's like pissing in a pond. You break the banks and then it leaks into the bigger pool, before long it's in the stream and then the river and before you know it the entire ocean is tainted with piss. It's what happens."

"I'll talk to Katherine and ask her to be discreet."

"I think you've done enough talking, don't you? I asked you to be discreet. Asking her to keep it quiet will only stimulate her interest and encourage her to ask more questions. No more, Niall. Is that understood?"

"I understand."

"You said that last time. If you're not cut out to be a Warder, with all the privileges and comforts that come with it, then other arrangements can be made. If you want to be a Warder then you need to start acting like one. I gave you a job. Have you done it?"

"Not yet."

Garvin sighed. "There are a group of them holed up in a squat in north London, an old factory. Amber will go with you."

"Amber?"

"Yes, Amber. Perhaps if you see how the job should be done, you'll get on with it. I've sent Fellstamp and Fionh elsewhere. If you won't do this, Dogstar, then I'll send some-one who will. Amber's waiting for you downstairs. She won't wait long. Get your kit and get moving."

I said nothing, pressing my fist over my heart in ac-knowledgement and left, pulling the door shut behind me, then leaned against the wall next to the door, breathing slowly in and out. Garvin was usually the measure of con-trol and diplomacy, but today I'd seen another side of him. If he'd sent Fellstamp and Fionh in search of some of the escapees then that was bad news. They would not treat them as carefully as I would. I needed to get on top of things if I was going to save any of these people, and keep my job.

I also needed to talk to Katherine, which meant going against what he'd just told me. If Alex turned up at her mother's then Katherine would need to know what the situation was, oth-erwise she might go complaining to the authorities, or draw further unwanted attention to Alex, when what we needed was a calm, careful, approach.

None of which were words I would normally associate with Katherine.

Alex always liked Oxford Street. All the top shops were there, all the ones with the clothes that her mother would never let her wear. Unsuitable clothes, matched with unwearable shoes. She loved it.

Of course, there were the designer shops, but even wrapped in glamour she didn't think she could get in and out of one of those without drawing unwanted attention. Those shops didn't have clothes on rails, and changing rooms you could just use. You had to have an attendant and someone to tell you how marvellous you looked. Having earned her freedom she was not so willing to risk losing it again.

Instead she wandered around the better teen shops, looking at the fashions and checking out what the other girls were wearing. Of course she could just shift her glamour and look however she wanted, but that wasn't the same as having the clothes for herself.

She went down a rail and picked out a top with a sparkly emblem, and a short denim skirt, a skimpy tee, some leggings, and took all of it to the changing room where a stern-faced shop manager gave her a token which showed how many items she as trying on. The woman was dressed in clothes from the store, but frankly she looked too old for them.

After a short wait in the queue, she slipped into the communal changing area. Inside, girls squeezed themselves into a variety of outfits, some with more success than others. There was a lot of chat, and a fair amount of swearing as girls found that they were no longer able to fit in a size six or whatever. One girl was fighting a losing battle with a bustier thing while her friend tried to stretch it around her. Alex smiled.

She shed the shapeless sweatshirt and jeans and wriggled into the short skirt, pulling the zip up hard when it stuck. She pulled the sparkly top over her head, stretching it over her budding curves and smoothed it down. Only then did she look up into the mirror.

The girl who looked back was a stranger. Alex almost looked around to see if she had caught the reflection from some other girl. Sure, she'd had a mirror in her room, and there were mirrors dotted around the courts, but this was full length widescreen. Alex blinked and her reflection blinked back.

She caught a smug look from the girl who'd been trying to squeeze into the bustier. Alex almost told her where she could get off, but then looked again at the girl in the mirror. The sparkly top was stretched tight across her bust – too tight. It bunched into lines and left a line of pale midriff where the over-tight skirt pinched in her waist, making her look like she had a roll of puppy fat.

Her face gave the lie to any weight gain. It was lean and angular. She brushed her cheek where the bones were outlined under the skin. Her unruly hair coiled around her fingers and she teased out the curl, wondering when this had happened to her. When did she become this bony angular waif?

She stepped sideways as one of the other girls edged in front of her for a better view of herself; giving her attitude, like Alex was hogging the mirror. Looking around the changing room, Alex was suddenly conscious that the other girls would see the strange girl, in clothes that were too small, in a bra that bulged in the wrong places.

Quickly, she stripped off the top, hearing the seams stretch and crackle as she pulled it over her head. She unzipped the skirt with relief and pulled on her jeans and shirt. There was no point in trying on the leggings and tee shirt – they were all too small. She tugged things back on hangers and headed out.

She passed the token back to the woman at the changing room entrance.

"Did you find anything you liked?" she asked.

"S'all too small," said Alex, handing back the clothes.

The woman took them from her and checked them before hanging them from a rail behind her.

She turned, assessing Alex and then checking the sizes on the clothes she'd just hung up. "These are eights and you're definitely going to need a ten," she said. "What size bra are you wearing?"

Alex told her, and the woman sighed. "It's very common with young women – you don't notice how your shape is changing. You're going to have to buy a new bra before you try anything else on," she said. "The one you're wearing is too small for you and nothing is going to fit right until you do. I'll ask one of the assistants to advise you, if you'd like?"

"No, really," said Alex, "I'm OK."

"Of course," she said. "You'll find lingerie in the far corner over there." She gestured towards the back corner of the store.

"Thanks," said Alex, drifting away.

Since she got back she'd been preoccupied, what with the birth of the baby and having lessons with Fionh. All the rules about what she could do and couldn't do – it was worse than Porton Down. Her appearance hadn't been an issue, though. Maybe it was the drugs she'd been given, but she didn't feel drugged, she just felt... different, as if she didn't quite fit in her own skin. She'd just thrown on the clothes she'd been given, only now she realised they were shapeless and baggy or just didn't fit.

She found herself in front of another full length mirror along one of the aisles. Her hair wound in dark curls around her face and her eyes looking hard and cold. She smoothed the sweatshirt down, trying to visualise the figure underneath. A girl with a dress walked around in front of her. She stood between Alex and the mirror and held the dress up against herself.

"Do you mind?" said Alex. "I was using that."

The girl glanced around at her, taking in the crumpled sweatshirt and the faded jeans. "Seriously?" she said. She turned and checked the dress again.

"Stuck up bitch," said Alex, but the girl had already moved away.

Alex stared at herself and realised that the girl had a point. She did look a bit of a state. The jeans hung from her hips and the formless top did nothing for her. Now that she was conscious of it, her bra was too tight in all the wrong places and she felt frumpy.

A couple of girls passed between her and the mirror, debating the merits of the skirt they had chosen for one or other of them. Alex had no one to debate with. Did anyone care how she looked? Did anyone even notice her? Standing in the middle of the shop, she felt the people moving around her. She felt each heartbeat swishing by, heard their chatter, was jostled and stepped around, but comprehensively ignored. She'd never felt so alone. Even at the worst of Porton Down, people knew you were there. They didn't just step around you.

It came to her that she could could stop it all. She could slow every heartbeat, cause the blood not to flow. She could make it thicken and slow and they would all die, all of them.

She twitched as she felt her hands wrap around the heavy blade, the handle slick with blood. She felt the weight of the blade in her

hand as she lifted it, heard her exhalation as she swept the blade
down, felt the shock travel up her arms as it bit into bone, biting into
the severed head in front of her...

She shook herself, wiping her hands down her front, trying to push the memory that had risen, unbidden, back
where it came from.

She shook her head, trying to clear it. "Stupid. Just stupid."
Her hands were shaking. She interlaced her fingers to quiet
the trembling.

"Are you all right?" A girl with a shopping bag slung over
her shoulder appeared at her arm, face filled with concern.
"You're very pale. Do you want to sit down?"

Alex shrugged her off. "I'm fine. Leave me alone."

"I was only asking," said the girl, but Alex was already
moving away between the racks.

She had to pull herself together. It was no good being flaky
when she was out on her own. It would only attract attention she didn't want or need. She needed to get a hold of
herself. She was tougher than this. She had been through
worse and survived hadn't she?

On impulse, she walked back down the racks. She checked
the sizes as she collected a violet skimpy tee, a teal bolero
cardigan and a blue and purple kilt that looked kinda funky.
She added to this a handbag, a pair of silver high-heeled shoes
and a bra with a bigger cup-size. Then she headed for the exit.

She didn't need to pay; she didn't have any money in any
case. She was cloaked in glamour, no one would notice. No
one would see. Even the CCTV wouldn't register her image.
Unfortunately she'd forgotten about the security tags on the
clothes and as soon as she passed the door the alarms went
berserk.

"Shit!" she swore and ran.

She dodged around people walking slowly down the pavement, hearing the heavy thumping of the security guard's boots on her tail. She intensified her glamour and swerved into a doorway. People walked past ignoring her. A large white guy in a blue uniform stopped in front of the the doorway. Her heart beat in her chest.

Don't look around. Don't look around.

Another guy in uniform, a tall skinny black guy, stopped, failing to notice the girl with her arms full of clothes in the doorway, just behind his colleague.

"Where'd she go?" said the black guy.

"I had her, and then she vanished," wheezed the other one, bending forward and resting his hands on his knees. "I'm getting too old for this. Either that or they're running faster."

"Come on, old man," said the black guy, punching the white guy on the arm playfully. "Did you see what she looked like?"

"Nah, but we'll get her on the cameras." They walked back towards the store, leaving Alex in the doorway with her prizes.

"You stupid silly bitch," she said to herself. "What did you do that for?"

But she had her prizes.

Eight

Returning to the suite I shared with Blackbird, I found her folding nappies into a drawer. I collected my sword.

"Going out again?" she asked.

"Garvin wants me to round up the escapees. He's sending Amber with me. She's waiting down at the Way node. If I don't get a move on, she'll go alone."

"I see. Pushing you up to the sharp end again, is he?"

"If Alex comes back, could you ask her to wait," I asked her.

"I'm not your secretary, Niall."

"Look, I have to go out, OK? If I don't go... who knows what Amber will do. I'm only asking that if Alex comes back while I'm out, you'd ask her to wait until I get back so I can talk to her."

"She's used to waiting."

"What does that mean?"

"Only that your daughter, like many other things, doesn't seem to take priority."

"She's not even here," I said. "I can't talk to her if she's not here, can I? What am I supposed to do? Sit around on the off-chance that she appears?"

"I'm sure you could find something to do," she said quietly.

I sighed. "I have work to do, and I really don't have time for this now."

"Off you go then. Have a good day at the office, darling." She smiled but there was no joy in it.

"You're in a strange mood. Is something wrong?"

"No. I'm fine. Go and save the world, or whatever it is you have to do," she said, turning back to the laundry.

I shrugged and left, unable to untangle whatever it was that Blackbird was not telling me. It was as if she was sending me a message I couldn't decode. She'd always wanted a baby, that much was obvious, and now she had one. She'd got what she wanted, so what was the matter? Didn't she like being a mother?

Heading down to the room where the Waypoint was, I found Amber leaning against the wall, showing no sign of impatience, or indeed any emotion whatsoever. The contrast between them struck me. I couldn't imagine having the conversation I'd just had with Blackbird, with her. Amber watched everyone, but no one watched Amber.

I made a point of assessing her. She had one black leather boot forward, where she leaned against the wall, the other boot was back against the wall, ready to propel her into action. I noticed for the first time that her boots had heels, not high, but enough to give a small lift. Her favourite weapon, a straight blade with a cord-bound hilt long enough to be wielded two handed, was slung from her hip in a black lacquered scabbard, over dark grey trousers. She wore a grey top loose enough to allow movement, tight enough not to snag or catch.

"Like what you see?" she asked, candidly.

"You're not used to being noticed, are you Amber?" It was

more a statement of fact than a criticism. I wondered if merging into the background was part of her glamour.

She watched me with dark eyes under the black tousled fringe while I took in her hard chin and sharp cheekbones; she was angular. Her shoulders were sharp and bony, she was lean without Fionh's curves or Blackbird's softness and that gave her a wiriness that none of the other Warders had. The only time I'd seen Amber show any emotion was at the memorial service held for Alex and the dead girls. After the speech, she had embraced me with tears in her eyes and told me to be strong. It was so uncharacteristic that it stuck in my memory like a thorn. There was no sign of that emotion here. It was another Amber, carved from something hard and uncompromising.

"I'm ready," I told her.

She smiled faintly, then stepped forward onto the Waypoint. There was a twisting vortex and she vanished. I stepped forward after her and felt beneath me for the rising wave of the Way. I could feel her track through the Way, not warm like Blackbird, but cold and precise.

I followed it.

Having nearly been caught stealing clothes, Alex was a lot more careful about what she took after that. She made sure that none of it had security tags, or if they did, it was a moment's thought to remove them. They were tamper proof, but that was against people, not fey. It was just an *opening*, after all, and with a little practice she could look at a security tag and it would fall off.

She was wearing the kilt and top. The high-heeled shoes she had stolen were ditched – they were party shoes; she could barely walk in the damned things, let alone run. It had taken more ingenuity to acquire the white calfskin baseball boots she now wore. She'd had to persuade the girl in the shop to let her try them on, then follow her quietly into the stockroom when she put them back. She had swapped the silly heels for the boots and walked out. When the next person wanted to try that size they would find the heels, but by that time she would be long forgotten.

She sat on the tube train in her new clothes looking at her distorted reflection in the curved window opposite. She had make-up in her new handbag, along with a comb and a rather nice purple silk hair clip. She'd tried the clip in three times before abandoning and stuffing it back into the bag. Her hair had a mind of its own, and rejected the clip no matter how firmly she pushed it in.

She'd stolen a sandwich too, and wolfed that down. She'd wanted a burger and fries but you had to order and pay for those, and she still didn't have any money. She'd considered stealing a purse, but taking from shops was one thing, stealing from people was another. Shop stuff didn't belong to anyone until it was bought, but people's stuff was personal. She wasn't a thief.

The train was emptying slowly as it got further out. Getting on board was child's play, and there were no ticket inspectors on the underground. All she had to do was wait and it would carry her home. She thought briefly about what her mum would say about her new clothes, but other than today, Mum hadn't seen her for weeks. With any luck her mum would assume Dad bought them, and vice versa. Besides, she couldn't wear clothes that didn't fit, could she? No amount of glamour would fix a zip that wouldn't close.

The woman opposite, three seats down kept glancing at her. Alex fussed with her hair, wondering if it was being unruly again. It had a habit of curling and uncurling on its own if she didn't pay attention. She met her gaze and the woman looked away. She had a nice tattoo on her arm, though. It was a butterfly with long tails on its wings.

Alex had wanted a tattoo for ages, but she knew her mum would go mental, and there was the added deterrent that girls like Tracy Welham had them. Of course, hers were gross and anyway, she was dead. Alex shifted uncomfortably on the seat.

She didn't care that the Welham girl was dead. She was evil. The reason Alex had the panic attacks was because of what they'd done to her – they'd made her lose control. She didn't feel guilty, no matter what the psychologists said. They should have left her alone. She'd told them, hadn't she? She'd warned them. Anyway, it was like Fionh said. They had challenged her, three against one, and they'd lost. Tough.

Her mind wandered back to the tattoo and she found herself staring at the woman. She was about thirty or something, what was she doing with a tattoo? She looked at her own arm. Slowly colours started to emerge, faintly at first, then stronger. The problem was that it looked more like one of the drawings on her school exercise book than the woman's tattoo. She scowled and it vanished. She couldn't turn up at Mum's with a tattoo anyway.

By the time the tube neared her station it was overground and she could look into the backs of people's gardens as she rolled past. They were little dramas, each of them, or little soap operas, except no one got murdered. She wondered if that was where the Welhams lived.

She hopped off the train at her stop and exited beneath the notice of the station attendant. No one challenged her, no one even noticed. She walked along the avenues, noting familiar landmarks, passing the shop where she'd bought sweets, the road which led to her school. On impulse she walked towards the school, wanting to see what had become of the chaos she had visited upon them. When she reached the gate to the school field it was locked. She left it open behind her. She walked across the open field cloaked in glamour, noting the new window-frames in the changing block and the emergency door newly set in the wall of the girl's changing rooms.

She laid her hand upon it and it clicked open for her. Inside was clean, silent and cool. There was no sign of the destruction she'd wrought. It smelled faintly of disinfectant, not the overpowering stench of raw sewage. The stalls were all new, some of the fittings still had tape on them to protect them. She walked around the changing rooms, trailing her finger across the surfaces, drawing an imaginary rising line along the walls. They had erased every mark of her. There was no memorial, no sign, no indication that four girls had died here. Well, one of them was very much alive.

She kicked out at the door to a stall. It banged loudly against the side of the stall. She kicked it again, and again, harder, until it broke off the hinges and collapsed into the stall. She turned to look at herself in the mirrors screwed to the wall. Her hair was a winding mass of tendrils, her eyes were filled with blue fire, her hands bunched into fists.

Her reflection admonished her but she was in no mood to be censured. The mirror was only liquid slowed down, and she was the queen of all things liquid. "Pah!" She spat an incoherent command, and the mirrors flew apart into a thousand fragments, an explosion in a glitter factory, surrounding her in a rain of tinkling, sparkling fragments.

"Who's there? What's going on?" It was a male voice coming from the gym, the caretaker. She looked down. Under the shower of glass she had coated herself in tiny glittering fragments, yet there was no scratch upon her. She stared at the particles and they dropped or dribbled, running together, merging with all the other particles until there was a single amoeba of flat green glass where the central drain had been. Across the floor, tiny fragments of foil from the mirror drifted like silver leaf litter. She left it that way, shutting the emergency door quietly behind her, and leaving them to figure it out. Now they would remember her.

She went back onto the field, leaving the gate wide open, taking the route home. She walked the familiar path feeling like a stranger. Even her footsteps sounded wrong to her. She marched around the avenues and cut through the short cuts. Finally she came to her road, her house. Barry's Toyota was there. He would be home. So would Mum. She caught site of herself in a neighbour's window. She didn't look like the girl that lived there. She looked wild.

It didn't matter. You could always go home.

She sneaked around the back by the garage, lifting the catch over the gate as she'd always done. She closed it quietly behind her. At the back door she hesitated, but then smiled to herself. It would be OK.

She let herself in, she didn't need a key. Where was the smell of boiled potatoes? Wasn't Mum supposed to be cooking supper? Raised voices came from the sitting room. She moved carefully into the hall.

"I'm telling you I saw her. She was right there!"

Barry was trying to calm her mother down. "Could it have been another girl, the same age perhaps?"

"It was her! She looked older, yes, but I know my own daughter, for God's sake!"

"I never said you didn't'"

"You never believe me. You always try and second guess everything I say. I'm telling you she was there and you're telling me I can't believe my own eyes. I'm not mad!"

It was kicking off, no mistake. They could be at it a while. When her mother got going there was no stopping her. No wonder there wasn't any supper. Alex turned away from the living room and quietly mounted the stairs, much as she'd done a hundred times when her mother and father had been arguing. She went straight to the room at the back of the house – her room, her sanctuary.

She stood in the doorway and looked around. There was a desk with a new computer on it that hadn't been there before. Where was her bed? Where was her homework table? What had happened to her dresser, her make-up, her hair clips, her clothes? Where was her posters, God! They'd even changed the wallpaper!

She went to the wardrobe and wrenched it open. Inside empty hangers clinked slowly against one another. All her clothes, gone. She went to the desk opening the drawers, looking for her pants, her tights, her bras, anything that might vaguely have been hers. The room had been stripped, cleansed, disinfected like the changing rooms at the school. Every trace had been removed.

The only remnant she could find was a small silver ring her father had given her for her birthday. She wasn't allowed rings at school, so she'd left it on a hook inside the wardrobe. They must have missed it when they took everything else she had and tipped it into the bin.

She grabbed the ring from the hook and pressed it into her palm. She looked around at the empty room, her eyes welling, the sharp edges of the ring pressing into her hand. The room had been stripped, cleansed, purged of all trace.

She ran out, taking the stairs two at a time, burst through the kitchen, slammed through the kitchen door, banging it wide. She veered around, blinded by tears, fumbling with the lock on the back gate until her numb fingers flicked it open. Running into the street, a car blared its horn noisily as she ran into the road. Behind her she could hear them, questioning, searching. She blundered across the road, then cut down a shortcut, smudging tears from her eyes as she ran.

Far behind her she could hear them calling, "Alex! Alex! Come back!"

There was no going back. You couldn't go back. You could only go on. The world erased you until there was nothing left. You left no mark, no sign of your passing. They pasted you over, just like wallpaper.

Until there was nothing left.

I followed Amber through a run-down estate in London, somewhere off the North Circular. Litter accumulated in the gutters and discarded takeaways overflowed the bins. Groups of youths in hoodies watched with resentful eyes as we passed, probably wondering whether we were bailiffs.

We went through an underpass below the railway and emerged into a deserted industrial estate. Half-demolished offices were open to the elements, ragged edges of floors jutting out into space, demolition left unfinished as demand evaporated in the teeth of recession. From the buddleia and elderberry growing in the exposed concrete, it had been like that for some time.

"You take me to the nicest places," I said to Amber. She ignored me.

Our path wound around piles of rubble and oil cans used for long-cold fires. If there had been watchmen, they were made redundant when it became apparent there was nothing worth protecting. Panel after panel of cracked glass looked down on us, as if someone had carefully cracked each pane, individually, as an art-installation statement. There was no one to appreciate their care.

I stopped. "The place is deserted."

Amber paused and turned. "That's what you're meant to think."

She walked on until she reached a long building at the end of the row, surrounded by verdant saplings and nettles. It had been a factory; the ducting for the heat extraction and where the cables for heavy-duty power had been stripped for their copper could still be seen. Floor upon floor of machinery, all gone – presumably sold for scrap or exported to the third world.

We circled round the end of the building and pushed through a door that had been kicked in until it collapsed inward. Inside corroded pipework networked the ceilings but the floor was bare, apart from the occasional rusty bolts sticking up, or a fragment of discarded mangled ironwork.

Light permeated through the crazed glass, showing distorted outlines of the outside world and intensifying the shadows at the rear. We moved along the building to the far end where concrete stairs led to the next floor. Above was the same, another gallery of despair, the machinery removed, the wiring stripped. We wandered that floor then went back to the stairway.

"Do you know what you're looking for?" I was beginning to suspect that we were on a wild goose chase.

She mounted the next set of stairs quickly, and I followed. The floor above had sacks and old tarps hung against the windows. The shadows were deeper, but the story was the same. Everything had been stripped away.

"Bring them down." Amber gestured towards the tarps draped over the windows.

I went down the gallery, pulling down plastic sheeting and old tarpaulins, spilling light across the floor. As I reached the far end, something stirred in the shadows at the back.

"Now what did you wanna do that for?" The voice came from a figure outlined against the dark, moving forward from the deeper shadows.

"Upstairs, Dogstar. I will handle this."

I moved back along towards the stairs only to be intercepted by others moving out from the shadows. They moved in across the gallery, converging on us – four of them, all male, wearing the much-vaunted hoodies. They had crude weapons, an iron bar, a piece of piping. One of them had a piece of wood with nails spiked through the end. My hand moved down to my weapon.

"Where you going, bro?" one of them taunted. "This party just startin'."

"Upstairs, Dogstar," Amber ordered. "Or we'll lose them."

The one nearest the stairs moved into my path, blocking my exit. "You outta luck. There's nothing here but us, and we ain't leaving," he said.

"Neither are they," the one closest to me chuckled, slapping the pipe into his open hand.

"This is not your lucky day," said the third.

"If you got any money, it'd be wise to hand it over now. It'll save us searching the bodies later," said the fourth.

Amber stood easily in the centre. I knew better than to move closer to her; that would restrict our opportunities for movement. Instead I moved apart slightly, forcing them to split their attention in two directions and spread out when they would have closed in. Their attempt to bunch us together faltered.

Amber stood, head bowed, waiting.

"Got nothing to say, little girlie?" the first one taunted.

Amber lifted her head. "How are you," she asked quietly, "on nursery rhymes?"

The one who'd spoken first laughed. "You're a long way from the nursery now, bitch. You're out in the wild woods is where you are."

"How about this one," she said. "One upon a time there were four little piggies…"

I blinked. Amber had gone. There was a whine from the one who'd spoken last. Amber was behind him, the bright slash of her blade held across his throat. He dropped the iron bar.

"This little piggy went to market," she said into the silence. I blinked.

The first guy was on his knees, holding his neck, the second fell to his knees, Amber's blade under his right ear.

"This little piggy," she said, "should have stayed home." I blinked again.

The third was staring about him warily, brandishing the nailed club. There was a flash as her blade swept up from behind, up the inside of his thigh, holding him on tiptoe.

"This little piggy was roast meat," she said.

"Don't you cut me, bitch!" His voice squeaked like the piglet in the rhyme.

I blinked.

The guy with the pipe stood there, swinging it back and forth. Suddenly his legs were kicked out from under him and he crashed backwards, the pipe bouncing out of his hand to ring noisily on the concrete.

"And this piggy's blood, will run and run and run…" The tip of Amber's blade was half an inch from his eye.

I blinked. She was in the middle of the circle again.

"Shall we try again?" She said quietly, "this time with real piggies?"

She paused. For one second they stared at each other. Then she smiled.

"Once upon a time there were four little piggies..."

They scrambled to their feet, abandoning their weapons and running for the stairs. They collided with each other in their haste to get down and away from the crazy woman and her nursery rhymes. I could hear the clatter as they went down the floors, the thud as they burst through the ruined door.

Her smile faded as the noise died away. The only problem was that I was left with the crazy woman.

"I said, upstairs," said Amber, sheathing her sword.

"They blocked my way," I protested.

"No wonder you have problems if you let their kind come between you and your quarry." Amber went to the staircase leading upwards and listened.

"Do you think there's more of them?" I asked.

"No. They were just the alarm system. The real quarry is upstairs."

She vanished upwards and I followed after her. When I reached the floor above I saw her standing at an open fire door, looking down a rusty fire escape.

"They've gone," she said.

"We could follow them?"

"And play cat and mouse when they know all the bolt holes and we're not sure which of us is the cat?" What she didn't say is that if I'd been quicker getting past the watchmen then we would have had them bottled in up here. As it was they were long gone.

The upper floor had been kitted out as a grand open living

space. There were multiple sofas, old metal cupboards, book-shelves and mattresses. They'd found a generator and wired up an Xbox to a flat-screen perched on top of a metal file drawer. The furniture was an odd mix of discarded seconds and the spoils of skip-diving.

"Expensive taste," she said, picking up a cashmere scarf carelessly draped over a tired sofa.

"You think they've got money?" I looked sceptically at the holes in the nearest sofa.

"No, I think they have light fingers. Anything too big to steal is second hand. All the small stuff is new." She walked through and around piles of CDs, DVDs, games and books. "There are a lot of books for teenagers."

"Some teenagers like books," I replied. "Mine does."

"Alfred Watkins, *The Old Straight Track*, and *Do What Thou Wilt: A Life of Aleister Crowley*." She tossed the books back onto the pile. "Dangerous rubbish."

"Sounds a bit New Age to me."

"We'll need to watch the cults and the nutcases," said Amber. "If they get a foothold with one of the extreme groups then we'll have a problem. The last thing we want is them setting up a new religion."

"How many are they?"

"Four, maybe six? They have beds for four but they could be sleeping together."

"Four could be difficult. They are fey," I pointed out.

"And we're Warders," she said. "Sounds like the odds are in our favour. Besides," she looked back at the fire escape, "the first sign of trouble, they abandon everything and scarper. They're not looking for a fight."

"They might come back."

"If they do they'll know we're here long before we see

them, so there's no point waiting. They'll make a mistake eventually, and then we'll see."

"What does that mean?"

"We'll know the answer to that question when it happens." She turned towards the stairs.

"You know, sometimes your accent slips and you sound quite the Londoner."

"You know," she said, "Sometimes you poke your nose in where it's not wanted."

"You could have killed them," I called after her. "Why didn't you?"

"Because then we'd have to dispose of the bodies, and I don't particularly feel like digging. Do you?" She glanced back and then headed back down the stairs.

I had hoped for a better answer, something about the nobility of human life, or at least of saving killing until the last resort. Instead I got cold practical Amber. Then again, if she had killed them I was sure it wouldn't be her doing the digging. I was grateful for that much at least.

I sighed and looked around. The factory was chaotic and squalid. I wondered what they used for toilets, or washing. They probably smelled to high heaven living like this. A life in the courts would seem like luxury, if only I could find a way to persuade them before someone like Amber shoved a blade through their hearts.

I picked out a book that had slipped down the side of the sofa. The title emblazoned upon the cover was *The Golden Dawn: The Original Account of the Teachings, Rites & Ceremonies of the Hermetic Order*.

Amber was right. Someone was filling their heads with dangerous rubbish and the sooner we found them, the better.

I tossed the book aside and followed Amber downstairs. She was waiting, leaning against the concrete.

"Amber?"

She lifted her chin slightly, indicating that she had heard me.

"Why are you always such a hard-arse? You could be really nice if you wanted to be."

The faintest of smiles touched her lips, and she shook her head.

Alex wasn't sure how long she'd been there. She'd done what she'd always done at the worst moments, the really bad times. She'd run to Kayleigh's house. Now she was standing across the road, waiting for something to happen.

It was getting late. Kayleigh's dad was putting on the lights and drawing the curtains, but still Alex hesitated.

Kayleigh's mum had always been great. She never asked too many questions about Alex turning up at odd hours and with no warning. She just let her in and left her to sort it out with Kayleigh. She'd even wait for a bit before calling Alex's mum and letting her know she was safe.

This was different. Alex wasn't safe. She was dead.

She watched Kayleigh moving around her bedroom upstairs, putting things away, tidying things up. Alex smiled. Kayleigh had always been tidier and more organised. Why can't you be more like her, Mum had demanded. Why can't you be tidy like Kayleigh?

Even from the road she could see the pop star posters on the wall, the trinkets and keepsakes arranged along the window sill. Alex tried to imagine herself with keepsakes, with a family, with a bedroom and a routine. Perhaps that was the answer. She could be Kayleigh's long-lost sister, or her cousin, come back from abroad. She could even look like Kayleigh, it wasn't that hard. Or she could be adopted, a late decision, not wanting Kayleigh to grow up an only child.

Except none of it rang true. She could imagine herself, using her new name, telling stories about places she'd never been. She could be someone else, a nice girl, Kayleigh's second cousin, except for the lies.

Blackbird had warned her it would get harder. She'd told her that the more she used her power, the harder it would be to lie. Alex had sniffed and ignored her, but now she could feel it – the tongue-twisted, wrong-fisted, numbness of saying something that wasn't true. If Blackbird were here, she'd be smug.

The phone rang inside the house and she heard Kayleigh's dad answer it. There was a pause, then he appeared outlined against the light from the front door. Looking up and down the road. Was Mum on the phone, asking vague questions? Just some light query, nothing that would make it sound like she was looking for Alex. Had he seen so-and-so? Was there anyone wandering around outside?

But no one saw Alex if she didn't want to be seen, not since Porton Down. They would pump stuff through the air ducts that made your stomach cramp and your joints ache, just to stop you using glamour, but not any more. Now she was free.

He went back inside. No sign of anyone. Who were you looking for? What would her mum say? Would she blurt it out? No, she would draw a line under it all and pretend it never happened. We can't be an embarrassment in front of the neighbours, can we?

She looked up again at the girl in the window. Poor Kayleigh. No one else would befriend her, no one else had the same ideas, the same loves and hates, crushes and crashes. As far as Kayleigh knew, Alex was dead, killed in a nasty accident.

She'd been there when it happened, seen for herself. She'd had to cope with losing her friend.

And that was the trouble. Alex was still lost.

The girl who was Kayleigh's friend died in the changing rooms, drowned in sewage. The girl she was now had seen and done things that Kayleigh couldn't even imagine, let alone understand. How could she tell Kayleigh about being held under water, about being drugged, beaten and starved. How could she explain that she was poisoned, stripped and left naked for all to see? Nothing in Kayleigh's world came close. Kayleigh could never feel the exhilaration of surfing down the Ways, or understand the intricacies of glamour. She was and always would be the way she was – kind, noble, straight-forward Kayleigh.

The hole in Kayleigh's life was the same shape it had always been, but Alex no longer fitted it. The Alex she'd been had wanted to be blonde and bubbly, and fun to be with. That Alex had been consumed, eaten away, leaving someone else in her place.

Alex looked down. Around her arms, strange vines and coloured leaves emerged in patterns on her flesh, winding down to emerge in coiled tangles around her wrists. There strange buds emerged, dark and shiny. They were a lot cooler than butterflies. She shook her head and her hair was long and wavy where it had been softly curled. It was tinted the deepest black, almost blue. She lifted her chin and felt her eyelashes darkened, her lips stained with raspberry tint. It would do for now.

Turning away, she shoved the silver ring on her finger, the last vestige of a life she couldn't have. She would keep it to remind her that there was no going back – only onwards. Walking away from Kayleigh's house, she headed back towards the tube station. She would have to find somewhere safe to stay, and that would be easier in town.

As she walked away, the faint sound of a phone ringing began again.

NINE

Back at the courts we were met by Garvin.

"No luck?"

"They were prepared," said Amber, "maybe even organised."

"That's a new development," Garvin commented. "Did you track them?"

"No point. They were settled in, but they knew we'd found them. We could go back when it's quiet, see if they return for what's left, but they've stolen what they had. My guess is they'll just steal some more. It's easier and safer than risking an ambush."

"So we wait," said Garvin.

"They'll pop up again. Their kind can't keep their heads down for long."

"Let's hope they don't pop up in a way that's public and violent."

It occurred to me that Garvin was more concerned about the publicity than the violence. He turned to me.

"Blackbird asked if you'd go and see her when you got back. I think she has another lesson planned."

"Where is she?"

"She was heading out to the courtyard, but she might be back inside by now."

"I'll go and find her."

Amber accompanied me as far as the stairs up to our rooms.

"Listen, thanks for not telling Garvin I messed up back there," I said to her.

"If I had told him, what good would it have done? You need to stop worrying about screwing up and focus on the job in hand. Garvin's the least of your worries. He's not going to crack your skull open with an iron bar."

"Even so, you could have told him and you didn't. I'm grateful."

"Don't get the idea that I'm on your side, Dogstar. I'm on my side. Always."

"I'll try and remember that."

"Go to your lesson. Seems like you need it."

I watched her retreating back as she walked away. Was she going soft on me? It was hard to imagine – Amber was an ice-cold exterior wrapped around an ice cold interior. Nothing touched her.

It left me wondering why she'd built such a wall around herself.

I found Blackbird upstairs sat on our bed. I glanced towards the darkened side-room where the door was ajar so that she could keep an ear out for our son. All was quiet, which I took as a good sign.

"Garvin said you were looking for me?" I said.

"Did he?" Her answer was curt. She'd been in a funny mood earlier and my absence didn't seem to have improved it.

I tried again. "Did you want me for something?"

"How was your trip? Did you find what you were looking for?" The question was lightly framed, and felt as if it should hold some hidden meaning, but I couldn't fathom it.

"No. I messed it up, well sort of. We were intercepted by some hoodies who wanted to mug us. Amber dealt with them."

"More to add to the body count?" she said stiffly.

"She scared them off, actually. She's not as bad as you make out."

"One Warder is much like another, I find."

That was a little pointed. "Does that include me?"

"I don't know, does it?" She was folding and unfolding a nappy on her lap, as if she couldn't get it right but couldn't stop until it was.

"Have I done something wrong?" I asked.

"How would I know? I haven't seen you all day," she said.

"Garvin said you wanted to have another session with me," I suggested.

"Have you done any of the exercises I set you last time?"

"I did try when I was waiting for Katherine, but I haven't had much chance to practice."

"That would be a no, then. Too busy galavanting around the country chasing hoodies, ex-wives and wayward daughters, I expect," she said.

This wasn't the time to ask if Alex was back. "No, it's just that I've been busy."

"Well," she tossed the nappy to one side, letting it fall haphazardly across the bed, "there's not much point in teaching you things if you're not going to practice, is there?"

"It's not that I don't want to," I said. "There are only so many hours in the day, you know?"

"I'm well aware of how many hours there are in a day."

"I'll try and find some time to practice later, maybe you could help me?" I suggested.

"Of course. I'd love to sit there and watch while you concentrate on creating stillness. I can't wait, thought the excitement may be too much for me."

"OK, then. I'll do it alone."

"Like you do everything else?" she said.

"What's that supposed to mean?"

"I'm simply remarking that your approach may not be as inclusive as it could be."

"Is this because I went out with Amber? You're not jealous, surely?"

"Why would I be jealous? What is there to be jealous of?" She brushed imaginary specks from her skirt.

"Nothing. If you think there's something between Amber and me you've got entirely the wrong end of the stick."

"I never said anything about Amber. It was you that mentioned her," she pointed out.

"Well, there isn't anything, OK?" I was feeling like I'd done something wrong, though I didn't know what.

"Whatever you say," she said.

"What do I have to do to prove that there isn't anything?"

"Well you could stop protesting about it. Drawing attention to it only makes it seem worse than it is."

"There isn't anything to draw attention to," I said.

"So you say."

"Is something the matter?" I tried to keep my enquiry neutral.

"With me? Why should any thing be the matter?" she asked.

"I'm not sure. You're acting strange, that's all."

"I'm acting strange? I expect it's probably my hormones."

"That might explain it."

She stood up, genuinely angry. "How dare you! What gives you the right to blame your conduct on my body? You know nothing about it. What makes you think you're so damned perfect?"

"Keep your voice down, you'll wake the baby. I only meant..."

"Meant what? That I'm not in command of my feelings because there are chemicals in my bloodstream? That I can't be expected to control myself because I'm female? Who do you think you are?"

"I wasn't meaning that. You're the one who keeps going on about how being pregnant changed everything. How do you expect me to know how it feels?"

"You can't possibly know how it feels. You swan off here and there, doing what you like when you like, you never offer to change him or look after him while I go out."

"Where do you want to go?"

"None of your damned business! I've been going to places and doing what I wanted to do since before you were born. Why should I have to tell you where I'm going?"

"You only had to ask," I protested.

"Ask? Why do I have to ask? Do I need your permission now? Is that what you think, that I'm sitting here like your bloody secretary, waiting for you to give me permission to leave?"

"No, I just meant that if you let me know you wanted to go out, I would come and look after him for a while."

"When you're not treating me like a secretary, you treat me like some kind of babysitter," she said.

"Oh no, that isn't true."

"Isn't it? You leave me here day in and day out. I never see the light of day."

"No, hang on a minute. You were the one who wanted a child. You were the one who suddenly got interested in me when you found out I was fertile."

She shook her head. "That's not true."

"Isn't it? When you found me that day on the Underground, you were all ready to abandon me to the Untainted, and then you found out I had a daughter. All of a sudden the old lady was gone and you were all long legs and shy smiles. *What would you like to do for your last day*, you said, all come-to-bed eyes and pouting lips. You think I didn't know? You think I didn't notice?" I was shouting now, but I didn't care.

"That's not how it was." There were tears in her eyes.

"You didn't think I'd make it through the night, did you? That's why you left me at Leicester Square. You didn't want to be around when the Untainted came for me. You damn near admitted it."

She shook her head, but she couldn't get the words out to deny it.

There was a knot in my throat, but I swallowed it down. "Even then, when I survived and you found I was wraithkin – it didn't put you off, did it? What could be a powerful enough incentive for you to overcome your revulsion? What would it take for you to put that aside?"

"No, no, no," she whispered.

"It wasn't me you wanted. It was what I could give you. All you ever wanted was a child. It was written all over your face at that inn in Shropshire. The first time you thought you might be pregnant you looked like the cat that got the cream. You hit the jackpot, and now you've got what you wanted you couldn't give a damn about me."

"It's not true," she whispered.

"Tell me truthfully. Before you knew I was fertile, did you have any interest in me at all?"

She shook her head, denying my question.

"That's not an answer, Blackbird. You never wanted me, did you? It was only ever about the baby. Now you've got what you needed, you want out. Don't worry, I know how it goes. I've been there before. I've got the bloody T-shirt."

She shook her head again, scattering tears, wringing her hands together. I turned and reached for the door handle. "Let Garvin know when you're leaving. I'll keep out of your way until then."

I stepped through the door and slammed it shut behind me. I was breathing hard, adrenaline coursing through my veins. My head felt like it would burst. I wanted to kick the door, the wall, anything. How could I have been such a fool?

I knew what she wanted from the start, but I kidded myself. I told myself that when she got to know me it would be enough – we would find a way to be together. I'd let my sex drive override my common sense and look where it had got me. Another bloody disaster. Another lesson in letting your heart rule your head. You'd think I'd bloody well learn.

Behind me, the door was wrenched open. I turned and she stood there, hands on her hips, colour in her cheeks.

"How dare you!" she shouted. "How dare you presume to tell me what I think and how I feel. What gives you the right?"

"Don't make it worse than it has to be."

"Worse? You stupid, stupid man! You idiot! What do you think you're doing?"

I shrugged. "It's over isn't it? What else is there to say?"

"Idiot!" she repeated. She grabbed my jacket and wrenched me back into the room, slamming the door behind me. She pushed me back against the door and pressed her lips to mine, hard. She kissed me hungrily, pressing her body against mine. It was such a change of tack that it took a moment for my head to catch up with my body.

"What are you doing?" I asked.

She kissed me again. "Shut up and undress me."

"You'll wake the baby…"

"He's downstairs with Lesley." She tugged my jacket off my arms and pulled my shirt out of my trousers, I could feel her nipples hardening under her blouse. I started fumbling with her buttons. She grabbed the blouse and ripped it open, exposing her breasts and shrugged it from her shoulders, then tugged at the belt of my trousers.

"But I thought…"

"Stop it! Stop thinking. You think too much. You pull things apart until there's nothing left. You analyse everything until it's torn apart. Don't think. Feel."

She tugged me by the belt towards the bed, pulling my shirt over my head and kissing me again. We fell on to the bed and kicked off our remaining clothes, wrapping our bodies together.

She bit my shoulder, making me squeal, "Ow! That hurts"

"That's for being stupid." She nibbled my ear, making me squirm, "and that's for thinking too much." She had her hands on my naked rear, wriggled beneath me. She kissed me long and languid, lifting her hips, and my body took over from my brain and I finally stopped trying to think.

A little while later I was staring at the ceiling, stroking her hair while she lay on top of me, resting her head on my chest. The length of her naked warmth was laid down my body, so that her legs rested between mine. I sighed.

"A pigeon for your thoughts," she said.

"It's a penny," I reminded her.

"You always say that, but it doesn't make it right."

"I hate pigeons."

"I don't suppose they're that keen on you," she said.

We lapsed into silence again; I could feel the rise and fall of her chest where she lay on me.

"You're not leaving me then?" I asked, tentatively.

She leaned over and sank her teeth into my side.

"Ow! Ow! That hurts! Let go!" I rubbed where her teeth had nipped the skin. I rubbed it with the palm of my hand. "I'm going to have a mark there."

"You shouldn't ask such stupid questions."

"Teeth are off limits. No teeth. OK?"

"That's not what you said earlier," she purred.

"That was different."

"You have to make your mind up then. Teeth or no teeth?" Her hand stroked across my chest, circling where my chest hair surrounded my nipple.

"Why is everything so complicated?" I asked her.

"It's not complicated. You simply have to decide what you want and what you're prepared to do to get it."

"Is that what you did?"

There was a long pause. I carried on stroking her hair.

"I admit, when I first met you I was thinking that you already had a daughter, so maybe another baby wasn't impossible for you. But you have to remember that you were marked by the Untainted. I'd never heard of anyone surviving to the next dawn in those circumstances. It was unlikely at best, and I offered what I could, partly from selfishness, it's true, but I would have made sure you enjoyed it."

"What changed your mind?"

"About you? I don't remember a specific moment. Between threatening to skewer you with a knife and losing you on the Way, something changed. I found I cared about losing you."

"Do you still care?"

She pressed her nails into the soft skin at each side with increasing pressure.

"OK, OK, I give in." The pressure relaxed

Lifting her head, she rose up on her arms to face me, studying my face intently.

"What?" I asked.

She shuffled upwards so that she could straddle my hips and sit across me, taking both my hands in hers and inter-twining the fingers, pressing them down so that her hands were over my shoulders. I leaned up to kiss a nipple, but she evaded me, looking serious.

There was a hint of green fire somewhere in the darkness of her eyes.

"Know this, Niall Petersen. I have loved you almost since the day I met you. I cannot promise to love you for ever, be-cause I do not know what the future will bring, for either of us, but right here, right now, I love you."

"I love you too."

She lifted her hand, mine still entwined, and pressed it against my lips. "Don't say that unless you mean it. I do not demand it of you. I do not even ask it."

"I do. When I thought you were leaving I was... I don't know what I would have done."

"Someone..." She stopped, and sighed, and tried again. "Before I met you, someone hurt you. Maybe it was Kather-ine, and maybe it was someone else, I don't know and I'm not blaming anyone for it. But you hold yourself closed, like any moment you expect the floor to drop out from under you."

I didn't say anything. The knot had reappeared in my throat and I didn't think I could speak.

"I just want you to know," she said quietly, "that I won't do that to you."

She leaned down and gently kissed my lips.

She added, "I might stick a knife in your ribs, or bash your head in with a rolling pin, but I won't do that to you."

I smiled, and she smiled too.

"Which might be sooner rather than later if you don't get me out of here. Seriously, if I have to change another nappy today I am going to go stark-raving mad. I love our son dearly, but he's a little shit-bottom."

"All part of the joys of parenthood," I said.

"Well if you don't want to find him skewered to a door post, you're going to have to do something."

"Far be it from me to tell Blackbird of the Fey'ree when she can come and go. The world is your oyster, Mistress." I hadn't forgotten her earlier words, despite our current rapprochement.

"That smart mouth will get you into trouble." She kissed it for emphasis. "I can feel my brain going to mush. I haven't had a decent conversation that doesn't involve nappy-rash for weeks. Don't look hurt, I don't mean you. It's just that I've always been active and enquiring; I spent the last thirty years as an academic. The lack of any kind of mental stimulus is driving me to distraction. I need something to get my teeth into."

"I'll see if I can come up with something."

"Maybe I could come with you on one of your Warder missions?"

"I don't think Garvin would approve," I pointed out.

"Stuff Garvin. I don't need his permission."

"Woah, I was just pointing out that Warder business possibly wasn't the best way to get some fresh air."

"You don't need to protect me, Niall."

"It's not that. I'm already feeling out of my depth. I meant it when I told you I messed up this morning. We could have caught them if I had been quicker on my feet."

"And then what happens to them?" she asked.

"Whatever. They join the courts? We all live happily ever after?"

"Something tells me that's not what Garvin has planned."

"I know you don't see eye to eye with him, but you don't have to see a conspiracy in everything he does."

"Where is Angela?" she asked, innocently.

"The seer? She's staying in the house, isn't she? Garvin said he'd ask Mullbrook to find her somewhere."

"Have you seen her since then?" she asked.

"Well no, since you come to mention it."

"So where is she?"

"It's a big house. There are plenty of empty rooms."

"It makes you wonder, doesn't it? What are they all for?"

"Now you really are going off track. I promise I will find something for you to do." She squeezed my hand, "For us to do together, then. Just don't rattle Garvin's cage any more than you have to, OK? He's already on my case."

"He probably wouldn't approve of you having sex when you're supposed to be on duty," she said, releasing my hand and stroking across my chest so it brushed my nipple.

"We won't tell him then, eh?"

She released my other hand and leaned down for a long slow kiss. She whispered warm in my ear, "He's probably listening at the keyhole." She lifted my hands to her breasts so I could caress my thumbs over her nipples while she stroked down my arms. She wriggled on top of me in response.

"I don't think so," I said.

"He knows far too much of what goes on in this house," she said, sitting upright and reaching round behind her to stroke her nails up the inside of my thigh.

"You're not serious," I asked.

She stared at me wide eyed, while her hands did something far from innocent behind her.

"We'd better give him something to listen to then, I suppose?" she said.

The West End got more crowded as the light faded – party goers, mates out for a drink, people choosing from menus outside brightly lit restaurants. Alex floated past them. At the end of the evening they would all go home. Late buses and last-ditch taxis would carry them back to their houses and they could crawl into their beds and dream of happy families.

"You all right, love?" A bloke with his mate in tow staggered towards her. She caught a whiff of the alcohol on his breath.

"Go away," she said. "Leave me alone."

There must have been more in her words than a simple request, because he veered away, dragging his friend behind him. She changed direction and walked into Leicester Square, weaving between couples arm-in-arm, avoiding the crowds of lads out for a good time, staying clear of the girls who were less than subtly touting for business at the edge of the crowd. The cinemas were emptying out after the late showing, the uniformed staff guiding the stragglers out into the square.

"It's your lucky night." The man approached her smiling, offering his card. "We're recruiting models and you have the look of tomorrow, you know that? Of course you do, a beautiful girl like you has her career ahead of her. Just take this card to the address on the back and they'll look after you." He proffered the card.

She smiled, "You really think so?" She took the card and turned it over. The address was in minute print.

He grinned at her. "Sure, you're a natural. You're gonna look great in pictures, Baby." He stepped in close, too close for her liking.

She reached up and tapped him lightly on the forehead. He stepped back, unnerved by her odd reaction. "I don't think it's your lucky night," she said. "I fact, I think your night's going to take a turn downhill." She turned away.

"Don't say that, Baby. You'll jinx me. I'm just doing my job."

She called back, "And don't call me Baby." Walking on, she wondered how long it would take him to realise that the word "pervert" was now tattooed across his forehead. She changed course and headed into Soho in case it was sooner rather than later.

As soon as she left the bright lights of the square she wrapped herself in glamour. These were streets she would be cautious around in daytime, even more so after midnight. Taxis rumbled down the streets and a garbage collection giant was grinding and squealing its way down the street, tipping containers of commercial waste out into its dark maw with mechanical efficiency while its minions ran around trying to keep the beast fed. She turned aside, heading vaguely towards Oxford Street and the lighted pillars of Centrepoint and the BT Tower.

The streets grew quieter, punctuated by the chinking rattle of bottles as the pubs cleared out the empties and the occasional roar of a motorcycle taking a short cut down the back streets.

The people out now were drunk, lost or lonely, and she didn't include herself in any of those groups. She walked down the edge of a square, a large patch of brown grass fenced off in the middle with park benches occupied by huddled shapes with draped newspaper, plastic bags and tins of cider. She'd a fair idea of how harsh that life could be and had no wish to join them.

The sudden whiff of a foul drain caught her off guard.

The tumbling rush of turning water, the gut-turning stench of shit, the gulped-off scream as one of them was dragged under....

She shook her head, lifting her hand to push away the mental images that crowded into her brain as she stumbled off the pavement into a doorway. *Not now.*

Leaning against the door to a swanky advertising boutique, pressing her forehead to the cool glass, she fought to control her breathing. The cold on her skin helped to calm her. She smoothed her hair back from her face, pushing down the memories, concentrating on the moment. She was OK. All that was past, and she had come through it. She could deal with it.

Even so, she couldn't stay the night in a doorway. She had to keep moving.

Despite the summer day, the night was chilling fast and she'd only the skimpy cardie to keep her warm. There was the momentary regret that she could have acquired something warmer, but then she pulled it close about her. She liked her new clothes. They made her feel better. She started walking again.

A movement across the square caught her eye. Something large had just bounded across the grass. She scanned the open space for movement, but there was nothing there. A dog? No, too big, and where was the owner? Something else? In her time at Porton Down she had seen things that she did not want to encounter in the dark London streets. She wrapped her glamour tighter and cut down an alley away from the square, heading back towards the bright lights.

She crossed over Shaftsbury Avenue, wondering whether to head up towards Tottenham Court Road or back down to Leicester Square. She'd been here in the day, shopping for a guitar when she'd discovered a boy she liked was into music and wanted to form a band. Her mum had suggested she sing, but she had balked at that. The kind of music he liked wasn't the sort of music you sang, and her enthusiasm for the guitar had evaporated when she'd discovered that you had to cut your nails and it made your fingers sore. They'd sold it on eBay for half what they paid for it.

Turning away from the music stores, she headed back to Cambridge Circus towards Neal Street. There were some nice boutiques that way and even though they would be closed she could still window-shop. She paused as she crossed Seven Dials. There were a couple getting out of a taxi outside a hotel, the man making a big show of tipping the driver, and it occurred to her that there were places in London full of empty beds that were there for the taking.

She ghosted past the reception where the couple were booking in and went to the lift. The buttons operated with a key-card, but that didn't stop her. She went to the top floor, opening out on a blank corridor with doors spaced along it.

The ones with trays outside were obviously occupied. The problem was figuring out which ones were empty. The receptionist would have it all on the computer, but there was no way to access it without attracting attention. She went to a door and listened. Was that the faint sound of snoring? She moved on.

Four doors down she found a room that was quiet. She put her hand on the door handle and the light blinked to green. The door opened easily. She opened the door and let herself in.

"Who's there?" A voice came from the darkness inside.

"Sorry Madame, it's... room service." The lie twisted on her tongue. "I've got the wrong room. My apologies." She slipped out again and pulled the door shut behind her, sliding sideways away from the viewport in the door. After a second she heard the lock behind her click shut and the rattle as the chain was put across. She slipped away down the corridor.

The doors all looked the same. If only she could figure out which ones were empty.

At the end of the corridor was a door with a brass plaque mounted beside it. The plaque said, The Seven Dials Suite. "In for a penny..." she whispered. She put her hand on the door control and it blinked green.

Pushing through she found a hallway with low-level LEDs leading like runway lights into the room. She let the door almost close and then rested it against the latch so she could escape quickly if she needed to.

"Room service?" She called, experimentally, into the room. There was no reply.

She edged forwards along the corridor and nearly jumped out of her skin when the latch clicked behind her and the door closed. Heart beating fast, she went to the end of the hall. It opened out into a room with floor-length glass windows looking out over the rooftops. The city light illuminated comfortable chairs with chic magazines arranged artfully on occasional tables, and doors leading off to other rooms. This was more like a luxury apartment than any hotel Alex had ever stayed in. She crept through the apartment, finding other rooms with huge beds freshly made and a marble bathroom with an enormous tub.

"How the other half lives, eh?" she whispered.

Satisfied that the apartment was empty, she went to switch

on the lights, but they were dead. She tried another switch, but that was dead too. Maybe there was a power failure? The LED lights in the hallway still worked, though. On an impulse she went back to the door and found a slot where your key-card would fit to switch on the power. She placed her hand on it, but nothing happened. I wasn't that it was locked, it simply didn't work.

On reflection, she thought that maybe it would be better if no one saw light coming from a room that should be empty. She could manage in the light from the windows and all she really needed was a bed. She locked the door from the inside and put the chain across for good measure. She went into the bathroom and washed her hands, then splashed her face in the sink, dabbing her face with the snowy towels. In the mirror her eyes glowed faintly blue back at her.

She glanced at her wrist. Dropping the towel, she went back to the main window overlooking the rooftops. Unlocking the balcony doors, she stepped out in to the night and examined her wrists. The buds that had been there had opened into dark flowers, black petals folded back to reveal long stamen. What did that mean? She rubbed at them, but they were dyed into her skin. Tattoos were supposed to be fixed, weren't they?

The night air was cool and it was somehow private up here. She tried to imagine herself staying here legitimately, but she could think of no circumstance where she would be accorded this kind of treatment. Maybe if she'd stuck to the guitar and been a rock star?

Closing the door on the balcony, she rubbed at her wrists as she wandered around the apartment. She found a fridge in a cupboard and opened a pack of cashew nuts and a mineral water, eating them laid out on the huge sofa. There was champagne in the fridge, but she wanted to keep her wits about her. This was no time to get silly. She would save the orange juice for the morning.

In the bedroom she stripped out of her outfit, telling herself she would need to acquire some clean underwear in the morning and that M&S in Covent Garden would be a good place to do that. She left the curtains open. Having spent so many days in rooms where it was always light, she liked sleeping with the curtains open. Climbing into the huge bed, she drew the light quilt across her and laid in the dark, listening to the city sounds filtering across the rooftops. She laid there, eyes open, long into the deep of the night, before sleep finally claimed her.

TEN

When I visited Alex's room the next morning, she was still not there. What with my argument with Blackbird and then the reconciliation, plus having to reclaim the baby to the knowing smiles of Lesley, I had convinced myself that Alex would return under her own steam and that she would be in bed this morning and I could take the opportunity to have a calm word with her.

It was a shock to see that she hadn't been back. The room was exactly as she'd left it. I returned to the suite I shared with Blackbird.

"She's not been back," I told Blackbird, who was feeding the baby.

"Stop pacing up and down. You're distracting him from his feed. Maybe she's staying with her mother?" Blackbird suggested. The noisy sucking resumed.

"If she is, then goodness knows what she's told Katherine."

"Perhaps it would be a good idea to get in touch and see what the situation is. Alex must realise that she can't stay with her mother long term. It isn't going to work, Katherine must see that."

"You don't know Katherine."

Blackbird went back to feeding the baby.

"OK, I'll call her. I'll go and find a mirror in one of the spare rooms and see if I can catch her at home."

"Are you cutting me out?" There was a note of warning in her voice.

"No. No, really. I just thought... Katherine may not be too pleased with me at the moment."

"If you start excluding me from everything again, I won't be too pleased with you either." She smiled to soften her words. "Call her. It's OK. I'll be quiet as a mouse and your son has his mouth full."

I went to the mirror and laid my hand on it. "Katherine?"

Condensation spread out around my hand as the temperature in the room dipped. My son grizzled, but then continued to suckle. There was a hissing sound of random static, then a ringing tone.

"Hello?"

"Katherine? It's Niall."

"Niall! Thank God! I've been ringing every number I have for you. None of them work! Don't you have a mobile that works any more?"

"No... it's complicated. Is Alex there?"

"That's why I was trying to get hold of you. She was here, last night."

"Where is she now?"

"I don't know. She ran out on me. I tried to call her back, but she'd vanished before I could find her. I've called Kayleigh's parents – they haven't seen her."

"What did you tell them? She's supposed to be dead."

"I'm not that stupid. I just asked them if Kayleigh was OK."

One of the changes in my relationship with Katherine was

that I could tell when she lying or being evasive, like now. I let it go. Now was not the time. "Has Kayleigh seen her?"

"No, no one has. Where is she, Niall?"

"She didn't come back here last night. Her bed's not been slept in. As far as I can tell, you were the last person to see her. What did you say to her?"

If they'd had some kind of row, that would go some way to explaining Alex's absence. She was probably sulking somewhere.

"I didn't get chance. She was in and out before either Barry or I knew she was here."

The evasion in her voice was getting stronger. "What are you not telling me?"

"I think... Maybe she got the wrong idea."

"About what?"

"After she... after she was gone... I just couldn't stand it, Niall. I couldn't bear seeing her room like that. It was like she was going to be coming home, but she never did."

"What's that got to do with her being there last night?"

"She was upstairs. She was in her old room."

"I don't understand."

"Barry's been working from home a lot. We'd converted it to an office for him. We had decorators in to do it."

"What about Alex's stuff, her things? She was going on about wanting her own things around her."

"I gave them away, Niall." Katherine sniffed down the phone. "I gave them to charity. I couldn't bear to keep them." She was crying down the phone now. I could hear her snuffling and making small noises of distress.

"But then... Oh God, Katherine. What have you done?"

"It wasn't my fault," she sniffled. "If you hadn't kept it all from me then I'd have held on to them for her. I'd have looked after them."

"But she's only been gone, what, a few weeks?"

"You didn't have to walk past it every day! You didn't have to see it every time you crossed the hall. You have no idea, Niall."

I could hear Katherine snuffling and sniffling down the phone.

"I've got to go," I said. "She may come back to you – there's just a chance – if she does, try and make it look like you want her back. I'll try and call you tomorrow." I dropped the call without giving Katherine chance to answer.

"That wasn't very kind, was it? The woman is clearly upset," said Blackbird.

"Oh she's upset all right. She knows full well what happened. Alex came back and found she'd been moved out. What's the girl supposed to think?"

"I don't think she meant it like that."

"You think it matters to Alex how she meant it? For all Katherine knew, Alex was barely cold in her grave, and she redecorates! She even has a man in to do it for her!"

"You don't know that, Niall. You're leaping to conclusions on precious little evidence."

"I know Katherine."

"Perhaps not as well as you think. It wasn't you having to walk past Alex's room every day, and you've had the comfort of knowing she was alive, even if you couldn't find her. Katherine hasn't had that luxury."

"Yeah, well. I bet it wasn't long before she was getting quotes for the job, picking out furnishings..."

"You're assuming the worst."

"Maybe."

"Either way, it doesn't help you find Alex."

"I know how to find her. I've done it before and I'll do it again."

I turned back to the mirror and placed my hand on it. "Alex? Where are you?"

Alex woke with the thought that there was someone in the room with her. She blinked against the harsh daylight spilling in through the tall bedroom windows but kept still, listening. She went back through her actions the night before. She was sure she'd put the chain across the door before she'd gone to bed. Surely she hadn't slept through them breaking in?

Under the city noise and hotel air-conditioning hum there was another sound, out of place. She lifted her head slowly and found the room undisturbed. She slid sideways from the quilt onto the deep-pile cream carpet and pulled her bra and top from the chair, slipping them on quickly. She crept to the door, scanning the sitting room beyond. It was empty. She went back, intending to slip into her knickers and skirt.

"Alex? Are you there?"

She nearly jumped out of her skin at the sound of her father's voice. It was coming from inside the bedroom. She retreated, scanning the room, looking for the source. Above the dresser, the mirror was misted in the centre.

"Alex, I need to talk to you."

It was definitely her father, and his voice was coming through the mirror. How was he doing that? Come to that, how did he know she was here? Then she remembered, when she had first been at Porton Down she had heard his disembodied voice. With all the drugs and the treatment she had thought it was a dream, but maybe not.

She reached forward with a tentative finger to touch the mirror.

"I know you're there. Answer me."

She jumped back. There he went again, treating her like a two year-old, telling her what to do and how to think. No one told her what to do, not since Porton Down, not even him. She frowned at the mirror and its surface rippled under her gaze, but still his voice came through, jumpy and broken but intelligible.

"Alex? Speak to me! Where are you?"

She grabbed her bag and pulled out the red lipstick she had stolen the day before. She wrote 'NO' on the rippled surface of the mirror. It was a crude warding, but it sufficed. Her father's voice ceased.

"Alex, what are you doing? Answer me this instant!" His voice was coming from the sitting room now. She dashed through, searching for the mirror. The sound was coming through the full length mirror near the door. She scribbled 'NO' on that one too and then went through the apartment, writing 'NO' on every mirror, every picture, every window, until the room echoed with the word.

Finally there was silence. She looked around. The room looked like it had been vandalised, the word 'NO' repeated like some blood red deranged message all around the room. She dropped the lipstick like it was hot and it rolled across the carpet.

"I'm not crazy. I'm not!" She was breathless.

She ran into the bedroom and pulled on the discarded clothes from last night, stuffing her feet into her boots. She grabbed her bag and pulled on her cardie. As she ran back through the sitting room she stepped on the lipstick and it smeared across the carpet.

"Shit!"

She stared at the red smear across the cream pile, her hands bunched into tight fists. Her breathing came faster, she couldn't take her eyes off the streak of red. She screwed her eyes shut, biting her lip.

Then she ran for the exit, wrenched back the chain and threw open the door. She almost crashed into the trolley the chamber maid was wheeling down the corridor. The door to the suite slammed behind her and she flew down the stairs and out through the fire exit, banging the door open in front of startled pedestrians and swerving to avoid the car that swept past.

She kept running, taking random turns left and right until she was lost in the back streets with no idea which way to run next.

"She locked me out! How could she do that?" I stared at the silent mirror, no longer responding to my touch.

"If you paid more attention to our sessions and actually practiced what I taught you, you'd know," said Blackbird.

"No, I don't mean that. I'm her father. She's not supposed to... hang up on me?"

"What, you're still going into the bathroom with her, tying her shoe laces, helping her dress?"

"No, obviously not."

"So she does have some privacy."

"This isn't a matter of privacy, it's..."

"What? I think she let you know in no uncertain terms that she wanted some space, some time to think things through," said Blackbird. "She's growing up fast, if you would let her."

"But she's only fourteen."

"Fifteen, Niall."

"Fifteen, then. It's no age for a girl to be out on her own all night."

Blackbird smiled. "On the contrary, she seems to be

managing extraordinarily well. She's certainly given you the brush off."

"This isn't funny, Blackbird."

"No, I don't suppose it is, but you're only going to make matters worse if you pursue her. I didn't help that you came over all Pater Familias with her."

"All what?"

"It means Head of the Family, with connotations of ownership of the estate and everything and everyone in it. It's Latin."

"I was just concerned, that's all. She's been gone all night. As her father…"

"That's just what I'm talking about. As her father you want to decide where she can go, what she can do, who she sees, where she lives."

"She's my daughter. It's my duty to look after her."

"She'll always be your daughter, no one can change that, but she's not a child any more. She's seen too much, done too much, to be comfortable living within the constraints of childhood. She was forced to grow up, too quickly and too harshly, that much I'll grant you, but she was. You can't undo what was done, Niall."

"So I should let her stay out all night, take drugs, get drunk, get pregnant?"

"You make those sound as if they're equivalent." There was a warning in Blackbird's tone.

"An unwanted pregnancy isn't what she needs, Blackbird. Even you must acknowledge that."

"She may not be able to get pregnant. Have you thought of that?"

"I'm not sure I want to find out just yet. I'm more worried that she'll be mugged – killed even."

"I think she can look after herself. She's proven extraordinarily resilient up until now. You brought her up well, and she's chosen her own path. Now it's up to her."

"She has no common sense. She'll do something rash. What if she's ill? What if she gets run over? She has no road sense at all."

"Listen to yourself. You're treating her like a four year-old. Have some respect for her. Did she sound like she was in trouble? Was she begging for assistance?"

"No, but…"

"You found her last time because she needed you. You rescued her when she couldn't help herself. This time she doesn't want to be rescued, especially by you."

"What do you mean, especially by me?"

"You're her father. You're the last person she wants to come to her aid. She wants a white knight on a charger, who'll tell her she's worth the slings and arrows that he faced to reach her. You have to face it, Niall. She's looking for a mate."

"A what!"

"Calm down. Not right away, and maybe not for some time, but eventually she's going to want to choose someone for herself, someone to be with."

I pushed my hand back through my hair. "I'm too young for this," I said.

Blackbird laughed. "She's been through a lot and she's endured. She's earned her independence. Anyway, there's nothing you can do about it. It seems she's been paying a lot more attention to Fionh's lessons than you gave her credit for, and now that's paying off. If she doesn't want to be found, you won't find her."

"She's not supposed to use it against me."

"She's using it for herself. You can't blame her."

"What am I going to tell Katherine?" I asked.

"Tell her the truth. Tell her you've tried to find Alex and failed. What can she say?"

"More than I want to hear."

"She bears some of the responsibility for this Niall. I think she knows that."

"You'd have to pull her teeth out to get her to admit it."

"Look at it this way, it solved one problem. You don't have to tell Katherine why Alex can't go back to living at home with her. She's chosen for herself, and there's nothing Katherine can do about that, any more than you."

"What if she gets hurt? Where will she sleep? What will she do for money?"

"Let her figure it out, Niall. She knows how to find you. All you have to do is make it clear that if she does come back, it's on her terms, and that you'll accept that."

"Her terms? What does that mean?"

"It means not locking her up in your ivory tower until you can find a suitable man to palm her off on."

"I haven't… there's no way…"

"The West Wing, then. Have you allowed her out? Has she been able to buy clothes, meet people?"

"She's hardly been in a state to be allowed to…"

"Allowed. That's an interesting word, Niall. Well, she no longer needs your permission or seeks it. She's taken responsibility for herself, and actually it's time. Now you have to trust her."

"That's harder than you think."

She looked down at our son who had eaten his fill and then flopped asleep in her arms. "Oh, when this little one wants to fledge and fly I expect to be biting my nails at the edge of the nest just like any parent, but it doesn't change what has to happen. They can't stay in the nest forever. That's just nature."

"Yeah, well let's just hope it isn't red in tooth and claw."

Alex sat on the steps outside a red-brick apartment block. The steps were stained with green algae, but she had a blister on her heel and she didn't care. She delved into her bag looking for a plaster or something to cushion her foot, but of course, there was nothing. She had make-up which she wasn't wearing, a hair clip that fell out, but nothing useful like a plaster.

She looked up and down the street. Away from the main streets where the chain stores made easy pickings, there were little corner shops with eagle-eyed shopkeepers who kept everything behind the counter, and long walks between them. She needed to head back to the high street where she could get what she needed. What she really needed, though, was somewhere to stay.

It was all very well being free to go where you wanted but if you had nowhere to go back to it wore thin pretty quick. Her feet were sore, the weather had broken and there was the threat of rain. Her thin cardie was no longer the comfort it had been. She needed shelter, and food, and a warm bed, and central heating, and chocolate.

Momentarily she thought about going home, but there was nothing there for her now. She had no clothes, no stuff, no room even. And her dad would be furious with her after she warded him out this morning. It would take him days to calm down. If she went back now she would be grounded for months. She couldn't even go to Kayleigh's. She had no friends now, there just wasn't anyone she could talk to, except maybe Tate.

Initially him calling her *Miss* all the time had annoyed her, but now she kinda liked it. He always treated her respectfully and asked her what she wanted to do. He offered advice, but didn't get all antsy if she didn't follow it. And he was huge. She caught herself wondering if he was that big all over, and found herself blushing. No, she didn't think of him like that. He was a friend, that was all.

She pushed her hands through her unruly hair – she couldn't go to Tate anyway. He was a Warder, just like Dad, and he would have to tell Dad where she was, and then there would be hell to pay. That wasn't going to work.

She stood and brushed at the green marks on her skirt, making them worse rather than better. She needed a change of clothes as well. She sniffed at her armpit and wished again that she'd made use of the shower in the hotel before running out like a scared cat. What was the matter with her? She'd had the situation under control, so why run? She shook her head at her own folly.

There were people she knew, though, weren't there? There were the other people like her, the ones from Porton Down. She wasn't the only one who had escaped, and she had an idea where one or two of them might have gone. Maybe she needed to be with her own kind, people who'd understand what she was going though?

Hoisting the bag back onto her shoulder, she headed back towards an area where there were sandwich shops and a high street chemist – somewhere she could get something for her feet. Then she would take a trip and see what she could find.

"Is this what Alex did when I tried to speak to her?" I was sitting on the fence overlooking the fields which rolled away from us.

"No. What she did, I think, was to ward where she was staying against you," said Blackbird. "A warding can apply to a place, or an object, or a person. Warding a place is simple and effective. You exclude anyone's magic but your own. In its finer form it can be used to clean and protect a place, a home perhaps, so that malicious magic cannot intrude, but even then it has limitations. Anything brought into that space which is tainted with another's power will disrupt the warding and release the magic. That's how you know that someone has crossed your warding – you'll feel the release and know it's been broken."

"So she pushed me out."

"There's no point in brooding on it, Niall. You invaded her privacy and she reacted. Instead of expressing your concern and asking if she was safe, you started making demands. It was not, perhaps, the best way to re-establish relations with your daughter."

"You always take her side."

"I take no side but my own, but I know Alex is precious to you and I'm trying to help. You need to stop thinking of her as a little girl."

"That was pretty cool, what she did, though, wasn't it?" I smiled.

"Crude but effective. She excluded you and prevented you from re-entering. Maybe she's more capable than you think, and she's certainly better at learning and not getting distracted by side-issues when someone is trying to teach them something."

"Sorry, where were we?"

"You were extending your awareness outwards and telling me what you feel."

I closed my eyes. Here beneath the trees the shade was

welcome, but the rustling of the leaves and the smell of the grass was a constant distraction from what I was supposed to be looking for.

"It's just trees and grass," I told her.

"Is it? Or is that what you're supposed to think?"

I let myself sink deeper into the sense of the place, hearing the buzzing of bumble bees, the far-off coo of a wood pigeon and the faint rumble of distant traffic. "It's peaceful."

"How peaceful?"

Now that she mentioned it, there was something. "There's a kind of dampening, a dullness spread around us. Is that what I'm looking for?"

"What can you tell me about it?"

"It's heavy, like a wool blanket but not warm like that, just heavy. Now that I can see it it's over everything. It's huge."

"Every day the Warders renew these boundaries." Blackbird said quietly. "Every day they reassert their magic over this ground. What you're sensing is the repeated warding of this place, layer upon layer, until it's so thick that it can no longer be broken, simply endured. It's one of the things I don't like about being here. It's smothering."

"Why didn't I sense it before?"

"Here at the edge it's easier to detect. You can feel the density of it change as it fades out towards the edges. Within the grounds of the house it's pervasive. It invades every space and seeps into every crack. There is nowhere not steeped in it. Like background noise that never ceases, after a while you don't notice it. I do though. It's like a constant niggle at the edge of my senses, a lingering doubt that things aren't as they should be."

"You could have said something."

"It doesn't seem to bother you, and as you pointed out it's

all very convenient having everyone on call, with all the facilities to hand."

"But I get to go out and leave for a while. I get some relief from it," I said.

"Indeed."

"Couldn't you set up your own warding, just in our rooms? You could exclude the Warder's magic and have a little island of peace."

"A bubble inside a bubble? Somewhat unstable, don't you think? I'm not sure that would even be possible. Besides I can't see Garvin allowing any area over which he has no control anywhere near the courts. He is responsible for security when all's said and done."

"I'm sorry. I didn't realise."

"It presents us with an opportunity, though. I want you to establish your own warding, right here at the edge of the courts where it's weaker. You will need to push their warding back to establish your own."

"How?"

"Do you remember when we were sitting outside the Church of St Clement's Dane in London and I was showing you how to establish your glamour?"

"I guess. I could feel the way your magic concealed us, as it spread across the area around the statue."

"Think of extending threads of magic outward, like a spider spinning a web. Push it out a little, connect it together, then push it out a little more. Keep extending the boundary."

"That's not how a spider builds a web," I pointed out.

"I know that. I'm just drawing an analogy. Think instead then of how wasps build a nest. They start small and then build onto it in spirals, shoring it up as you go."

"I don't even know what it is I'm shoring up."

"It's like territory, like putting your stamp on it, as if you were claiming it."

I tried to imagine myself claiming the area around the fence. Nothing happened. "It's not working."

"OK, forget that. Come down here and lie down." She hopped off the fence and smoothed her skirts before sitting on the grass.

I stepped down and sat down with her and then lay back onto the grass so that my head was near to where she was sitting.

"Look up in the tree and allow your eyes to defocus – better still close them, not tightly, but so that the sunlight filters through your eyelids. Imagine the tree is still there."

"It is still there."

She tweaked my nose.

"Ow!"

"Shut up and listen. The tree is above you, extending its branches out into the air, leaning up into the sunlight. Let your magic extend around your body, let it relax into the earth, so that it seeps into the soil, down among the roots and worms. Let it follow the roots of the tree, in your mind, in your imagination, up through the trunk, out along the branches, onto the twigs."

"It feels light and warm."

"Follow the light out along the twigs into the leaves. Feel the sunlight in the leaves, feeding the tree, bathe in the sunlight at the tips of the leaves."

"This is really very restful. You're not going to be offended if I fall asleep are you?"

She ignored me. "Leave a sense of yourself, a presence there at the leaves, but now float from the leaves into the air, following the shifting breeze, drifting with the wind."

"Is this how a seed feels when it falls? Oh, hang on, there's something here. It feels like a fungus or a fuzzy mould."

"You've reached the edge of the warding. Send a root of your own into it. Explore it with your senses" she suggested.

"It tastes sour, not like the tree."

"It's very old, layer upon layer. But like all layers it has weaknesses. Explore the cracks. Push your way into it. Find the fault lines and wheedle your way into them."

I could feel the weight of the warding ahead of me. Somehow it left the taste of decay in my mouth, along with the smell of the forest floor and something beneath that – a bitter sourness that crept onto the tongue, making my mouth flood with saliva.

"What do you think you're doing?"

It was Fionh's voice and I opened my eyes, squinting up against the light. She was standing next to the fence we had been sitting on. I blinked, glancing at Blackbird.

"I asked you what you thought you were doing," she repeated.

"Blackbird was showing me how wardings work," I explained.

Fionh raised an eyebrow at Blackbird.

"It seemed a good way of demonstrating how a place can be warded over time," she said.

"You know better than to interfere with the wardings of the courts," said Fionh. "And getting Niall to do it in your place will not help you."

"I don't think I know what you mean," said Blackbird.

"I think you do." She looked down at me. "Don't do that again. There are things in the wardings which you do not want to encounter. They're there for a reason, and not to be meddled with."

"Sorry, I had no idea it was so sensitive," I said.

"No. You didn't. But she did." She looked from me to Blackbird. "You're supposed to be teaching him."

"Oh, I think that lesson was an excellent demonstration, Fionh. Thank you for your assistance."

Fionh's mouth hardened, but she turned and walked away with whatever was on her tongue unsaid.

Eleven

———

Alex was beginning to think she had come to the wrong place. The estate looked abandoned – surely no one lived here? Cracked windows looked down on her, and rubble had been heaped into random piles.

Had she remembered correctly? Some of her memories of her imprisonment were distorted by drugs and the regime she had been put through. She knew not to trust her sense of time, but there were other things. At times her dreams and reality seemed to merge and she wasn't sure she could differentiate between one and another.

The memories that stuck, though, were ones of other inmates. Meetings like that were brief, and often at least one of them would be spaced out on something. She'd been taken by surprise the first time, lying on a trolley and doped up with muscle relaxant. A face had appeared in her vision.

"I'm Donna," she said. "I like movies and romantic stories. Quick, tell me about yourself, something, anything!" She had shaken Alex's shoulders.

"I'm Lexie." Slurring her words, she sounded drunk, but she didn't feel drunk. "Where are we?"

"It doesn't matter. Tell me something about yourself, something normal, something you'd tell a friend."

"There's the cool guy at school," she slurred. "He's called Jamie... he's got a really nice arse."

"That's good Lexie. Now we're friends. They can't break you if you're with friends. We're all in this together. Find someone else. Do the same with them. We can beat them together."

The door opened and a woman entered. "What are you doing?"

"She was mumbling something. I think she was trying to talk to me," said Donna.

"Don't worry about her, Donna. Come along. It's time for your assessment."

Lexie watched as Donna was led away, but the memory stayed.

She'd done the same with others, forming connections, however brief. She could remember all of them, every name, every face.

It was funny, she couldn't remember the staff – except for Watkins.

The bloody severed head of Doctor Watkins was in front of her. The shock travelled up her arm as she chopped the heavy blade down on his open-eyed skull, splitting the bone and sending fragments of gunk splattering outwards, sticking to her arms, her face. Blood and slime slicked her hands. Tugging free the blade, lifting it again, her breathing loud, heart thumping. The exhalation as she chopped down, "Heeuagh!" The swish and crunch as the blade glanced off the skull, slicing off an ear.

She shook her head, pushing the memory away, staggering momentarily at the disorienting vision. She couldn't afford to lose focus like that. She deliberately slowed her breathing, unclenching her fist with the other hand, massaging the spasmed muscles. It was over. She'd had her revenge. He was dead.

A train gave an electric whine as it ran along the banked-up tracks behind the estate. The normality of the sound helped to steady her. She'd seen Gina in a corridor; a two-second conversation. They'd exchanged addresses. When Gina told her it was an industrial estate, Alex questioned her, but there was no time. They'd been separated and she'd not seen her again.

And here it was, except it wasn't here any more. No one had done anything industrial here for quite a while. The buildings were derelict, some of them half demolished, others cracked and vandalised, sprayed with tags and slogans. She navigated through the piles of broken bricks and half-burned timber and came to the building she was looking for.

She turned around slowly, looking for signs of life. A siren wailed distantly, seagulls flapped their lazy way across the overcast sky. What a dump. Had Gina come back here? Is this what she found? Except this wasn't recent, so maybe she was here after all. She looked up at the green slime running down the walls under the broken gutters, the way the rubble had sunk and settled, the big patches of nettles and bramble – all this happened ages ago.

She worked her way around the nettles to the side door. Someone had kicked it in, probably looking to see if there was anything left to steal. Alex couldn't see what the attraction was, but she squeezed past onto the factory floor beyond. It looked like a film set, one of those abandoned warehouses where they stage shoot-outs and blast all the windows out, except that the windows were wire-reinforced and simply sagged where they cracked. No film crews here. Hey, perhaps that was what she should do – go and find a film crew and make herself useful. She could be an extra, or an actress even. She smiled and shook her head.

She reached the end of the gallery and wandered up the stairs, wary of rats and pigeons. Nothing to scavenge here, though, so she was probably OK. The floor above was the same – cracked glass and scuffed concrete. She went up another level, and here there were signs of habitation. Someone had put up plastic sheets against the light. The gallery was striped with long slivers of sunlight which only intensified the shadows. In the dimness a mattress was laid against the wall. Surely Gina wasn't meaning this?

She walked forward, keeping near the windows where the light was better. "Gina?" Her voice sounded hollow in the dark. "Gina, it's Lexie. You remember?"

There was a scuffle in the shadows. Something moved. Maybe she was here after all?

"We ain't had this good luck in a loooong time." The voice was male.

"I'm looking for Gina," Alex called out. "Is she here? Do you know where she is?"

"Ain't no Gina here, sweetness," another voice, also male. Alex backed towards the stairs but a shadow separated from the dark and moved between her and the exit.

"I'm just looking for my friend," she said, glancing between them. "I don't want trouble."

"Ain't no trouble here, we all welcome, sugar." They moved apart, spreading out to form a half-circle around her. Alex backed towards the window. She reached behind her and tugged the plastic sheet. It slid down behind her.

They squinted against the light. "That's a shame," said the one with the gang-pattern in his buzz cut. "You seen our faces now, and we ain't happy with no witness."

"I didn't see anything," she said. "There's nothing to tell."

"It's not what you seen," said the one with the diamond ear-stud between her and the stairs, "It's what you gonna see."

To her left, the guy with the buzz cut grabbed her handbag. She shrieked and held the strap for a moment, but had to let go or be dragged towards him. He laughed, and then turned the bag upside down and emptied it on the concrete in front of her.

"You ain't got no money," he kicked through her make-up, the hair clip, the half-eaten bar of chocolate and the plasters she'd stolen. "She gonna have to find some other way to pay," he said to the others.

"You leave me alone," she warned, her fists bunched.

"Oh, come on sweetness. Give it up for us and we'll treat you nice?"

"You better leave me alone. You don't want to…"

A shadow moved in behind her. She glanced around and met a fist coming the other way. Her face made a sound like a pile of wet meat hitting a slab and she flew backwards. Bright flashes trailed across her vision and she felt suddenly sick. Her mouth tasted thick with blood. She opened her eyes to the glare from the windows above her. Buzz-cut was holding her hands above her head while the others pulled off her clothes. She had been thrown on the mattress which they must have pulled out towards the windows

"Let me go! You bastards!"

She kicked and struggled against their grip. Her shouts were mumbled where the punch had swollen her lip. She wrenched at her wrists, but Ear-stud had his weight on them and his grip was like iron. He just laughed down at her and tried to lean down for a lewd kiss. She twisted her head aside as her skirt was pulled down off her legs.

"Get off me! Help! Help me!" she hollered.

Her shouting and squirming only seemed to excite them more. They grabbed her ankles, tugging off her shoes. One with knife scars all down his arm took handfuls of her top and ripped it open down the front. She screamed as they pulled the sleeves off one arm and then the other, ripping it off her.

"That was my best... you've torn my best..." she was crying and kicking, and at the same time couldn't get her breath. Arm-scar struggled to tear her bra apart, but the elastic proved more resilient and wouldn't tear. Eventually he just pulled the clasp apart at the back, pulling it up her arms and off while Ear-stud held her down.

Arm-scar pinched her nipple hard. She spat at him, but he just smiled. "This is the best bit. I love this bit." He grabbed her knickers and yanked them down in a single swipe. There was a moment of silence as Alex lay in shocked nakedness.

"You a peach, Babe." Arm-scar stood, staring down at her, while the other two grabbed her ankles and braced themselves against the mattress, stretching her wide. She watched in stunned fascination as he dropped his pants and pulled a huge erect penis out of his boxers.

"Is it your first time, sweetness? I'll make it good for you." He grinned, flashing brown-stained teeth. Alex heaved against her captors, but they had her all stretched out. He knelt down between her legs.

"Nooooo!"

Her cry was echoed by a low moan from the structure of the building. Something tinkled to the floor along the gallery. A slow ticking started in the pipes where they criss-crossed the ceiling. Arm-scar glanced up and then back at her.

He shook his head, refusing to be distracted. "Ain't no one gonna save you now, Peach."

A sound like popping valves travelled down the gallery towards them. The fire suppression system sprayed out where it ran through the network of pipes across the ceiling. Freezing cold water rained down on them all, to the shouts and calls of the men.

Arm-scar looked up into water raining down on them, and then down at Alex. "Makes no difference to me. A wet peach is still a peach."

"You don't understand," said Alex, through gritted teeth. "But you will."

Heads turned as the water started running across the floor towards them. Drops gathered into pools and pools ran into rivulets. It gathered into a wave that swept across the floor and crashed over the mattress.

"What the...?" The man knelt between her legs faltered. He glared down at Alex. "If it's you doing this, I is gonna teach you respect." He drew back his fist.

Water ran up his legs like quicksilver, streaming up his body, defying gravity. He flicked his fist, trying to shake it off, but it clung to him like a second skin, covering him in a film of moving liquid. Too late, he realised that it was covering all of him.

He shouted, "What the fuck?" leaping backwards, trying to flick it from him, pushing it away from his face, his nose and mouth.

In seconds he was enveloped in a moving bubble of oily water exactly formed around him. He clamped his mouth shut against it but it ran into his nose and ears, covered his eyes. The others watched in horrified fascination as he floundered about, the water still spraying down from the pipes, adding continually to the liquid invading every orifice. He tried to scream but was choked off as the water rushed down his throat, gulping off his cry in a bubbling hiccough. He flailed his arms and fell, splashing to the floor as the water pooled around him, smothering his cries.

Alex was suddenly released as the others grasped how wet and vulnerable they were. While their friend thrashed and clawed at his throat for air, they scrambled to their feet and backed away from her. Whatever it was they saw in her eyes, it terrified them.

They turned as one to run, but the water was under their feet, making them slide and stumble, grabbing out to each other for support. They crashed, entangling each other, splashing into the water which covered the floor. They clawed each other for purchase, crawling over each other, shouting and swearing, trying to be the one furthest from the liquid sheet flowing towards them across the floor.

Alex pushed herself up from the mattress, unaware of her naked state, eyes filled with a swirling blue fire as she focused her anger on them. Her hair writhed around her head as if seeking something to grasp and choke. As the thrashing from Arm-scar slowed and subsided, the water around the remaining three started to rotate into a slowly whirling pattern.

"You miserable little shits!" she spat. "You pathetic excuses for humanity."

"We weren't gonna do nothing," shouted Ear-stud in panic as he tried to pull his way over the other two. "It was Naylor was gonna do it."

Alex glanced at the figure trapped under the faintly heaving bulge of water across the floor.

"Don't worry," she said. "He got what he deserved." She paused for effect. "And now you're getting the same."

The water rushed inwards in a spiral vortex, clinging to them where it splashed. They hollered and screamed trying to throw it off. It ran up their legs and arms, coating their skin and covering their clothes while they scrambled over each other to get away from it.

"Enough!"

The voice came from a figure by the stairway. Another figure gestured and a wind whipped down the gallery tearing the sheets from the windows, flooding it with light. In the glare, the water sparkled malevolently. Alex saw that there were three of them, the young woman who had spoken and two males who flanked her. They were standing at the edge of where the water sprayed from the ceiling. She realised they weren't much older than her.

"Who are you to tell me what to do?" said Alex in a low voice that rang with threat and anger. "You didn't see what these... these... worms, were going to do."

"But by the look of it, Naylor has paid the price," the newcomer said. "Inconvenient, but no doubt necessary." She was taller than Alex, with spiky black hair and a nose-stud. Her hands were tucked into the pockets of her motorcycle jacket, and she put her head on one side, affecting disdain.

"You said you'd protect us from the likes of her," said Buzz-cut. "You said if we kept the place clear you'd see we had it to ourselves."

Alex looked from Buzz-cut to the newcomer. "You mean these shits work for you?"

The woman's voice was calm. "They kept unwanted visitors out in return for small favours. It looks to me like they've seriously overstepped the mark. Is Naylor dead?"

"If he isn't he soon will be," said Alex, turning back to where Naylor was floating in the unnatural blob of liquid.

"Leave them, Alexandra. They are beneath your notice."

She turned back. "How do you know my name?"

The newcomer leaned back and said something quietly to one of the young men beside her. He disappeared upstairs.

"We've met before, though I think you were indisposed and are perhaps unable to recall. We were in a place we both know well and were glad to leave."

Alex tried to place her. She'd thought she'd remembered everyone, but then there were the gaps between the dreams and reality. She shivered and suddenly became conscious that she was naked and cold. The spray from the ceiling slowed and then stopped, leaving only a sporadic dripping along the gallery. She clasped her hands together to stop them shaking. She knew in her head that it was shock. She had almost been raped and now she couldn't stop shaking.

"My clothes..." she said. "Those bastards, they tore...they ripped my..."

The one who'd gone upstairs returned with a blanket, which he passed to the young woman. She approached Alex as if she might bolt any second. "Here, put this around you. That's it." She wrapped the blanket around Alex's shoulders. She guided her as she splashed in bare feet to the stairs. The other two stepped back to allow her through.

"Take her upstairs," she instructed the one who'd brought the blanket.

Alex was gently ushered upwards. Behind her the unnatural mound of water holding Naylor suddenly collapsed leaving the wet body lying on the concrete. She could hear the woman issuing orders.

"Get this stuff cleared out," she said. "I want this place looking like nothing happened."

"What about Naylor," one of them asked.

"Take the body and dump it where no one will find it."

Here was a mumbled protest Alex didn't hear.

"I don't care," she replied. "You reaped the reward you deserved. You're lucky she didn't drown the lot of you. Naylor was an arrogant fool and mean with it. I, for one, will not mourn his loss."

Alex was guided up to what looked like a cross between an apartment and a warehouse. They steered her to a sofa where she sat on the edge and shivered. She kept thinking about what had almost happened, and all the things she could have done. Why hadn't she done any of them? She could have drowned them in their own spittle, sucked all the water from their blood – any number of things. They wouldn't have even known she was there if she didn't want them to. Why hadn't she done any of them?

The young man with the blanket brought a throw from one of the other sofas and handed it to her. "You're shaking like a leaf, girl. Here, put this over your legs."

He sat down beside her.

"I'm Mark," he said offering his hand, "but you can call me Sparky. That's Chipper. He don't say much." Chipper lifted a hand and then went back to looking out of the window.

Alex untangled her hand from the blanket and shook his. It seemed an odd formality given the situation, but he gave her a toothy grin.

"Wh... wh... who's..." She couldn't stop shivering. Clinging to the blanket, she wrapped herself tighter, trying to stop her teeth chattering.

"Eve? Don't mind her. She's a bossy boots, but she knows some stuff. She must like you though. She don't take to strangers normally."

"Wha... wha... this place?"

"Oh, it used to be a squat, somewhere to chill out, you

know? They used to do raves and stuff here, but Eve cleared them out. It was attracting too much attention."

"You're from P... P... Porton Down?" She was finally warming up and getting the shivering under control.

"That's where we met Eve. She knew Gina, and Gina came up with this place, except there was a bust up about them nicking some of Eve's stuff. As they say, Gina don't live here any more."

"Where is she now, do you know?"

"Gina had an accident," Eve spoke from the stairway. "She bit off more than she could chew."

"You killed her," said Alex.

"She took something that wasn't for her. I simply took it back."

"And you killed her for that?"

"You killed Naylor," Eve pointed out.

"He was going to rape me!"

"Sometimes it's kill or be killed. I would have thought you'd understand that."

"She was one of us," said Alex. "She was at Porton Down."

"She was there, but she definitely wasn't one of us. You don't steal from your friends. You don't sell you friends out for drugs, money, sex or whatever else you want. We look after each other, because no one else looks after us." She walked over to stand in front of Alex. "And what about you Alexandre?"

"We didn't meet at Porton Down, did we? No one calls me Alexandre, except maybe my mum," she challenged.

"We did meet, or at least I saw you there. Three girls dead. It was in your file. That's quite a tally."

"That was an accident. How did you get access to my file?"

"Those girls, you drowned them, like you accidentally drowned Naylor?" asked Eve.

"How do you know about that?" asked Alex.

Eve studied her for a moment. "When everyone else ran, I stayed. While others screamed and died I went through files looking for what I needed. Why were you looking for Gina?"

"I dunno. I guess 'cause we're the same. We all went through the same things. I thought maybe she'd have somewhere I could hang out for a bit until I get my shit together."

"Why don't you go home to mummy?"

"Can't, can I? Burned that bridge."

Eve turned away and went to stand behind Chipper, looking over his shoulder out onto the desolate estate. She stood so close that Alex wondered whether they were an item.

"I need someone," she said, still staring out the window. "Gina died, not because she stole – though that was reason enough, but because she knew things – she'd done things. Through her treachery she proved that she would sell us out for a fix, or a bottle, or something she wanted, sooner or later. We couldn't risk that and she paid the price for her indiscretion."

She turned away from Chipper without touching him. No brush of affection, not even a sidelong look. "If you would even dream of selling us out, Alexandre, you would be better to leave now, while you can."

"Are you offering me a place to stay?"

"Here? No. This place is compromised. We only came back to retrieve certain items. We'll be gone soon and you won't be able to follow us."

"So where are you going?" asked Alex.

"We move around, but there are places that can provide what we need. The rules, as I think you already know, do not apply to us. *Do what you wilt shall be the whole of the law.*"

"That's a line from a movie isn't it?" said Alex.

"Hardly," said Eve. "We are engaged in a struggle that goes beyond anarchism and political structure. We will change the world itself. Our goal is more fundamental than tinkering with the system. All of that will be swept away."

"Are you a bit bonkers?"

Eve turned on her like a snake, her eyes narrow, her voice squeezed out between her teeth.

"There are some who cannot encompass the vision of what we will do, and they may think it outlandish or impossible, but they are limited by their feeble imagination and stagnant ability. They are bound by convention and compromised by their own wants and needs. We are none of that, and we will change the world."

There was a fervour in her eyes that alarmed Alex, but she could hear that Eve believed it. She glanced sideways at Sparky. He shrugged, as if it was obviously true.

"What kind of change?" she asked.

Eve smiled. "This world was not made for us. We do not fit. We are not accepted in any part of it. We are alien and unwanted, rejected at a fundamental level. But what if that could be changed? What if we could remake this world as we want it?"

"I don't understand," said Alex.

"You don't need to," said Eve, "you just need to want it enough to be prepared to act. Sacrifices will need to be made. The only decision is which end of the sacrifice do you want to be on – the one making the sacrifice, or the one being sacrificed?"

"Is that a threat?"

"You can't change the world without changing everything," said Eve. "But you can decide which side of the change you're on. The world will change whether you like it or not. Work with us and you can be part of it."

Alex turned to Sparky. "Is she for real?"

He shrugged again. "I've seen some weird shit. Hell I've done some of it, but she's right. We don't fit. They're not going to change the world for us, so we have to change it for ourselves."

"This is your decision, Alexandre," said Eve. "You can walk away now and what will happen will happen. But if you stay, you're part of it."

Alex looked from Sparky, to Eve, to Chipper, who still stared resolutely out of the window.

"OK," said Alex. "I'm in."

TWELVE

The home of the Seven Courts isn't so big. Yes, there is the main house, the east and west wings, the solar, the garden, the orangery, the cellars, the stables, and the ice house, all of which is very grand and mostly deserted, but it isn't so big that you can permanently lose someone. Where, then, was Angela?

She and I had arrived unexpectedly, and there had been the session with the vision, and despite my less-than-optimal condition after that experience I distinctly remembered Garvin insisting that Angela would stay. So where was she?

The only signs of habitation in the west wing was where Alex had been staying and that was deliberately away from the other residents. I had been in all the rooms, even the pokey attics and servant quarters on the third floor, and there was no sign that anyone had been living there. The ground floor of the east wing was where a number of the staff were living, where the kitchens and laundry, the offices and the pantries were, and despite the curious looks from many of the staff when I poked into cupboards and crannies, I had not found her there either.

The upper floor was where Blackbird and I had our suite of rooms. I was sure I would know if anyone else was staying there, or in the rooms above. Even so, that didn't stop me looking.

After a circuit of the gardens, the orangery, the stables and the outbuildings I was starting to get irritated. Of course, I could go and ask Mullbrook where she was being housed, but that would get back to Garvin, but I might as well ask Garvin myself if that was the plan.

No, I wanted a conversation with Angela without Garvin's assistance and for that I needed to know where she was – unless she wasn't anywhere? It had crossed my mind that Garvin might simply be disposing of the people I brought back, but why go to all the trouble of bringing them in if you were going to kill them anyway? While Blackbird questioned Garvin's motives, I thought he was straight. Garvin did what Garvin said he would do. There was no pretence about him, and in this case, Garvin wouldn't waste the resources. He'd have someone kill them where they were and save time.

I walked back through the gardens, and went back to Alex's room in the west wing. I still hoped to walk in and find her on the bed, sulky and resentful, but that hadn't happened. I'd tried to locate her through the mirror, but she had shielded herself from me. My attempts had been met with a blank wall, which at least meant she was still alive. I dreaded the vague dissipation that occurred when I used my power to find someone and they were no longer findable. Losing her had been bad enough the first time, I didn't think I could deal with that again.

That didn't stop me using the same power to find Angela, though. I placed my hand on Alex's mirror and felt the glass chill under my hand.

"Angela?"

The glass clouded, and the sound in the room opened out. "Angela? Are you there?"

There was a restless shuffling under a background that sounded not unlike the room I was in. It was like listening to a live broadcast and the real thing at the same time. Sounds were repeated moments apart – a crow cawed and then re-peated itself in a softer echo a second later. The sound of the breeze was resonant rather than distant.

"Can you hear me?"

Unless there was a mirror in Angela's room, or something that acted like a mirror, she would not be able to speak back to me. It was clear, though, that she was close, wherever she was. Yet I was sure I'd been all through this part of the house and seen no sign of her.

I opened drawers in the chest below the mirror and then in the bedside cabinet. In the top drawer of the cabinet I found what I was looking for – a small portable mirror that Alex must have used for plucking her eyebrows or some sim-ilar personal ritual. I rested a finger on it.

"Angela, can you hear me?" This mirror also clouded, but now I could hold it near to my ear as I left the room. I walked down the corridor, first one way and then the other, trying to discern whether the sounds came more into sync or less. The difference wasn't great either way.

There were spiral stairs at the end of the west wing, with windows looking out on the lawns and over the countryside. Stepping quickly downstairs, I went back along the lower gallery. If anything the sounds were fainter here, and louder from the mirror. Was that because most of the doors were closed down here? I opened the door into a drawing room, the curtains half-drawn and dead flowers on the grate. No, the sound was definitely fainter.

I closed the door behind me and went back to the stairs, going up two flights to the smaller corridor on the top floor where it was hotter in the summer and colder in the winter. These slanted roof rooms would have been given over to domestic staff originally, but now those that weren't used to store redundant furniture were empty and unused. There was loads of light, but it felt oppressive and stuffy. I walked along and found myself back at the stairs in the main house.

Looking back along the corridor, I was sure I had been all the way along and yet it didn't seem as far as it had to walk along the lower floors. Was this floor shorter? Surely they were all in the same building on top of one another and all the same length? A suspicion formed in my mind. I walked back along the corridor and found myself back at the spiral stairs, but too quickly, too easily. It left me with the irrational desire to measure the corridors and see if they were the same length.

I held up the mirror to my ear. There was still a difference, but less so, than downstairs, or maybe that was simply that we were higher up and more open to sounds from outside? Nevertheless I had the sense that I was missing something.

Positioning myself in the middle of the corridor, facing the opposite end, I closed my eyes and walked forward, counting five paces. I stopped and opened my eyes. The corridor was still there, it hadn't changed. I repeated my actions, and then again. Each time I opened my eyes and checked where I was. By the time I reached the end I was fairly sure I hadn't missed anything, yet I couldn't shake the feeling that something didn't fit.

If I gathered enough power into myself, I knew that I could see the world in a different way. Raffmir, my old enemy had taught me how in order to get me into Porton Down and rescue my daughter. He'd given me the ability to see the fabric of reality itself and even step behind the curtain to cross distances. Fortunately the rest of his plan hadn't worked, and both Alex and I had escaped the fate he had planned for us, but having learned the trick of it, I knew I could do it.

At the same time, if someone was hiding something here then I did not want to call attention to the fact that I'd found it. Blackbird always admonished me for using power without subtlety, as a blunt instrument. Here was a chance to prove I could be subtle if I wanted to.

I had noticed that every time I called power there was a sharp drop in temperature. It was as if I was taking the heat from my surroundings and converting it somehow. That sudden cooling marked my use of power like a red flag – it had given my presence away before. There was, however, plenty of heat up here near the rafters.

Closing my eyes, I tried to empty my thoughts in the way that Blackbird had taught me. At the same time I reached inwards to the core of power inside. It flared inside me and I felt the surroundings cool, forcing me to release it again. That was too much. I wanted something smaller.

I tried again, letting my senses expand, feeling the warm air drifting with dust and musty smells. I imagined the air cooling slightly, just enough to start an air current to bring more warm air. The core inside me remained closed and the air remained warm. The trouble was, air just wasn't my thing. Blackbird could twist the breeze through her fingers but to me it was just air.

And perhaps that was part of the problem. I was trying to do what Blackbird did, but she was a creature of fire and air. My element was the void, the space between things. So how could I use that to my advantage?

The void was a curious thing – the Feyre believed that

everything was made of four elements, Earth, Air, Fire and Water. This made sense because their power was expressed in four distinct ways which loosely correlated to these elements. The void was different. It was what held everything apart and stopped the other elements from collapsing in on themselves. It was the space in which everything else existed, and where the other elements shared space with each other. In contrast, the void and the wraithkin, whose element it was, existed alone.

So if the corridor really was the wrong length, I would know. If somehow the space had been compressed or altered in some fundamental way, as a son of the void, that should be obvious to me in the same way that if someone made the wind blow the wrong direction it would be obvious to Blackbird. Therefore it had not been altered.

But I was also aware that it wasn't the length it should be. On some fundamental level, the corridor was wrong and it set my senses jangling to walk down it. It was just...odd. I had an idea that with enough power I could change the nature of a space and distort it – bend it – to my will, but this was not what was happening here. That would take far more power than was apparent.

But what if the corridor was not changed, but only the appearance of it, like a glamour? That would take considerably less power and would leave the corridor fundamentally unchanged but apparently shorter.

I closed my eyes and let myself drift, sensing around me. It was hard among the layers of wardings in the courts to discern one thing from another – like listening for a coin spinning on the floor of a busy railway station – but it was there. The corridor had a net stretched along it, like the glamour I used to turn eyes away when I did not want to be noticed. It lay along the corridor like a multidimensional mesh of misdirection and concealment.

I found the threads and followed them, gradually teasing them apart, unravelling the magic until it finally snapped apart and the corridor shifted. I opened my eyes and the formerly light corridor had acquired a dark section, within which was a door.

I stood outside listening. There was no discernible sound from inside but maybe that was also cloaked in glamour. I turned the handle and pushed the door open. Inside was a plainly furnished room with a chair next to a table with a book open upon it. It looked clean but bare. The windows were set low and looked out over the countryside, and there was a door through to another adjacent room. I looked as if it had been occupied recently.

I stepped in, intending to see if there was anyone in the next room. The door swung closed behind me and it was only the glimpse of something out of the corner of my eye that made me veer away. A heavy chair crashed against my shoulder and I was thrown sideways by the impact.

"What the...! Angela? What are you doing?"

I nursed my shoulder where the chair had collided with it. Angela was stood behind the door holding the back of the chair like she was going to ward me off with it.

"Niall? Sorry, I thought you were that woman."

"You nearly cracked my head open. What on earth were you trying to do? What woman?"

"The blonde one. Fionh."

"You're lucky it was me and not her. She would have spilled your guts onto the carpet and sliced your head off for good measure. What were you trying to do?" I rubbed my shoulder where the chair had caught me.

"I was trying to leave."

"Can you not just use the door like any normal person? Do you have to hit people with chairs?"

"You don't understand," she said, "Until you came in there was no door. Once she leaves I'm trapped in here. I thought if I could stun her, I could lock her in here while I found a way out."

"Put the damn chair down, or are you planning to hit me with it again?"

"No, no, I…" She took the chair and placed it back against the wall.

"That would never work anyway. It's her glamour that's keeping the door hidden. She could unravel it as soon as you closed the door and follow you, and you would not like what she would do to you after you bashed her head in."

She glanced at me, then made a dash for it. Fortunately she had to get past the door to the open doorway and I managed to grab hold of her.

"Let me go! You don't understand. They're going to kill me!" She struggled and kicked until I threw her onto the floor and put myself between her and the door. She was breathing hard and looked up at me with narrowed eyes. "You're with them, aren't you?"

"I'm not with anyone."

"Yes you are. You're a Warder like she is."

"I don't know what you're talking about," I said.

"You kill people. You bring people here and haul them up in front of the Lords and Ladies and then when they don't meet some arbitrary standard, you kill them."

"I've never k…" I could hear in my own voice that she would hear the lie in that. "OK, that was different. Those men were drowning young girls. I've never killed anyone that didn't deserve it."

"I expect that's what Fionh says too," said Angela.

"Look, this has to be some sort of misunderstanding. They'll find you a place in the courts. Garvin said they would."

"Oh yes. They'll find you a place all right, as long as you fit within their narrow definition of what it means to be fey. Only problem is, I don't"

"What do you mean you don't? You showed me a vision. You have the power. Garvin was there, he saw everything."

"Except that's not what Teoth is looking for. He made me create a vision for him. We saw things – most of it I barely understood – but it was all the past, not the future. I watched them as they made some kind of deal, he wouldn't say what it was for. I saw them culling their own kind. They killed children, even before they'd grown into their power. They executed innocent people because their power wasn't true, whatever that means. I saw them do it."

She was staring around her now, looking for a way out. "I don't really know how I see things or why, I just do. Teoth kept asking me about you – that phrase – 'The sun will rise and they shall fall' – he kept asking me what it means. He said my power is corrupted, that my humanity has poisoned my power. It's why I can't see the future, only fragmented versions of the past. He says I'm not worthy."

"Not worthy? What does that mean?"

"It means that sooner or later they will kill me like they did the others. You've got to get me out of here, before it's too late."

"You're overreacting. Why would they kill you? You're not doing any harm."

"No, but I've seen what they're doing now. They're not going to let me take that knowledge elsewhere, are they?

You got me into this. You brought me here. You've got to get me out of here."

I glanced at the door. In the doorway, out of sight of Angela, Fionh stood listening. Angela saw me look and her face fell.

"Fionh," I said. "Fancy seeing you here."

"You're not supposed to be here," Fionh said.

"I think I gathered that from the way it was concealed," I said.

"Garvin wants to see you," she said.

"How convenient."

"Now," she insisted.

"And if I leave, what are you going to do?"

"My job," said Fionh.

"Promise me you won't harm Angela."

She reached in and grabbed my sleeve, tugging me out of the room. I caught a glance of Angela's mouthing the words, *help me*, as I was pulled out and the door closed. Fionh placed her hand on the door and I felt the glamour creep back into the passage.

"You've got her well hidden."

Fionh said nothing but walked away and then waited for me to follow.

"It's not like she's a danger to anyone, is it? I mean, what's she done that's so terrible?"

"You're asking the wrong question," she said.

"Why?"

"You should be asking yourself how much patience Garvin has and looking to your own position. You're not here to question the wisdom of the courts, Niall. That's not your role."

"Oh, and who is then?"

"The courts are the final arbiters. That's rather the point."

"Maybe it's time things changed," I told her.

"That's not for you to decide." She led the way downstairs to where Garvin waited.

Garvin was not taking this well. "Tell me again why you think you have the authority to overrule the High Courts of the Feyre."

"That's not what I said," I replied.

"You told Fionh that someone should challenge their authority with the clear implication that the person making that challenge should be you."

"You're putting words in my mouth."

"No, Niall. You're talking treason. Let's not beat around the bush here. As a Warder you serve the courts, not the other way around. The Lords and Ladies do not need your permission, or your consent, or even your knowledge. As far as the Feyre are concerned they are the final and only court. End of story."

"But that's the point, don't you see? The courts are the be-all and end-all for the Feyre, but these people aren't fey, not completely. They're part human – all of them grew up in human society. They have no knowledge of fey culture or fey rules, and how would they? This is all as new to them as it was to me."

"This is not about you, Niall. Don't make it personal."

"It is personal. You sent me after these people. That makes me responsible for them. I can't stand by and watch you execute them!"

"Who says they're being executed?"

"Are you guaranteeing they won't be?"

"If they are accepted into the courts then they'll be able to live peacefully for as long as they survive."

"If? You said if."

"It isn't up to me."

"That's what I'm talking about. Teoth told Angela that her power wasn't good enough, that she was insufficiently… endowed. So now what?"

"She awaits the courts pleasure. That's not unusual."

"For how long?"

"For as long as it takes to decide. I expect Teoth is trying to work something out for her. He's not a barbarian. He'll try and accommodate her." There was a hint of dissembling in that sentence and Garvin knew I could hear it. "Either way it is not, I repeat, not, up to you. No one stands between the Warders and the justice of the courts and survives. You do not want to test that."

"So now you're threatening me?"

"I'm not threatening anyone. You're making a huge assumption that Angela will be rejected based on what? Gut feeling? Hearsay?"

"But if she is rejected she will be… what's your word for it? Terminated? Disposed of?"

"She may be allowed to return home."

"Why can't she do that now? She can wait at home as easily as she can wait in that room up there," I suggested.

"Teoth asked for her to await the court's decision. That's normal, and hardly cause for this kind of hysteria."

"I would remind you that her life is at stake. That's hardly hysteria."

"We put our lives at stake every time we act. Life is risk. It's no different from what we do every week," said Garvin.

"No, there is a difference. We choose what we do. We don't have to sit there and wait for the axe to fall."

"You're overreacting."

"Am I? Or have you got so blasé about killing that the taking of a life no longer seems important to you," I challenged.

"I'm not going to be provoked, Niall. You're wasting your time and mine."

"And I'm not going to be the person who brings these people in for execution. You said Teoth isn't a barbarian, well neither am I."

"You can't resign, Niall. This isn't that kind of job. Being a Warder is about making hard choices. It's about doing what no one else will do. You know that."

"Surely, being a Warder is not about killing innocent people? Isn't it about justice? You told me it's about doing what needs to be done, not executing people for the sake of... what? Convenience? That's not justice, that's just protecting vested interests."

Garvin stood, and for a moment I thought he would draw a weapon, but he simply placed his hands on the table.

"You have an overblown sense of your own importance," he said, but there was something in the statement that didn't quite sound true. It made me look at him afresh.

"What is this about, Garvin?" I was sure he knew more about this than he was letting on.

"It's about your ability to carry out the tasks assigned to you. We've had this discussion. These people are dangerous."

"When Angela granted me her vision, she said that this all started long ago. She said it was about me. What did she mean?"

"If I knew the answer to that question, I'd be a lot happier," he said.

"You know something," I accused him.

"I know lots of things," he said, "I know that if you won't bring these people in to the courts then I'll have to get someone else to do it. "

"You can't coerce me into imprisoning people so you can have them killed."

"Once again you wilfully misunderstand me. Your role as a Warder depends on your ability to do the job. If you won't do it then I'll give it to someone who will. Until then, stay away from Angela."

"What about Teoth's decision."

"She will be informed in due course."

"With the sharp end of a blade?"

"Don't push it, Niall. My patience isn't infinite."

I turned and left.

"He knows more than he's saying," I told Blackbird. I was pacing up and down our room while Blackbird sat near the window with her book.

"Garvin, devious? That should hardly come as a surprise," she said.

"Angela told me that Teoth asked her about that phrase, 'The sun will rise'."

"'And they shall fall,'" said Blackbird. "Prophesy is notoriously bad at predicting the future, Niall. Half the time it's better not to know. By the time you've figured out whether the prophesy is causing the future or the future is causing the prophesy, you may as well not bother."

"You took me to see Kareesh. That was for a prophesy."

"I was desperate. Extreme circumstances call for extreme measures. It worked, didn't it?"

"I'm not sure," I said. "Maybe the jury is still out on that one."

"You survived. Sometimes that's all that counts," she said.

"I couldn't have been there before, could I?"

"Been where?" She closed the book and set in on her lap.

"To see Kareesh. I couldn't have been there without you, could I? Before we met?"

"You didn't even know about the Feyre, Niall. How could you have been there without me?"

"I'm... in Angela's vision, I saw myself with Kareesh. You weren't there but Gramawl was."

"That's not how it happened," she said.

"I know, but in the vision it was real. She said things, she referred to things that happened later. I was there."

"I don't use the words 'notoriously unreliable' by accident," said Blackbird. "Prophesy at best is a view of what might be, the nodes and points of the future that are most likely to happen."

"But this already happened. This was the past, not the future."

"How do you know? How do you know that next week you're not going to have that conversation with Kareesh?"

"Teoth said – Angela's power is corrupted. She doesn't see the future, she sees the past."

"I would take issue with your use of the word corrupted. Different, perhaps?"

"I'm only repeating what Angela said. But if Angela sees the past then it is certain, because it's already happened."

"But you also said there was a burning man on the Underground platform. Was he burning when you saw him that day?"

"No. He was normal, like anyone else."

"There you are, then. Yes, she showed you the past – your past – but your brain interprets that in its own way. It inserts imagery and assigns meaning, even where meaning doesn't exist. Some things just are, Niall. They don't mean anything."

"She couldn't make me forget, could she?"

"Angela?"

"Kareesh. She couldn't bring me there and then make me forget?"

"Why? Why would she do that?" Blackbird spread her hands in frustration. "She didn't even know who you were until I introduced you."

I tried to sift through the tangle of images and things I knew. If Angela's vision was true then who was the burning man? No, it was like looking into a distorted mirror. But what if I had met Kareesh and Gramawl before Blackbird had taken me to her?

"You didn't answer my question," I said.

"Which question?"

"Could Kareesh make me forget meeting her and Gramawl so that I didn't even know it had happened?"

Blackbird stared at me for a long moment. "You know quite well that your perception of the world is governed by your senses and your senses can be manipulated, by glamour and other magic. You have to trust what's true, though. You have to find the truth and hold on to it. Otherwise you will mire yourself in a tangle of speculation and you will never get free."

"But she could have done it?"

"Yes," she confirmed. "Even I could have done it."

"Did you?"

"Niall." She was exasperated. "That is exactly what I just asked you not to do."

"Sorry. It's just… There's something going on. All this stuff about 'the sun will rise' means something. Garvin won't reveal what he knows and Teoth was probing Angela about it. Something important is going to happen and I'm involved."

"That may be true," she said, "but you can't rely on prophesy. 'The sun will rise' – a literal sun? A particular day? Another sun? Not a sun as in sunshine but a son as in a child? That's clearly what Deefnir thought."

"Maybe he knows something too."

"'And they shall fall'? Who will fall, Niall, and why? How far will they fall? Will that be a literal fall or a metaphorical fall... it's all useless until it happens, and you're only messing with your own head thinking about it."

"So you don't think we should try and find the book?"

"What book?"

"The one with the pages open to show the six symbols."

"There may not even be a book," she said.

"I'd bet money on it."

"You want to look for a book – one among how many? Millions? You don't know what it's called, or who it's by, or where it's kept."

"It was in a library."

"Well that narrows it down." She shook her head.

"It was old, and the person reading it was using lamps. That means it'll be even older now."

"There are a lot of old books, Niall. Some are in private collections. Some are in museums, galleries, libraries, private houses... you need somewhere to start looking."

"There was a design in the middle with four shields in a circle. Three symbols to each side of it."

"There are entire books filled with symbols, the sole purpose of which is to get their readers to contemplate what they might mean. They were meant to provoke and inspire, to get people thinking about eternity and their place in it. They were not meant to be interpreted as literal truth."

"You were an academic, though. You know how to research things in books, don't you?"

"You mistake my meaning. You're not talking about a needle in a haystack now, so much as a piece of hay in a haystack, among other haystacks, when you don't even know what field it's in."

"But if I could prove that Angela's prophesy was worth something, that it gave us a vital clue to what is happening, then maybe Teoth would accept her into the courts. At the moment he's dismissing her out of hand."

"The problem is not the prophecy but whether you can change the attitude of the courts. At the moment they want their cake and eat it – bring in the part-fey humans, but reject them when they're not fully fey. They can't have it both ways," she said.

"How long do you think she's got?"

"Angela? You can't save everyone, Niall."

"I brought her here."

"And you think that makes you responsible? The responsibility lies with those taking the decisions. You've said your piece. You can't blame yourself if they overrule you."

"She wouldn't be here but for me."

"Garvin would have sent someone else, and how that would be better?" she asked.

"Maybe I wouldn't feel so responsible?"

"It wouldn't prevent it from happening. You need to learn to accept what you not going to be able to change."

"Perhaps, or maybe I need to stop being part of something that I think is wrong," I said. "You said yourself that this all comes with strings. You said we should leave."

"I did, but think about this. You and I are the only ones challenging the status quo. If we leave, there's no one to gainsay them. They will continue as they always have. Maybe we are here for a reason, and maybe that reason is to be the thorn in their thumb."

"I think Garvin would say pain in the arse."

"Now that," she smiled, "is a noble cause in itself."

Thirteen

Alex leaned over the wall and looked down on the people walking below. "It's pretty busy," she said. "I've never seen so many tourists."

"They'll thin out towards the end of the day," said Eve. "They have coaches and trains to catch. The guards will stay, though."

"It's not the police we're dealing with here, is it? These guys are military," said Alex, looking at the soldiers in red uniforms and flat black hats posted around the courtyard and in front of the White Tower.

Eve sat on the edge of the wall and conversationally pointed out the guards posted at the gates and those leading gaggles of tourists around. "They're military," she said, "but at the end of their careers. This is a cushy number for them. They just have to stop tourists from poking their noses where they're not wanted and there's almost no chance of getting shot. It's a better gig than Afghanistan."

"Beefeaters, aren't they?" said Alex.

"They're called Yeomen Warders. Beefeaters is a nickname."

"My dad's a Warder," Alex spoke before she meant to, eliciting an inquiring look from Eve. "He's in security," she said dismissively, "he spends all his time looking after people with too much money."

"Interesting," said Eve. "You must get to meet lots of famous people."

"Nah," said Alex. "This is old money. They keep it amongst themselves and they're totally stuck up. They don't mix with normal mortals."

"Sounds horrendous," said Eve.

"You don't know the half of it," said Alex. "So what are we after? The crown jewels?"

Eve glanced reprovingly at Alex. "The crown jewels are the obvious target. They're very heavily guarded. It's all just glitter, though."

"Some glitter."

"Chipper and Sparky are going for those, but there's too many alarms – heat sensors, pressure pads – this place is state of the art. Even we can't get in and out without anyone noticing," said Eve.

"So how are we going to steal them?"

"We're not. They're a distraction, not the main event. The idea is that Chipper and Sparky keep the guards busy while we focus on the main targets."

"Like what?" Alex stared around.

"One of those." Eve nodded towards an enclosure at the far end of the courtyard.

"A crow? What are you going to do with a crow?"

"They're not crows, stupid. They're ravens. As in Nevermore?" said Eve.

"'Quoth the raven, nevermore'. Yeah we did that in English. He was a funny guy, Poe," said Alex.

"The ravens are symbolic. It's said that when the ravens leave the Tower of London, the monarch and the country will fall."

"Is that what you're planning?" asked Alex

"No, that's just superstition. Besides, we don't want a whole raven, just a feather. A pinion of the raven's wing."

"This gets better with every moment," said Alex. "Have you seen the beaks on those things?"

"We need a feather Alex. And once this goes off, security here is going to go berserk. We won't be able to attempt it again this year."

"Why don't you go and get it?"

"It's time for you to earn your keep," said Eve. "We looked after you. We found you new clothes and sorted you out after you got in a mess. You wanted in, Alex. Either you can get me a feather, or you can't."

"Yeah, well you hold onto the bird while I get the feather out. How's that for a plan?" Alex's chin was up.

"I'll be otherwise engaged."

"Doing what?" challenged Alex.

"It's all a matter of timing. We could take a crack at the jewels now, and the feather is easy – you'll be fine. The other thing we've come for is harder. It's only exposed for a limited window, and we need to get in and out before the place is locked down."

"What are you after?"

"A key," said Eve.

"What's so special about a key?"

"This key opens more than just locks. It's kept in the ward-room near those houses just near the main gate. Every night they have a ceremony where they lock up the tower and set all the security up."

"So we're coming back tonight?" said Alex.

"No. We're not leaving. That's why we sneaked in in here in the first place. They count all the tourists in and then out again to make sure they all leave, except we weren't counted."

"So they won't know we're here," smiled Alex. "If it's all locked up, how do we get out?"

"We wait until the sun goes down. Most of the guards will change out of their Yeoman Warder gear into military uniforms. As soon as that happens it gets serious. There's a group of guards who will go up to the gate to escort the tourists through the ceremony of the keys."

"I thought you said the tourists went home?"

"There's a small party led through the ceremony. I checked and there are no spare places for tonight. We should have a full party. They're led through to the tower, it all gets locked up, and then they're escorted out."

"What about us?"

"We hit them just as they start to lock up. Sparky sets the alarm off at the jewels, you get the feather, and for a brief few moments the key will be unattended. I grab the key, we meet down there by the gate. They'll want the tourists off site as fast as possible. We just merge in with the party as it leaves. In the confusion, they'll never know they escorted us out as well."

"You make it sound easy."

"No magic until after the alarms are triggered and then only glamour so they don't notice us. We don't know what they have set up. They may have infrared, night-vision, all sorts of stuff. I told you, it's state of the art. They may look like toy soldiers but they have real weapons with real bullets."

"What if we get caught?" asked Alex.

"Don't. It's not theft, it's treason."

• • • •

Borough market is a great place to shop, but not an easy place to find someone. It's crowded, noisy, and there are lots of ways in and out, so that you can't just watch the entrance and wait. You have to wander.

It's also smelly. Not in an odorous, noxious way, but it's filled with smells. The cloying scent of frying onions mixes with the ripe pong of French cheese. Sticks of broken celery stalks compete with the sickly sweet of overripe strawberries. There are spices and herbs, complex high-notes from the flower stalls overpowered by the meaty wafts from the butchers' stalls and the fishmongers. All of this is laid on the faint odour of river water and mud from the Thames, only a few hundred yards away.

The smell is distracting, and so is the noise, but I was here on business and tried to focus. This was the haunt of one of the escapees, Andrew Warner – Andy to his friends. He'd been picked up here originally and taken to Porton Down, and he'd been under surveillance for some time before that.

His file indicated that he was classified low-risk, high potential, and talked of fragmented personality disorder, and morphological instability, whatever that might mean. I was hoping it meant he wouldn't try to kill me.

It also said that he'd tried to bring together the inmates at Porton Down into some sort of community support group, to help them help each other. The idea hadn't been popular with the leadership and there was much discussion of cross-contamination and the introduction of combined effects into experimental data, plus concerns about collaboration from the security people where there was any kind of gathering.

The idea had been scrapped, but not before Andy had managed to pull together an initial meeting and put the idea before some of the other inmates. The doctor responsible for

that meeting had been sacked, and the report roundly con-
demned his actions, but a first meeting had already taken
place. If Andy had met some of the other inmates, there was
a strong chance he would know more about them, and might
even be able to communicate with some of them.

The chance to open up a dialogue and offer them sanctuary in the courts, while at the same time being able to
negotiate with the courts as a group rather than on an individual case-by-case basis had brought me here. If I could
pull people together, then maybe we could make this work.
Otherwise there was a strong chance that Garvin would lose
patience and send in the dogs, and then there would be
blood.

Of course, I had Andy's photograph from the file, but I was-
n't sure that would help me. Appearance is flexible among
the fey, and if he really didn't want to be identified then he
had every chance to change his appearance and disappear. At
the same time I'd noticed that the fey had a habit of returning
to certain ways of looking. It was as if changing your image
too much, too often, left you looking like everyone and no
one. I had felt this myself, and although I looked younger
than I used to, most of the time I still looked like me.

Blackbird was one of the few fey I knew who could switch
her appearance between multiple personalities without slipping back to her usual appearance after a while. She could
stay an old lady, or a young girl, for an indefinite period. I'd
asked her about this after the baby was born and she got her
glamour back. I knew what she looked like without glamour, and I'd got used to it while she was pregnant, so I asked
her why she switched her appearance as soon as her power
returned.

"Habit," she told me.

It didn't seem like much of an answer, so I pressed her on it.

"When you've looked one way for long enough, you don't forget," she said. "Before I met you I was Veronica for what, forty years? Before that, I was someone else. And before that too. I can be any of those people if I want to."

"Why can't you be you?"

It was the wrong question to ask, I could see that from the crinkle at the edge of her lips, but having asked it, I couldn't let it drop.

"This is me," She gestured at herself. "When I lost my power, I would look in the mirror and see a face I didn't recognise. I was looking into the eyes of a stranger. It was one of the things I didn't like about being pregnant. It made me feel exposed – almost naked."

It was a moment of rare vulnerability, and I held her close for a long while after, switching the conversation to safer subjects, such as what she would wean the baby on and whether Garvin was going to get me killed.

On that subject, I'd let my mind drift from the task at hand while I wandered through the stalls, which was not a good way of ensuring survival.

My eyes drifted to a guy in a long coat. He was holding out a rounded jar of amber liquid to one of the stall-holders. It caught the light, somehow absorbing stray rays of sunshine and magnifying them so it looked like he held a pot of shining gold. The stall-holder was shaking his head and holding up his hands but the guy was persistent.

There was a brief exchange of words and the guy's shoulders dropped. He turned towards me, tucking the jar back into a rucksack, searching the stalls for new opportunities and our eyes met. It wasn't his face I recognised. He'd grown a stubbly beard and his hair was longer than it had been in the photo. It was the look in his eyes, the look of someone who's been hunted, imprisoned, and tortured.

He turned away and then casually walked back towards the stall he'd visited as if he'd just thought of another reason why the guy should take the jar from him, but when he reached it he kept going, accelerating along the aisle. I jolted myself into motion, hurrying after him, trying to keep track of the long brown coat in the crowd. If I lost sight of him he could change appearance and I would never find him. I had to keep him in view.

He swerved around a lady with a shopping trolley and diverted sideways down a passage between the stalls. I took a risk and dipped into the next row and managed to catch a glimpse of him as he crossed between stalls and carried on towards the edge of the market. I sprinted down a parallel aisle, half expecting to find no sign of him as I emerged, but he was there, running down the edge of the stalls, scanning behind for any sign of me.

I carried on, exiting onto the lane that ran alongside the edge of the market and then swerved back in to intercept him. As I did I caught sight of a brown coat as it billowed out and half-caught on a pillar as the owner ran out into the lane I'd just left.

The next gap was yards ahead and I sprinted, closing the gap while he couldn't see me, striving to keep my momentum as I veered out through the exit on the lane after him. As I did he was at the end of the lane, looking back. As he saw me he bolted down a side road towards the railway arches and I followed.

"Wait," I shouted after him, "I only want to talk."

I couldn't tell if he'd heard me. I ran after him anyway, coming out onto the side road and finding an empty street. It was too long for him to have reached the far end so quickly, so I slowed my pace, scanning alley's and arches for signs of life. If he was hiding he could have switched his appearance as soon as he was out of sight – he could look like anyone by now.

The entrances to the arches were dimly lit and boarded up, with most barred and bolted with substantial padlocks which, while they wouldn't be much of a barrier to someone with fey ability, would be difficult to lock again from inside, so I looked for a loose lock or an unbarred doorway. The alleys were more of a problem as they had side doors and big commercial bins – the rear access to commercial properties on the main street on the other side of this row.

It was at the opening to such an alley that I found the brown coat, stuffed between a drainpipe and a wall beside a large black bin. The alley was shaded by tall brick buildings on either side – the only obvious access into the buildings was a door that looked like no one had opened it in the last decade. Around the door, the mortar between the bricks was crumbing leaving the ground sandy underfoot.

Down the alley I could see vague shapes huddled in the corner. I drew my sword, conscious that as I moved into the alley my eyes would take a moment to adjust. A sword would make anyone intending to jump me hesitate.

"Andy? The sword is only for protection," I called into the dimness. "This doesn't need to be a fight. I just want to talk to you."

I moved carefully into the shade between the buildings. The alley opened out again further in. Drainpipes ran down the walls and high letter-box windows set on either side. I checked the windows to see if anyone could have squeezed through, but the soot and grime in the cracks showed they had been painted shut long ago.

At the back of the alley was a roller shutter door, set a few feet off the floor for loading and unloading into vehicles. Piled high in the corner next to it was a mound of black bin-bags, big enough for a person to hide in. I edged towards it and used the end of my scabbard to poke into the pile. A cloud of flies erupted from the bags, buzzing around my head and face before settling back on the bags. The base of one of the bags had ruptured spilling rotting vegetables and split tomatoes. There was no one hiding there.

I looked at the roller shutter. Had there been time for Andy to open it enough to crawl through and close it again after him? I didn't think so. I pulled the base of it upwards. It was locked, but that didn't mean much. What could be locked could be unlocked, but it would be heavy to lift and slow to move; those things make a tremendous racket. I would have heard it, wouldn't I?

I moved cautiously back to the opening of the alley, collecting the coat from the drainpipe on the way. It was a good coat with a wool lining, and the inner was still warm. He had abandoned it in a hurry. I went through the pockets looking for clues and came up with a roll of five pound notes and plastic bag of pound coins tucked into the inside pocket.

I scanned the walls up the skyline above me, half expecting to see someone peeking over the parapet above. No one did. Still, I couldn't help feeling that I was observed. I let my heartbeat slow after the chase, and then extended my senses into the alley. It was not like the hallway at the courts – there was no underlying magic laid layer upon layer to bind and confuse. This was clean, though filaments of power hung in the air like trails of smoke. Someone had used power here, but whatever they'd done, it was dissipating fast.

Glancing up again at the high walls, I could see that with

the loose mortar, something with sharp claws might have scaled those walls, though they would have had to climb pretty quickly to avoid being caught. It made me momentarily glad I hadn't apprehended him in the market. Dealing with such a creature in a crowded place would not have been easy.

I stuffed the notes into the bag with the coins and put them in my pocket, then rolled the coat into a bundle. Now I had something of value to him. If I couldn't catch him, maybe I could tempt him to reclaim his possessions.

I walked back to the market, checking behind me frequently. No one followed. I found the rucksack tossed behind a waste bin along the path he'd used to run. Inside were more jars of the viscous amber liquid. It looked like honey.

Making my way to a coffee shop I ordered a cappuccino and took it to a stool by the window placing the coat on the counter beside me, and looking out over the stalls. I took my time drinking it, looking for people who didn't move with the crowd or who lingered too long in the wrong places. Eventually I had to concede that he wasn't going to reappear. If he was here then he was hanging back, concealed by glamour and unwilling to show himself.

I drained the cup and took the bundled coat, stuffing the money into an inside pocket. At the counter I asked for a biro and wrote on a napkin.

Andy – I only want to talk. Here's your coat and money back as a sign of good faith. Be here tomorrow and I'll buy you a coffee. I have an interesting proposition for you – more money than you have here. Meet me tomorrow, at midday.

I tucked the note in with the money and buttoned closed the pocket, then went back to the stall where I'd originally seen him. The stallholder looked hopeful for a moment until I showed the coat.

"Do you know Andy, the guy selling honey?"

He shook his head at me. "He wants too much money for it. He's gotta appreciate we're talking trade prices, not retail."

"I'm not negotiating on his behalf," I said. "But I found his coat and rucksack. He must have left it behind."

"What d'you want me to do about it?"

"If I leave it with you, can you make sure he gets it, next time you see him? It's got his float in it. You'll make sure he gets it, won't you?"

"What do I look like, Salvation Army?" he protested.

"Oh come on, someone will pinch it otherwise – it's his stock, and it's a good coat."

"Yeah, well. Give it over then." He took them from me and tucked it down behind the counter. "If he don't come back for them, I'll give 'em into one of them charity shops. They'll take it."

"Don't worry. I'm sure he'll stop by. Thanks, you're a gent."

"Too bleedin' kind-hearted is what I am. Yeesh."

I walked out of the market down the main aisle, making sure I was visible long after I left. I would return tomorrow and see what happened.

Alex wasn't good at waiting, and the time between five-thirty when the tower closed to the public and nine o'clock when they shut the tower up for the night was spent in increasing impatience and irritation. She wanted to get on with it, to get what they came for and leave, but Eve was insistent. They had to wait for the key.

Cloaked in glamour, they clustered up on the wall near the Water Gate, watching the Yeoman Warders pace through their duties, checking each building and arming the alarm systems that protected the crown jewels and the tower. As the light faded the shadows became deeper and the activity ramped down. Patrols still walked the yards and checked the doors, but their frequency diminished as the human guards transferred their trust to electronic surveillance and security systems. There was joking among the guardsmen and a degree of ribald humour that was reserved for when the public had left.

"Right," said Eve. "Chipper, Sparky – you've got the difficult job. You have to get close enough to the jewels to make them think it's a real raid, but not so close you get caught."

Sparky grinned in the twilight. "Don't worry, we're cool."

"I do worry," said Eve. "I worry that your arrogance and hubris will bring disaster down on our heads. These are some of the most sophisticated systems known to man, but their weakness is that they are aimed against other men, and they are protecting the jewels, not our true targets. By creating a distraction you will draw their attention, and that is both good and bad. They have automatic weapons, infrared vision – for all we know they have a satellite trained on us right now, or the ability to co-opt one for their use. Don't take chances. Take out everything you can see but be prepared for things you can't. Infrared lasers, x-ray scanners, we just don't know. All you have to do is draw their attention. Give us five minutes. That's all we need to get in and out. Stay out of sight and keep concealed until it's time. Once the operation begins we will be out of contact and hidden, even from each other. There's no going back and we'll get one chance, so don't bottle it."

"We won't bottle it," said Sparky.

Chipper's eyes shone in the darkness. He looked more

alive than Alex had ever seen him.

"I'm not worried about you." Eve glanced at Alex.

"I'll be fine," said Alex. "In, out, we're done. I've done this before," she confirmed.

"Not like this you haven't," said Eve. "If it comes to it, be prepared to use whatever means you have. We cannot afford to get caught, understand? We meet up outside the bar, The Hung, Drawn and Quartered on Great Tower Street."

"Got it," said Sparky. Chipper nodded. Alex licked her lips, which were suddenly dry.

"Alex, you understand your part?"

"One feather, black, coming up," she said.

"The ceremony of the keys begins at nine sharp. They'll escort in the tourists and walk them around. When they are furthest from the gate down at the White Tower, that's when we hit them. Don't screw up," said Eve. "We're not coming back for you if you get caught. You all have positions. Cloak yourselves, we're on."

Chipper sprinted away into the dark, followed by a flash of a smile and Sparky was gone too. That left Eve with Alex.

"Stick to the plan," said Eve. "It'll be fine."

"Yeah," said Alex. She wasn't sprinting for anyone. She walked away along the wall, hugging the shadows and cloaking herself more deeply with every step.

Alex had avoided the paths, figuring that if she was in charge, that's where she would put the pressure pads. Instead she took the stone steps up onto the wall and dropped quietly onto the roof of the aviary. She landed as quietly as she could, but still the birds set up a raucous cawing when she landed. She balanced at the peak of the roof, listening for sounds of human alarm. If there was any, it was drowned out by the birds.

She edged along the peak of the roof and then slithered down to the eaves on her belly, amid the caws and calls from the occupants. No matter how quiet she tried to be, they got more and more agitated. This wasn't making her job any easier.

"Shut up, bird brains," she muttered under her breath.

Below her was a wooden wall with a window covered over with wire mesh. Even if she could get past the wire mesh, she had no guarantee the window would open. She pushed herself sideways along the roof, positioning herself above the door. As she reached it, a figure loomed out of the dark on the path.

"Ere, what's up with you lot, eh?" said the figure. He was dressed in uniform, but as far as Alex could tell he was unarmed. He didn't look up, failing to notice the girl sprawled across the roof, but went to the door of the aviary, rattling keys until he found the right one.

"All right, all right, keep your feathers on. Anyone would think there was a snake in there with you."

He pushed through the doorway, clicking on a light so that it spilled out into the pathway.

Alex waited, counting heartbeats, listening to the old man chatting away to himself and the birds. It was clear that something had agitated them, but so far he had no idea what. When she got to forty-six, three uniformed figures sprinted across the courtyard, heading for the White tower. There was no alarm sounding, but then who were they going to call? The police? They already had the military here, if they couldn't handle it, who could?

The guy in the aviary hadn't seen them. It was now or never.

She moved sideways and rolled over the edge, making as little noise as possible. The birds went wild, cawing and screeching, providing ample cover for her descent. She pushed herself to her feet and slid along the outside wall. He was talking to them like they were people.

She leaned around the doorway. The old man was watching the birds flapping around inside a large cage, talking to them quietly. One of the birds fixed her, turning hits head sideways in curiosity, so that it could focus on her with the black bead of an eye.

"Caaaaawww," it said.

The man spun around, following the gaze of the bird. Alex had seconds to react. She stepped in close as he turned, placing a hand on his chest as his eyes widened in surprise at the sudden appearance of the curly-haired teenager in front of him.

His eyes rolled upwards and he dropped like a tree, falling full length, sawdust billowing around him as he crashed to the floor.

The birds started a cacophony of calls. "Aaark! Arrk!"

"Shut up!" shouted Alex. Surprisingly, they did.

Alex looked at them. They regarded her, turning their heads to train first one black eye on her, then the other.

"You can speak?" asked Alex.

In answer, one of the birds hopped down off one of the bare branches they had been provided with and stalked across the floor to where the keeper lay full-length, eyes rolled up, breathing shallow.

"Aaark?" It said.

"It's all right, calm down," said Alex. "He's not dead, just unconscious. He'll be fine in the morning."

"Caaaaaw," said another bird from the safety from the branch.

"You're in there, and I'm out here, right?"

The birds fluttered back and forth in the cage, but they

seemed to calm at her words. They watched her carefully, cocking their heads and listening to her.

"You think I'm coming in there with you lot, you've got another thing coming," she said.

They cawed in rasping agreement, as if they were laughing at her cowardice. The birds hopped sideways. To Alex's ears, they seemed to find it funny.

Alex watched them. "But you understand me, yeah?"

Quietly they cawed to one another as if they were arguing about the situation. The birds exchanged looks. "Caaaw," said one.

"So here's the deal," said Alex. "You give me a feather, a long one mind, none of your pissy ones, and I leave. Your friend wakes up later and no one's the wiser. Deal?"

There was a chorus of cawing from the birds.

"Or…" said Alex, "I can boil the water in every one of you and make you explode. Then I can walk in and take the feather for myself, geddit?"

The birds erupted in another chorus of argument. "Well?" said Alex.

One of the birds strutted down the branch while another bent down, as if it was bowing to Alex. There was a flash of beak and the bird had a long black feather. It hopped down the branch and approached the mesh of the cage cautiously.

"You needn't think I'm putting my hand in there," said Alex.

The bird angled its head and then hopped up to the mesh and poked the feather through, dropping it on Alex's side. Then it flapped over the branch, turning to watch her. She collected the feather and placed it in the resealable plastic bag that Eve had given her for it.

"A deal's a deal," she said. She knelt down beside the old man, placing her hand on his chest. The birds flapped about in agitation. "It's all right," she said. "I'm just rebalancing the flow. He'll have a headache tomorrow, but no more, I promise. OK?"

The bird that had produced the feather bowed once, dipping its beak and raising its tail feathers high in a wide sable fan. Alex nodded to it, acknowledging the bow, and left.

Outside, the courtyard was bathed in light. She slipped sideways but there was no longer any shade to hide in. She might as well have walked across the middle of the courtyard for all the good it did. Even so, she worked her way around the outside, heading for the gates which led across the expanse of moat to the outer walkway.

When she reached the gateway, it was locked. Four grim looking soldiers stood to either side of the locked gate with automatic rifles held across their bodies, barrels down but ready to fire. Of Eve, Sparky and Chipper, there was no sign.

"Fuck!" she swore under her breath. "Now what am I supposed to do?"

Fourteen

"I want to make it clear," the Scot seated at the end of the table said, "that this meeting never happened. You were never here. These words were never spoken. We'll deny it all."

Garvin lifted his chin very slightly. "You're saying this for whose benefit?"

Garvin looked at me and I raised my eyebrow very slightly. I wasn't even sure why I was here. I knew these meetings went on, but I'd only ever been to one, and that was in rather unusual circumstances.

The Great Hall of Oakham Castle was special – its walls were home to hundreds of horse-shoes, gifts from visiting dignitaries over the centuries. Whether by design or accident, the proximity of the horse shoes had the effect of dampening the sense of truth and falsehood that all who were fey possessed. It meant that within these walls, the fey visitors did not have the advantage of knowing whether their human counterparts were telling the truth. It levelled the playing fields for negotiations between humanity and the Feyre, at least in part.

The guy at the end of the table had been in charge of security during my last visit, but not part of the negotiations.

Secretary Carler had conducted those and I was wondering whether this was the new guy's way of letting us know he'd been promoted. That also made me wonder what had happened to Secretary Carler.

"Questions have been asked," said the Scot, "and denials have been issued."

Garvin folded his hands on the table and looked from one to the other. "As I understand it," he said, "our meetings are with Secretary Carler or his replacement. I don't have a remit to negotiate with anyone but the Secretary himself." He looked pointedly at the security guard at the door, the goatee bearded tech across the table, and then at the Scot.

"We're not here to negotiate," said the Scot.

"Then what's this about?" asked Garvin.

"Certain material has come into our possession which implicates certain other people in acts which may compromise the agreement between our respective principals. I have been tasked..." he paused for effect, "...with making certain that this does not become a security issue."

"What are you referring to?" asked Garvin.

"Show them," the Scot said to the tech, who sat with an expensive looking widescreen laptop computer open in front of him, positioned so we couldn't see the screen. The portable white screen which had been set up on a tripod stand at the end of the dais glowed blue and then white as it came to life.

"This is all pre-event," said the tech, "and I'll fast forward through it. It's really just to show that everything was working fine up until the incident."

The screen showed an array of tiled feeds in a composite grid view from cameras around a large building. I counted six rows of eight cameras. I was trying to think why the view was familiar, and then I caught sight of Tower Bridge in one of the views.

"This the the Tower of London," I said.

"Cut to the chase," said the Scot. "Show them why they're here."

The tech sighed and operated a control on the laptop so that the tiles flickered forwards in time and then paused.

"Nine twenty-seven, the gate guards are there to collect a party of visitors from the front gate. The visitors were checked and vetted before entry and there's no sign of collusion. They were as surprised as everyone else." The feed showed two soldiers in uniform marching up to the gate and allowing a small group of tourists inside.

"Nine thirty-four they arrive at the main gate. They're challenged and allowed through. They meet with the Yeoman Warder who is escorted to the keys. Now watch here," He used a laser pointer to circle on one of the tiled images. It was stepping through a single frame at a time. For a moment in one frame a shadow passed across the courtyard, but in the next frame it had gone.

"See it?" he asked.

"See what?" said Garvin. "Is this a ghost sighting? Is that what you brought us to see?"

The tech backed up a frame. There was a streak of darkness across the grass. "These cameras are taking twenty-four frames a second. Whatever it is, it appears to be moving very quickly."

"Or it's simply a trick of the light?" said Garvin. "It could be a moth close to the lens so that its relative movement appears fast?"

"No, it's not close to the lens and there's no point of origin for a shadow," said the tech.

"It's a glitch in the system," said Garvin, "You brought us here to show us this?"

"It gets more interesting," said the Scot. "Roll it forward."

"We're moving frame by frame now, so each one of these is a twenty-fourth of a second." The views of the walls and courtyards continued, as the frame count and time-stamp in the corner advanced. Then in ones and twos the images disappeared from the screen.

"What you're seeing here is a systemic attack. The cameras are being taken out one by one, very rapidly."

Progressively the pictures were blanking out. "Power failure?" I asked, earning a look from Garvin, but intrigued by this development.

"There was a power failure, four seconds after this, but these cameras have separate power supplies and battery backup. Also, if this were a power failure then they would all fail at once. These are going out one at a time." He continued until the screen was blank.

"Any comment?" said the Scot.

Garvin shrugged. The Scot looked at me.

"Some sort of software failure?" I suggested.

"Evidence says not," said the tech. "The systems returned to full working condition, but not until later. Fortunately we have a backup." The screen glowed white again and then showed a wide-screen monochrome view of the castle courtyard from the river side over the wall.

"This view is from the top of Tower Bridge, the only remote camera with this angle – consequently the resolution isn't brilliant, but it's apparently far enough away to be unaffected by whatever is causing the disruption."

He zoomed in on the courtyard and then started advancing frame by frame. "Three, two, one... now." The screen showed two indistinct blurry images entering the courtyard. They appeared to be in no rush, though the image was unstable, as if it was looking through intense heat-haze. He stepped through the images until they crossed out of sight.

"The internal cameras are time-matched so this is the same scene we saw before, but as you see, internally they're only recording a tiny fragment of the data coming from the high remote camera, which implies that some sort of editing has taken place, yet the integrity of the frames is valid – they have not been tampered with." He looked up, expecting some sort of response. Garvin and I stared back.

"The alarms start shortly after. There are generalised power failures, a number of incendiary devices were used though we have yet to identify the accelerant. It appears to be extremely volatile leaving little trace. The White Tower came under sustained assault, the building was accessed and a number of the secondary alarm systems were triggered, though as in the case of the outside cameras, the inside feeds were ineffective."

"The White Tower is where the Crown Jewels are kept," said the Scot.

"How much did they get away with?" asked Garvin.

"Nothing, at least not from there," the Scot said. "The jewels are separately secured overnight, and there's no ready access. It's not like the Queen phones up overnight and sends for the crown to be sent round to Buckingham Palace on a whim."

"So they left empty-handed?" I asked.

"Not quite," said the Scot. "You're going to love this bit."

The tech went back to the camera, zooming out to full field view. He let it run fast-forward for a few minutes and then slowed it to normal speed.

"There was a disturbance in the outer courtyard during the alarms – we assumed that this was a backup team or an exit strategy, but that isn't played out by what followed. The tourist party shadowing the ceremony of the keys was immediately detained, pending investigation. In the event it appears they were innocent bystanders. The gates to the courtyard were secured, though, and armed guards posted to the exits in accordance with security procedure. They were attacked by one or more assailants and physically assaulted. The gate was opened and there is a brief glimpse here…"

He panned the view to the corner of the screen where three shadows crossed open grounds and disappeared under some trees. "Injuries to the guards were not severe, though there is a disciplinary pending on how four armed soldiers can't defend one gate from what appear to be a group of un-armed teenagers."

He panned back again into full-field view.

"More interesting is just under six minutes later." He fast-forwarded and then slowed. "Watch here."

A dark blur slipped along the top of the wall facing the river. It seemed to cling to the edges and veer around like a candlelight shadow in a breeze, flickering and dodging. It hesitated, then continued, tracking along the wall, then hesitating.

"She's looking for a way out," said the tech.

"She?" said Garvin.

The shadow slipped along the wall to a gate structure, flanked by square towers.

"Traitor's Gate," said the Scot. "Quite appropriate in the circumstances."

The tech continued. He seemed "The water gate itself is wood reinforced with iron. It's old and not really intended as an effective barrier. On the other side of it, though, the entrance to the Thames has been bricked up and there's a significant barrier. The Thames is high, as you can see, but the water doesn't enter the tower itself. The water behind the wall is quite shallow – a few inches only. The tide turned twenty-three minutes before this and is on the ebb. The current is downstream towards the estuary."

He panned across the wall where the gate had been sealed. "According to witnesses there was no splash or ripple, and they initially discounted the water as an exit route. It's not as easy a way out as it appears and has trapped the unwary before. Instead they focused their attentions on the parapet and any attempt to abseil or scale down the wall. Only when the water started to move did they realise where's she'd gone."

"That's the second time you've used a female pronoun," said Garvin.

"The wave oscillated three times, initially moderately but with increasing force. On the third oscillation the gate is forced open. That's when the outer wall starts to collapse. Within moments there's water flooding through. A section of the wall collapses and the Thames is through."

He looked up at them.

"The wall was inspected a month before. There was no sign of any weakness then, though subsequent inspection shows water damage to be the cause. We're at a loss to explain it. That would have been it," said the tech, "except that there are cameras under the bridge which monitor boats passing underneath. One of them caught this image…

The screen changed to a black view with a small white spot in it. He zoomed into the spot until it resolved into a face in the water. The girl had her eyes closed, arms extended, carried by the strong current downstream. It was Alex.

Garvin and I exchanged glances.

"Good," said the Scot. "I thought you'd recognise her."

Garvin interlaced his fingers on the table. "We are not un-aware of this individual's activities."

"Excellent," said the Scot, opening a file in front of him. "The girl has been identified as Alexandra Dobson, née Petersen, daughter of Katherine Dobson and Niall Petersen, who, if I'm no mistaken, is about three feet to your right at the moment. Any comment?"

"We are not currently aware of her whereabouts," said Garvin quietly.

"Not currently aware? Is that shorthand for you've fucking lost her?"

"You try my patience," said Garvin.

"We're not talking a bit of mindless vandalism here. These are the crown jewels. They are a symbol of this country's integrity and lawfulness. Can you imagine how embarrassing it would be if we'd had them stolen?"

"About as embarrassing as having it discovered that you're conducting illegal and immoral experiments on human beings?" said Garvin.

"They weren't human," said the Scot.

"That's an interesting point of view," I said, earning a sharp look from Garvin.

"Nothing human can do that!" the Scot said, pointing at the screen.

I was standing before I knew it, the power boiling up inside me, aching to be released. Garvin was up beside me, pressing down on my shoulder, making me sit, pushing me back down, and the power with it. If we hadn't been surrounded by the dampening effect of the horse shoes, I don't think I could have contained it. I allowed myself to be re-seated, slowly and carefully, acutely conscious of how close I'd come to killing him.

The Scot was elated that he'd provoked a reaction. "You're on every alert list we have, Petersen," he said. "The only thing missing is a bounty on your head."

"Are you threatening me?" My voice was low and level, but far from how I felt.

"Enough," said Garvin. "Niall, hold your tongue. You're not helping and there's more at stake here than you're dignity."

"It's not my…"

"Enough!" Garvin stared me down. When I looked away he turned to the Scot. "You've already admitted they didn't take anything. I'll ask you again, is there any point to this exhibition?"

"I didn't say they didn't take anything," said the Scot. "I said they didn't get the jewels"

"So what did they get?" he asked.

"Will you stop pacing up and down?" said Blackbird, "You're distracting the baby."

I looked down at our son, resting in Blackbird's arms and watching me rather than latching on to her to feed.

"Sorry." I sat down, but that just provoked a bout of wriggling and tipping his head back until he could reach a position where he could see me again. He was developing fast, and had become much more aware of his surroundings in the last few days.

"Here, you take him for a moment. It's you he wants to see anyway. You might as well hold him."

I took him from her and he kicked his legs while I manoeuvred him into a comfortable position resting on my forearm. He waved his arms around until I gave him a finger to hold, at which point he promptly pulled it to his mouth and started to suck and gum it.

"You see?" I said to him. "You were hungry after all, and you're not going to get much out of that, are you?" He continued sucking my finger, despite my advice. Sometimes children just don't listen.

Blackbird stacked up some pillows on the bed, made herself comfortable and then offered her arms. "Shall we try again poppet, and your father can sit down and keep still this time."

I passed him back to her and in a moment he got the idea and settled down to sucking noisily.

"So what exactly are they accused of taking?" she asked me.

"Alex was identified by one of the Yeoman Warders as the girl in the aviary. They're trying to establish whether she can be tried for treason for interfering with the ravens, assuming they can catch her. According to the man responsible, one of the ravens has a tail feather missing and Alex is being blamed for it."

"I wouldn't fancy taking a tail feather from a raven. They're big birds and they tend to put up a fight. Maybe it fell out on its own," she suggested. "Proving any of this is irrelevant anyway, it's never going to come to court."

"Maybe not a human court. I don't know what the Feyre courts are going to think of this. At the very least it's an embarrassing incident, and at worst a treaty violation. Who knows what Kimlesh will say."

"Alex isn't part of the courts. She never joined, and therefore she's not anyone's responsibility. Unfortunately she doesn't have any of the court's protection either. If she's caught, she could just be killed without a hearing."

"That's comforting," I remarked.

"Sorry, Niall, I didn't mean it like that, and it's not like she's stolen anything of national importance. It's a feather for goodness sake. The bird can grow another one."

"That doesn't apply to the other item that was stolen," I said.

"Oh?"

"Supposedly the Queen's keys are stored in the gatehouse and used to lock up the Tower of London at night, but not all the keys fit the locks."

"And why would that be?" asked Blackbird, shifting our son from one breast to the other in a nifty move that was too quick for him to wail before another breast was presented. There was some wriggling and waving of arms, and then he settled again.

"One of the keys was a gift to the crown, found as part of a treasure trove in long barrow in East Anglia, buried with a Angle nobleman."

"The Sutton Hoo burial?" asked Blackbird.

"No, a smaller horde, but in some ways more significant. Some of the items were hard to identify – the key was out of time. The metallurgy was too sophisticated for the period and therefore the key was thought to have contaminated the find at some later point and somehow been included with the horde as a less valuable item."

"An anachronism."

"Except that the horde was otherwise intact. The items were very well preserved and various valuable items were included, which would have been stolen if the horde was discovered by treasure hunters."

"Something shiny like a key could have been dropped in a hole by a magpie, and just ended up with the rest of the horde by accident," she pointed out.

"Except it wasn't shiny. It was dull grey, and the exact metal it was made of was never determined."

"Dull grey?" she asked.

"Not tarnished silver, and iron would certainly have rusted. It was the wrong colour for gold and was unlikely to have been aluminium – far too early for that. Where else have you seen a dull grey metal object that's hundreds of years old?" I asked her.

"You're comparing it with the Quick Knife, the knife from the Quit Rents Ceremony?"

"I'm trying not to leap to conclusions, but I'm running out of alternatives here. The key was not corroded, even though it is easily over four hundred years old, and may be more like a thousand. It was made of an unidentified grey metal."

"Perhaps it was an aluminium key which got mixed up with the horde much later?"

"It was given to Elizabeth I in 1593 as part of the horde, but the key was passed to the Tower of London for safe-keeping. Nothing else from the horde was taken there, though there may have been other items that weren't documented. Aluminium wasn't discovered in a metallic form until the eighteenth century – I checked."

"Perhaps it was discovered earlier than we thought?" she said.

"Perhaps it wasn't aluminium. Why else would a team of part-fey teenagers break into the Tower of London and steal it?"

"Are you sure that's what they were after?"

"The only other thing unaccounted for was the feather which Alex took. The group made a big fuss around the jewels but made no serious attempt to steal them."

"A distraction."

"Quite. But how did they know there was a key there? It's mentioned in the internal inventory of the tower, but you'd have to know where to look. It's not a published treasure of the tower and even the museums were unaware of its existence."

"If you wanted to hide a key, where would you hide it?" asked Blackbird.

"Amongst a lot of other keys?"

"Inside a guarded Tower with soldiers and a sophisticated alarm system," she added.

"The alarms are a recent addition."

"But they replaced earlier alarms, which have been upgraded by each generation according to the times. Someone tried to protect it, both physically and by hiding it, which implies that someone knew what it was and what it opens."

"You think it opens something?"

"It's a key, Niall. That's what keys do."

"It could be decorative?"

"If it was purely decorative then why steal it? No, whoever took it knows what it's for, and when we know that, we'll know why they stole it."

"What about the feather?"

"Another distraction? Who knows? You can get a raven feather anywhere there are ravens, but there looks to have been only one key like that one."

"So how do we find out what the key is for?"

"You ask a man who knows," she smiled.

"A locksmith?" I asked.

"No, a wizard," she smiled.

"You sodding well abandoned me!" said Alex. "You saved

your own skinny arses and left me there for the ravens."

"Nonsense," said Eve. "You're here now, aren't you?"

"No thanks to you. You could have waited for me. You could have stayed at the gate, I was seconds behind you."

"And therein lies the problem," said Eve. "We didn't have seconds. You were told to be at the gate at the appointed time. You weren't there. They had armed guards and reinforcements on the way. If we'd stayed we would have been caught."

"Chill out," chimed in Sparky. "We'd have had to started killing people if we'd stayed any longer."

"Which would raise the profile of our little adventure a tad too far," said Eve. "Much better that you made your own exit."

"I could have drowned," Alex said. "I could have washed out to sea and then you'd never get your sodding feather."

"You can't drown," said Eve. "I don't think it's possible for anyone with your abilities to drown, even in sea water. Besides, you've shown yourself to be resourceful and quick-witted, independent and capable of defeating the best security that man can devise. You should be proud of yourself."

"It was a pretty cool way out, wasn't it?" said Alex.

"It rocked," said Sparky. "Even I wouldn't have thought of that."

Mollified, Alex flopped down on the old sofa, the springs protesting as she sank into it. "This is messed up," she said. "We need a new one."

"When we're done, the world will be at your feet," said Eve. "Where's the feather?"

Alex looked up. "Somewhere safe."

Eve held out her hand.

Alex sighed, and pulled down her top and fished into her bra, while Sparky made a show of not staring at her cleavage while she did it. Chipper was too busy playing Xbox to notice anything. She extracted a polythene zip-lock bag containing the long feather and handed it to Eve.

"You kept it dry, that's good," said Eve.

"It's a tail feather."

"I really wanted a wing pinion," said Eve, examining the sheen. "But this will do well enough, I think."

"I had to bargain for it."

Eve's head lifted. "You spoke with the birds?"

"Kind of," said Alex. "They understood what I was saying, or maybe they're like that with everyone?"

"No, you are favoured, Alex. The birds have knowledge beyond human comprehension, and they must have seen something in you to act so. They have acknowledged what I saw in you when you first came to us – the capacity for great things."

"Great thing, huh?" Alex shrugged it off, but she was smiling as she did.

"Your time will come Alexandre, and when it does you should not flinch from the task. It will take courage and faith, a leap into the dark to gain a path to enlightenment."

Alex shook her head slowly, sceptical of Eve's grand words. She glanced at Sparky who raised an eyebrow slightly, implying that even if Eve wasn't all there, she had engineered a theft from one of the most closely guarded places in the country. She deserved their respect simply for that.

Alex folded her arms. "So what's next? What's the next step in the plan for world domination?"

"We seek not dominion, only the reordering of the universe, to better reflect that which resides within us," said Eve.

"Yeah, whatever," said Alex, but she watched Eve admiring the feather twirling between her fingers.

"Our assembly is almost complete. Once we have the key, the well will open. Then we will hold the fate of the universe in our hands."

"I thought we already had the key?" said Alex.

"That is only a part of the key, one piece of the whole. We will have the other parts soon and then we will see what can be done."

Alex watched Eve's intense fascination with the blue sheen on the feather and wondered not for the first time whether Eve was firing on all cylinders.

"I should have stayed with the baby," I told Blackbird. "You don't need me for this."

We were marching down yet another corridor of the maze of buildings in Bloomsbury where the University of London has whole blocks dedicated to academic pursuits. Blackbird had reverted to her older persona of the older lady I had first met in London a year ago. I still found it hard to reconcile the young vibrant Blackbird I knew with the lecturer in medieval history from Birkbeck – the role she adopted to fit into human society.

"He'll be fine. Stop worrying," she said over her shoulder.

"What if he cries?" I asked her.

She stopped and turned. "Will you stop it! This is the first time I've managed to get away and I will not have you spoiling it for me by reminding me at every verse-end that I've left him behind. If he cries then I expect Lesley will change his nappy. That's what I would do if he cried. For goodness sake, Niall, you have to stop fretting. You've been a father before; you know they don't die if you leave them alone for five minutes."

"Yeah, well. I felt more in control the first time, and look where that got me."

"So that's it, you're not fretting about the baby, you're fretting about Alex." She turned and continued down the corridor.

"I tried to reach her again last night."

"And?"

"Little fragments of things, but nothing you could make any sense of. She's still blocking me. Who knows who these people are that she's fallen in with."

"She doesn't want you interfering, and the way you've been behaving I can hardly blame her." Blackbird stopped at a T-junction in the corridor. "They've repainted all this since I was last here, but it's this way. At least I think so." She marched off along the corridor again.

"What if something happens to her? What if the authorities catch her and imprison her again?"

"Do you honestly think they're going to catch her? The guards at the Tower couldn't, so what makes you think the police are going to do it? And if they do? What are you going to do about it? March in there and demand her release? Bring the penal system crashing down around their ears?"

"I rescued her last time," I pointed out.

"So you keep reminding me," said Blackbird. "Down here." She took the staircase that led down to the floor below ground.

"Who is this guy, anyway?" I asked her as she pushed through double doors into a corridor lined with small rooms, mostly vacant, with the occasional sign indicating that offices were occupied by postgraduates or administrative staff.

"I met him at an academic gathering and we got chatting. He was very charming and said I should look him up."

"You mean he chatted you up?"

"Well I don't think he was interested in my research, if that's what you mean."

"Did you sleep with him?"

Blackbird stopped and turned so fast that I almost walked into her. "That's a very ungallant question, Niall Petersen. Could it be that you are pricked by jealousy?"

"It's not me that was…"

"Enough! Stop that," she said. "It's unbecoming and quite inappropriate. I've had many lovers and I do not intend to discuss them with you. Who I chose to take to my bed before I met you is none of your business."

"Except we're going to meet this guy and I'd like to know how the land lies," I pointed out.

"We have not spoken for some time, and I am expecting that he will be surprised to see me. We are old friends and nothing more."

"If you say so." Already I didn't like the guy.

"I do, and we are here to ask a favour, so I would prefer that you refrain from upsetting him."

She continued down the corridor through another set of double doors. In this area the lights came on as we approached, making it look as if no one had been here in days.

"I haven't said a word."

"You don't have to," she said. "We need Gregor's knowledge if we're going to figure out what Alex and her friends are up to before Garvin does. I think that's in everyone's interests, don't you?"

She came to a side corridor and turned down it, coming to a wooden door with a sticky note on it. The note said, "Abandon All Hope, Ye Who Enter Here".

"Hell?" I asked Blackbird.

"Gregor's lab," said Blackbird, knocking on the door. There was no answer. She knocked again louder.

"Maybe he's not home and it's been a wasted journey," I suggested.

"Except for the notice on the door. It's his little joke," Blackbird explained. She knocked again louder and opened the door.

Inside was an expansive room well-lit by overhead fluorescent lights. There were three large benches, each crammed with equipment and scraps of notes. Broad-leafed plants stood in tall glass cylinders wrapped around with copper wire connected with crocodile clips to an array of car batteries. A tank of liquid stood to one side, filled with murky looking water and illuminated by a black-lamp that hummed quietly. It looked like the specs floating around in there were glowing.

"What subject did you say he was teaching?" I asked.

"I didn't. He teaches modern history, we met at an academic convention."

"This doesn't look like history to me."

"His research follows a rather wider remit. Gregor is a scientist and a magician – he's into all sorts of esoteric ideas and sees no distinction between science, philosophy and magic. Last time I was here he was trying to show me a perpetual motion machine."

"That's not possible," I stated with some certainty.

"You're a fine one to talk about what is and is not possible," she reminded me. "Gregor, are you here?"

"Can't you see I'm busy?" A voice came from a smaller office attached to the lab. "The tutorials have all been rescheduled – new dates have been sent out by email. Check your spam filter – it's probably in the spam folder."

"Gregor, I'm not one of your students," she called through to the office.

"Then what are you doing in my..." His face appeared around the door. "Veronica! How absolutely delightful to see you. How long have you been there?"

A barrel chested, moustached grandee of a man swept out of the office and picked up Blackbird in a bear-hug embrace, kissing both her cheeks noisily twice.

"Mmmwa! Mmmwa! It is fantastic you are here. I have something to show you. Have you heard of wave energy stimulation? Do you have a bodyguard now?"

"Gregor, this is Niall. He's helping me with some research and we wanted to pick your brains."

He turned to me and extended a hand. "Gregor Leyon-avich, at your service." He wore generous sideburns which almost connected with his moustache. Taking his hand, I shook it firmly and slowly.

Gregor smiled. "Sword callous, right hand, a long weapon and heavy by the feel of it, not a practice weapon and not one of those toys, those lightweight foil things. I was joking about the bodyguard, Blackbird, but maybe this is not a funny joke?"

I glanced at Blackbird.

"Sherlock Holmes is one of Gregor's heroes. He observes everyone and everything," she said.

"Sherlock Holmes never existed. He was a fictional character," I pointed out.

"Quite so, but in his genius, Conan Doyle invented the ultimate rationalist," said Gregor, "sceptical about everything but assuming nothing, evaluating all possible alternatives. You have muscle underneath that jacket, which means you work at it. Your weight is balanced towards your toes, so you have been trained. You are no amateur, I think. Your right shoulder is higher than your left, which implies a bias to one side, so not a master swordsman, but very competent. Not often you come across a trained swordsman these days. But when you have eliminated the impossible, whatever you have left, no matter how unlikely, is the truth."

"In my experience the truth is in the eye of the beholder," I said.

"Well said, my friend, but without truth we cannot have beauty, which brings me back to the delightful Veronica. My dear, they told me you had sold your soul to the Americans."

"I'm back for a little while," said Blackbird, "but I am not advertising my presence. I have no wish to get sucked back into academic rivalry."

"An overrated occupation at best," agreed Gregor. "Come, let me show you my wave energy demonstrator." He gestured across the lab to a machine in the corner. "One day, machines like this will power entire cities."

He went to a bank of switches and relays on the wall and clicked on a pair of large red switches. Boxes began to hum and lights flashed on displays. A laptop computer stopped showing screensaver pictures and began displaying a graph with flat-line red and green readings.

"The matter we wanted to discuss..." said Blackbird.

"A moment only, I promise," interrupted Gregor. "This is impressive; wait and see."

An orange indicator turned to green and Gregor threw a switch with a flourish. A laser emitted a blue-white beam which was split by a half-silvered mirror and bounced around various prisms before hitting another pair of prisms which brought the beams together again into a single beam aimed at a detector. Gregor carefully adjusted an instrument that was receiving the beam.

The prisms and the mirror were inscribed with odd symbols – It made me wonder what his native language was. Something Eastern European by the sound of it.

"Watch the display," he said. "The red one shows total energy input while the blue one shows the energy released."

The lines on the graph started to climb until they levelled off about half-way up the screen, the red line on top indicating that energy input exceeded energy released by about a third again. A digital read-out measured the difference at just over minus twenty-seven per cent.

"This is the default state. The gaps between the lines indicate the energy used by the system," he explained.

"Gregor, this isn't what we came to talk to you about," said Blackbird.

Gregor ignored her, intent on the rig. "Now," he said, "I'm using microwave transmitters to introduce harmonics into the beams."

He turned a dial and the blue line began to climb towards the red.

"That's just increasing the energy input to the system," I pointed out.

"It would be if the beams were absorbing energy from the microwaves," he argued, "but that's not what's happening. The energy in the microwaves is all accounted for in the measurements. There's no direct transference, or rather there is, but it's already been subtracted from the read-out."

The red line rose slowly as he increased the input, but the blue line rose faster, until it passed the red line and stabilised above it. The read-out said plus eleven point two per cent.

"You must have an energy source that's not accounted for," I stated.

Blackbird kicked my ankle hard enough to get my attention. "What Niall meant to say is that we have a question we'd like your view on."

"No," he ignored Blackbird again. "It's all in the measurements. What's more, you can increase the input to the laser, and the percentage yield stays constant without increasing the microwave input." He adjusted the input to the laser and the blue line climbed even further away from the red one.

"That's not possible." I was sure I was right. "Energy has to come from somewhere."

"Niall. You're only encouraging him," said Blackbird.

"You're missing something, surely?" The experiment was interesting, but there had to be a source for the increased energy. It couldn't come from nowhere. It was a long time since I'd done any physics, but it was a basic law of the universe that you don't get something for nothing.

"That's what I thought," said Gregor, "but I'm damned if I can find it." He flipped the master switch and the system clicked off. The lines on the laptop dropped to nothing. "What was it you wanted to ask me?"

Blackbird glared at me, but I shrugged. He was clearly enthusiastic about his experiment. What harm could it do to let him demonstrate it?

"A couple of items were stolen recently," she explained, "and I thought you might be able to tell us what their significance might be."

"What sort of items?"

"A key from an Anglo Saxon burial mound and a tail feather from a raven," I told him.

His eyebrows lifted. "Not the usual sort of thing," he stated. "What makes you think these thefts are related?"

"They were stolen at the same time," said Blackbird, "from the same place."

"The Tower of London?" said Gregor.

"How did you know that?" I asked.

"Give me another instance where ravens and keys are kept in the same place," he said. "I cannot think of one. Besides, your question answered mine."

"What do you think, Gregor? What are they doing with these things?" asked Blackbird.

"You haven't mentioned jewels, so I assume they didn't succeed in stealing those?"

"As far as we can tell," I said, "they didn't even try to steal them. They used the jewels as a distraction but then went for things that are worthless."

"They are only worthless to someone who does not value them," said Gregor.

"And you would?" asked Blackbird.

"Perhaps. A key and a feather are both potent symbols. A key is for opening, and as a symbol of secrets – things locked away. A feather is also a symbol. The Egyptians believed that the feather represented truth, and that in the afterlife their hearts would be weighed by their gods against a feather of Maat."

"Maat?" I asked.

"The essence of truth, usually represented by an ostrich feather."

"This was a the tail feather of a raven, not an ostrich," Blackbird pointed out.

"But the symbology may transfer," said Gregor. "Symbols are all about the power you invest in them. They could have taken a feather from an old hat, and it would still be a feather, but because there was nothing invested in it, it would have little power."

"So the fact that this feather was stolen from the Tower of London gives it power?"

"In a sense, yes, perhaps."

"So what is it for, Gregor? Why do they need a feather and a key?"

Gregor rubbed his chin, thoughtfully. "I do not know," he

said finally. "I am not aware of any rituals that would use just those symbols. They are too ambiguous – too loose, do you see?"

"I'm not sure I do," said Blackbird.

"Most magic is the art of converting something you don't want into something you do," he explained.

"Like alchemy," I suggested, "transforming lead into gold."

"A simple matter. You sell the lead to someone who needs it and they give you money, which you turn into gold."

"That's cheating," I said.

"Is it? Or is it simply using a path which people who do not think do not see? Much of magic is like that – trading one thing for another."

"You make it sound ordinary," I said.

"True magic, though, is very much rarer. In true magic you extend the bounds of the universe to include the infinite, where limits become meaningless and therefore exchanging one thing for another becomes like getting something for nothing. You can appear to get more out than you put in, like my wave energy demonstrator. If I am right, it is drawing power from the universe itself, and therefore exhibits a resource which is, for our purposes, limitless."

"So is it science or magic?" I asked.

"A great question," said Gregor. "You must tell me when you have the answer. A feather and a key? They have no unifying symbology, no theme to draw upon. They do not in themselves define the boundaries of anything."

"You're saying they are insufficient in themselves?" said Blackbird.

"Indeed I am, Veronica. Much of logical deduction is not knowing the answers, but knowing the right question."

"What's the right question?" I asked her.

She grinned at Gregor. "What else have they taken?"

"Correct," he said.

FIFTEEN

The market was near closing time. My visit to Gregor with Blackbird had delayed me and I had almost forgotten my invitation to meet Andy the honey-seller at the cafe. It was an outside chance that he'd appear, but having made the offer I felt honour-bound to at least turn up.

I sat in the cafe window, watching the market traders beginning to pack up their wares and close down their stalls. The idea of using someone to set up some sort of bridging arrangement with the fey courts appealed to me, but it needed someone the inmates would trust to front it. Andy had the potential, but I had to find him before I could pitch it to him. I'd been here for an hour, but there was no sign of him.

The trader I'd left the coat with said he still had the coat under the counter, so Andy hadn't been and gone without seeing me. Of course, it was possible that I had scared him off – having been arrested and carted off to Porton Down can't have done a lot for his trust for authority. He might have decided to abandon coat and money, cut his losses and run, but I thought not. He'd been arrested here in the first place. He'd returned here after the escape. Something was bringing him back, and I was hoping he would show himself sooner or later.

I had to admit, though, it didn't look like it was going to be today. Maybe if I came back tomorrow I would have more luck. I thanked the waitress who cleared my cup away and headed out into the market. I stopped at one of the stalls selling fruit. The stallholder was bemoaning the figs he had for sale, saying they were too ripe to hold onto and he was going to have to chuck them out the next day if someone didn't buy them. I hesitated, wondering if Blackbird liked figs.

That was when the half-seen figure crossed my vision. It wasn't that I recognised him, but that I didn't really see him. When I turned to look there was no one there. He was using glamour to conceal himself.

I left the fruit-seller and walked swiftly to a parallel row, following along with the path I'd vaguely seen from the corner of my eye, trying to catch a glimpse of shadows that shouldn't be there or places where I had the sudden urge to look away.

I tracked back towards the stall where his coat was, being careful to keep out of view. I circled around, keeping stalls between me and the path he was likely to take, and came out near where I had left his coat. Andy was talking to the owner of a stall selling Caribbean foods with his back to me. The owner pointed to the stallholder with the coat. He thanked the guy and walked over to the stall, taking my bait.

I waited out of sight until he was talking to the stallholder. The coat was produced and he grinned, clearly pleased to have it back. He slipped into it, shrugging it onto his shoulders and patting the pockets. He pulled out the money I'd secreted and hefted it, making some remark to the stallholder. I edged forward, waiting for him to read the note I'd left with the money. As I did, the stallholder lifted up the rucksack and then noticed me, pointing me out to Andy.

Andy's reaction was immediate. He sprinted for the aisle, knocking over a tray of apples in the process, scattering them across the concrete. The stallholder shouted after him, gesturing after him as he raced away.

I was already moving after him, heading down a parallel row of stalls, catching glimpses of the flying coat as he ran ahead of me. He turned into the side street, heading back where he went before. I accelerated, figuring he was going for the same exit. As I tuned into the back street he was running ahead of me, coat flying out behind him. He didn't even look back, he skidded into the blind alley.

I slowed to a halt at the mouth of the alley. A little way in the coat was sprawled across the floor, abandoned. The bag of money was discarded too, thrown against some of the bin bags further in. Of Andy there was no sign. I drew my sword and edged into the alley, scanning the walls and the high roof, looking for an outline that didn't fit. I'd been only seconds behind him. Unless he could fly or run up sheer walls he had to be here somewhere.

"Andy? Come on out. I won't hurt you. I want to talk to you."

There was no reply. After a few moments I summoned up the courage to explore deeper, finding only old bin bags and rotting vegetables. I turned around in the alley, looking for hand-holds and climbing places. There was no obvious route upwards, but he'd used this alley twice now. Was there some means of escape that I was missing? I rattled the thin windows and checked the roller shutter again. Did he have some way of opening and closing it quickly and quietly?

I put my sword away and placed may hand on it, willing it to open. The cold metal was unresponsive, and when I tried to lift it, it clacked noisily but wouldn't budge. It left a finger-width gap, but that was all.

Turning slowly, I looked for trapdoors or drain-covers that might hide an exit underground, kicking aside bin bags to see what was underneath, but there were none. Walking slowly back along the alley I picked up the coat and the money. I hefted the money as he had done.

This clearly had value to him, he'd been pleased to receive it back. So why abandon it? The same with the coat, it was bulky, yes, but why leave it behind? I was beginning to think he was sprouting wings and flying away over the rooftops, which might explain the coat, but not the money. Why not take it with him?

Shaking my head I took it back to the market. The stall-holder was not pleased to see me.

"He was fine until you turned up. Owe you money does he?" he said, hefting boxes of fruit onto a sack truck.

"I just want to talk to him."

"Maybe he doesn't want to talk to you? Thought of that, have you?" He carried on loading.

"Look," I said. "If I don't talk to him he could be in trouble."

"Police are you?" he asked. "Show us your badge."

"Not police, this is a private matter, and I think Andy will want to keep it that way."

"Bonking someone's missus is it? The quiet ones, they're always the worst."

"As I say, it's a private matter." I let him come to his own conclusions. "He's come to you twice now, he'll come back for the coat when he thinks the coast is clear." I held out the bundled coat.

"I ain't looking after it. Look what happened, you scared him into tossing my stock half-way round the market."

"You still have the rucksack, and I apologise for the damage to your stock." I fished out a tenner from my wallet. "That should cover any damage."

"Nah, I don't want your money. Give it 'ere." He took the coat from me.

"I've slipped a note into the inside pocket for him, make sure he knows it's there."

The stallholder tucked the coat away. "You've warned him off now. Can't you let him alone? He don't mean no harm."

"He's not in any danger from me. I only want to talk to him."

"Yeah, funny how those sorts of conversations end up with broken bones, ain't it?" he remarked, assessing me.

"Just make sure he gets the message," I said.

"All you have to do is find them and bring them in. That's it," Garvin said. "That's the job."

"It's not as simple as that," I said. "Amber and I went after this group and they were prepared. Now they know we're after them they'll be even more careful. It's not just me that can't find them, Amber hasn't been able to track them either."

"Meanwhile you want to give that Scottish git more ammunition," said Garvin.

"He has access to information that we do not," I pointed out. "We need to know what else has been stolen – not just trinkets and home comforts, but odd things – items that might have some symbolic significance."

"Why do you need to know this again?"

"Blackbird thinks they might be trying to create some sort of ritual, or to prevent one. You remember the fuss about the Quit Rents Ceremony? She thinks it might be something like that."

I carefully didn't mention Gregor. Garvin wouldn't be keen on Blackbird's involvement, but getting an outsider involved would not meet his approval at all.

"Is there nowhere else you could find that out?"

I thought for a moment about asking Sam Veldon. He worked for the security services and might have access to this information, but it would be outside of his normal sphere of interest and asking the wrong questions in that environment tended to draw attention. I had used most of my favours with Sam getting Alex back – he was unlikely to be helpful.

"Unless you have some other contacts with access to the police computer systems? That'll be the quickest way to find out what's going on – if we can narrow it down to thefts from museums, private collections, art galleries and anywhere else with artefacts which might have symbolic significance, stolen between the summer solstice and now, that should give us enough to work on."

"And if I get you this list, what are you going to do with it?" he asked me.

"That depends what's on the list," I demurred.

"You're sure this isn't one of Blackbird's games?"

"To what end?"

Garvin sighed, "It's enough that she goes off on wild goose chases, Niall, without sending the Warders off on one as well."

"Aren't you always telling me to find out what I'm walking into before I engage?" I asked.

"Don't quote me back, Niall. I haven't the patience for it."

"We know they've stolen a feather and a key. The question is, what else have they stolen, and what will they go after next? I thought you'd be pleased that I was following my training."

Garvin raised an eyebrow, then folded his hands. "OK, I'll

put a request in today. I don't know how long it will take them to respond. I'll get back to you when they do."

"Thanks," I said, standing. "Oh, and I'd like to borrow Amber, if I may?"

"Amber? Why?"

"I've tracked one of the escapees down, but every time I have him cornered, he disappears. I think it would be easier with some backup."

Garvin studied my face for a moment. "Very well. I'll talk to her."

"I've already mentioned it to her. It's OK with her if it's OK with you," I said.

"She's a Warder, she doesn't need permission," he said.

"She seemed to think it would be best to clear it with you first," I said.

Garvin looked at me long and hard. "Amber hasn't asked my permission to act on anything for a very long time."

"I'm only saying what she said to me."

"I'll speak to her," said Garvin, "but it's fine. In fact, I encourage you to work with the other Warders. Maybe some of their experience will rub off on you."

"Thanks for the vote of confidence."

I turned and walked away.

"It's kept them alive," Garvin called after me. "You might want to bear that in mind."

At whose expense, I wondered.

"You don't need me for this," said Amber. "It's a job for one."

"You agreed to help," I pointed out.

"I thought he was dangerous. From what you've said, every time he spots you he takes off. That's hardly a threat."

"I still haven't managed to catch up with him."

She shook her head. "You're making it too easy for him – approaching in plain sight, announcing your presence before you need to – no wonder he gets away from you. If you're going to use those tactics you're going to have to learn to run a lot faster."

"I don't want to scare him. I'm trying to build trust."

"Perhaps that's not working out so well for him?" she suggested.

"Look, Amber, are you going to help me or not?"

She studied me for a while, and then nodded.

"Twice now I've chased him and each time he's come to this alley. Where he goes, I don't know, but he comes round here and then vanishes."

She turned around slowly, checking walls, floor, the roll-down shutters and the slot windows. "Not many places to go. Are you sure he isn't hiding out until you've gone?"

"Where?" I asked.

She drew her blade and poked through some of the bin-bags, finding only discarded waste and flies.

"My plan," I explained, "is to wait for him to appear and then introduce myself. I'll try and talk to him. If he bolts then he'll likely come here, where you can be waiting for him."

"Cornered animals fight harder," she remarked.

"I only want to talk to him. There's no reason for a fight."

"On your part, at least," she said. "We don't know about him."

"He hasn't shown any inclination to fight up until now. Let's keep it that way, shall we?"

"It would help if you knew what talents he possesses – evasion is clearly part of it."

"There's not enough information in the files to make any sense of it. We'll have to play it by ear. Are you OK with the plan? You'll have to wait here."

She leaned against the wall by the down-pipe. "I'm good at waiting."

As I watched, she closed in on herself, settling into stillness. After only a moment or two she might as well have been part of the wall.

"Great," I said, wishing I was more confident.

I made my way back to the market, wandering through the aisles and keeping a low profile, hoping to see Andy before he saw me. I looked for signs of someone using glamour – the faint heat haze in the air where someone is trying not to be seen, the unaccounted urge to look away when someone passes. As it was, I needn't have bothered. Half an hour later, Andy walked through the market wearing the coat, carrying the rucksack I'd left with the stallholder. Having escaped twice, he'd developed a boldness to his approach and sauntered casually through the stalls, greeting regulars by name.

I followed him through the stalls, watching him ply his trade. He sold jars of honey to a couple of stallholders, exchanging the golden jars for coins and notes. I began to see that he wasn't trying to supply the market with honey in bulk, but was selling jars individually to the stallholders themselves. The comment the guy who'd kept his coat had made about him charging retail price began to make sense. He wasn't looking for trade, he was looking for customers.

I followed him to the guy I'd left his coat with, and he stopped there and spoke with him. He passed over a jar, gesturing that he would take no money for it. It was a reward for returning the coat, perhaps. I waited out of sight until he finished his conversation and moved on, winding his way through the stalls. I placed myself in a position where he would be coming towards me on his way back out again, leaning casually against a pillar so that he could see I wouldn't chase him.

As he turned the corner and scanned the stalls he spotted me. I tried for a wave of the hand as a casual greeting, but he interpreted my move as a threat and bolted for the side street. I ran after him, tracking his progress out of the market into the street, heading for the alley.

I was only moments behind him. He had the rucksack hampering him and the coat flying out like a banner behind him as he ran. As soon as he came to the alley he dipped sideways.

I came around the corner to find him standing, arms raised and held out from his body. In front on him, Amber held her sword level with his throat, the tip of the blade only inches from him. Poised, she stood like a dancer. He looked back at me as I caught up behind him.

"It's OK," I said, slightly winded, "We only want to talk. She won't hurt you."

"Buuddzzz," he said.

I looked at him. "What?"

There was something strange about him. His skin became bumpy, as if some disease was erupting from within him. His form rippled as he swayed drunkenly, Amber's blade following his movement. It was as if he was no longer able to support his own weight.

Amber said, "What the...?"

His skin broke into fragments and evaporated, falling away to reveal a living crawling mass of tiny creatures. They streamed into a flying mass, spiralling out from the man-shape, the coat and rucksack falling to the ground amid them. Amber and I staggered back from the swarming, circling mass as they filled the alley with their buzzing, rising and swirling upwards in a harmonious melée, spilling out over the roof until they vanished out of sight.

"Bees." I said, finally grasping what I'd seen. "He's made of bees!"

"Shapechanger," said Amber, "and not one I've seen before. Come on." She headed out of the alley.

"Where are you going?" I asked. "We're never going to catch him now."

"That's where you're wrong," she said.

I raced after her as she headed down the side street, rounded the block and turned back on herself into the shopping street that fronted the row. She scanned the skyline.

"Not far then," she said.

"What's not far?"

"You see any bees?" she asked.

"No."

"Quite." She ran along the row, counting the shops until she came to a vegetarian cafe. "This is about right," she said.

She glanced to either side at the private doorways to flats on either side, choosing a black door that looked newly painted. "Black's my favourite colour," she explained.

"Where are we going?" I asked.

"You'll see."

She put her hand on the door and it popped open. Inside was a short hallway with stairs up to the first floor. We mounted the stairs quickly, running along the corridor past a door from behind which a heavy reggae beat was thumping, to the next set of stairs. She didn't hesitate but kept moving upwards. The next floor was quieter, but we went up again. This stairway was narrower and came to a plain door at the top of the stairs.

"Make a wish," she said.

"What kind of wish?"

"Too late." She laid her hand on the door and pushed it open. Inside was a small one room bedsit that looked as if it had been ransacked. There were clothes on the floor, hanging from door handles, in piles on the bed. Books and magazines were strewn among the mayhem.

"Is this where Andy lives?" I asked.

"I doubt it," said Amber. "Now that would be a coincidence. Besides, I can't see Andy finding this kind of chaos comfortable. He'll be a man who likes things in their place."

"How do you know that."

"I don't. But I know bees."

She threaded her way through the flat until she reached a window overlooking the rooftops at the back. From here you could see the market across the way.

"Perfect," she said, sliding the window up. She stepped out onto a small balcony.

I followed to the window. She stepped on a planter with an array of brown dead chrysanthemums, up onto the balcony rail and walked around until she could climb upwards onto the flat roof above.

I stepped out, looking over the balcony three floors down to the side street below. My stomach sank as I realised I would have to climb up on the rail. I turned away, looking up to where Amber stood on the flat roof above the window.

"You better come up," she said. "You're going to love this."

Less confident with heights than Amber, I moved the planter to the side where the rail met the wall and then mounted the rail to lean against the wall and scrabble to the roof. When I stood up I saw what prompted her remark.

The rooftop was a repeated pattern of leaded flat roofs and gabled peaks. All down the row, wooden hives had been placed where flat roofs offered a sheltered spot. There must have been eight or nine hives, each one circled by bees visiting or leaving. They flew past us, oblivious of our presence, heading off to roof gardens, parks and window boxes to return with nectar and pollen.

"This is why he keeps coming back," I said. "I couldn't figure out why he didn't head off somewhere else where I wouldn't look for him."

"And now you know," said Amber.

As we watched, the bees became more active, circling an area near the centre of the hives. Bees circled inwards, landing and climbing on one another until a mound appeared which grew and formed into the shape of a man – a man that became Andy.

"You shouldn't have come here," he said darkly. There was a hoarse rasp to his voice which made me wonder how much of a struggle maintaining that shape had become.

"I'm not here to hurt you," I called across the roof.

"In this place, you cannot hurt me," he said. The buzzing from the hives increased and a column of bees rose from each one, circling menacingly as if looking for a target.

Amber's eyes turned hard as glass. "You might want to take things easy," she said quietly.

"Or what?" he said. "Will you cut me with your sword? You can kill a few of us, but we are many, many more than you can imagine."

In answer Amber held out her arm and flames licked up her wrist up onto her hand, rising until heat haze shimmered from it. "We all have our talents," she said.

"Enough," I said. "Stop it. Amber, please don't. It's not helping. Andy, I'm sorry, it seems like I've been pursuing you but actually I want your help."

"You have a strange way of asking for it." The circling of the bees continued.

"I know, and I apologise. Can we talk? I think you may find what I have to say interesting, and it could help you and potentially others like you – like us."

"Us?"

I glanced at Amber. "As she said, we all have our talents."

"What's yours?"

"I could show you, but I'm not sure your bees would like it. Another time, maybe."

"I don't want you here. Go away," he said.

"I wish it were that simple. I know where you were taken, what they did to you."

He shook his head, denying my words. "How can you know? You weren't there. You don't bear the scars. I should know." There was anger in his words now, and remembered fear.

"I was there, but at the end. I was the one who broke in, a… colleague and I, we stopped it. We were the ones who finished it and set you all free." It felt wrong portraying myself as a hero, when what I'd done felt far from heroic, but perhaps Andy needed something to believe in, something to connect with.

"Why? Why should I believe you?"

"Because you can hear it in my voice. Because you know I'm telling the truth. I didn't go there to rescue you, it's true. I went to free my daughter who was there with you. I rescued her, but I set you all free."

"You brought the darkness?"

To him, as an inmate of Porton Down, where the lights blazed twenty-four hours a day every day, it must have seemed like that. Raffmir and I brought darkness to a place that knew only light.

"I brought the darkness. As she said, we all have our talents."

He looked thoughtful, glancing across at the hives and then back at us. Then he came to a decision.

"Go away," he said. "Leave the hives alone."

"I need to speak to you."

"Go back down, and I will come to you. Go back to the market. I will find you."

"You'll come?"

"If you leave now."

I glanced at Amber.

"It's not like he can run off somewhere," she said quietly. "He'd have to take the hives with him, and it's not easy moving them. The bees know the area. They're creatures of habit."

"OK," I called to him. "I'll wait for you."

We climbed down and made our way back through the flat, locking the door after us.

"How did you know where he was?" I asked Amber.

"Bees fly horizontally unless you give them a reason not to. There were no bees at ground level, so they had to be up a height somewhere. The rooftop is an obvious place. Plenty of room, and no one to disturb them."

"He keeps the bees, and they keep him," I said, remembering him selling the honey.

"He is the bees. What do you want to say to him?" asked Amber as we made our way back to the street.

"I want his help in bringing together the escapees. He tried to organise them in Porton Down, so he knows some of them – more than most, anyway."

"He tried to organise them," said Amber. "Figures."

"I think he could be helpful," I said.

"Bear in mind he won't travel far," she said. "He's ruled at least partly by his animal shape. By winter he's liable to be mostly dormant."

"The other inmates may trust him. You've seen how little they trust anyone else."

"Well, you don't need me for this. Are you OK to find your own way back to the courts?"

"I'll be fine. I'll join you later," I said.

A smile touched her lips. "Don't get yourself stung to death."

When I got back to the courts, Garvin wanted an update.

"So you didn't bring him in?" he challenged.

"I'm not sure anyone could make him go anywhere he didn't want to go," I said.

"Amber did say it was unusual."

"He's tied to the hives in ways I probably can't comprehend. He can't move anywhere any more than the bees can. If I brought him here, he couldn't stay for more than a short while. It's not a choice, it's how he is."

Garvin raised an eyebrow. "Do you think he can have children?"

"What kind of a question is that?" I asked. "Can Lord Kane? Or is there a risk of kittens?"

"You need to be careful, saying things like that," said Garvin.

"Because Kane's fey, or because he's a Lord of the Seven Courts?"

"Both, and because he's liable to tear your heart out and eat it," said Garvin.

"He's promised not to harm me."

"Then it's his word that's standing between you and sudden death. How far do you want to test it?"

"Point taken."

Garvin folded his hands. "I'd rather you didn't test his level of patience."

"My point is that it's not an appropriate question in either case. Sure, Kane is one of the Lords and Ladies, but why is it anyone's business whether Andy can be a successful father? That's between him and his partner, if he has one, surely?"

"The courts have an interest in the fertility of the half-breeds, you must understand that. It's why they exist."

"No," I said. "It's how they came to be, but it's not why they exist. They exist for themselves, not because someone in power called them into existence, and not because they live to serve. They are themselves. We have to stop thinking of them as an experiment, and start thinking of them as people. Otherwise this will all fall apart. Don't you see?"

"I live to serve," said Garvin, "and I don't see anything wrong with service."

"Then that's your choice," I pointed out, standing, "but it's not their choice and you can't force it upon them."

I left him with that thought, and as I left I thought I heard him make some comment behind me, but it was lost in the background noise. It seemed to me that Garvin was more difficult to deal with each day, but perhaps it was simply that I kept bringing him more and more unsolvable problems.

I stretched my back and rotated my shoulders. It had been long day and I needed rest. I resolved to go and find Blackbird and try for an early night, though my son might have other ideas.

Sixteen

I was woken by a familiar sound. I lay in bed with Blackbird breathing softly beside me, listening to our son grizzling to himself in the next room. Miraculously we'd managed an early night and collapsed into bed with the zealous vigour that parents of young children have when given the chance to be in bed together – we were both rapidly asleep. Now we were paying the price. My son was awake and hungry, and shortly he would make himself heard whether we were asleep or not.

I slipped from under the covers, tucking the quilt around Blackbird so the chill of the night air wouldn't wake her. If anything, she'd been more exhausted than I was, so I would take the opportunity to feed the baby without waking her, and let her sleep.

Our son was mostly breastfed, but I could make a bottle up if needed and if he was hungry enough, he would take it. It wasn't quite as comforting as the warmth of his mother but at three in the morning he would have to take what he could get. I pulled on a T-shirt and some sweat pants, and went through to his room.

There was a dim red light, placed in one of the electric sockets by the stewards, so I could see he wasn't exactly awake yet. That wouldn't last, though, as he was already restless and would toss and turn until he woke himself up and demanded food. I reached down and picked him up, resting him against my shoulder while I wrapped a blanket round him. He made small noises, but was momentarily appeased by another warm body.

I padded back through our bedroom, grabbing the change bag on the way through, and slipped outside into the hall, closing the door softly behind me. Blackbird turned over, but didn't wake.

Outside it was chillier, but it was too late to go back for something warmer to wear. The temperature in the old house dropped at night – the product of bad insulation and rooms with high ceilings. As a Warder, trained to steel myself against adverse conditions, I could put up with cold feet.

I walked through the house in near silence, punctuated by the occasional hoot of an owl outside. There were no people, no stewards. The whole house was asleep.

As we made our way downstairs, my son nuzzled against me and then started chewing his hand – a sure sign of impending hunger. I navigated through the halls and rooms in darkness to the back kitchen. The light in the fridge came on when I opened the door, and I found that Lesley, bless her, had left a feed made up, saving me the task of making one up and then waiting for it to cool. I ran some warm water into a pan to take the chill off the milk.

My son woke up to the fact that food was imminent and started making a lot of noise. I walked up and down with him a few times, but it wasn't going to distract him. Hungry babies are not easily distracted. They are very focused people.

Carrying my noisy bundle back through the house to one of the abandoned sitting rooms. I dropped the change bag on one side, placed some pillows to support my back and made myself comfortable. I tested the milk on the inside of my arm out of habit, finding it only just warm enough. Still, he would eat it cold if he was hungry enough.

Even though I placed the teat of the bottle against his lips where he could feel it, the yelling continued for a few moments, then ceased, to be replaced by a rhythmic sucking. I breathed a sigh of relief, pushed back into the armchair, and got comfortable. I talked to him as he fed, telling him stories about bears and unicorns in the sort of stream-of-consciousness story that fathers make up at three in the morning, and gradually the slurping slowed as his hunger eased.

Now we had the difficult bit. I smiled at all I'd learned from Alex. It was no good trying to feed a sleepy baby. They ate some, slept for half an hour and then woke you up again for more. You needed to get their attention, and cold nappy cream was the way to do it.

I spread the change mat on the floor and laid my semi-comatose child on the mat. As soon as I started to undress him he woke up with a vengeance, screaming blue murder that I was not only changing his nappy, but using freezing cold nappy cream as well. I endured his protests and ineffectual attempts to fend me off, and in a few moments he was dry and clean, the dirty nappy set aside and his milk waiting for him. That didn't stop him yelling.

By now, though, he was awake again, and placated with some more milk, so I could sit back and let him finish it off. He was comfort eating now that his initial hunger was sated, but I wanted him to last until morning.

"You do that very well."

"Amber! What are you doing here?" There was a shape across the room which I'd taken for a shrouded chair, but which now resolved itself into a sitting person. My son shifted at the alarm in my voice, and then went back to drinking as I relaxed again.

"I didn't want to disturb you," she said.

"Hmmph. If I'd dropped him we would have disturbed the whole house." The shape didn't move. Even though I knew she was there, she was still difficult to see in the dark. "How long have you been there?"

"Since before you came in."

"How did you know I was coming in here?" I asked.

"It's where you came before."

"You've watched me do this before? Without saying anything?"

"Only once. I didn't disturb you then. You seemed content." She sat up and moved to another chair where I could see her better.

"Well don't creep up on me like that again, It's... creepy." At three in the morning it was hard to come up with a better description. "What are you doing up, anyway?"

"Patrolling – renewing the wards."

"Aren't you supposed to be scouting the grounds?"

"You're the only person awake for miles – you and your son."

"Ah, well. Glad we could entertain you." My sarcasm was ignored.

"It brings back memories," she said.

"Of what?" I asked.

"My daughter."

I was momentarily taken aback. Amber had never mentioned a daughter. As far as I could tell, none of the Warders had children. I had assumed it was part of the job description and yet another reason I wasn't very good at it.

"No one said you had a daughter," I said.

"I don't talk about it. It was a long time ago."

"Where is she now?" I asked.

"She died."

Now I felt really bad. "Amber, I'm so sorry. Here I am, being so insensitive. I'm really… I don't know what to say."

"It's OK. She was old. She had a good life."

"Old?" The question was out before I realised what I'd said.

"She was human, like her father. Completely and utterly as human as could be. She lived into her eighties – not a bad age. At the end… I'd like to think she knew me, but it was hard to tell. The drugs they gave her in the hospital made her memory bad." She thought for a moment. "I think she knew me."

"But you must have been… you didn't age."

"I know. It's strange. She started out as my daughter, and by the end I had to play her granddaughter – too young even to be her daughter then. She would touch my face and tell me I had such good skin."

"Didn't she tell anyone? I mean, it must have been strange. Did she know you were her mother?"

"Yes. It was our secret. She used to laugh at how I never aged a day while she grew older every year – until it wasn't funny any more."

She paused, thoughtful for a while.

"We tried," she laughed, but there wasn't much humour in it. "We tried to bring it out, to activate the magic within her. It didn't work. Nothing did. In the end it just hurt her."

"That's… terrible."

"Is it? Yes, I think it might be. You're either fey, or you're not. You don't get to choose."

"Amber, I'm so sorry. You must miss her very much."

"I wouldn't change it. If I could swap a year of my life for a year of hers, it would be different, but that's not the way it works. Instead you are given the years that are yours. Her years were wonderful. She was a beautiful girl."

"I don't know what to say."

"As I say, it was a long time ago."

"It's strange, Amber. You've never mentioned her before. I never even knew you had a daughter. Why are you telling me this now?"

"It brings back memories – mostly good ones." I caught a glimpse of her sad smile in the half-light. "You're very lucky."

I looked down at the child in my arms. "I like to think so."

"You already have one child who's come into her power. She will outlive you, perhaps, but you won't see her age and die."

"I hadn't thought of it like that."

"Your son – well you won't know until it happens. With fey power on both sides, he stands a better chance, but there are no guarantees."

I looked down at him. He'd stopped drinking, his eyes were closed and his limbs had gone floppy. I withdrew the teat and he made a half-hearted attempt to get it back, but quickly turned his head into my chest and went back to sleep.

"At one time," I told her, "all I wanted for my daughter was that she would grow up as a normal girl with a normal life."

"Be careful what you wish for," said Amber. "It's not easy watching your children die, even if they have a good life. It's not something you ever get over."

"No. I don't suppose it is," I agreed.

"Treasure every moment, Dogstar. You have no way of telling how long you have." She stood, sliding across the room with lithe grace. "Good night, sleep well."

She vanished into the dark and I sat quietly with a lightly

snoring baby for some time before I made my way back upstairs. Settling him back into his cot, I wondered what would become of him. I went back to bed, listening to Blackbird breathe in the dark, and by the time I went back to sleep, the first signs of dawn were showing behind the curtains.

The next morning I woke up late and was immediately summoned to see Garvin.

"I have a list of items for you. I hope you know what you're looking for."

He placed a folder in front of me. I opened it to reveal several sheets of paper with typed lists of items on them. "What's all this?"

"It's what you asked for, a list of all the unusual items stolen since the release of the prisoners from Porton Down."

"Can't they narrow it down a bit?" I turned over the first sheet to find the list continued on the next, and the next.

"They could if they knew what they were looking for."

"A seventeenth century chalice stolen from a church near Toxteth, ceremonial robes from another church near Barnstable, a replica sword stolen from a museum in Burgess Hill. How are we supposed to narrow it down."

"That," said Garvin, "is your problem. You have the list. Now you need to tell me what they're doing with it all."

"But these weren't necessarily stolen by any of the escapees. They could have been nicked by anyone."

"Then you need to identify which of it is important, don't you?"

I went down the list. "Well, I guess we can eliminate anything that's a replica, can't we?"

"I don't know," said Garvin, "can we?"

I slid the papers back into the folder. "Let me work on it,

see what I can figure out. There must be a pattern to this somewhere."

"Fine," said Garvin, "but in the meantime these people are still running around loose. I want them caught and dealt with, and whatever it is they doing stopped. If you find them, you can ask them what all this is for yourself, can't you?"

"If we find them," I pointed out.

"You're not going to find them in there," said Garvin, nodding towards the folder.

"Perhaps," I said, "but we're not having much success finding them anywhere else, are we?"

"We'll see," said Garvin.

"When are we going to do something?" Alex was pacing up and down the office floor between the empty desks. "We never do anything."

"We are doing something," said Eve. "I'm reading, or I was until you interrupted me. Chipper is doing whatever Chipper does when he's plugged into that machine, and Sparky is... What are you doing, Sparky?"

Sparky looked over the monitor across the cluster of desks. "The internet is still working – I'm downloading movies. There's this Chinese site – you can get anything on here."

"Anything good?" asked Alex.

"I've got Evil Undead 3 if you want to watch?"

Alex sighed. "Don't you ever watch anything but zombie flicks?"

"I watched that thing the other night with the bald guy in it. That didn't have zombies."

"No. It had aliens instead. Why can't we watch something that doesn't involve the human race being wiped out."

"What could be wrong with that?" asked Eve.

She said it jokingly, but Alex caught something in her tone that didn't follow the joke. Alex watched her, but Eve just shook her head and returned to reading.

Sparky went back to browsing files for download. Alex walked up and down the office again. It was an odd place. Eve said the company that owned it had gone bust, so they'd sounded the fire alarms and marched everyone who worked there outside and locked the doors. The desks and chairs were just as they'd left them, newspapers open, coffee mugs half-full of cold coffee with lines around it where the water had evaporated. It was spooky, as the people had been disintegrated leaving everything else in its place. There was even an empty pair of shoes under one of the desks as if the person wearing them had simply vanished.

"Why don't you read a book?" said Eve.

"What? One of your weird-arse mystical relics, or that one about the universe being two-dimensional?"

"Flatland," said Eve. "It's a very thought-provoking book."

"It is not good. It is boring. B-O-R-R-I-N-G, spelled D-U-L-L."

"That's not how you spell boring, Alex," said Eve.

"It's how I spell it. Why do we never go anywhere or do anything, except when we're stealing some bizarro artefact from a lost civilisation? Why don't we go clubbing or something? We could have some fun!"

"You are free to go clubbing if you wish," said Eve, coldly.

"On my own? And yeah, Gina went clubbing. Look what happened to her."

"Gina had other problems."

"We could go and find some decent food, instead of living off noodles and chips. My skin feels like an oil slick." Alex rubbed her finger up and down her nose to demonstrate.

"Vanity does not suit you," said Eve, "and we are supposed

to be keeping a low profile. We can hardly do that by skipping out of restaurants without paying. Besides, Chipper doesn't want to leave his computer."

Chipper was wired into a PC with three screens that he'd cobbled together from equipment around the office. He wore huge headphones which sometimes failed to deaden the sound of staccato gunfire and the screams of the dying.

"That's all he ever does! What's he playing now? Some World War Two thing that goes on forever. He'll be all night on that. What am I supposed to do?"

"You can go out if you want to. You're not a prisoner," Eve pointed out.

"And this office – the chairs are all on wheels, there's no beds to sleep in, the lights are on whether you want them on or not."

"As Sparky pointed out, it has internet and power, it's clean and dry. There's a basic kitchen with a microwave. What more do you want?'

"A bed?" said Alex.

"Sleep is highly overrated," said Eve.

"I don't get it," said Alex. "You're in all this hurry to get hold of the stuff and then we wait. What are we waiting for? Why don't we change the world now? Today?"

"The timing must be perfect. You don't understand."

"You always say that, but you never say when. You're worse than my sodding parents."

"It will be soon, Alex. You must learn patience." Eve glanced up sharply. "What was that?"

"What was what?" said Alex.

Eve looked back along the line of desks in the deserted office space to the doors where the lift lobby was. "Why is there no light in the lift lobby?" she said, her voice acquiring an edge as she rose to her feet. She picked up a stapler and threw it towards Chipper so that it bounced off the monitors.

"What'd you do that for?" said Chipper, tearing off the headphones.

"Trouble," said Eve. "Police?" She picked up the book and stuffed it into the satchel she carried, tucking it in beside other items stashed in the satchel, slipping it over her head and across her body.

She was collecting a long silver arrow from the desk where she'd been reading when Sparky spoke.

"Er, guys?" Sparky stood up slowly, his hands held up and away from his body. As he stood it became apparent there was someone standing close behind him holding a long curved knife to his throat. "Problem here?"

"Fellstamp?" Alex said his name before she could stop herself. She immediately recognised the broad-nosed face rising behind Sparky. "What are you doing…?"

"You know him?" asked Eve, incredulous.

"Kinda," said Alex. "He's one of the people who work with my dad."

"Just everyone relax and no one gets hurt," said Fellstamp. "We're not looking for a fight – just being cautious. If we wanted to hurt you, you'd be dead by now."

"We?" Said Eve. "There's only one of you."

"No, there isn't." A figure appeared near the door to the lift lobby, where seconds before Alex could have sworn there was no one.

"Fionh," said Alex, turning to face her. "You're not taking me back. I won't go!"

"Shut up, Alex. This is not about you," said Fionh. "You," she nodded towards Eve, "put down the arrow, drop the bag and any other weapons, place your hands high where we can see them."

"You know these people?" said Eve, shoving Alex in the chest so that she staggered back against a desk. "You brought them here?"

"No," said Alex. "They must have tracked us here. I didn't tell anyone, honestly."

"In two," said Eve, quietly.

"What?" said Alex. From her position she saw Chipper pretend to lift something from the desk, cradling it to him. Eve paused for just a second. Sparky was gripping the top of the monitor in front of him. There was a faint smell of electrical overheating. A wisp of smoke rose from the back of the monitor. Sparky nodded.

"Don't try anything," said Fellstamp, "Or your friend will grow a new smile."

"Two," said Eve.

There was a blinding white flash from Sparky. In the after image burned into Alex's retina, long trails of jagged lightning forked out all around him. Fellstamp flew backwards, a bright arc lancing into his chest. To Alex, blinking through the green spots floating in front of her eyes, he seemed to float in the air as he sailed backwards, arms out-flung.

Chipper made a gesture that looked to Alex like he was launching a grenade. A great gout of flame erupted in front of Fionh, the pulse of heat throwing Alex forward so she landed across one of the stupid office chairs and toppled sideways onto the floor.

Her ears ringing from the twin detonations, Alex crawled to her knees, coughing at the bitter-tasting smoke that was roiling down around her. A high-pitched alarm was screeching. Emergency lighting flickered into dim illumination.

Alex pulled herself up on the desk in time to see Fionh striding through the smoke towards Eve with a long straight blade held easily, but as she advanced her steps faltered. Fionh glanced down, suddenly unsure of her footing. Even as she hesitated, the floor appeared to ripple and bow underneath her. Carpet tiles up-ended into a dip in the floor which expanded, swallowing everything as it flowed outwards.

Fionh leapt forwards, the ground under her sagging and collapsing, leaving her sprawled across the shifting carpet tiles as they were sucked inexorably into the slowly whirling vortex that had opened up in what had been a solid floor. It rippled like water, and sighed like sand. Fionh crawled forward while the floor slipped backwards into the dark hole that had opened up in the floor.

"Die bitch!" said Eve.

"No!" said Alex. "You mustn't!"

Eve glanced at Alex and then stepped forward and slapped her, flat-handed, across the face. Alex staggered sideways at the force of the blow. Tears welled into her eyes.

"Never!" Eve's eyes blazed with anger. "Never ever tell me what I can and cannot do!"

Alex held her hand to her cheek where her cheek burned. "There are more of them," Alex blurted through the tears. "If you kill them they'll come with more, better armed, better prepared."

"They'll have to find us first," said Eve. "Out!" she called to Sparky and Chipper. "Emergency exit. Now!" She grabbed Alex's hair, lifting it and pulling it back so that Alex's throat was exposed. In her hand, the tip of the silver arrow glinted menacingly.

"Did you bring them here? Did you?" asked Eve.

"No!" Alex gasped. "I swear."

Eve paused, on the cusp of a decision. Alex readied herself, trying to think of something she could do, something she could say.

Eve threw her forwards. "Go! Follow them down. I'll be right behind you."

She pushed Alex towards the emergency exit. Alex stumbled forwards, her footing uncertain. The whole floor was shifting and bucking like it was a living thing. The foul-smelling smoke drifted around her, forming into drifts like ghosts in the still air. She glanced back. Outlined against the dull flicker of the flames, she could dimly see Eve's outline.

It was too late to help anyone now.

It was so rare to see people running in the courts that I couldn't help but follow the commotion down to the source, the room where the Ways converged, under the house.

When I reached the room I couldn't quite believe what I found. Fionh was sprawled on the floor, covered in smears of dark soot, showing livid bruises and singed hair. Garvin was knelt beside her giving her water from a glass. I'd never seen Fionh look anything but crisp and business-like. It was a shock to see her in such disarray.

Beside her, Fellstamp was laid with his head in the lap of one of the female stewards, his eyes closed. In normal circumstances he'd be enjoying that sort of attention, but he lay quite still, eyes closed. She held a cloth pressed to his forehead, murmuring down to him. There was an acrid smell of burning plastic and another smell I couldn't identify.

People were bringing in bowls of warm water and blankets. They didn't seem to know what else to do.

"What the hell happened to you?" I blurted out.

Fionh pushed the glass away. "Your daughter and her friends, that's what."

"Alex did this?" I was incredulous.

"Her friends did. We underestimated them badly. They

looked peaceful enough and we went in hard. Fellstamp took one of them hostage. We thought we had it under control but there was some sort of electrical discharge, I've never seen anything like it. It caught Fellstamp full in the chest. He hasn't moved since."

"Perhaps it was an accident. They don't have much control."

"You joke!" said Fionh. "While one of them was throwing fireballs at me, the other did something to the floor of the building. It was like quicksand, dragging me down."

She coughed and Garvin gave her some more of the water. When she could speak again she continued.

"The leader is a girl, not much older than Alex. She was carrying a bag slung across her chest and a metal arrow, it looked like silver. She had a book as well, but she put that in the bag as soon as she realised they weren't alone." She coughed again. "When the others had gone, she leaned down at the edge of the pit that was dragging me down. She watched me struggling as I was sliding slowly backwards. She didn't offer a hand, or even blink."

Fionh's gaze turned inwards at the memory.

"She said to pass on a message. She said not to come after them. She said if we did she would take a city and do the same with that as she was doing to me. She said she would drag all of it down and send it to hell, which was what it deserved. Then she stood up and walked away without a backward glance."

"And you left Alex with these people?" I asked.

"Your daughter?" She laughed without humour. "She's in on it – one of them, calm as you like. They had a bit of a tiff when the leader thought she'd given away their location, but she went with them all the same. She's one of them, Niall."

"She can't be. Alex wouldn't associate with anyone like that," I protested

"She's changed, Niall. She has tattoos all down her arms now, and wears her hair jet black. She probably calls herself Dementia or something."

"She's just playing along with them."

"No, Niall. She's one of them."

Mullbrook arrived, bringing in two stewards with a makeshift stretcher made from a tabletop, which they guided down beside Fellstamp.

"He hasn't moved since he was hit," said Fionh, watching them carefully lift him onto the low wooden platform. "I had to carry him down the Way."

Naturally pale, his skin looked like it had been powdered white under the soot and the grime.

"You need to rest," said Garvin. "When you feel up to it we'll get you cleaned up. You'll feel better when you've had some sleep."

"I don't want sleep," she said. "I want revenge." She tried to push herself up, but Garvin rested his hand on her shoulder and gently pressed her back down.

"That's why you're not going after them," Garvin said. "It'll take a cool head and careful planning. I'll take Amber and Tate. We'll do what needs to be done."

"What about me?" I asked.

Garvin looked up at me. "My instructions will be to kill on sight. I don't think I can ask you to do that, Niall."

He paused.

"Not when it's your own daughter."

Seventeen

"We've got to do something!" I paced up and down in front of Blackbird. "They're going to kill her."

"They'll have to find her first," said Blackbird, reasonably.

"They've already found them once. How long before they give themselves away? This time they won't give them chance to draw breath. They'll just kill them all and have done with it, Alex included."

"I thought Alex didn't do anything?"

"She didn't. It's guilt by association. And when I said that to Garvin, he said that she didn't lift a finger to help them either."

"That's no reason to kill someone."

"That's what I said, but you know what Garvin's like."

"Indeed I do," she remarked, "he thinks he's judge, jury and high executioner, and unfortunately he's not disabused of that by the High Court."

"I have to try and find her." I said. I found myself dry-washing my hands, and stuck them in my pockets to stop myself.

"Where would you start? You've been looking for her for days and you haven't found her yet. For that matter, how did Fellstamp and Fionh find them?"

"They were tipped off. Apparently the building where they were squatting is part of a territory given to one of the fey in Teoth's Court. They were spotted entering and leaving and a complaint was raised with the courts. Garvin realised who it was that was disregarding territorial boundaries..."

"...and sent Fionh and Fellstamp in heavy-handed," Blackbird finished.

"Apparently Fellstamp took one of them hostage – sounds like he picked the wrong one."

"And that worked out well, didn't it?" she said. "How is he?"

"His condition hasn't changed. Half the female stewards are walking around as if they're in mourning, and the other half are looking as if they've had a lucky escape."

"He's such a rogue."

"You're smiling. Don't tell me you're smitten too?"

"You have to admit, he is very charming," said Blackbird, off-handedly.

"Not at the moment, he's not."

"He'll come around, you'll see." She could see I was worried about him.

"I hope so. I don't know what Garvin will do if he doesn't pull through. He's very protective of his people."

"Apart from you," she said.

"The same with me. Up to a point."

"Quite."

"I only seem to cause him trouble," I admitted.

"And that's your fault, is it? You do this deliberately?"

"Of course not."

"Then he can hardly punish you for it, can he?" she said.

"It's not me he's punishing."

"Isn't it? He must know how you feel about them going after Alex. She is your daughter."

"He knows, but it doesn't change anything. He says she's brought it on herself."

"The excuse of the despot throughout history – they brought it on themselves; they forced my hand; they made me do it."

"I have to find her," I repeated.

"Perhaps there is a way. You said that this girl had a silver arrow with her?"

"Yes, and a book."

"Then it's time we went to see Gregor again. We know they have a key and a feather. Perhaps he can shed some light on what they're doing, and from that we might be able to figure out where they are before Garvin does."

Alex was backed against the wall in the alley. "I didn't tell them anything, I swear." She looked from Eve, to Sparky, to Chipper, and back to Eve. "You can tell I'm not lying, dammit!"

Sparky rubbed his neck thoughtfully. "They found us somehow, didn't they? And I damned near got my throat slit."

Alex folded her arms. "So you automatically blame me."

"You knew them," said Eve. "None of the rest of us knew them."

"They're Warders, I told you. Everyone at the courts knows them, at least by reputation," said Alex.

"But you know them personally," said Eve.

"My dad works with them. He's sort of in the same bit of the courts. They all work for Garvin."

"And what does Garvin do?"

"Garvin's freaky. He's not quite right up here." Alex tapped her temple. "He makes my flesh crawl."

"But what does he do?" asked Eve.

"I told you, he leads the Warders, and they do the bidding

of the courts. It's all about who's top dog and who's allied to whoever. The Lords and Ladies have absolute power, and what they say goes, but they don't necessarily agree with each other. When I went to see Kimlesh, she told me that I could join the Nymphine Court, but that meant accepting the rules and abiding by her rulings, and in return, she'll defend me from the others."

"So she decides where you live and what you do?" asked Eve.

"No, not exactly. You can live wherever you like, but if you get into a dispute with another fey, maybe you take something that belongs to someone, then the court will rule. Maybe you get to keep it, or maybe you give it back. It stops them killing each other."

"And all of them are members?" asked Eve.

"Pretty much. Except for us. They don't really know what to do with us. We're not human and we're not fey. There's a big debate over whether half-breeds should be able to join."

"But Kimlesh offered to let you join her court?" said Sparky.

"The Nymphine court is the only one I can join because my elements are water and air. Kimlesh wants the half-breeds to join the courts. It's her choice who joins and who doesn't, so if I join, it tips the balance, see? She gets what she wants. But the others, Teoth, Krane, some of the others, they're not opening up. If I joined, it could force their hand, and they won't like that."

"So you ran away," said Eve.

"I was leaving anyway," said Alex.

"And they're following you because they want you to join, or because they don't?" asked Eve.

"Both, I guess. Kimlesh says I can join because there's a precedent. Yonna admitted Blackbird to the court of Fey'ree years ago, so it's been done before. There were others, but most of them died when the Seventh Court betrayed the courts and killed all the half-breeds they could find. There are supposed to be a few of the older ones dotted about, but most of them are in hiding."

"So they're killing the half-breeds, even the ones that are part of the courts?" said Eve.

"That's the Seventh Court, the Wraithkin. They're different. They don't like any of the half-breeds. They don't think we should exist."

"But the Seventh Court are part of the courts?"

"Yeah," said Alex, "I guess. They're the seventh one."

"I still don't get how they found us," said Sparky.

"They found us because they're hunting us," said Eve. "And if they catch us, they'll kill us."

"I don't think Fellstamp would have hurt you," said Alex. "He's not like that really. He was just trying to take control."

"They'll kill us when they find us," said Eve, "or they'll take us back to their courts and kill us there – if the Seventh Court don't kill us first."

"It's not that clear cut," said Alex.

"No," said Eve. "But it's what will happen. Whether it's an accident or on purpose, the outcome is the same. We can't afford for them to find us again. Take off your clothes."

"My what?" said Alex.

"Your clothes. Take them off," said Eve. Chipper smiled slightly. Sparky openly grinned.

"No! I'm not stripping for you or anyone else."

"They found you somehow, Alex. They did it once so they can do it again. They could be tracking you through your clothes, your jewellery, anything. You have to get rid of them."

"I stole my clothes," said Alex. "Even my underwear is new."

"Do you have anything from you past life?" asked Eve.

"No," said Alex, putting her hand behind her back.

They all heard the lie.

"Give it to me," said Eve.

"It's nothing. It's such a small thing. They can't be tracking me with that."

"Give." Eve held her hand out.

Alex shook her head, but Eve moved in swiftly, grabbing her hair and her arm, twisting her around and pressing her against the wall.

"No! You can't have it! It's mine!"

Alex balled her fist so that the ring was tight on her finger, but Eve twisted it behind her, pushing her into the wall and prying her fingers apart. The ring was stripped from Alex's finger.

Alex screamed, "No! No! No! No!" She twisted and fought to get free.

Eve tossed the ring to Chipper. "Stamp on it."

Chipper caught it and put it carefully on the floor, resting it under his trainer and then leaned his weight on it, while Alex screamed in Eve's grip. The ring twisted and bent, then folded in half. He stomped on it twice for good measure, breaking it into two pieces. He picked up the pieces and threw them down the alley.

Alex sobbed, taking great gulps of air and wailing.

"Grow up, little girl," said Eve. "You have no family but us. You have no friends but us. We are everything you have and don't you forget it. When we change the world none of this will matter. Then you'll thank me."

Eve let her go and Alex stumbled away, screaming abuse at those behind her, but knowing in her heart that she had nowhere else to go.

• • • •

"A library? Why does he want to meet in a library?" I asked Blackbird. "What's he going to do, stick a pin in an atlas? Borrow the Observer Book of Strange Rituals?"

"It's not the sort of library that lends books."

We were walking down Euston Road, the constant roar of motorbikes and the growl of taxis and buses almost drowning out our words as the traffic stop-started its way along one of London's busiest thoroughfares.

"What's the point of a library that doesn't lend books?" I asked.

"It's a hidden library," said Blackbird, "and it has a copy of almost every book that's ever been published, including some extremely rare volumes. When I spoke to Gregor on the phone he said to meet him here. He has a reader's ticket."

"You need a ticket to read books?"

"You do when they're as rare as these."

We turned through huge iron gates that sang with a discordant note that made me pass as far from each of them as I could. Blackbird ignored them and we walked through to a huge courtyard in front of a monolithic block building that looked like a modernised version of a 1930s movie set. A huge clock adorned the frontage.

"Is that it?" I asked.

"The British Library," said Blackbird, "or at least the bit you can see."

"Where's the rest of it?" I asked.

"You're standing on it."

I looked at the paving that stretched away around the building. "Below this is just books?"

"Not just books, no. Manuscripts, maps, documents, scrolls. This is a palace dedicated to the written word. Beneath our feet are rows and rows of shelves, and beneath that, the same, and below that more and so on, downwards. You should come and walk around the galleries one day. The public exhibits are worth seeing."

"Let's find Gregor and see what he wants to show us," I said.

He was waiting for us on the upper floor, where he rushed over to greet us as we stepped off the escalator.

"Veronica, it is simply wonderful to see you again. Is it not a truly marvellous building; such architecture, such vision."

He gestured around us, then grabbed my hand and shook it enthusiastically. "You must be so proud to be a part of a nation that builds such wonders, yes?"

"I suppose?" I said.

"Ah, always the citizens do not see the wonders around them. You take them for granted until they are taken from you. Only then do you discover what you have lost." His moustache wobbled from side to side in disapproval.

"And what have we lost?" asked Blackbird.

"Come," he said. "I wish you meet Julian. He will tell you the story, just as he told it to me."

He asked each of us to wear yellow Visitor badges and then led the way through to the back of the building, through a door into offices away from the public space. We got a few suspicious glances, but Gregor flashed an orange badge at them and we were allowed to pass. We came to a small office. Inside a thin man in a grey shirt with a black tie looked up at our approach.

"Julian, this is Veronica and her friend, Niall. They are interested in the book I asked you about."

"We are?" I said.

"I am," said Blackbird, extending her hand. "Veronica Delemere, formerly in Medieval History at Birkbeck."

He took the outstretched hand and smiled. "I think we have one or two of your books here, Dr. Delemere."

"Really? How charming," she said. They all smiled, ignoring me. I was just a friend, apparently, and not worthy of attention.

"The book, Julian. Tell them," said Gregor.

He looked up at Gregor. "Ah yes. Well, a bit of an embarrassment, really. We're not used to this kind of thing."

"What kind of thing?" asked Blackbird.

"It seems that someone has borrowed it," he explained.

"You see," I said. "They do lend books out."

"What Julian is saying," said Gregor, "is that the book has been stolen."

"Is that possible?" asked Blackbird.

"Ordinarily, no," Julian confirmed. "We have inserts in every book that will set off detectors at any exit. You can't even walk out with one by accident. In addition, the staff are spot-checked randomly to discourage anyone with ideas of taking anything; a necessary evil."

"That seems a lot of security for a load of old books," I said.

He glanced at Blackbird and Gregor. "You have no idea. We have the first draft manuscript of Thomas Hardy's *Tess of the D'Urbervilles* here. There are copies here of the Lindisfarne Gospels."

"If they're only copies then surely they are not worth much?" I knew I was flaunting my ignorance, but the snooty attitude was annoying. I wanted to rattle his cage a little and butt into the conversation.

"Well, if you consider that they were copied by hand in the year 687, you might revise your opinion," he said.

"How much?" I asked, rubbing my finger and thumb together.

"Priceless," Gregor said, "and completely irreplaceable."

"Priceless generally has a price, though, doesn't it?"

"They are not for sale," said Julian, "but a stolen copy would be worth millions to a private collector. Of course, when such a work is so readily identifiable, the collector could never show it to anyone, but then such people rarely have any interest in other people. And that's just one work. The library has many such items."

"So your security is set up accordingly?" I asked.

"There have been attempted thefts before," said Gregor, "and though some have escaped with their liberty, they have left empty-handed."

"Not this time, though," said Julian, "though the work that's missing isn't one of the high security items. It was kept in the general vault, though even that's not exactly accessible."

"What is it?" asked Blackbird.

"An oddity," Julian remarked. "Unique in that it was annotated, but we have other copies."

He opened his desk drawer and extracted a bundle wrapped in black fabric. Pulling on a set of white cotton gloves he unfolded the cloth, revealing a brown leather book. The cover was plain brown leather, unadorned, burnished through handling. I was momentarily filled with the desire to ask Julian to wrap it up and put it away again. It was an odd sensation, as if there was something in the book that should not be revealed. I shook myself.

"Ah, you feel it too?" said Gregor, "Good, you are sensitive for a philistine."

"Who are you calling a philistine?" I challenged.

"A man who asks the price of a hand-copied Gospel?"

"Hmm, fair cop," I said. "What's the book about?"

"It is a journal, of sorts," said Gregor. "I read it many years ago, but then I received Veronica's call on the telephone and she is telling me that your thieves have stolen a silver arrow along with the other things, yes?"

"We think so," I agreed.

"This is the journal of Aleister Crowley, or a copy of a copy, in fact. I read it many years ago, but the mention of the arrow along with the other things set me thinking and I came to the library to consult the work directly."

Julian explained. "When we went to retrieve the book concerned it had gone. There's no record of it being taken out recently, and no movement record indicating it had been archived or moved to secure storage."

"Perhaps it has simply been misfiled?" Blackbird asked him.

"You don't understand," said Julian. "Each shelf contains many thousands of books. We can't possibly manage them all manually. There is a robotic system which tracks along the shelves, registering the tags for the books. Essentially, the system registers all the books before we hand any out, and then registers them all back in again. We would know if one was not returned, and if it was misfiled it would show up somewhere else and the system would throw up an alert that tells us where it is and where it should be."

"So how did it leave the library?" she asked.

In response, he opened the drawer and placed a page on the desk. "This was left in place."

"It's the tag?" I asked.

He nodded. "Someone has removed it from the book, which probably means they damaged it to take it out." He made it sound like an accusation of rape.

"So someone did take it," said Blackbird.

"Someone who got past the security staff, opened the door to the vault, found the book amid the myriad of other works stored down there, took out the tag and then left, also without setting of an alarm or leaving any trace," said Julian. "The management are convinced it's an inside job and anyone in the vault that day is under investigation. Thankfully I was off sick that day or the investigation would have included me."

"Unless that was a useful alibi?" I suggested.

He scowled at me. "Don't make suggestions like that around here. It isn't funny any more."

"Sorry," I said.

"Show them the diagram," said Gregor. "This is what I brought you here to see until we encountered this... setback."

Julian carefully opened the book at a bookmark. "Bear in mind that this is a copy. There were several made and this is one of the less valuable ones because it has some variations that were not in the original but have been added by the copyist as their own contribution, though that in itself makes it interesting."

He opened the book at a page with a diagram that was overlaid on a complex geometric pattern covered in the sort of symbols that I'd last seen on Gregor's wave energy demonstrator. Around it were six symbols, and in the centre a seventh. I recognised them immediately from Angela's vision, but was careful not to react in case they thought it was me who had somehow stolen the book.

"What are these symbols?" I asked, expecting Gregor to answer.

Instead, Julian spoke. "They are an arcane notation used by members of the Hermetic Order of the Golden Dawn – for them it was a kind of shorthand for universal forces, or mystical invocation."

"The order of what?" I asked. "Hang on, I've come across that name before." I racked my brain trying to think of where

I had seen it. The only thing I could think of was the library at the courts which was full of all manner of strange books.

"They are a group of people dedicated to acquiring knowledge of the universe through arcane means," said Julian. "They've been around for along time. Aleister Crowley was a member, as was Alfred Watkins whose book *The Old Straight Track* started the nonsense about ley lines."

"They're just called leys," said Blackbird, "not ley lines, and Watkins didn't invent them. He just pointed out that some things were remarkably well-aligned."

"Don't tell me you're a believer," said Julian.

"Like Gregor, I have an interest in all manner of things," she said, "but no, I don't believe in ley lines."

I glanced at her and there was the tiniest smile on her lips.

"So what do the symbols mean?" I asked.

"Gregor thinks…" Julian started, but then ceded to Gregor to explain.

"Like many symbols they represent different things on different levels, but they are all symbols of opening, one way or another. At the same time they can also represent physical objects, talismans or tokens."

"Like what?" I asked.

"These symbols on the left could be said to be a sceptre, a key and a feather, while these on the right could be represented by a cross, an arrow and a scourge."

"I don't understand," I said. "What language is this?"

"My dear friend," said Gregor, "language is the wrong word. It is an interpretation of a symbol written in a codex that has no words. Would you speak mathematical symbols? Or musical ones? This is not a translation, it is an interpretation, but given what you have told me…"

I looked at Blackbird.

"You said they were symbols of opening," she said to Gregor.

"Indeed," said Gregor, "and interesting for that alone. The sceptre is the symbol for the opening of the mind, the key is for revealing secrets. The feather is a symbol of opening of the heart, while the cross is an opening of the spirit."

"The cross is a Christian symbol," I pointed out.

"The cross was adopted by Christianity because of the crucifixion, party because of this connotation, but this predates Christian symbology," said Gregor.

"It's a symbol of a cross," pointed out Blackbird. "Rather than a representation. They're not going to be crucifying anyone." Then she looked at Gregor. "Are they?"

"Unlikely. As you say, it is symbolic. The arrow will not be shot by a bow, the scourge will not be used to whip anyone. They are tokens."

"What do they mean?" I asked.

"The scourge is symbolic of self-flagellation like the monks of old, and symbolises opening the body, while the arrow is symbolic of opening distance, or space. All together they are a powerful configuration of opening and would represent a key of significant power."

"Like the key that was stolen?" I asked.

"What key?" asked Julian. He was ignored by all of us.

"No," said Gregor. "That key is only a component of a larger key comprising all the components, which would be used to open something else."

"What?" said Blackbird.

Gregor smiled apologetically. "I can't tell you that. The four lobes of this central symbol indicate something, but it is not part of the symbology around it." He indicated the central symbol which expended in four rounded lobes from a central point.

"Then we are no better off," I said.

"Oh, we are," said Gregor, "because while I can't tell you what, I can tell you where."

"You can?" said Blackbird.

"Oh yes." Gregor grinned. "Show them Julian."

Julian turned the pages to reveal an engraving of a church.

"There," said Gregor.

"Where is it?" said Blackbird.

"It is a church in Herefordshire."

"A church," I said. "Then it is connected with Christianity."

"Not everything done in the name of the church is religious. They had immense wealth and significant power. The nature of this could as easily be secular as sacred," Gregor pointed out. "This was built by the Normans in the twelfth century, along with adjacent fortifications. It predates Crowley and the Hermetic Order by several centuries."

I looked at Blackbird. She was obviously thinking the same thing. If this was twelfth century and post Norman invasion then it would have been from around the same time as the Quit Rents Ceremony.

"Very well," said Blackbird. "Where is it?"

"I will come with you, of course," Gregor said.

Blackbird and I looked at each other. If we went without Gregor we could use the Ways and be there in minutes. If we went with Gregor it would take much longer.

"What?" he said. "I am as curious about this as you. Do I not deserve to share the discovery? Have I not given you the vital clue to unlocking the mystery?"

"It's not as simple as..." said Blackbird.

"Simple? This is simple. He closed the book in Julian's hands and wrapped it back into the black cover, giving it back to Julian. "Replace this copy in your vault, my friend. There is one fewer now, so this one is even more precious. Do not let it stray."

We watched as Julian replaced the book in his drawer and locked it.

Gregor broke into a huge grin. "Now, when are we setting off?"

Eighteen

"You know what you have to do?" said Eve.

Alex stared at the ground, sullen and unresponsive.

Eve folded her arms. "How long are you going to carry on sulking? It was just a ring, for God's sake. It wasn't even pure silver."

"I'm not sulking," said Alex.

"Well you could have fooled me," said Eve. "This is your chance. This is your opportunity to make your mark, and what are you doing? Staring at your shoes. I swear I've never met anyone so self-centred. It's not the end of the world, Alex."

There was something in that sentence that made Alex look up. What had Eve given up to do this? She never talked about her background or where she'd been before Porton Down. Maybe she did understand what it was like to lose everything.

Eve watched Alex intensely, willing her to get herself together.

Alex sighed. "The ring was the only thing I had left."

"In that case, you're well rid of it. We don't need their gifts, their ties, their tokens. They bind us to an emotional attachment that's only there to perpetuate their control, and we don't want to be controlled. We won't be told where to go and how to live, not anymore. We're free of all that, understand?"

Alex lifted her chin but didn't say anything. Eve smiled and put her hands on her shoulders, shaking them gently back and forth.

"You can do this, and when it's finished you'll have done as much as any of us. You'll be part of it."

Alex's lips twitched in what might have been the echo of a smile.

"OK. Just look like you ought to be there. Use your glamour and no one will question your presence. Take the rod and come straight back out. It's a doddle," Eve said.

Alex looked across the open square to the Houses of Parliament. There were armed police and camera's all over the square, but she knew none of them would see her. "OK." She walked away, glancing back to where Eve waited only to find she'd already vanished.

She reached the road and merged with a group that was crossing. Her glamour gave her a smart skirt suit, low heels, minimal make-up. The tattoos were hidden and her hair was a mousey brown in an unfashionable style that would draw no one's eye. She carried a bag that was half handbag and half briefcase. Eve had said they would expect her to carry something, and she'd put some of Eve's less valuable books in there so it would have the right weight and heft.

The plan was simple. The office of the Gentleman Usher of the Black Rod was at the south end of the palace of Westminster, as he was nominally in charge of security in The Lords, though the police did the actual work.

All she had to do was walk in with someone and slipstream

into the building. People were closely scrutinised on the way in, just in case they were carrying a bomb or a weapon, but on the way out they were only watched as they left. The rod was half Alex's height and would normally be difficult to conceal, but with glamour that wouldn't be a problem. She could just walk out with it and no one would be the wiser.

Alex lingered near the external security gate until someone came along that looked as though they were entering. She selected a man with grey hair and grey suit, a civil servant maybe. Adjusting her glamour so that she was noticeable but unremarkable, she let herself be pulled along in his wake. Everyone assumed she was with the bloke she followed, though he never knew she was there. She smiled at the police as she walked through the barriers. They noticed her, but ignored her.

I'm just part of the furniture, thought Alex. Nothing to see, no cause for alarm.

She followed the man up to the building and then into the entrance. Inside there were scanners like in the airport with armed police holding stubby sub-machine guns, angled to the floor. She could feel the adrenaline building in her system as she watched the civil servant put his keys and phone into a tray so they could go through the scanner. She waited politely and then did the same with her own phone and put the bag on the belt for the scanner.

I'm supposed to be here.

She walked through the cream arch of the scanner, her heart beating in her chest. She half expected the alarms to start blaring, but they didn't even bleep.

She collected the bag from the belt and headed for the half-glazed door into the rest of the building.

"Excuse me, Miss?

Alex froze, then turned slowly. They weren't supposed to notice her.

I'm supposed to be here. It was her mantra.

One of the police approached her. She readied herself for the fight, marshalling her resources. A glance at the armed policemen and she was calculating how long it would take them to react before the guns came into play.

"Your phone, Miss. You left it by the scanner."

She almost hiccoughed with relief. "Sorry," she gulped. She accepted it from him. "Thanks."

"No problem." He walked back to the security station.

She turned and pushed through the half-glazed doors, greeted by the smell of floor polish and old wood. The building was dimly lit, high windows sending slanting sunlight to create islands of warm tones which were reflected back by the gold leaf on the ceilings. Alex suppressed the urge to giggle. She had expected the centre of government to be really sombre and stuffy, but this was completely over the top. It looked like some nineteenth century dealers had gone mad in a bling frenzy. There were statues everywhere. Faces of white polished marble watched her from every nook and cranny, piled one on top of another up the columns, looking down from pedestals in every corner.

She crossed a hallway and headed around to where the office was supposed to be. Walking down the row, she looked for a name or a number. Various options presented themselves; media suites, interview rooms, even a whip's office, which left Alex wondering what sort of thing they got up to in here. None of them were security or the Office of the Gentleman Usher of the Black Rod.

She stopped at a junction.

"Can I help you, Miss. You look a bit lost?" She hadn't noticed the old duffer on the bench seat under the window.

"Oh, you made me jump!" she said, holding her hand to her chest. She had to peer into the gloom under the window to see him.

He shrugged. "You have the manner of a person who's looking for someone and hasn't found them," he said.

How had he seen her? She would have to be more careful. "I'm supposed to be presenting myself at the office of Black Rod," she said, "but it's really dark in here. I think I must have taken a wrong turn." She kept her language formal, responding to his odd way of phrasing things.

"Ah," he said. "When you get to my age, you don't want it too bright. It keeps you from your afternoon nap."

Alex smiled and shifted from foot to foot, unsure of how to respond to that.

"Black Rod has moved office," he said helpfully. "I'm surprised that whoever sent you this way didn't know that."

"Me too," said Alex, nervously. He might be old, but the old gent was as sharp as a pin.

"It happened some little time ago," he said. "Take that corridor until the third turn to the right, and it's the second door along."

"Thank you," said Alex. "Third turn on the right, and second door. Got it." She waved her thanks and headed off.

"He's not there at the moment," called the old gent after her.

"It's OK," she said, speeding up. "I'll leave him a message."

She marched down the corridor as fast as she could, her footsteps echoing loudly on the patterned tile floor. She thought of running but that would only attract attention. People didn't run here.

She took the turn sharply and counted along to the door.

It was locked, but the label confirmed it was the right door. It was also half-glazed, but the glass was frosted so she couldn't see if anyone was inside.

She knocked in case he was in there, asleep. There was no answer from within and no sound of snoring, so she put her hand on the door. The lock tumbled and the door swung open. She clicked on the light in the absence of an external window, conscious that others would now see it if they passed. She wouldn't have long.

Inside the room was an old desk, a green-glass shaded lamp positioned over pile of paperwork. To her right the wall was lined with books, each one leather bound and inlaid with gold so that the room was scented by them. To her left was her prize; a long display case high on the wall that held an ebony staff about the size of a walking stick. The ebony gleamed dull in contrast to the bright gold of the ferrule in the middle and the lion's head mounted on the end.

She shifted the visitor's chair so that she could stand on it and reach the case. Scanning around the case for alarms or sensors, she found none. It appeared to be locked, but although the lock was a good one, it was brass and so opened with minimal effort.

She opened the case and lifted out the rod. Its surface was smooth and felt almost soapy. She pushed the case closed with a click and turned to step down. The old gent from the corridor was watching her from the doorway.

"I see you found what you were looking for," he said.

She narrowed her eyes. "Don't get in my way," she said.

"On the contrary, young lady, it's my job to get in your way. This is, after all, my office."

"You?" Alex exclaimed. "You're Black Rod?"

He smiled. "The honour is mine."

She stepped down from the chair. Even without the heels she would have been taller than he was. "I'm leaving with this, and you won't stop me."

"What you hold in your hand is not in itself terribly valuable. It's a symbol, and as such is immediately recognisable. You won't be able to sell it without getting caught."

"I'm not going to sell it," she said.

"A trophy hunter. I see. What makes you think it will look better on your wall than on mine?"

"Get out of my way," said Alex.

He stepped back, but a burly looking policeman in an anti-stab vest took his place. "I think it would be best if you put that down, Miss," he said.

"You brought reinforcements," she said to Black Rod.

"It's not a game, young lady. I gave you the chance to put it back."

"Put the staff down, Miss, or it'll go badly for you," said the policeman. "You're not going anywhere." He pulled out a nightstick from his belt and flicked it so it extended with a snap.

"How many did you bring?" she asked the old gent.

"I think the officer would like you to surrender," said Black Rod. "It would be a shame if you were hurt in the arrest, but he's quite prepared for that eventuality."

"You've got it all wrong," said Alex. "I gave you the chance to back off. Remember that later."

The policeman stepped in, making a grab for her arm. She wrong-footed him; instead of moving away she stepped in close, lifting her hand to his face. He flinched, expecting a slap, but her hand was gentle against his cheek. He grabbed her shoulder and twisted her arm back painfully. Alex grimaced, but she had the advantage and she knew it.

The policeman's face went grey, his eyes unfocused and he let out a sigh as he dropped to the floor as if he'd been pole-axed. "That's what happens when you stand up too fast," said Alex. "All the blood rushes to your feet."

She stepped over the ungainly heap to find Black Rod in the doorway. "You'll never get past security with that. Give up now and I'll put in a good word for you."

She glanced back at the collapsed policeman. "I think they might not listen to you after what I did to him. Are you gonna stand in my way, or am I gonna do the same to you?"

He stood aside. "You're a very misguided young woman," he said. "Violence is not the answer."

"It's one answer," she said, "especially when no one's listening. Get inside." She stepped outside and nodded towards the office.

He glanced towards the corridor.

"You can try that," she said, "but I bet I can run faster than you."

He smiled grimly and she backed him into the office. She yanked the cord on the phone out of the wall and left him leaning against the desk. Outside she pulled shut the door and laid her hand on it. It wasn't coming undone any time soon. Inside, she could hear him talking quietly but urgently. He had a mobile phone, she should have thought of that.

She ran down the corridor and then stopped. Running would only attract attention. She leaned around the junction in the corridor. There were two policemen turning the corner at speed. She shifted her glamour. The black rod became a nightstick, the skirt suit shifted to a black uniform and stab-vest. It wasn't a perfect match but in the gloom it would do.

She turned the corner, pointing across the junction. "Down there! Man down! I'm going for help."

They didn't see her, only glanced at the uniform and made the turn at speed, pounding down the adjoining corridor. She wondered how long it would take them to process that she sounded like someone from a TV cop-show. Not long.

She ran back towards the entrance. Everyone was running now, so she wouldn't look out of place. She swerved around the corner, barely missing an officer going the other way who yelled something at her as she passed. Beyond that was the security station and freedom. She straightened herself and pushed through the doors into the well-lit area.

"Quick!" she said. "They need help!"

She expected them to move, but the first of the two armed officers watching the door turned hard eyes on her.

"That's not uniform," he said. The second turned to follow his gaze. The first lifted the muzzle of his weapon. "On the floor! Now!"

From behind him there was a searing flash and the second officer sailed backwards into the cream scanner arch, toppling it sideways onto the bag scanner so that the people manning that scattered under the assault.

The officer pointing the gun at Alex turned to meet the new attack and Eve was there, right behind him.

"Surprise," she said as he turned, reaching up to him in a gesture that looked like she was reaching for a kiss. She held his chin and twisted it sideways with a sharp snap. He dropped like a rag-doll.

"Out! Now!" she shouted at Alex.

Alex stumbled forward, looking at the vacant expression of the policemen on the ground whose head was at an entirely unnatural angle. Eve grabbed her by the collar and dragged her round the body, through the debris into the daylight, accelerating into a run. Alex caught a brief glimpse of the gatehouse where bodies were piled inside like drunks after a long night out.

"Are they dead?" she asked as they ran past.

"It doesn't matter," said Eve, taking the rod from Alex. "Very soon now, none of it will matter. Now run!"

Down the road from the House of Commons entrance, people were running towards them. The crack of a pistol shot echoed from the grand facade of the mother of parliaments. Alex shifted glamour with the rest of the group, splitting up and merging into the scattering crowds, becoming one of the fleeing tourists before heading for the rendezvous.

Once in the safety of the crowds, they might as well have been invisible.

Hours later we were still on the train. I had forgotten what it was like, queuing for tickets, standing around waiting on platforms, and then the interminable journey. The only thing the railway and the Ways had in common was that they didn't necessarily take you where you wanted to go. We'd taken a fast train to Newport in South Wales and were now coming back on ourselves to get to Hereford. After that it would have to be a taxi.

"How are you doing?" Blackbird asked.

"I'm OK."

The presence of so much metal around me wasn't comfortable, but it was bearable. I glanced over to where Gregor was asleep in the corner seat against the window.

"How can he sleep like that?"

She smiled and shrugged. He had talked animatedly about anything and everything for the first part of the journey and then when we boarded the slow train to Hereford, he tucked himself into the corner, closed his eyes and slept. It was like there was a hidden Gregor switch; he blinked and was off.

The carriage in which we travelled had few other passengers, but even so I leaned across the gap between the seats to speak more privately.

"Do you trust him?" I asked Blackbird.

She shrugged again, "Do we have any choice?"

"We should have gone back to the library and looked at the book ourselves. We could have been at the church hours ago."

"I can't read the symbols, Niall. It's some sort of code," she said. "If we get to the church and it's all in code, what are you going to do?"

It was my turn to shrug.

"Quite," she said, glancing sideways. "He's just curious – about everything."

"That's what worries me. We all know what curiosity did. Do you think he's involved with this society, The Hermetic Order of the Golden Dawn?"

"It's possible," she said. "They were supposed to have had a schism in the mid 20th century, but it would come as no surprise if fragments of the society were still in existence, or that Gregor would be part of it."

"While he was prattling on, I remembered where I'd seen that name before. There was a book, *The Mysteries of the Hermetic Order of the Golden Dawn*, or something like that. It was sitting on one of the old sofas in the abandoned industrial building when Amber and I went after the escapees. I thought at the time that someone was filling their heads with dangerous rubbish."

"It could be more dangerous than any of us suspected."

"There's something else," I said to her. "In Angela's vision, there was a library, not the British Library, but a much older one. There was a man reading a book and the book had the symbols in it – similar to the ones that Gregor showed us in the book, or very like them.

"Who was the man?" she asked.

"I don't know, maybe it was that guy, Crowley? How would I recognise him?"

"We could probably have found a photo if you'd said something earlier," said Blackbird.

"I didn't want to say anything in front of Gregor or Julian. Who knows what else he's aware of that he's not telling us?"

"That's not what worries me. 'The sun will rise and they shall fall – The Order of the Golden Dawn'? Is that a coincidence?"

"It may be just that, a coincidence," I suggested.

"Even Deefnir thought it was important. There's something big coming, Niall. I can feel it."

"Deefnir thought it was to do with our son," I pointed out. "You don't think he's in danger do you?"

"There have been plenty of opportunities to try something," said Blackbird, "but we've seen nothing of the Seventh Court since you brought Alex out of Porton Down."

"They'll be lurking somewhere, I don't doubt."

"No, if they were here then Raffmir would take the opportunity to taunt you. He couldn't resist it. He'd be appearing at every opportunity, pretending to know more than he really does."

"Then what's it all about?"

"I don't know," she said. "Alex may have triggered something. These people she's with, perhaps they have something to do with it?"

"Aren't you the one who is always telling me how useless prophesies are?"

"That's the frustrating part. If we only knew what we were looking for…"

Gregor stirred, his eyes flicked open. He sat upright. "We are almost there, yes?"

The train began slowing as we tracked around the outskirts of Hereford and then curved around to cross the river into the city.

"Now," said Gregor, "we shall see what can be seen."

Gregor's instructions to the taxi driver were to take us to the village of Kilpeck, which turned out to be about ten miles or so south-west of Hereford. The taxi dropped us near a country pub, one of those that had once been a local for the villagers but had been transformed into a restaurant catering for the owners of sports cars and four-by-fours. Gregor paid the taxi driver and asked him for a business card so that we could ring when we needed to get back to the station.

We walked up the lane past farm buildings and village houses towards the church, topping a small rise at one end of the village. It was a squat building on a rise of meadow grave-yard with walls of pinkish stone and a slate roof rising to a sharp peak, a bell-cote at one end. The roof stepped down twice to a rounded end that looked as if it might have been added as an afterthought.

"It's Norman," said Blackbird, "and in surprisingly good condition. When did you say it was built, Gregor?"

"Construction was in the twelfth century, sometime around 1140. There was a motte and bailey castle on the western side but alas, that has not survived. Only the church remains intact."

Gregor walked through the churchyard gate straight up to the ornate doorway. I recognised it from the drawing in the book he showed us, and from Angela's vision. It was the same portal, there could be no other like it, surely? The heavy wood had been weathered to an almost stone-like grey with huge iron hinges bracing the door, while the stone archway had been detailed with carvings of mythical creatures with vines twining around and in between them, bound together with celtic knots. If anything, the reality was even more impressive than the vision had been.

"Wow!" I said. "That's some door. Was this place important at some point?" I looked back to the village behind us, which hardly seemed to merit the ostentation put into the church. Gregor ignored my comments and focused on inspecting the carvings around the arch.

I turned to Blackbird, intending to try and indicate that I had something to tell her out of Gregor's earshot, but she was already moving away.

"Look at these corbels," said Blackbird, heading off around the side of the church.

"These what?" I asked, following her.

"The stone projections under the roof-line," she explained. "Decorations carved under the roof-line. These are superb. I've never seen anything like them."

Along the wall, under where the supports for the roof jutted out were stone carved heads looking down at us. Some were recognisable; a hound nestled against a rabbit and an owl's face peered down at us. Others were oddities, creatures that looked like aardvarks or men in strange helmets.

I looked back to see if Gregor had followed us, he was standing by the portal watching from a distance. "I've seen this place before," I said to Blackbird in a low tone that would not carry to Gregor.

"You have?" she said.

"In Angela's vision. There was a man here, talking to the priest. They were talking about something the man wasn't comfortable doing. He talked about protecting something."

"Hmm," said Blackbird. "Perhaps he was talking about the corbels, Well, look at that."

"What am I looking at?" I asked her.

She pointed out a rather grotesque figure. Its hands seemed to be pulling apart its abdomen.

"That's a Sheela Na Gig," said Blackbird. "It must be one of no more than a handful that survived."

"What's it doing?" I asked her.

"She's showing us her genitals," said Blackbird, "which as you may imagine, did not go down well with the puritans. I thought they'd destroyed them all."

"What an odd thing." I looked up at the strange image. "Why would you put that on a church?"

"Where's Gregor?" said Blackbird.

I looked around. I had assumed that he was waiting for us, but he was nowhere to be seen. "He must be in the church," I said.

"Come on," said Blackbird. "He's up to something."

She walked briskly back around the church and placed her hand on the door. It clunked and swung open under her hand. Inside the church to our left was a font, an ancient-looking parish display and wooden steps leading up to a choir gallery. To our right was the body of the church with dark-oak pews arranged to either side.

Beyond that was the apse, where the altar was placed, and between was a tall arch, similar in shape the main door, but larger. Gregor was beyond this, muttering to himself.

"Look," I said, pointing out the carvings on the arch to Blackbird.

On either pillar there were monks carved into the stone, one above another. They looked grim, each bearing a token as if it were a great weight. On the left the monks were holding a sceptre, a key and a scourge, and on the right they were holding a cross, an arrow and a feather.

"I guess we're in the right place," I said to Blackbird.

She was watching Gregor through the archway. He was kneeling behind a pew which was placed on the far right of the arch. For a moment I thought he was praying. On the stone flags beyond the arch he had chalked the six symbols we saw in the book.

"It has gone," he muttered to himself. "What will we do? How? How can this be?"

"What's he saying?" I asked Blackbird.

In one motion he jumped to his feet. "You!" he proclaimed. "You know who did this! You must tell me." His words boomed around the church.

"Did what?" asked Blackbird. Her words were spoken quietly, encouraging him to calm himself, but he was not calmed.

"Thief!" He proclaimed. "You do not know what you have stolen."

"I haven't stolen anything," said Blackbird.

"I saw you," said Gregor. "The tarot does not lie. The Priestess and the Hanged Man, you were in my laboratory."

"You said I should visit you," said Blackbird. "Gregor, you invited me."

"What's he raving about?" I asked her.

"You came to me with stories of travel to the Americas, but there is no trace of American in your accent, your clothes are from England and your skin is as pale as ever it was. You were never in America."

He looked from her to me. "Your friend, he trains with a sword, walks like a warrior and speaks of thieves with concern in his voice. He worries for them, why?"

"What have you lost, Gregor?" she asked him.

"No!" he said. "You know who has taken it. You will tell me or you will not leave this place."

He sketched a sign in the air, and the door behind us slammed shut with a sharp bang.

Blackbird glanced back and then at Gregor. "Party trick?" she asked.

"I will show you party tricks," he said. He sketched another sign in the air and it was as if all the air had been sucked from the room. I found myself suddenly gasping for breath.

Gregor seemed to grow in size. "Tell me!" he roared.

Blackbird was unaffected. "You dare to call upon air with me?" she said with scorn in her voice. She snapped her fingers and the air was restored.

"Blackbird?" I said. This situation was getting out of control.

"I knew it," Gregor was elated. "You will pit your mastery against mine! You will return to me what was taken!" He gestured grandly and the room vibrated to his words.

"I haven't taken anything," said Blackbird, "but you are not quite what you appear to be, are you Gregor?"

"I challenge you!" he shouted. "Your mastery against mine."

"I do not accept," said Blackbird. "This is not a game. Something was taken and you will tell me what it was."

"You already know," said Gregor.

"I do not, but I will soon." She went to walk forward, but he waved his hand and a shimmering curtain came into being across the arch. "You are not leaving here until you tell me," said Gregor. "I am master here." He smiled at her from beyond his barrier.

"You do not understand," said Blackbird. "I am not playing games." She shrugged her shoulders and her image wavered. Before me she transformed into the younger Blackbird.

"Is that wise?" I watched as Gregor's eyes went wide.

"You are the priestess," Gregor intoned. "Just as it was foretold."

She clapped her hands together and it was like thunder in the room. The barrier shredded into tatters before her and she strode forward. Gregor shrank back, sketching some defensive symbol in the air. Blackbird barely paused. She swept it aside with the merest gesture. He fell backwards and sprawled before the altar. He held up his hand to ward her off.

"Mercy," he whimpered, his eyes squeezed shut.

"Get up, you old fool," she told him. "I am tired of your games."

"You will spare me?" His voice recovered. "You will not take my soul?"

"Take your soul?" she demanded. "How in the world would I do that, you bumbling idiot? Now get off your knees and tell me what they have taken before I lose patience and beat you to death with a prayer cushion."

He looked from her to me and back to her. "I do not understand."

"No," she said, "you don't, and you probably never will, but something here is very wrong and you will tell me what it is."

He pushed himself to his knees and then rose hesitantly to his feet. "But you... you have lost decades. You are a young woman."

"Far from it," she said, "and getting older by the second." She went to the corner where he had been kneeling. "What is this?"

I went over to peer behind the pew. She was looking down at a slab of stone carved with the symbol that had been in the centre of the six symbols in the book at the British

Library. It was a cross of sorts, made from four separate lobes like shields, arranged inside a circle.

Gregor edged towards her, still hesitant. "I am sworn to secrecy."

"You test my patience," she said. Somehow her quiet words developed more menace than his booming had.

"Yes, but… I promised to keep the secret until death."

Blackbird narrowed her eyes. "That," she said, "can be arranged."

He blanched under her gaze, but still he said nothing.

"Let me help you," she said. "Something was stored here, protected by some kind of warding. The key was in that book; six items brought together will open the warding and whatever was inside is yours. Someone has taken it."

"You know who did it," he said. It was part statement, part question.

"Perhaps," she relented. "This has been planned from the beginning. Someone has been researching this for some time and their plan, whatever it is, involves what they have taken."

"It is not for humankind," said Gregor.

"That's OK," said Blackbird, "They're not exactly human."

Gregor's eyebrows shot up at this. "It must not be used until the end of days," he said. "It is to be kept until the final battle when it will open the gates for the Gods themselves to intervene."

"We do not believe in Gods," said Blackbird.

"The four horsemen, the pantheon, the end and the beginning," said Gregor.

"You're babbling nonsense again," said Blackbird.

He stepped forward. "Each of these represent a dimension, Earth, Air, Fire and Water," he said, pointing at the shields, which were actually more like lobes.

"I am familiar with the concepts of classical philosophy," said Blackbird, icily.

"No, you misunderstand," said Gregor. "These are not elements like chemical elements. Our universe exists, if it exists, in the interstitial space between four pure planes - surely you know this. Each one is anathema to the others. Fire, water, earth and air; they are not literal. These are labels, expressing a fundamental difference and separateness – they might as well have been called truth, beauty, strangeness and charm. Each is distinct, each has its own properties and energies. Only here, in the space between universes, can they exist together."

"The void," I said.

"Yes!" said Gregor. "We exist in the void between universes. True magic is the borrowing of energy from these planes, bringing new energy, new matter, into the void. What we call our universe is a scratch, a blemish, on the heart of reality. Aeons from now it will be absorbed back into the four planes, but for a while, all that we know exists."

"You can't bring things from another universe," said Blackbird.

"They are not universes like our universe," Gregor said, "and not bring, only borrow. All that is taken must be returned. We are a vibration in space-time, and that vibration can be tuned so that it resonates with the planes beyond. With skill, we can sing to the universe and it will join us in our song. We can become giants."

He went to the centre of the apse and sketched the six symbols in the air above each mark on the slabs. When he sketched the sixth symbol, the circle with the four lobes fell into a deep lightless hole in the stone. "This is where it was kept."

"Where what was kept?" asked Blackbird.

Gregor came to kneel again beside the hole and put his arm into it, as if he could not quite believe it had gone. His arm vanished where it entered the hole as if he was dipping into the blackest oil.

"An orb," he said. "Older than the pyramids; it was brought here from Egypt long ago, but it did not come from there. Perhaps it fell from the heavens, or was stolen from the Gods."

"What does it do?" asked Blackbird.

"Do?" said Gregor. "It does not do. It simply is."

"Let me put that another way," said Blackbird. "Whoever has taken it, what can they do with it?"

"They can sing to the universe. They can wake the Gods themselves," he was still fumbling in the hole.

Blackbird reached down and pulled Gregor up by his shirt front to look him in the eye.

"We do not believe in Gods," she told him slowly, "so what will it actually do?"

"It will restore balance and harmony. It will purify reality and leave everything as it was meant to be. It will cleanse the blemish that formed between the planes and make it as if it never existed."

"You're talking about ending the universe," I said.

Gregor looked up at me. "Yes," he said, "that too."

"Where?" said Blackbird. "Where are they taking it?"

"It doesn't matter," said Gregor. "Soon there will be no here or there, no good or evil. Everything will be still, cold and silent."

"If they could just do that here, it would already be done. Where have they gone?"

"I do not know," he said. "It takes power to use it. They will need a nexus, a convergence. There are a few such places. The great stone circles, perhaps, or one of the old places."

"That's not good enough," said Blackbird. "How can we find them?"

"Even if you find them, it will not help you," said Gregor. "It wards itself. Once it is active, no one will be able to get near enough to stop it."

Blackbird dropped him and he collapsed onto the stone floor, all the energy drained from him.

"We have to find them," she said. "We have to reach them before it starts."

"But where?" I said.

She turned back to Gregor. "You said it wasn't meant to be used until the end of days. Where would you take it then?"

"I do not know," he wailed. "It was meant to be at the final battle, but where the battle will take place is… obscure."

"An old place," I said. "He mentioned a stone circle."

"There are lots of stone circles," said Blackbird, "and the obvious ones are not the oldest."

She went back to Gregor, dragging him up to his knees. "If we hadn't waited for you, we could have been here first," she told him.

"That's not helping," I said to her. "He's wretched enough as it is."

Gregor's eyes were puffy as if he was going to cry. All the stuffing had gone out of him.

"Do you have your cards," she asked him.

"What cards," I asked.

Blackbird smiled thinly. "He knows what cards."

Gregor's expression changed, and suddenly he looked sly. "You will not take them. They won't work for anyone but me."

"I don't want to take them, you buffoon. I want you to use them. Tell us where they've taken the orb."

"I suppose I could…" he wavered. "But only if I come with you. You must promise to take me with you."

"We're not waiting for you," said Blackbird. "There isn't time. If you fall behind then so be it."

"Agreed!" said Gregor. "I will not fall behind. You'll see. We'll be there together to witness the end of all things."

"We will if you don't get on with it," said Blackbird.

Nineteen

Gregor took a box from his pocket from which he extracted a deck of cards.

"Tarot cards?" I asked her. "Are you serious?"

"I need a table," said Gregor.

"We can use the altar," said Blackbird, turning towards the end of the apse.

"No!" I said. "You can't use an altar for tarot cards. That's… that's…"

"Oh for goodness sake," said Blackbird. She grabbed Gregor's lapel and dragged him through the church to the back where a table had been spread with souvenir leaflets and postcards. She swept the lot from the table in a single gesture.

"Do it," she commanded.

He sat down and took the deck from its box. "I can't do it with you staring at me like that," he said.

She turned her back ostentatiously. I stood in front of her. She caught her tooth on her lip and narrowed her eyes.

"What does it say?" I asked Gregor over her shoulder.

"I am still shuffling the cards," said Gregor.

Blackbird balled her fists. If he didn't get on with it there would be blood.

"I will do a simple reading," said Gregor. "We do not have time for a more sophisticated divination."

"Really?" whispered Blackbird under her breath.

"The fool. Oh," he said, "I think that must be me."

Blackbird shook her head in despair.

"The priestess and the hanged man. You see? I told you."

"Get on with it," she called behind her.

"Have patience. These things cannot be hurried. Do you wish me to make an error?"

I could see her holding back her retort.

"The Sun, The Moon and the Star? Where have they come from? I do not understand. One more – the Devil. There is evil in this."

"We're getting there." she said, "Slowly."

"Now we come to it," he said. "The world, flanked by justice and judgement. A moment of truth."

"Nearly…" she said.

"The lovers, and the wheel of fortune, flanking the seven of swords. Everything hangs by a thread," he said, "but why the seven of swords?"

"One more…" she whispered.

"Death." His voice held the loss of hope.

"Do it again," she said.

"It makes no difference," he wailed. "We will only repeat what we have in different ways."

"The last card," she insisted. "Turn it again!"

There was a pause. "The Tower," he said, as if he was seeing clearly for the first time.

"Glastonbury," she said. "Glastonbury Tor, that's where they are."

She grabbed my hand, pulling me towards the aisle of the church.

"We will go together," said Gregor. "I will call the taxi. We can hire a car in Hereford."

"Sorry Gregor," she said. "I told you, we won't wait." She mouthed a single word to me.

Follow.

She stepped into the aisle of the church and I realised what I had missed in all the fuss. We were standing on a Waypoint. It hummed beneath us, under the flags. She stepped forward and the air twisted. She vanished.

"What the...?" I heard Gregor behind me and turned.

He stood with his mouth open.

"Sorry," I said. "You heard what she said."

"Wait!" he called, but I was already turning and stepping, feeling the Way rise beneath me, whirling me away on the breath of night, into the dark.

Eve held the orb out in front of her, cupped in her hands as she walked up the path towards the summit. As she moved, the colours in it swirled and twisted. It reminded Alex of photos she'd seen of the planet Jupiter, except there was no red spot.

"It knows where it's going," said Eve.

"Which is more than I do," said Alex. "This is the middle of nowhere."

"On the contrary," said Eve. "This is the middle of every-where. Everything converges here – human and fey – everything and everyone."

"But there's no one here," said Alex, scanning the top of the hill.

"Don't worry," she said. "They'll know when it's time. You can be sure of that."

Eve pushed on for the summit. Alex thought they would head for the empty windowed tower, but Eve stopped short in the flat space before it. "Here," she said. "This is a good place."

Alex exchanged glances with Sparky, who was carrying the bag with all the things they'd stolen in it. He shrugged, "I don't need to go any further if you don't." He dropped the bag, holding it out and letting it fall from his outstretched hand.

"Careful!" Eve glared at him. "If you damage anything in there at this late stage, you'll suffer for it."

"All right," he said. "Keep your hair on."

"Save your flippant remarks. We are at the culmination of years of research and painstaking study. Have you never wondered what happened? Where they all went?"

"Where who all went?" asked Alex.

"Long, long ago," said Eve, "the world was a different place. Creatures walked the earth that we now think of as myths and legends, but were as real as you or I. Griffons, manticores, dragons – even unicorns. The universe was a different place. Magic was a core part of existence. Without magic you were meat, something to be caught and eaten."

"Lovely," said Alex.

"Then came the universe of men, shaping the world to suit themselves. They forced the world of magic back where it came from, shaping the world into a poor facsimile of what it was, the world we see spread out before us now." She gestured out to the land around them, fading into distance in the haze. "But we can change it back. We can remake the world as it was."

"But we're part human," said Alex. "It's what we are."

"And they despise us for it," said Eve. "We are not of either tribe, but a melding of both. We are as much human as we are fey, but neither will have us. They have refused us at every turn, they have tortured us in their hospitals, and their laboratories…"

For a moment there was an expression on Eve's face that frightened Alex, but then her face softened.

"…and when we turned to our brethren, our true heritage of magic and power, they turned their backs. They sent their assassins, their killers, they held the knife to our throat."

She smiled, looking at Sparky, then at Chipper, then at Alex.

"But we are better than them. They are old and weak, and we are young and strong. They were arrogant and complacent, and we were ready for them. Weighed down by concepts as irrelevant as honour and duty, by corrupt deals done in dark corners, they have shown themselves to be unfit to carry us into the future."

She held up the orb. "We are the torch bearers; it is up to us to show them the way."

"What do we need to do?" asked Sparky.

"Gather the items together. Alex, take the rod and the key and stand there."

She pointed to a spot in the grass. Sparky dipped into the bag and handed her the items. "It'll be OK," he said quietly. "You'll see."

"Chipper," said Eve, "take the scourge and the feather and stand there."

Chipper moved to collect the items and stood in his appointed place. Alex watched him, thinking that for once he was here in the real world with them, and not some virtual reality. For once he looked focussed and attentive.

"Sparky, bring the arrow and the cross and stand there." Eve pointed to a spot that would mean they formed a large triangle around her.

He moved across, winking at Alex as he passed. When he

was in his place, Eve turned slowly, checking each was in position.

"Now," she said. "Now we will change everything. Hold out your arms to each other."

They did as she said, and as they did, each felt a connection being formed.

"It's working," said Sparky. "I can feel it."

"The circle is complete," said Eve. "Four elements for the four corners of the universe: earth, air, fire and water."

Alex could feel the power vibrating in the air. She grinned nervously at Sparky. On the other side of her, Chipper's eyes were wide open as he lifted his face to the sky above. She looked up and saw that the clouds were changing. The cloudscape twisted around them, pulled inwards. A giant spiral formed in the air above the Tor, dipping down over the spot where they stood. For a moment Alex was afraid it would form some sort of tornado, but it stabilised above them twisting tattered streams of cloud, tighter and tighter.

Eve lifted the orb in her hand and held it high in the centre of the triangle. Above her the clouds dilated, opening gradually into a circular aperture.

Alex stared upwards, fascinated by the sight that greeted her. Above the clouds it should have been the last vestiges of the autumn sunset, but what appeared was far from that. She was looking into the heart of the universe, she was sure. The spirals she saw mirroring the way the clouds turned around them must be galaxies, and the dust that formed them must be stars.

"It's beautiful," she said quietly.

"Everything that ever was, and will be," said Eve. 'The universe in our hands, to remake as we will."

• • • •

The Ways carried me towards Glastonbury, but as we approached something changed. Usually the Ways resonated to the sound of echoes of lost voices, and I was used to that, but now those voices built to a screeching wail across the dark, and the fabric of the Ways shivered as if with heat haze. When we reached Glastonbury there was a moment where I wondered whether I would be able to exit. It clung to me with threads of violet fox-fire before reluctantly releasing me.

I staggered forward, looking back in an unconscious gesture to see if I had dragged the threads back into the world, but there was nothing to see.

"You felt it too?" said Blackbird.

"What's wrong with it?" I asked her, looking around at the smooth lawns, mounds of stone protruding where the ancient abbey once stood. It was getting late in the afternoon and though the grey overcast sky threw no shadows across the grass, I could tell the sun was sinking.

"There should be a Way-Node here to take us to the Tor. It was once a meeting place where humanity would come bearing gifts to petition the Feyre for favour. The soil is rich in iron, which offers some protection for the unwary, and it is one of the oldest places of true power. The Way-node should take us there, but it isn't here."

"What do you mean it isn't here?"

"It was here, and now it's not. It must be the orb. It's doing something to the Ways. We should hurry."

She headed briskly for the exit from the Abbey Gardens. I felt her glamour intensify, hiding her from unwelcome eyes. I followed her lead, turning away curious glances. At the entrance the staff were packing away, closing up the shop and putting away signs advertising ice creams and discount membership. We walked between them, but they neither turned nor made any remark as we left. We let the concealment fall away as we merged with the people on the street outside.

"We don't have time to walk," she tutted at the empty taxi rank opposite. "Wait here."

She went back to the shop, leaving me to view Glastonbury. It gave the impression of a sleepy little place of old stone houses and historic buildings which had been contaminated by new-age tourism. The magic shops nestled by the tea rooms, and signs in windows offered crystal healing alongside bikes for sale. It left me wondering whether there was another Glastonbury underneath the tourist glitz, and whether the people around me were as innocent as they appeared. I found myself jumping at the approach of passers-by, even though they showed no interest in me.

Blackbird appeared again at my side. "They've called us a minicab. It shouldn't be more than a few moments."

"Good," I told her. "This is not somewhere I'd want to stay for any length of time."

Blackbird placed her hand on my arm. "I feel it too. This is one of the old places. It should be a sanctuary, a place where you can rest. For the Feyre, this is neutral ground; no one claims dominion here." She wrapped her arms around her body. "I feel like I'm being watched. As if at any moment something will leap out at me. It shouldn't feel like this. Something is deeply wrong, Niall."

I put my arm around her shoulder and drew her to me. "It'll be OK," I said, but the lie was apparent to both of us.

As I held her, I glanced up at the sky. The clouds had formed into a layer across the sky, like an featureless upside-down landscape with valleys and hills, reflecting the landscape below in grey monotones. The air felt heavy, dampening sounds.

People around us carried on regardless, seemingly unaware of the change in atmosphere.

The minicab drew into the entrance to the car-park, ignoring the car indicating right in the middle of the road, trying to turn in. The cab was a seven seater people-carrier, and it stopped in the middle of the car-park entrance, so that the car waiting to turn into the car-park from the other direction blared its horn. I pulled the sliding door open and we got quickly into the cab, not wanting to hold things up more than necessary.

"And the same to you!" shouted the driver from the open window. He pulled back into the traffic, nearly colliding with another car that was driving past.

I glanced at Blackbird, wondering whether a minicab had been the right thing to do. Even London cabbies weren't usually this aggressive.

"Even they feel it," she said. "It's nothing they could put a name to, but everyone's on edge."

"Sorry about that," said the driver, unaware that we could both hear the lack of sincerity in the apology. "Where to, Matey?"

"We'd like to go Glastonbury Tor," I told him.

"Load of old cobblers, that is," he said. "Nothing to see but a stupid old hill."

"Nevertheless," I asked him. "That's where we'd like to go."

"Please yourself," he said. He accelerated up the road, ignoring the speed limit. I reached over and buckled myself into the seat belt, indicating that Blackbird should do the same. It would be a shame to be killed in a car crash on the way to save civilisation.

"Will Gregor follow us?" I asked.

"Most likely," she confirmed, "but whether he'll be in time – who knows?"

"I don't understand how you could tell from Gregor's tarot that it would be in Glastonbury," I said.

"Like many who profess to learn magic," Blackbird explained, "he's learned to trust his intuition and interpret things in unconventional ways. It's not the cards themselves, it's how he handles them and what they mean to him."

"But he turned over The Tower. That's how you knew where they'd taken the orb."

"He's using the tarot to learn the location of an object – it's like dowsing, but with cards. He's standing on the top of a Way-node, where the whole of the Ways are being distorted by the thing he's trying to find. Even then he was nearly overwhelmed by his own premonition of death."

"Is he going to die, then?" I asked.

"We're all going to die, Niall. It's simply a matter of when. Like much of humanity, he's obsessed with his own mortality. As he gets older, it gets worse."

"I suppose the Feyre don't have that problem," I said. "Living so much longer frees them from that obsession."

"Only to be prey to other obsessions," she said. "Look at the sky."

I leaned across to look out. The edge of Glastonbury had given way to fields, trees and hedgerows, but where before the sky had been a uniform layer of grey moulded hills and valleys, now it had twisted, forming a bruised huge spiral, tinted with purple and yellow. I had a feeling I knew where the spiral was centred.

"Has that just happened?" I asked her.

"It's getting worse as we get closer."

"You mean we can see more of it as we get closer?" I said.

"We should have been able to see this from Glastonbury, it's big enough, and it hasn't just formed. The weather is different here – not just a change in the same weather, but different weather."

"But it's the same sky," I said.

"Is it?" As she stared at the sky, there was an ominous flickering within. "I'm not sure we're even looking at the same world any more."

The cab slowed down and halted in a gateway. "This is as far as I go," he said.

I could see the Tor stark against the moving sky, through the trees ahead. "Can't you take us a bit further," I asked. "It'll be quite a walk from here."

"I'm not going any further," he said, leaning forward and looking up through the windscreen. "I've seen storms, but that's a bad one. If you want to get out here, you're welcome, but if I was you I'd come back into town, find a nice tea room and sit it out."

"We'll get out here," said Blackbird.

She shuffled across, and I slid back the door so we could exit. As soon as we were out, he revved the engine and did a rapid U-turn, not even waiting for me to close the door.

"Hey," I called, "we haven't paid you!"

There was a harsh grating sound as he missed the gear and then accelerated back down the lane, leaving us standing by the side of the road. As the sound of the engine died away, I realised there was absolute quiet. The wind had dropped and there was no birdsong, or even the distant sound of a tractor or a motor-bike. That changed as there was a flicker in the clouds, passing from one to another along the outward spiral, so that it seemed that even the lightning wanted to escape. A few moments later there was a low rumble, more felt than heard.

"Come on," said Blackbird. "With luck we'll get there before it decides to rain."

She set off towards the outline of the tower on the Tor.

Thinking on what Blackbird had said, it occurred to me that what we were looking at might not be real. What if she was right? What if we were looking at a different world, a kind of pocket of existence with the orb at its centre. Was it like the Glade, the pocket world inhabited by the rogue fey who lured unwary sleepers there to feed on them by proxy? I had escaped that by pricking the heart at its centre. Could I do that here?

I let myself relax and began absorbing energy from my surroundings. I gathered power from the road beneath me, the air around me. The air chilled, making the hairs on the back of my neck stand on end. The world dimmed and I began to see the world with my wraithkin sense. It was filled with lines of force, distortions in the very fabric of reality like lines made by a magnet in iron filings. From nowhere, something cannoned into me, knocking me backwards.

I staggered back, missing my footing on the edge of the road and tumbling backwards into a dry ditch at the edge of the road. Winded, I lost my grip on the power and it slipped from me, returning my vision to normal. Blackbird was lying on top of me.

"What…?" I said, still winded.

"Idiot!" she said. "Look up!"

From my position on my back underneath her, I looked up at the sky. In the giant spiral centred over the Tor, another mini-spiral had formed, right over my head, circling within the greater spiral. As we lay there, all the hairs on my body stood on end.

"Stay down!" she warned.

There was a painfully bright flash, right where I had been standing. My ears popped as the sound-wave hit us and the world echoed with a crack that shook my bones. The smell of chlorine and ozone, and the taste of burned metal, filled my mouth and nose.

I swore loudly, but though the word formed on my tongue,

I couldn't hear myself. It was like being wrapped in cotton wool. Blackbird pressed me down, waiting, glancing briefly up. The spiral above me whirled away down the arm of the greater vortex, stabbing down occasional arcs of brightness onto the surrounding fields, accompanied by sharp cracks which even my muted ears could hear.

Gradually my hearing returned to normal.

Blackbird levered herself up hesitantly, pressing her hand on my chest.

"It's OK," she said. "Not safe, but OK."

She scrambled up out of the ditch and I crawled out after her. In the road where I had been standing was a small smoking pit where the tarmac had melted.

"What happened?" I asked.

"When you use power, you take some from your surroundings," she said, "and the largest source of energy nearby would be that huge cloud above your head. Did you never think to look up?" she asked.

"I was too busy looking at… it's all being pulled inwards," I said. "Space itself is being pulled in."

"If you decide to do that again, make sure you're nowhere near me," she said, and turned and walked away.

I ran after her as she walked briskly up the lane towards the hill with the stark tower on the top.

"I'm not sure you heard me," I said. "It's already started."

She stopped. "I know. What do you want me to say? Shall we just stand here and wait for the end?"

I shrugged. "I'm not sure there's anything we can do."

"You're worse than Gregor," she said. "Never ever give in, even unto the end of the universe itself. There's always hope, Niall."

Nevertheless, when she started back down the lane to the Tor, she was running.

TWENTY

After the hurried dash down the lanes, the Tor was a climb I didn't need, no matter how much fitter I'd become. Even so, Blackbird paced ahead of me. We made our way up the path, but we could already see it had begun. The clouds twisted down and opened out over the summit, revealing a dark vista on infinity. I ran up the path after her, but then slowed as I met an invisible resistance. I caught up with her where she pushed against it.

"What is it?" I asked, grimacing as I pushed against the unseen barrier.

Beyond, at the peak of the hill I could see three figures clustered around a fourth. It was easy to recognise my own daughter as one of them.

"Gregor said that the orb wards itself," she said, gritting her teeth and trying to pull herself onwards. She made a final effort, but was then physically thrown back. I caught her in my arms as she was propelled backwards.

"It's no good," she said, "it's too strong. We have to find another way."

We backed off a few paces where we could stand more

easily against it. It was like being blown back by a high wind, but there was no sense of moving air.

I picked up a stick that was abandoned on the grass, possibly from a dog-walker, and leaned back to throw it at the barrier. I drew my arm back and launched it.

"No!" said Blackbird.

The stick sailed overhead, but then turned and swung back, accelerating towards me so that I had to dive sideways. It flew past me, missing my head by inches so that I heard the rush as it went past, sailing out over the edge of the hill and down.

I stood watching it sail away down the hill, lost for words.

"Everything you put in is returned threefold. If you push against it, it will push back three times as hard. If you strike it, it will strike you. It's an old warding, but nonetheless effective for that."

"So how do we get inside?" I asked.

"We don't," she said, looking over towards the four figures arranged in the centre.

Eve gently let the orb go, and it hung in the air where she'd left it. "You can let go now," she said. "Everything is in place."

Alex experimentally let go of the rod and it turned for a moment in mid-air, like a compass finding north, until it settled, pointing at the orb. She released the key and it simply rotated slowly where she'd released it. "Freaky," she said.

The others released their objects too. Gradually the objects adjusted their positions until they were equidistant from each other.

"How do they know where to go?" Asked Alex.

"How does a key know which way to turn?" said Eve.

"But a key has someone turning it," said Sparky. He

reached out a finger and touched the arrow, which slowly rotated before finding its position again pointing towards the orb.

"I told you," said Eve. "It's not six things, but a single key with six components. They will turn when they are ready."

At her words, the objects stirred into life and began slowly turning around the orb, each in position relative to the others. The hole in the sky above them dilated further.

Alex shivered. "I should have brought a cardie," she said. "It's getting chilly up here."

"It will get colder," said Eve. "Always colder."

Alex wrapped her arms around her body. "When's it going to do its thing?" she asked. "I'm freezing my arse off."

"This is its thing," said Eve staring at the rotating objects. "We have set in place the key to the universe. The lock is turning. Now everything will change."

The orb rotated with the items, the patterns on its surface falling into step with the objects that rotated around it, and then slipping out again as the pattern formed and reformed.

"Well how long's it going to take?" said Alex, her lips trembling. The others looked as cold as she felt.

Eve turned back towards them, smiling. "Until the end of the universe."

"The end of the universe? We'll all be dead long before then."

"No," said Eve, shaking her head. "The end of time is mere hours away. All the chaos, all the fuss and nonsense of stars and galaxies, all of it will cool until the universe itself is entirely and utterly still. What you feel here is happening everywhere, and every-when. In mere hours, time itself will cease to have any meaning and there will be no more hours. They will be no future and no past. Everything will be wiped clean."

"But you said we were changing the world," said Alex.

"And so we are," she said. "Not just the world, but the entire pattern of existence. We will erase everything that ever was, or ever will be. It'll be like we never were."

"But you said we'd have dragons," said Sparky.

"And manticores," said Alex, "whatever they are."

Alex glanced at Chipper, and saw the strangest expression. It was as if light had dawned for him. His smiled matched Eve's.

"What the fuck have you done?" said Alex.

Eve turned back to the slow ballet of spinning objects. "Sacrifices must be made. There can be no life without death, no renewal without decay. Something must be given up in order for something to be gained."

"But you said we were bringing back unicorns," said Alex. "How can you lie? Why can't I hear you lying?"

She turned back to Alex, that same quiet smile playing on her lips. "Patience, child. From the stillness that comes, another universe will be born. You won't have to wait – time will not exist. You only wait when there's time. There will be no time." Her expression darkened for a second. "No one will ever make me wait, ever again."

For a moment Alex saw something in her eyes that was beyond pain. Then it cleared and the smile returned. "No more waiting. It is happening now, and tomorrow and yesterday, but we made it happen. She looked back to the turning objects. "I made it happen."

"You're fucking nuts!" screamed Alex.

She never saw the blow. Chipper back-handed her across the mouth and she sprawled backwards across the grass. "Watch your mouth," said Chipper. "You don't speak to her like that."

It was the first time Alex could remember Chipper speaking. His voice was broken and rough, as if he used it so little he had forgotten how to form words. From behind him, Sparky watched open-mouthed as he loomed menacingly over Alex.

Alex pressed her finger to her swollen lips, all the while feeling the temperature drop still further.

"You stupid sod," said Alex. "You're going to die. She's going to kill all of us. Don't you get it?"

Chipper smiled. "It's you that doesn't get it. What do you think we're here for? This is it. This is everything. We'll be more famous than anyone who ever lived. We'll be the people who brought it all down."

"You dolt," said Alex. "You won't be famous because there won't be anyone left."

He smiled and looked at Eve. "That doesn't matter."

"Fashionably late as always," said Blackbird.

Moving fast up the path from the base of the hill came a group of four figures. Niall easily recognised Garvin in the lead, with Tate close behind, flanked by Amber and Fionh.

"It's not like we couldn't use the help," I said. "We're getting nowhere fast."

"That sort of help I can do without," said Blackbird, but we waited for them below the crest of the hill, nevertheless.

"What's the situation?" said Garvin, not in the least out of breath as he reached us.

"See for yourself," said Blackbird. "The end of the universe has begun and you arrive just in time to witness it."

"How long have you known about this?" he asked me.

"That's right," said Blackbird. "Start with the blame and work backwards. Don't worry, Niall. There won't be time for sanctions."

"If you gave as much time to finding a way to stop this as you do to smart remarks," said Garvin to Blackbird, "we'd all be better for it."

"Why don't the two of you go somewhere quiet and bicker while the rest of us try and find a way in," I said. "Wait! There's something happening."

On the summit, the tallest of the lads stepped across to Alex and struck her. I winced involuntarily. "They're fighting over something," I said. It was too far away to hear the argument, but there was an obvious threat in the way he stood over her. "Stay down," I muttered, knowing she couldn't hear me. "Wait your chance."

"Tate," said Garvin. "Check the perimeter. If there's a way in I want to know. Amber, How high does it go? Fionh, check out the tower, see if we can use it."

Tate slipped away, testing the edge of the warding with his hand as he moved. Fionh went the opposite way, heading around the warding to the ruined tower on the summit. Amber stood for a second, lifting her cupped hands to her lips. She blew into them and a glow formed within, escaping between her fingers. She threw her hands wide and hundreds of pale butterflies erupted from her hands, circling like a flickering cloud around her. They rose and circled, fluttering out over the surface of the warding as they scattered. From the pattern of their flight we could see that the warding extended up and over forming a sphere around the orb.

"Even if we could climb it," said Blackbird, " there's no way to get inside."

"I wasn't thinking of getting inside," said Garvin.

"Then what were you thinking?" I asked. It took me a moment to catch on. He was suggesting that I use my power to create a weapon and drop it inside the circle.

"It won't work," I said. "As soon as I try and draw power the clouds open up and drop thunderbolts on me." I glanced over to the group on the hill, my daughter sprawled on the ground. "Even if I was prepared to do it."

"It won't matter what you do to her shortly," said Garvin. "Either to you, or to her."

"How did you know we were here?" asked Blackbird.

"You jest," said Garvin. When Blackbird's expression didn't change he explained. "Half the power grid for the country is out, the Ways are erratic and dangerously unstable and there are landslips, floods and local tornados everywhere, all centred here. I thought's that how you'd found it."

"No," said Blackbird, "We used our brains."

"For all the good it did you," said Garvin.

"Just stop it!" I told them. "I'm going to work my way round, see if I can attract someone's attention." I walked away, hoping that my exit would persuade them to stop bickering and put their heads together.

Away from the path, the land sloped away more steeply. Here the land was formed into shallow terraces that followed the hill almost like visible contours. I stepped down as the edge of the warding forced me to drop another level. From this position I could see less rather than more. Wondering what was going on at the top of the hill, I worked my way around until I was climbing again. I came up between the dark outline of the tower against the sky and the edge of the warding. Ahead of me were two figures, twenty feet apart. They faced each other. One was my daughter, and the other was Tate. I ran forward to speak with her, but as I did she turned her back and headed back into the circle.

I reached Tate, finding him absorbed in watching her walk back towards the orb.

"What happened?" I asked.

"She tried to leave, but she can't. They can't get out any more than we can get in."

"What did she say? Why didn't she stay?"

Tate turned to me.

"She said, whatever happens, no matter how things turn out, however long we have left, she wanted you to know that she loves you."

I pressed myself against the warding, watching her retreating back. "Alex!" I shouted after her. "*Alex!*"

She kept walking, never looking back.

As Chipper watched Eve, Alex scooted backwards, got to her feet and ran across the frost covered grass.

"There's no point in running," Eve shouted after her. "Very shortly there won't be anywhere to run to."

She kept running towards the tower until she encountered the barrier. It threw her back and she bounced back onto the grass. She got up, brushing the grass from her skirt, her dignity more hurt than the rest of her, and then realised that there was someone watching her from beyond the barrier.

"Good evening, Miss," said Tate.

He stood in the half light under the clouds. He might have been a stone, or the trunk from some ancient blasted oak. Except there were no stones up here, and no trees, only a broken windowless tower that looked like no one had ever used it.

"Are you going to pretend we're out for a walk again?" she called across the grass that separated them.

"Why," he asked. "Is there somewhere you'd rather be?"

She laughed, "Yeah, I guess you could say that."

"Glastonbury Tor is a beautiful spot, Miss" he said. "The Isle of Avalon. You should have seen it before it was drained."

"Yeah," she said, gazing round at the fields below the Tor where they faded into grey in the half-light under the clouds. "I think I'd have liked that."

"You could leave?" he suggested.

"Can't, can I? Little Miss Mayhem over there has got the whole hill locked up tighter than a duck's arse."

He smiled.

"What are you smiling at?" she asked.

"I was thinking that even ducks have to go sometime."

"Yeah," she said again. "Except when it all goes down the toilet first."

"Except then," he agreed.

They watched each other across ten paces of grass. She thought she would have liked to accompany him in a walk around the hill, but that probably wasn't going to happen.

"Are you scared, Tate?"

"Of what, Miss?"

She laughed again, "Of that," she said, pointing up at the sky. "That's what's happening. She's going to end the world and herself and me and everyone else with it. She's barking mad is what she is."

Tate looked up at the black hole in the sky, then back at Alex. "People don't do things without a reason, Miss. She'll have her reasons, even if they seem strange to you."

"You know, I've played this game before, though not for real – never for real." She looked up at the hole.

"What game, Miss?"

"If you had one hour before the end of the world, what would you do with it? Have you ever played that, Tate?"

"No, Miss. I don't think I have."

"Yeah, well. It turns out that what I'd do in the last hour before the end of the world is freeze my arse off. I wish I'd brought something warmer. Aren't you cold?"

"I don't feel the cold, Miss. At least not yet."

No, she thought, you probably don't. But you will.

"What's it for, Tate?"

"What's what for, Miss?"

"All of it? Life? What's it all for?"

"Does it need a reason, Miss? Does it have to justify itself? And if so, to whom?"

"Maybe we're about to find out," said Alex, staring upwards at the wonders of the universe above her.

"Maybe we are," he agreed.

"It doesn't seem fair," she said. "I was just getting the hang of it and now it's all going down the tubes."

"There is no fair, or unfair," said Tate. "There is only doing, and not doing."

"You forgot," she said.

"Forgot what?" asked Tate.

"You forgot to call me Miss," she reminded him.

He shook his head. "No, Alex. I didn't forget."

She watched him for a long time, but he neither moved nor changed expression. He met her gaze calmly, levelly, while she thought about everything she'd done, and everything she'd not done.

"I've fucked it up, haven't I?" She wrapped her hands tighter around her, shivering against the bone numbing chill.

"Have you, Miss?" he said.

"There you go again," she said, throwing her hands up and walking around in circles. "I just don't get it."

"Yes you do," said Tate.

She stopped suddenly. "Are you winding me up?"

He simply inclined his head, which might have been a yes, and might have been a no.

"You've got a nerve, haven't you? I mean, the world is about to end and you're... what are you doing, Tate?"

"Talking," said Tate.

She watched him. "Yeah," she said. "I 'spect you are."

She looked back at the centre where the things they'd stolen rotated slowly around the orb. Eve and Chipper were standing together. It was clear to her now. Chipper had the hots for Eve, he would do anything for her. Sparky watched them, a little way apart.

"I've gotta go," she said, turning back. "Do me a favour?"

"What is your wish?" he asked her.

"Tell my dad... whatever happens, however it turns out... never mind, just tell him I love him. Tell him I'm sorry."

"I'll tell him you love him, Alex. Don't worry."

She glanced to the right. She could see her father mounting the side of the hill, trying to reach her.

"I gotta go," she said.

"I know," he said. "I'll tell him."

She turned and strode back towards the orb and the people stood around it. Behind her her dad's voice rang out, calling her name, but she daren't look back.

TWENTY-ONE

"Jeeezus! It's cold." Alex crunched across the grass, leaving footprints where the brittle strands simply snapped under the pressure of her feet. She went to where Eve and Chipper stood in the freezing air. "You've got it all wrong," she said, her teeth chattering as she spoke.

"Finished sulking now, have we," asked Eve. "Sulk all you like, there's nothing you can do."

Eve seemed unaffected by the cold. Perhaps she welcomed it.

"I wasn't sulking," Alex said. "I was thinking."

"That's a first," said Eve. Chipper grinned.

"I was thinking that the real problem here is you," she said to Eve. "Whatever your problem is, you're determined to take it out on everyone."

"You don't know what you're talking about," said Eve.

"Don't I?" said Alex. "Little Evie, left all alone? Little Evie, with no one to turn to?"

"Shut up!" screamed Eve. "I'm going to make you regret you ever opened your fat stupid mouth."

Chipper, loomed over Alex. "You better shut up, like she says."

"Leave her, Chipper. I can handle the likes of her," said

Eve. "She doesn't understand. She's standing on a hundred thousand tons of stone and she wants to challenge me? We don't have to wait for the end of the world. We can kill her now, and bury her. Not necessarily in that order."

Alex felt the ground soften beneath her feet.

"You stupid little girl," said Alex. "You think you're the big thinker with your highbrow books and your pothead philosophy, but you can't see beyond your childish little nose. You accuse me of sulking, but isn't that what this is? One giant hissy fit to show the world once and for all that you want things your own way, or not at all?"

"Say that from the grave, bitch," said Eve.

Alex spread her feet keeping her balance as the ground shifted and sank beneath her. She fought the urge to struggle as she sank knee deep into the earth. She wouldn't give Eve the satisfaction or watching her try to crawl out of the hole that was forming around her.

"We shouldn't be fighting like this," said Sparky. "We should stick together – help each other."

Eve ignored him.

"It's not about sticking together, is it Eve?" said Alex. "It's only about you, isn't it? Everyone else can go screw as long as you get revenge for being left. No wonder you're alone."

Alex felt the ground shift under her when she mentioned being alone.

"Do you know the real irony?" Eve said. "I couldn't have done it without you. I needed four elements to activate the orb, or it wouldn't work. When Gina stole my books and found out what I was planning I had to deal with her, but that left me short one element – your element, Alex."

Alex sank to her waist so that she was forced to look up at Eve. She ignored the grit and stones trickling into her clothes

and her shoes. She dismissed the sensation of the earth sucking her down. She had to wait. She knew what she had to
do, but it would only work if she had support. She daren't
look at Sparky. She daren't even acknowledge his existence.

"I want you to know," Eve continued, "that it will take you
a while to die. Suffocation won't happen quickly and you'll
be around long enough to keep the orb stable – long enough
to trigger the end of the universe."

Alex realised then that she could save the universe. Eve
had given it away. All she needed to do was end herself and
it would all fall apart. Eve needed Alex for her element until
the orb became self-sustaining. Without Alex, it would fail.

"Why, Eve?" Alex asked softly, meeting her malevolent
gaze calmly. "Do you even know why they left you? What
happened that they would leave you like that?"

Eve's hands were in fists, her teeth gritted and her face
blotchy with rage. "They didn't leave me, you stupid bitch!"
she screamed. "I killed them. I killed all of them! I buried
them alive, which is exactly what I'm going to do to you!"

"Alive?" said Sparky. "Who? Who did you bury alive?"

"Everyone!" she screamed. "My brother, my sister, my parents! The entire house came down. It buried all of us in
rubble and bricks. I was the only survivor. I was the only one
able to survive."

"You caused it," said Alex.

"It doesn't matter; nothing matters any more. In a short
while it will all be gone and it will be like none of it ever happened. History itself will cease to exist. Time will cease to exist."

Alex shook her head. Her next words would have to be
chosen carefully. She could not afford to lie, but nor could
she afford the entire truth. She hoped it would be enough.

"You picked the wrong person," said Alex. "I'm not ready

to end it all. There are still things I want to do, places I want to go. There are things I need, people I need. There's so much we could become, and you want to choke that off before it's even started."

Finally she looked at Sparky. His expression was full of uncertainty, he looked from Eve, to Alex, to Chipper.

Chipper still watched Eve. He had the face of someone who finally understood – and accepted, no matter what the cost. Alex could see the doubt in Sparky. Was it enough? She couldn't wait any longer.

"And whose idea was it to come here, to Glastonbury Tor?" asked Alex. "Whose bright idea was that?"

"Mine," said Eve. "It's one of the old places – a nexus of power. And it's your grave."

Alex shook her head. "I don't think so. When you picked it, you forgot something. You're so far up your own arse the only thing you can see is your own shit."

"What are you talking about?" asked Eve.

In answer, Alex lifted her arms and began rising from the hole. Though Eve visibly struggled, and the hole around Alex spread outwards so that even Chipper and Sparky were forced to move back, Alex continued to rise.

"A hundred thousand tons of rock, didn't you say? Only a hundred thousand tons?" asked Alex.

The ground around her turned brown and then milky as water rose up through it, lifting her like venus from a mud-bath.

"Your little rock is in the middle of a lake twenty five miles across. It's been drained now, but as far as you can see in every direction was water – and it remembers – it knows what was lost and it's just waiting for a chance to reclaim it all." Alex shook her head in dismay. "It wasn't called the Isle of Avalon for nothing. This is my domain, Eve, not yours."

She could see Eve visibly fighting for control as the rocks beneath her vibrated with the force of the rising water. Eve was so linked to the earth that she was trying to squeeze the water out, to push it back with the sheer weight of stone, but that's not the way water works. Close off one way, and water will always find another. Alex could feel it seeping up through the cracks and crannies, feel the weight of power moving up through the hill.

She knew what must happen. She didn't want it, but she knew it must come, and she would not flinch from it now. Groundwater oozed onto the surface, pooling around Eve's feet, soaking up into her jeans, even as she struggled against it.

Chipper glanced from Alex to Eve, and back to Alex. He could see Eve was losing. Chipper hands bunched. Then he extended his fingers into a pistol, miming the cocking of the hammer, extending his arm until his fingers pointed at Alex's forehead. His eyes flared with anger and hatred. He was doing this execution style, pistol-grip held sideways, arm straight.

"No!" shouted Sparky.

Alex squeezed her eyes shut, curling herself into a ball. Momentarily, she pushed the water back from her skin, giving herself an insulating layer of dry earth, surrounding herself in a thin mist to direct the force away to the ground.

Beyond her eyelids, everything went white. The flash etched into her brain. The shockwave was simultaneous, a physical blow. There was a double sound wave, Crack-Crack! Her bones shook, her teeth ground together, the blood pounded in her ears.

For a while she couldn't seem to breathe. She opened her eyes slowly, green and purple spots floated in her vision. Uncurling her body, she heard the crack rumbling back in echoes from the distant hills.

The first thing she noticed was the grass, splayed out in a radius from the still smoking hole where Chipper had been. Behind him, Sparky's face was frozen, staring at the thing on the ground near the hole. The clothes had vanished, leaving something that looked like a flayed corpse with burned and blackened skin. As the smell of cooked meat steamed into the frozen air, Alex's gorge rose. Mercifully the body blackened further as Chipper's magic consumed his body, leaving only his outline in ashes, soaking into the wet ground.

Eve didn't look much better. She had finally earned the release she was looking for, though not in the way she wanted. Her eyes were open, but had turned milky white and stared sightlessly up into the black sky above. Her hair was in spikes where it stood out from her head and it looked like every muscle she had was in spasm, pulling her lips back from her teeth in a rictus grin with her fat tongue protruding, her twisted body arched over onto its side so that she looked like she was sticking her tongue out at the vanishing remains of Chipper.

"Too highly strung," Alex said quietly.

Then, to Alex's astonishment, Eve's leg kicked out in a spasmodic twitch. Her body was racked with pain, but somehow, for a few moments, she held on to life. Could it be that at the end, Eve wanted to survive? Then Eve's clawed hand reached out towards the orb, as if she wanted to hold it one last time. Her hand slowly crept across the grass.

Alex walked around Eve's body and stood on her fingers, preventing her from crawling forward, feeling it sink into the wet earth beneath her shoe.

"No more," said Alex. "It's over."

Eve convulsed, her entire body gave one final spasm and she lay still. Beneath Alex's foot, Eve's hand crumbled into dust. Alex watched as her corpse slowly collapsed in on itself, falling into dust that mixed with the wet earth.

Alex asked herself what she felt. She ought to feel sympathy. She ought to feel relief, shouldn't she? What she actually felt was glad. Eve had earned her fate, and had sent enough people to their deaths to deserve it.

It was the orb that pulled her attention from the fading shape. It was spinning faster, the objects turning around it orienting in random directions as if they had lost their compass north. She watched it momentarily and then realised what it meant. She scrambled over to grab Sparky's arm.

"We have to go," she said, shaking him.

He continued to stare at where Chipper's corpse had been.

"Now!" she shouted.

She wrenched at his arm, making him stumble forward. She pulled him along as the sound of rushing air built behind them. She glanced back and the objects were a blur where they whirled in perfect symmetry around the orb.

"Come on!" she shouted, as the sound from the orb rose like the buzzing of a million flies.

They hit the slope of the hill and gravity kicked in, taking hold of their feet. There were people ahead, Alex thought she recognised Blackbird. They started running towards her, converging on her and Sparky. She screamed at them, "The other way! Run!"

They hesitated, then looked up and turned as one.

Alex risked a glance backwards and saw the clouds had funnelled down towards the orb, flickers of lightning pulsing randomly within the column, giving it a sense of hunger as it spiralled down.

She ran on and saw a growing shadow run away from her, growing taller by the second as the light grew from behind.

She yanked at Sparky's arm, tumbling him over, and leapt to land on top of him. A sound like a giant oven door slamming hit them from behind them, and for a second Alex thought she could see not only her bones through her skin, but Sparky's too.

The two of them were picked up by a wave of force and hurled down the hill, tumbling and turning together until they hit the grass and rolled, over and over, one entwined in another, over the grassy bumps and hummocks, until they finally bumped to a halt.

Alex opened her eyes to see Sparky staring up at her. His eyes didn't change. They stared at her silently, mute and still. She shifted her weight, wanting to disengage from this dead thing, and he blinked.

"You're alive!" she said, and kissed him full on the lips.

He lay still and then responded so that the kiss turned into a longer one than Alex had intended. She disengaged. She hadn't meant it like that. Sparky's face was filled with... what? Beneath her, where her body lay across his, something stirred between them.

She pushed herself upright. "How! How can you possibly think of sex now? We nearly died! We nearly worse than died!"

Sparky grinned up at her from his position laid out on the grass.

"We're alive," he said.

It took a moment to disentangle myself from the hedge where I'd landed. Snagged by thorns, I had to pull myself out. By the time I was free, Blackbird was brushing the grass from her clothes, watching as the sky changed.

The clouds that had pulled into a spiral were flattening out, erasing the strange distortions caused by the orb. The giant hole in the centre was fading into a uniform grey. A few muttering rumbles of thunder drifted overhead, like memories of what had been, but all the anger had gone from it. The light was changing and the clouds no longer had a luminous quality of their own, but faded to a night-time gloom, reflecting only the orange of street lights from nearby towns.

"What happened?" I asked Blackbird.

"Something good," she said, taking my hand in hers and squeezing it.

Around us a new sound emerged. From all over the hill, tiny springs emerged, running in rivulets of muddy water down the hill.

"What the... Alex!"

I ran up the hill in the dark towards the place where I had seen Alex running down towards us. I found her halfway down the hill with a boy not much older then her. She was standing while he lay on the grass, but I couldn't escape the feeling that I had just interrupted something between them. Something was amusing the lad because he had a big grin on his face, while Alex scowled down at him.

I stopped a few paces short. "Alex?"

Now she was here I didn't know what to say to her. Even in the dark, I could see she was filthy dirty, her hair was in disarray and her clothes were torn. She looked battered and bruised, though even through the grime I could see that she had gained elaborate tattoos down her arms. When had she had that done?

She looked thinner, leaner and more hungry. The Alex that stared back at me was another version, a different Alex than the one who had sulked and refused to get out of bed. This one stared back defiant and independent.

"Alex?" I repeated.

I wanted to open my arms to her. I wanted to rush up and grab her and lift her up, whirl her around, kiss her hair, but I was scared that if I did any of those things she would bolt again and I would lose her.

Then she rushed towards me, tumbled into my arms and hugged me round the chest as fiercely as I could ever remember. I wrapped my arms around her and she pressed her head onto my shoulder, squeezing me with a strength that belied her lean frame. I kissed her muddy hair and stroked her head and pulled her close.

"I'm so glad you're safe," I whispered to her. "I couldn't bear to lose you again."

In return she squeezed me harder, then lifted her face to mine, the tears running down her cheeks unheeded, making lines of wet clean skin amongst the muddy smears. Then she was hugging me again and we were both laughing.

I became conscious of Blackbird standing close.

"It's all right," I said. "She's OK."

"At the risk of interrupting your reunion," Blackbird said, "we have a problem."

She moved sideways, revealing Garvin, Tate, Fionh, and Amber.

Garvin stepped forward. "Alex Petersen, Mark Handborne, I am arresting you in the name of the Seven Courts. You will accompany me to the High Courts of the Feyre immediately or suffer the consequences."

His long blade was bare steel in his hand. I suddenly felt the lack of mine and wondered for the life of me where I had last seen it. Nevertheless, I released Alex and stood forward between my daughter and her friend and the Warders.

"You can't arrest them, Garvin. They saved us."

"That's for the Courts to decide," he said. "Stand aside, Niall. This is Court business."

"I will not stand by and let you arrest my daughter," I told him.

"I have my orders, Niall. They all have to be brought before the Courts, without exception. Your daughter was granted a reprieve while her case was considered but she has yet to receive judgement. Either she comes before the High Court or she dies here. That's the way it has to be." He lifted the blade slightly, the threat plain. "I'll go through you to get to her, if you make me."

Alex pushed in front of me. "I'll go," she said.

"What?" I was flabbergasted. "What are you doing?"

"Come on, Sparky," she called to her friend. "We have to go."

The young man stood, and walked forward between Blackbird and I to stand beside her. He glanced down at the long blade hanging easily in Garvin's hand. "Steel," he said. "It's a great conductor."

Alex swept her hand sideways and slapped him gently, back-handed, him in the chest. "Stop it, you can't solve everything like that."

"You'd be dead before it happened," said Garvin.

Sparky glanced at him, challenge in his eyes, and then at Alex, who shook her head minutely. Sparky sighed. "OK," he said. "Take me to your leader."

I wished again that I knew where my sword was, but perhaps it was for the best. Four against one was not good odds, especially not these four.

The Warders came forward, weapons drawn, Amber stepping between me and Alex and Fionh and Tate steered Alex and Sparky away from Blackbird and I, separating us. Something passed in a glance between Tate and Alex, and for a second I wondered what had been said between them up on the hill, but then they slid away into darkness.

"Amber," said Garvin, "see if you can find anything of the orb, or the other items, and bring them back to the Courts. Niall, give her a hand. The court will be in session just as soon as the Lords and Ladies are assembled. You'll want to be there," he said as he turned and followed.

Amber stayed between me and the rest of the Warders until they faded into the dark. I thought perhaps she was less comfortable with the situation than was evident from her actions, but maybe that was speculation on my part. I knew she would do her duty whatever happened.

When they had gone, she nodded and walked up the hill to look for what was left of the orb.

"Why didn't you do anything?" I asked Blackbird.

"What would you have me do?" she asked.

"I don't know, come up with some rule that you can't arrest someone who's saved the universe?" I suggested.

"You know as well as I do, if the Courts summon you, then you're summoned," she said. "It will do them no good to run. Besides," she said, "your daughter is taking responsibility for her actions. She's growing up, Niall."

"She is, and will continue to as long as they don't execute her and the lad she's with. You know as well as anyone what the mercy of the Courts is like."

"The Courts are just, by their own values. We just have to make sure they make the right decision."

"And how," I asked, "are we going to do that?"

"I have a proposal," she said.

TWENTY-TWO

Alex sidled up to Blackbird under the watchful eye of Fionh. "When's Dad getting here?" she said.

"He'll be here," Blackbird told her. "Don't fret."

"I thought he was coming back with you," she said.

"He had to go and see someone first. He'll be here as soon as he can."

"There's always something more important," she said.

Blackbird turned to face her. "Child, there is nothing in the world more important to your father than you. Believe it."

"Then where is he?" she asked.

"Patience," she counselled.

Alex looked across at Sparky, standing between Tate and Amber. He grinned at her, but she could tell he was nervous. She had already played twenty questions on the subject of the Courts, their inner workings and what might happen to them. He hadn't been cheered by it.

He'd quietly suggested that they make a break for it, until she explained that even if they escaped they would spend the rest of their lives being hunted, always looking over their shoulders. Alex'd had her fill of that, and when it came to it, so had Sparky.

So they waited.

When the door to the Courts opened, Alex visibly jumped. Garvin beckoned them in. "They will see you now."

Blackbird smiled reassuringly and shepherded them through the double doors.

"Where's Dad?" she mouthed at Blackbird.

In response, Blackbird mouthed the word, *soon*.

Garvin stood by the door until they were through. "Tate, Amber, keep watch from here." He pulled the door closed as Fionh went through.

Alex had been in the courtroom when it was empty, and in daytime. At night with the court in session it felt entirely different. Whereas before the sunlight had streaked in through gaps in the shutters on the high windows, now the only lit area was the central design of a seven pointed star patterned into the floor, around which were arrayed seven thrones. The rest of the room was shrouded in shadow.

Alex looked up at the inside of the dome, and was reminded somehow of the strange little church at Kilpeck where Eve retrieved the orb. The creatures carved into the stone around the door of the church were not unlike the ones portrayed in the frieze inside the dome. She thought again of their attempt to bring back unicorns and manticores. She still didn't know what a manticore was.

"Come forward," said Kimlesh, from her seat at the end of the arc of thrones.

Alex glanced at Blackbird and received an encouraging nod. She stepped forward onto the star that was patterned into the floor. After a moment, Sparky followed her and they stood together. Out here she felt more exposed, and the sense of a brewing storm intensified. A shrug from Sparky confirmed that it was none of his doing. Even so, a thread of power prickled across her skin.

"Well come," said Kimlesh. "Alexandre, you have returned to us in unexpected circumstances."

"Yeah, well," she said. "Shit happens."

There was a sound that might have been a hiss behind her. Someone had drawn a weapon – a reminder perhaps that manners were required. She was well aware that this was a dangerous game, but she was done with arse-kissing. She wasn't here to beg.

"And this is...?" Kimlesh said.

"This is my friend," Alex said. "Lords and Ladies, this is Sparky. Sparky, meet the Lords and Ladies of the High Court of the Feyre."

Sparky looked uncomfortable for a moment. "Pleased to meet you," he mumbled.

Mellion leaned forward, his silver chain glinting as his dark eyes focused on Sparky, who shifted uncomfortably under his inhuman gaze.

"You would do well to remember where you are," said Lord Krane, who lounged in the throne at the centre of the group.

Alex met his gaze unflinching. "Yeah," she said. "And you would do well to remember that there still is a where, and a when, which there wouldn't be except for us."

"You have a high opinion of yourself," said Teoth, folding his arms, "which conveniently neglects to account that you are at least partially responsible for the events that transpired."

"We didn't know what she was going to do," said Alex.

"Then perhaps," said Barthia, "you should be more careful with whom you associate."

"She would have found someone else," said Alex. "It wasn't us she needed, just three people who were stupid and naive enough to follow along."

"Then you acknowledge your culpability," said Yonna. When she received a blank look, she tried again. "You accept the blame for your part."

"I 'spose," said Alex.

"That in itself is enough," said Krane.

"If she'd found someone else," Alex said, "we wouldn't be having this conversation. You and everyone else wouldn't exist. From what she said, we'd have never existed." She shrugged, "I don't understand that bit."

Teoth leant forward. "An unravelling of causality. Interesting."

"We've heard enough," said Krane. "Let's not complicate the issue."

"There is still the matter of our promise," said Kimlesh.

"What promise?" asked Alex.

Yonna spoke. "We promised your father that you would have a place in the courts, if you came into your power."

"That's hardly relevant now," said Krane.

"A promise is a promise," said Kimlesh. "Would you have me break my word?"

"What about me?" said Sparky.

Kimlesh shook her head. "There was no such promise regarding you, my child."

"I'm not a child," said Sparky, "and I'm not yours."

Alex thought a little of her defiance had rubbed off on him, which was not necessarily a good thing.

"The ruling of the High Court takes precedence over a single court in matters that affect us all," said Krane. "There is no doubt in my mind that this affects all of us. Indeed, it could be said to affect everyone and everything."

"Quite," said Teoth.

"That may be so," said Yonna, "but all of us promised that Alex could have her place. A promise of the High Court takes higher precedence still."

"It won't help her," said Barthia. "She may take her place or not as she pleases, but her fate is still a matter for the High Court."

"I don't want your place," said Alex. There was a silence in which Alex could hear her own heart beat.

"Be careful what you say, child," said Kimlesh. "You do not know the consequences..."

"I don't want a place because of some promise that you made my dad," Alex said. "Sparky and I, we did some things, but none of them were that bad."

"There is the matter of Fellstamp," said Garvin from the darkness behind them. "He has not woken."

"That is not a matter for the High Court," said Yonna.

"He serves the High Court," said Garvin, a note of challenge in his voice, "and deserves your protection and favour."

"Garvin has a point," said Krane.

Kimlesh ignored Krane. "The Warders place themselves in danger," she said. "We acknowledge their service, but we cannot demand blood price for every slight, no matter how grievous."

"The Warders serve only the High Court, Lady. Can we not rely on the Court's protection in return?"

"You have our protection and confidence, Garvin, as you well know, but injuries happen. We have every hope and confidence that Fellstamp will recover and rejoin your ranks."

"And if he doesn't?" said Garvin.

"Then we will hear your petition at that time," said Yonna.

"This does not resolve the issue before us," said Barthia.

"We are not here to consider the injury done to Fellstamp, but to consider the fate of these two, who have transgressed but also given good service."

"Only through a desire to save their own skin," said Krane.

"Can you support that statement?" asked Yonna.

Krane waved a hand. "I am merely stating the obvious."

"Then we agree, it is insupportable," she said.

"Not insupportable," said Teoth, "just difficult to verify."

"Are we allowing conjecture, now?" she asked Teoth.

Teoth folded his arms, refusing to be drawn to comment.

"The girl has said that she declines an offer of a place in the Courts," said Krane, "and the boy never earned one. We are here to consider the matter of disposition. Come, this is hardly complex. Are they more dangerous alive or dead? While admittedly they played a part in preventing calamity, they also came perilously close to precipitating the end of the everything. The two do not bear comparison."

Mellion gestured, using one brown hand to separate two imaginary parts, one from the other.

"I think what Lord Mellion means, is that one happened," said Yonna, "and the other did not."

"You are splitting whiskers," said Teoth.

"She is stating truth," said Barthia. "One is fact, the other is extrapolation."

"You know what I think," said Alex, in a voice that cut across the argument.

They stopped arguing and turned their attention on her.

"I think," she said, "that you have no idea what you're talking about. You're all sitting here pontificating about something when you weren't there. You don't know what happened, or why? Do you?"

"We have a thorough report from Garvin," said Barthia.

Alex gave a bitter laugh. "What? The same Garvin that stayed down the bottom of the hill out of sight? That Garvin? He doesn't know what happened," she turned. "Do you?"

"I have reported as I witnessed," said Garvin.

"Just say no," said Alex. "It's easier to understand."

"While it's clear you played a significant role..." said Garvin.

Alex ignored him, turning back to the array of faces at the edge of the darkness. "You take a half-seen story from someone who's already said that he wants revenge for the injury to Fellstamp," said Alex, "which conveniently neglects to account for the fact that Fellstamp and Fionh attacked us. Fellstamp was holding a knife to my friend's throat," she said. "Did you forget to mention that as well, Garvin?"

"Is that true, Garvin?" asked Kimlesh.

"The Warders were doing their job," he replied.

"So he was, then," said Yonna.

Krane cut across them, "The issue here is not whether Garvin's testimony is accurate. The child has already admitted her part in what happened. This is not in dispute. Rather, we are here to decide what must be done and I think that, at least, is clear."

"But you still don't know..." said Alex.

"Enough!" bellowed Barthia, in a voice which even quieted Alex. "Krane is right, the issue is clear. We must decide."

From the back of the room, a small disturbance was developing. The main doors opened onto the corridor. Alex turned to see her father entering behind her, initially with relief, but then with confusion. Beyond him, a number of disreputable looking people were being held back by Tate and Amber, filling the corridor beyond them. Even Garvin was taken aback, until he stepped forward, long blade drawn.

"What is the meaning of this?" Garvin demanded.

• • • •

As I entered the court, I wondered for a moment whether Garvin would lose it and precipitate a bloodbath. I was relying on him to be his usual dispassionate self, but it was clear that I'd hit a nerve. His face was flushed and I thought I saw the reflection of light from the long blade quivering with contained rage.

"Lords, Ladies," I said quickly, "I beg your indulgence and your consideration."

"Warder Dogstar," said Kimlesh. "Please explain yourself. Who are these people?"

"And what are they doing in Court?" asked Garvin.

I turned briefly to Garvin. "You asked for them," I said. "You said they were all to be brought before the court – without exception."

His face registered surprise, then anger.

I turned quickly back to the High Court. "If I may explain?"

"I wish you would," said Teoth.

"These," I said, "are the children of mixed blood, those that some call mongrels and others call half-breeds. Each of them has been through a great deal, not least because they were imprisoned and subjected to experiments at the research facility at Porton Down. They are the children of both humanity and the Feyre."

"Get these people out of here," said Krane to Garvin.

"Wait," said Kimlesh. "I would like to hear what Dogstar has to say."

"And I," said Yonna.

"Are we in danger?" said Barthia.

"I will vouch for their conduct," I said. "I have persuaded them to come before you to hear your deliberations on their fate, not one by one, case by case, but first-hand as a group of people who share a common cause and a common heritage."

"This is preposterous," said Krane. "How can we deliberate their fate when they are standing there watching us?" he asked.

"How can you deliberate their fate without seeing them?" asked Kimlesh. "Come forward, all of you, into the light, if you will."

They filed into the court around Alex and Sparky, until they were arrayed in a semi-circle that echoed the thrones before them.

"Have you a speaker?" asked Kimlesh.

There was muttering between them and I caught Andy's eye. He stepped forward. "I'll speak, if you'll let me?" There was a general muttering of assent.

"What is your name?" asked Kimlesh.

"Andy – Andy Warner, from Southwark."

"And what are your sympathies, Andy of Southwark?" she asked.

"My sympathies?" he said.

"What are the aspects of your power?" she asked. "What elements call to you?"

"I don't know what you mean," he said. "I keep bees. Is that what you want?"

"An honourable craft," said Yonna, "and an ancient one."

He smiled at that.

"Do you know who we are?" asked Yonna.

"Not so much," said Andy. "Niall here, he explained some of it, but there wasn't much time."

"Do you know why you are here?" asked Barthia.

"Maybe," said Andy. "It's to do with all of us, isn't it? Whether we'll be able to live in peace and keep to ourselves." The others murmured agreement around him.

There was another commotion at the back. I saw Angela coming forward into the group.

"You I do know," said Teoth, recognising her.

"I have been your guest, my Lord," said Angela, "but though the accommodation is more comfortable, and the regime kinder, perhaps, I find a prison is still a prison."

"You rush to judgement at your peril," said Teoth.

"I do not rush, my Lord," she said. "It's been some days and I have had no word."

"Well now that we've all got to know one another," said Krane, "Can we clear the room? We have matters of import to decide."

Blackbird came forward. "If I may speak?" she said.

Yonna inclined her head.

Blackbird walked to the front of the group. "I stand here with Niall, and all these people who have come before you by their own consent. They have come as one to hear your judgement on matters which concern all of them."

"Why, what have they done?" asked Krane.

"They are not being judged for what they have done," said Blackbird. She reached behind her and pulled forward Alex and Sparky to stand beside her. "Even these two are not judged for their actions. We have already heard that they saved us all, at risk to themselves. In other circumstances we would be thanking them."

"We are not in other circumstances," said Teoth.

"Instead," said Blackbird, "they are being judged for what they are. Even Angela here, is held a prisoner at Lord Teoth's disposal. What has she done to merit this imprisonment? Nothing."

"She petitioned for a place in the courts," said Teoth. "I must consider the matter carefully."

"Must you?" said Blackbird. "If any other fey were to petition for a place they would be granted it without question."

"But they are fey," said Teoth, waving towards Angela. "I do not know what she is."

Angela bristled at this, stepping forward, but Blackbird stayed her with a gesture.

"That is my point, my Lord. You are not treating them as fey."

"Because they are not," said Krane.

"And yet they are not human either," said Blackbird. "These are the children of your grand experiment." She swept a hand around the people in the arc. "They are few in number, but there are more children here than the Feyre have seen in five hundred years, are they not?"

"If they are fey," said Krane, "which we have not yet established."

"You mistrust them," she said. "Oh, please, do not deny it. They are not what you expected, are they? What you wanted was a generation of fey children to swell your ranks and rejuvenate the Feyre. In short, you wanted yourselves, only younger."

"That's not true," said Barthia.

"Then what did you want?" said Blackbird. "You sowed the seed in humanity and expected to reap what, exactly? How did you expect them to return to you?"

"Are we done with this?" said Krane, affecting boredom.

"Lord Krane. You are Lord of the Eldrekin Court. You represent those who can take another form, the shape-shifters and were-creatures."

"This is not news," said Krane.

Blackbird reached to pull Andy forward. "Will you accept this man into your court? Will you give him sanctuary and protection according to the customs and traditions of the Feyre?"

"He's a shape-shifter?" said Krane. "What shape does he take?"

Blackbird turned to Andy. "Show him."

"What, now?" he said.

"Yes," said Blackbird. "Right now."

Garvin moved forward, but Andy's frame wobbled and for a moment it looked like he would fall over. Then he spilled out into a swarm of insects that flew out in an expanding cloud to fill the hall with buzzing.

"Bees?" said Krane. "He changes into bees?"

"Have you ever seen anything like it?" said Blackbird, almost shouting to be heard over the noise.

One or two of the other half-breeds were swatting at the insects, there were so many filling the hall. The crawled on people's clothes, flew into their hair, it was only a matter of time before someone got stung.

"*Enough!*" shouted Garvin. "Clear the hall! Everyone out.

He and Fionh came around the ragtag group and stood before the Lords and Ladies, but there was little they could do against so many tiny insects. Kimlesh stared in wonder around her, while Yonna seemed immensely pleased with the situation. Not so Krane and Teoth, while Barthia sat stoically while the insects crawled on her.

"*Out!*" shouted Garvin. "Everyone out!"

Tate and Amber came in from the hall and shepherded the half-breeds outside. Gradually the hall emptied, and when the space was clear, the bees began landing, building into a giant pile, which wavered and became a man again.

"Zorry," he said. "She zaid I had to show you." Andy grinned shyly.

"I think we've seen enough," said Kimlesh. "Please wait outside. We'll call if we wish to speak with you further."

"I hold you responsible for this, Niall," said Garvin.

"I was merely following orders," I told him.

"I'll speak with you later," he said.

"Garvin may be upset with Niall, my Lords, my Ladies," said Blackbird, "but it was essential that you see this for yourselves. This is the reality of your great experiment. This is the result."

"Then we need a new experiment," said Krane.

"Do you?" said Blackbird. "Have you seen such ability before?" she asked.

"Of course not," he said "It's bizarre. How can he take the form of so many? He'll lose all sense of self."

"And yet he survives," said Blackbird, "and prospers, apparently without your assistance. If it was not for the harm done by humanity he would be living quietly still. He asks for little except to be left to live in peace, and you would deny him even that."

"We're not denying him anything," said Teoth.

"On the contrary," said Blackbird. "You are demanding that, like Angela, they present themselves at court to be deemed worthy of a place, and then you reject them because they do not fit your definition of what it means to be fey. They cannot win."

"It is not a game, Blackbird," said Barthia, "and I have not refused anyone."

"Shall I bring someone forward, then?" Blackbird asked. "Will you grant them a place?"

"Bring them forward and we shall see," Barthia said.

"And you will judge them to see if they are worthy to be called fey?" asked Blackbird.

"I will judge whether they are worthy of the court in which they are to be offered a place," said Barthia, "As I would any other."

"But the others are all fey," said Blackbird, "and these are not. They are mongrel fey who have grown up with human customs and human values, some with odd or strange abilities, some traumatised by their treatment at the hands of humanity. They are not ready to join the courts, any more than you are ready to accept them."

"What are you suggesting," said Krane. "We cannot just let them do whatever they want. Look at the damage they've caused already!"

"What damage?" asked Blackbird.

"There are floods in Somerset," said Barthia, "and the storm has done much damage."

"Within a year, a memory," said Blackbird, "and forgotten in ten."

"The Secretariat is aware that the storm is not natural," said Garvin. "They have demanded an explanation."

"Demanded?" said Teoth. "They are making demands, now, are they?"

"A bad choice of words perhaps, my Lord," said Garvin, correcting himself, "requested then."

"Hmmf," said Teoth.

"Nevertheless," said Barthia, "our agreement with humanity is clear. If we cannot curb the excesses of the Feyre, then we are in breach."

"But they are not fey," said Blackbird.

Barthia shook her head. "It makes no difference. We are obligated."

"Perhaps we should consider starting again," said Krane. "I know we've come a long way, but…"

Mellion mimed the turning of an hour-glass.

"There is not time," Yonna agreed. "Our numbers diminish each year, while the Seventh Court have only to wait."

I cleared my throat. "By starting again, I assume you mean genocide?"

"That's an ugly word, Dogstar," said Barthia.

"It is an ugly thing, to consider wiping out a population because they do not fit your preconceptions," I said.

"We have done worse," said Teoth.

"That was long ago," said Kimlesh.

"And yet the stain remains," Teoth remarked.

There was a sober pause while I wondered what exactly they had done.

"We are caught between the deep and the dark," said Barthia. "Blackbird is right. We should accept them into the courts and deal with the consequences."

"That's not what I said," said Blackbird. "Can we not let them live peacefully?"

"Bound by what?" Krane asked. "It is only a matter of time before one of them succeeds where the girl, Eve, did not."

"She was an exception," said Blackbird.

"I wish it were true," said Barthia. "We have not excelled in our duty to protect and preserve. We left them to their fate and these are the consequences. You are right, we cannot have them, but nor can we let them be."

"Then we must grasp the nettle," said Krane, "and do what needs to be done."

Mellion stood from his chair. They all watched, expecting some grand gesture, but he walked forward to Fionh, standing close and making quick elaborate hand gestures to her. She glanced at Garvin and then left quickly through the double doors.

"My lord?" said Garvin.

Mellion went back to his seat, interlacing his long fingers, and resting back against the chair.

"Is there something you wish to put before us," asked Yonna.

After a moment, the double doors opened and Fionh appeared with Tate, carrying a large chair from the dining rooms along the hall. Mellion nodded and they brought it forward, placing it alongside him, and withdrew.

"What is the meaning of this, Lord Mellion?" asked Teoth. "We already have an empty seat, we do not need another."

Kimlesh leaned forward, and then smiled. ""Of course," she said. "It's perfect."

"What's perfect?" said Yonna. Then she glanced back to the empty chair. "You're not suggesting…?"

"A mongrel court?" said Barthia. "Lord Mellion, this is a radical suggestion indeed."

He shrugged.

"An elegant solution," said Kimlesh, "my compliments, Lord Mellion."

"No!" said Krane. "This is preposterous. Who would lead such a court?"

I glanced sideways, seeing no one move. I looked around the people beside me and saw what must be done. It would be risky, and dangerous, but it would secure my daughter, and all the others like her.

I stepped forward. "My Lords, Ladies, I would be willing, if you will have me?"

There was a long pause. Then Kimlesh spoke.

"Warder Alshirian Dogstar, your offer is… generous, and warmly received I assure you, but it is not you we would wish to lead the mongrel court."

I stepped back in confusion. I felt rejected, but also relieved. But then who?

"There isn't anyone," said Krane.

"It's Blackbird," she said.

• • • •

"Me?" said Blackbird. "Why me?"

Kimlesh stood and approached her. "You are of mongrel heritage, are you not?" she said.

Blackbird had a look of mild panic about her. "I am, but…"

"And you are among the oldest of the mongrel fey?" she continued, walking around Blackbird.

"Yes, but…"

"You were brought up among the Feyre and yet you have lived among humanity for most of your life. You understand their customs, and ours."

"I suppose, though…"

"This cannot happen," said Krane. "Blackbird is a member of Yonna's court. We cannot have a mongrel court that is led by a member of another court, can we?"

"I relinquish my claim," said Yonna, "in the interest of us all."

"Wait," said Teoth. "This is madness. We cannot create another court. It's unheard of."

"Why?" said Barthia. "Seven courts cannot have sprung from nothing. Who is to say that once there were not three, or four, and others were added as need demanded."

"That's a huge supposition," said Krane.

"It had to happen somehow," said Barthia. "The wraithkin have always claimed to be the oldest court, with the clear implication that the other courts followed afterwards."

"A turn of phrase," said Teoth.

"Our brother cannot have it both ways," said Barthia.

Kimlesh took Blackbird's hand and led her towards the seat. It was neither as grand or as elegant as the seats beside it, but the symbolism was not in the least diminished.

"Wait," Blackbird said, drawing Kimlesh to a halt. "If I am to do this, then I want your agreement. All of you."

"That you will never receive," said Krane, "for our brother Altair would never agree to such a thing."

"He is not here," said Kimlesh, "and we took the decision to go down this road against his wishes, even while he was present."

"Then there must at least be a majority in support," said Blackbird. "I will need your support, if this is to succeed."

"Then I will pledge my support," said Kimlesh.

"And I mine," said Yonna.

Mellion held his hand to his heart and opened it, then offered it to Blackbird.

"I cannot, in good conscience, give my assent to something that I know will drive a further wedge between us and the Seventh Court," said Krane.

"Nor I," said Teoth.

"Then the balance is with you, Barthia," said Kimlesh. "With your support we will found a court for the mongrel fey, those that are of neither race or both, but who need a home nevertheless."

"I cannot be my decision alone," she said.

"Nor is it so," said Kimlesh. "Yonna, Mellion and I have pledged our support. With your assent we will have a clear majority, even counting Altair's wishes. Without it, we will be three for, and three against, with Altair holding the balance, though I think we all know which way that will go."

There was silence, while they all watched Barthia. She chewed her pierced lip in consternation, looking from Krane to Teoth, from Mellion to Yonna, and then to Kimlesh, who still held Blackbird's hand in hers.

"If we cannot make a decision," Kimlesh reminded her, "then we still have to decide what to do with the mongrel fey who wait at our door. They are few in number now, but they will grow, while we will not. It is why we first began this enterprise."

"Altair warned us this would happen," said Krane. "It is the beginning of the end."

"I have heard these arguments before," Barthia said, "when we first considered mixing our bloodlines with humanity. At that time I chose life and an uncertain future, instead of a the certainty of eventual demise." Barthia, folded her arms. "We will have an Eighth Court."

"No!" said Krane, "We cannot make this decision without Altair having spoken."

"We did it before," said Kimlesh, leading Blackbird to the vacant chair. "There is precedent for such a decision."

Blackbird hesitated, and gently disengaged Kimlesh's hand.

"Make no mistake," she said. "I understand that this is not the wish of you all, and I will do all in my power to make this work for you," she said. "But I am not doing this for you. I am doing this for those waiting outside, and those waiting beyond these walls, who will face an uncertain fate if I do not."

And she sat down.

TWENTY-THREE

As the news spread from the enclosed hall there was ragged cheering from the group waiting outside. It rapidly became apparent that continuing the High Court in session was not possible, especially when Krane and Teoth withdrew to consider whether the decision could be further challenged.

Blackbird stood up looking bemused and worried, and was taken aback when Kimlesh, Mellion and Yonna all embraced her, kissing both cheeks formally. After a moment's hesitation, Barthia did the same, acknowledging Blackbird as Lady of the Eighth Court.

Mullbrook appeared with vintage champagne and glasses, and the seven thrones and the single chair were moved away so that the other guests could spill into the hall. There was an urgent hubbub of conversation, speculation and deliberation, which was brought to a temporary hiatus by Yonna, who clapped her hands loudly for silence.

She stood in front of Blackbird.

"Child of the Court of Fey'ree," said Yonna. "Do you wish to be released from your vows, and let free of all obligation, let or lien, such that you no longer receive the protection of the Court or any of its bounty or benefit. You will be a free woman. Is that your wish?"

"It is," Blackbird said.

"Bring me a knife," said Yonna.

Mullbrook appeared with an ancient wooden handled knife, crudely made, but with a keen edge that glinted.

Blackbird offered her hand and Yonna drew the knife across her palm without hesitation.

"By your blood you are released," said Yonna.

"I am released," said Blackbird.

"By your heart, you will serve none but your own, and owe allegiance to none."

"I will owe no one allegiance," said Blackbird.

"By your mind, you will abide by your own consideration, saving the advice of those you trust."

"I will," said Blackbird.

"Your power is your own," Yonna said. "None may bind you, none may hold you, and may none stand against you."

She stepped forward and kissed Blackbird on both cheeks again. "You are free, sister."

Blackbird looked pale, and for a moment I thought she might faint. I moved quietly round behind her to catch her if she fell, but she rallied as the cheers rang up around her from the assembly.

"Is there a vow to swear me into the High Court?" she asked Yonna.

Yonna shook her head. "No my child. We are owed allegiance, but we offer none." She turned to face the assembly. "Your Lady has sacrificed much, this night. More than many of you know. Vows will be made later, oaths that bind and promises that hold. That is for tomorrow.

Who will come forward this night, and offer allegiance to the Eighth Court?"

There was a muttering among the assembly. I saw Garvin glance across at me as if I might lead, but as a Warder my allegiance was to all the courts, not a single court.

After a moment, Andy stepped forward. "I would offer my allegiance," he said. "How do I do it?"

"A simple bow will suffice," said Yonna.

He came and stood before Blackbird, who turned to face him.

"I would offer my allegiance, Lady." He knelt on one knee and bowed his head.

"Accepted," said Blackbird. "We will engage in formalities in due course, Andy, but for now be welcome to the Eighth Court."

There was a round of applause, then a shuffling as others came forward.

As they did, Garvin made his way around the group to stand next to me. Others copied Andy, descending to one knee before Blackbird.

"You must be very pleased for her," he said.

I glanced at him, then back at Blackbird. "Maybe when I find out what she's volunteered for," I said.

"You will have plenty of time to think about it. You went against my wishes, this night," said Garvin. "You put the High Court in danger and you prejudiced a decision that will affect the balance and harmony of the High Court for years to come. You're suspended."

"I'm what?"

"From this night, you are suspended from duty pending consideration of your conduct."

"Garvin?" said Kimlesh. "Is there a problem?" She appeared at Garvin's shoulder in the middle of his last statement.

"Warder business, Lady. No cause for concern," he said, making sure he had eye contact with me.

"Did I hear that you were suspending Warder Dogstar?" said Kimlesh.

"My Lady, as always, your hearing misses nothing."

"On what basis, may I ask?" she said, lightly.

"On the basis that he went expressly against my wishes, and brought a group of people of unknown disposition and un-qualified power into the High Court, placing the High Court in danger," said Garvin.

"You believe I and my colleagues are endangered by a bee-keeper and his friends?" said Kimlesh.

"Any one of them could have been an assassin," pointed out Garvin.

"Sent by whom?" said Kimlesh.

"That doesn't matter."

"I believe, that you expressly asked Warder Dogstar to bring the escapees from Porton Down before the Court as soon as possible," she said.

"As ever, Lady, you are well informed. I asked for that, yes," he said.

"Did you specify that they were to be brought individu-ally?" she asked.

"No, not exactly," he said, "but common sense dictates that…"

"So he was following your orders," said Kimlesh, "which were unfortunately phrased."

"I suppose," said Garvin, "but…"

"And do you serve all of the courts of the Feyre," Kimlesh asked.

"Indeed, Lady, but…"

"I think you may reconsider the suspension, in the light of

the decision of the High Court to recognise Blackbird as the Lady of the Eighth Court, which was undoubtably facilitated by Warder Dogstar. We are grateful for his unorthodox approach, and there was no actual danger, was there Garvin?"

"The bees, Madam…"

"…were an irritation at worst, and an excellent demonstration of how things are developing," she said. "Of course, the disposition of the Warders and the duties assigned remain entirely a matter for you, Garvin."

"Of course, my Lady."

"Good. Then we understand each other." She moved away to join the group that had already pledged their allegiance to Blackbird.

I was tempted to speak, but held my tongue.

"Warder Dogstar," said Garvin.

"Yes?" I placed my closed fist over my heart.

"The Eighth Court will be needing close attention in the months to come. Do you feel able to provide that protection."

"I do," I said, making sure I didn't leak the least trace of a smile.

"Then get to it," said Garvin. "I hold you responsible."

"Indeed," I said, repeating the gesture.

"And Dogstar?"

"Yes, Garvin?"

"I want you to remember that this was your choice. This isn't the end of it, not by any means, and I want you to remember that I tried to keep you out of it."

"I don't want to be kept out of it," I told him.

"As long as you understand," he said, turned and walked to the double doors. Fionh fell in beside him.

As they left, I saw Yonna talking quietly with Mellion. Yonna shook her head and Mellion made a complex hand gesture ending with an opening hand stretched wide, palm down.

They spoke for a moment more and then separated to speak with others. I was pulled away into a collection of people with questions for which I had few answers. More champagne was poured and Mullbrook and the stewards appeared with trays of snacks to keep the party going. It was a celebration to remember, and Blackbird was at the centre of it. I think she spoke with everyone there – fey, mongrel fey, warder and steward alike.

Lesley appeared with our son, bathed and fed, and Blackbird held him for a while and then tried to gently pass him to me, but he clung to Blackbird and would not be parted, so she had to carry him around a while longer. He earned much comment and gazed at everyone intently as if he must remember them all.

Finally people dispersed, with Tate and Amber shepherding people out and back to their lives after promises to return and swear allegiance to the new court, and Mullbrook finding rooms for those who said they had nowhere to return to and would stay. I was surprised when Angela said she would remain at the courts, though she did check first to establish that she wasn't going to be locked up again before she let one of the stewards guide her to a bed.

"I'm exhausted," said Blackbird as the last of the visitors left, "but you're still ready to play aren't you?" she said to our son. She handed him to me, and he finally allowed himself to be passed across. He must have been a little tired because he rested his head against my shoulder, watching the stewards move around the room.

"I think we could go to bed," said Blackbird, "before it's morning and this one wants feeding again."

"Where's Alex?" I said.

Blackbird smiled. "Still fretting after all she's done? It's OK, she hasn't disappeared again. She just said she needed some air and said would take a walk around the gardens."

"But it's raining," I said.

"Then she is in her element. Come Warder Dogstar, take me to my bed before I fall asleep standing up. It's tomorrow already, and it's going to be a long day."

She took my hand, and I carried our son up to the suite where he graciously allowed that he might sleep for a few hours. When I finally left him, I found Blackbird awake, staring at the ceiling.

"How goes it with the Lady of the Eighth Court?" I asked her.

"She's still trying to figure out whether she's done the right thing," she said. "How is our son?"

"He's asleep, as we should we be. Oh, by the way," I asked her, "what does this gesture mean?" I copied the opening hand gesture I had seen Mellion make earlier.

"Where did you see that?" she asked.

"Mellion made it in conversation with Yonna at the gathering this evening."

Blackbird frowned, a little wrinkle appearing in the centre of her forehead. "It's a gambling expression," she said. "It means to make your play, roll the bones, or something like that."

"What a strange thing for him to say," I said.

"Especially for Mellion, who does not indulge in games of chance," she remarked. "But that, along with a host of other problems, can wait until tomorrow."

I switched the light off and climbed into bed, glad of the opportunity to rest.

"There is another thing Mellion could have meant," she said into the darkness.

"What's that?" I said, rolling over onto my side so that I could see the outline of her face in the moonlight seeping around the edge of the curtains.

"He could have meant, the die is cast. We are in the hands of fate."

"Why would he say that?" I asked her.

"That," she said, "is the question I've been asking myself."

"Go to sleep," I told her, laying back down. "Even the Ladies of the High Court of the Feyre have to sleep sometime."

"Yes," she said. "For the day will come soon enough, and who knows what surprises it will bring."

"Good night, Lady."

"You don't have to call me that," she said.

"Oh, I think it quite suits you." I smiled in the dark.

She nudged me gently in the ribs. "Good night, Warder Dogstar."

"Sleep well," I told her.

I listened for her breathing to deepen as a sign that she slept, but was quickly overtaken by tiredness myself, and slipped into a deep sleep.

I knew immediately that I was dreaming, mainly because I had no idea how I got here. Come to that, I had no idea where here was.

The street looked ordinary enough; a wide suburban row of semi-detached houses and bungalows, a few cars parked on the road but most pulled onto driveways or tucked away for the night under carports or into garages. The street was lined with the skeletons of trees, stripped of their greenery by autumn chill – somehow the seasons had slipped and the leaf-fall was upon me. Deep piles of papery autumn leaves rustled against fences in the night-breeze and swirled around my feet in spiral dances.

I was standing beneath one such tree, looking across the road at a bungalow that had been extended into the roof-space so that warm light spilled from the upper window out onto the roof. A figure darkened the window, a middle-aged woman, who turned to make some remark behind her and then drew the curtain closed so that they glowed with inner warmth. I saw her shadow drift away behind the drapes.

A car travelled down the street, a large grey saloon, headlights brushing across me. It rolled smoothly past, the driver's gaze fixed on the road ahead, neither accelerating nor decelerating until its rear lights glowed harsh red before turning the corner at the end of the street.

From the room beneath the bedroom, the flickering blue-grey glow of a TV came through the lace curtains and I could hear the faint sound of canned laughter. Drifting with the breeze came the lingering scent of boiled vegetables and baked pastry.

Upstairs, the light flicked off, leaving only a faint glow. After a moment the lights came on in the downstairs room, and I could see the woman moving around before pulling the curtains closed on that scene too.

I wondered again what I was doing here, watching this play of domesticity, when the curtains in the upper room drew back. The glow from a hallway door caught across a small face that I recognised. It was Lucy, the girl who had hidden from the beast beneath her bed, the girl I carried across the rooftops. Was this her new home, then?

She vanished for a moment, and pushed the bedroom door

closed so that even that small light was extinguished. It seemed to me then that this was a strange act for a girl that knew there really were monsters.

Is that why I was here? Was there some new threat? I scanned the gardens to either side, looking for a white flash of long tooth or the ripple of sable fur. The long yowl of a cat startled me, but it was merely an ordinary moggy, claiming territory against its neighbours. No slinking nightmare emerged from the shadows.

Perhaps there was another reason I was here. I never did discover whether she was the child of the man who carried a beast within him. If she was his child then she might carry those genes, and perhaps discover as I had, that not only were there monsters, but that she was one of them. With the founding of the Eighth Court there could be a place for her. Was that why I was drawn here?

But then why borrow trouble against the future? Right now she had a home, a life, and people who cared for her. It would be some years before her path was decided, and by then the Eighth Court might have a more secure future to offer her. She deserved the chance of a normal life, if she could have one.

Looking up to Lucy's room I found that she had opened the window to the chill night air, though she wore only a nightie against the cold. She leaned out of the window and looked up, straining to see something far above her.

I moved out from under the tree to see what it was she was looking at, and saw that the night was crisp and sharp, so that stars barely glinted. There was no aeroplane or flying owl. I could see no comet, and the moon was absent. The dark was as deep as it could be, here in the suburbs. What then was she looking at?

Then a sound drifted across to me through the darkness, and I understood.

In her small voice, she was naming the stars.

About the Author

Mike Shevdon was born in Yorkshire, grew up in Oxfordshire and now lives in Bedfordshire, so no one can say he hasn't travelled around his English homeland. Mike is a technologist by profession, which is the nearest thing he could find to Sorcerer in the careers manual. He has also studied martial arts for many years, including Archery and Aikido. He is also a keen cook – he is the proud inventor of Squeaky Cheese Curry, particularly loves food from South East Asia, and is on a life-long quest to create the perfect satay sauce.

Mike draws his inspiration from the richness of English folklore, and from the history and rituals of the UK. You can follow him on Twitter using *@shevdon* and his fascinating, lore-packed website is *www.shevdon.com*

ACKNOWLEDGMENTS

Once again, I am indebted to the Shevdon Irregulars, that band of dedicated helpers who read my drafts and offer invaluable feedback, ideas and comments. I am particularly grateful this time because the deadline coincided with Christmas which is a busy time for everyone, putting everyone under pressure. Bless you all, you still came up with the goods and dedicated the time and energy to making this book better.

Thanks to Andrew, Jen, Jo, Lauri, Leo, Peter, Rachel, Simon and Sue. I am particularly grateful to Peter for his ideas on the approach to the character Chipper, to Jen for her expertise on bees and beekeeping. I would also like to thank Lauri for her inside knowledge of the Ceremony of the Keys and for her US perspective on the book. Your knowledge and ideas have shaped this book. Meanwhile I continue to enjoy the Wellie Writer sessions with Andrew and am grateful for the perspective and encouragement provided, as well as the opportunity to share. You are a true friend.

I would like to thank Anabel Portillo for the prize-winning idea of embedding a memory in a glass of water, and Andy

Warner, who seeded the original ideas of how his character would play out in a discussion over a pint or two.

My gratitude, as always, to the professionals – to Jennifer Jackson of the Donald Maass Agency for her input and advice as well as her agenting efforts on my behalf, and to the guys at Angry Robot Books – Marc Gascoigne, Lee Harris and Darren Turpin, who recently joined ARB. I am also indebted to John Coulthart who designed the superb covers. You're a lovely bunch of people and a pleasure to work with.

Another group of people who deserve my thanks are the reviewers and bloggers who have taken the time and trouble to write about the books. I have been blessed with some very kind words, and I am grateful for the time and trouble taken to review my work. My appreciation also to the readers who email me with words of encouragement or appreciation and to the people who have chatted to me after readings, or approached me to have a copy signed – thank you for your kind words. They are much appreciated.

Writing can be tough, not just on the writer, but on the people they live with and who support them. I continue to be amazed at the level of tolerance and support from my family, and from my extended family and close friends. What an amazing bunch of people you are. These books would not exist without your love and support, for which I am continually grateful. Special thanks and love to my son, Leo, who is away at university much of the time now, but who still puts up with his Dad's ramblings and occasionally offers a few of his own.

Finally, and once again, my thanks and love to my wife, Sue, for her dedicated support and for enduring the painful process that is my writing. You can always be relied upon to come up with remarkable events, fascinating snippets and obscure references that inspire the best stories. Your positive encouragement and patience are what keep me going.

You make me proud and immensely grateful.

Thank you.

STRANGER AND MORE CHARMING

Many of you will be aware that I enjoy blending real history into my stories, and *Strangeness and Charm* is no exception. As with my previous books, some of the more unlikely elements turn out to be true.

The first of these goes back to the Genre for Japan auction of 2011, following the disastrous Tohoku earthquake and tsunami which devastated the Pacific coast of Japan. The auction was organised by a fine bunch of genre enthusiasts and reviewers who asked for donations that could be auctioned to raise money to provide relief and shelter for the victims. Part of my contribution included the opportunity for the winning bidder to have a character named after them in my next book.

Andy Warner won that auction and is included in this book as the one character named after a real person. I cannot reveal how much of the magic that Andy manifests is real, and leave you to reach your own conclusions on that. I would also like to thank everyone who bid for my contributions and made the auction a success for the organisers, especially those who donated even though they did not win the items. Your actions do you proud, and demonstrate what a fine bunch of people genre fans are.

Some of the places and traditions mentioned in Strangeness and Charm are well known. The Tower of London, which was built on orders from William the Conqueror and completed in 1100 is immediately recognisable, and the superstitions around the ravens are well-documented. The Ceremony of the Keys is less well-known known, perhaps, and has been performed since 1555 under the following instructions:

> *And it is ordered that there shall be a place appointed under Locke and key where in the keys of the gates of the saide tower shall be laide in the sight of the constable, the porter and two Yeoman Warders, or three of them at the least, and by two or three of them to be taken out when the[y] shall be occupied. And the key of that locke or coffer where the keys be, to be kepte by the porter or, in his absense, by the chiefe yeoman warder.*

The Ceremony of the Keys has been conducted nightly at 9:53 pm, with the exception of one night in the Second World War when the old Victorian guard rooms were struck by an incendiary bomb. The resulting shockwave blew over the Chief Yeoman Warder and his escort. There is a letter from the Officer of the Guard apologising to King George VI that the ceremony was late, along with a reply from the King saying that the soldier concerned was not to be punished as the lateness was due to enemy action. The ceremony continues to this day, and limited numbers of the public are permitted to accompany the Chief Yeoman Warder in the ceremony by prior arrangement.

The Houses of Parliament are another well-known landmark, though the Gentleman Usher of the Black Rod, an office created by letters patent in 1350, is usually associated with the State Opening of Parliament. Black Rod is sent to summon the Members of the House of Commons to the Lords to hear the Queen's Speech. By tradition, they slam the door in his face as a symbol of Parliament's independence from the Crown.

Much less well known is the Church of St Mary and St David at Kilpeck in Herefordshire. This is a fine example of an early Norman church and is unique for the corbels which are spaced around the roof-line under the eaves. Many of the fine carvings have survived and they include one of the best preserved Sheela na Gigs in existence – the origin and meaning of these stone carvings of females with exaggerated and exposed vulva is obscure.

The south doorway to the church is set in a splendid arch-way of pinkish stone carved with all manner of strange creatures – angels, birds, beasts and creatures both real and imaginary are carved all around the doorway in exquisite de-tail. Inside there is an arch between the apse and the body of the church and on the arch are carved six figures. They are monks and each holds a token. On the left side they hold a rod, a key and scourge, and on the right they have a feather, an arrow and a cross. Within the apse and on a slab in the floor to the right is a circle within which are carve four shield-shaped devices arranged in a cross.

What is truly astounding is that the motte and bailey castle not more than a hundred yards from the church was slighted by puritan Parliamentary forces during the English Civil War to prevent the castle being recaptured and used by the op-posing Royalist forces. There are only rudimentary earthworks to show where it once stood. The church with its pagan carvings of dragons, manticores and serpents, and a very apparent Sheela na Gig, was completely untouched.

Whether Aleister Crowley ever visited the church is not known, though he is known to have attended Malvern College in the early part of his life, which is not more than thirty miles away on the other side of Hereford. Crowley was an occultist and practiced ceremonial magic, and was a member of The Hermetic Order of the Golden Dawn under the name Frater Perdurabo, which means "I shall endure to the end". Crowley left the Order during one of the many schisms which fragmented it, but continued to pursue mystical and occult objectives throughout his life. The Order is known to have had links to Masonic organisations and manuscripts and symbolic cyphers are known to have passed from the Freemasons to the Order of the Golden Dawn.

The British Library is one of the most remarkable repositories of books, manuscripts and maps known to exist. It contains many superb and priceless works including copies of the Lindisfarne Gospels, the original manuscripts of famous novels and works which are completely irreplaceable, many of which are frequently on display to the public. I'm not sure whether they have a robotic cataloging system, though. If they don't, then perhaps they should.

Glastonbury Tor is one of the most famous natural monuments in the British Isles. The Tor was formed from sandstone reinforced by ferrous oxide from the Chalice Well, a freshwater spring at the base of the Tor. When the surrounding land eroded, the reinforced Tor did not.

It stands in the Summerland Meadows, which form part of the drained fenland that encircle the Tor, but it would once have formed an island in a very large area of wetland. The water extended for miles around, though parts of it may have been cultivated in summer when it was drier, leading to the name, *Sumorsaete*, Land of the Summer People.

The Tor is terraced into seven distinct terraces which are neither agricultural, nor caused by livestock grazing. Nor are they defensive as far as anyone can tell. Their purpose and origin remain the subject of speculation.

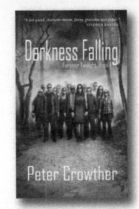

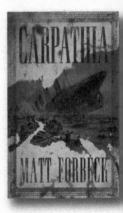

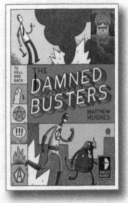

And so are you.

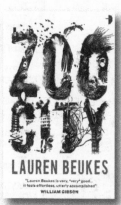

Twitter @**angryrobotbooks**

ANGRY ROBOT

WHO NEEDS FOOD?
Own the complete Angry Robot catalogue